The Green Lady

and other

Shorty Tales

By

Major Ursa

Burlington, Vermont

Book Cover Art by Ashley Evans

Inside Back Cover Art by Elias Ghigliotti

Copyright © 2025 by Ursa Books

Onion River Press
47 Maple Street, Suite 214
Burlington, VT 05401
info@onionriverpress.com
www.onionriverpress.com

ISBN: 978-1-966607-15-1 Paperback
ISBN: 978-1-966607-16-8 eBook
Library of Congress Control Number: 2025909241

Acknowledgement

This book is for all the heroes in my own life. For my great grandfather who never let his blindness or the occasional telephone pole stop him from living or being happy. For all the times he stirred my ketchup with his finger to make it taste better. For my father who served his country with honor. He faced bout after bout of cancer with courage. They were incredible role models for a young boy and later as a man. They were not the only heroes in my life, but their impact is beyond measure. Welcome to the team, Amber. Your inputs were awesome.

Thanks again GD for all your hard work.

Dedication

To the many people that have helped me to be more than I had any right to be, thank you. For those that helped me up when I grabbed for things just beyond my reach, God bless you. For those who stood at my side through good times and bad, you are my friends. To my wife who cringes every time I take my stick and go for a walk by myself, I love you too. And to those in the world that think I can't just because I am blind, look out. This old man is going to leave you in the dust.

And lastly to my son who died on his birthday last year while I was writing this book, I miss you. A part of me regrets that you got the RP from me. But a bigger part of me was so proud that you didn't give up. I saw more growth in you that last two years as the blindness came on fast. You can't imagine what I would give to see who and what you would have become if your life hadn't ended so tragically.

Author's Note

Every book is special in its own way, but some are more significant than others. This was one of those books for me. The Green Lady is more than just another tale where a hero and heroine fight to overcome every obstacle the world puts in their way. The heart of this story is the battle with self and the personal demons that we must confront each day of our lives. Happiness can only be achieved by recognizing our own limitations and striving to overcome them. Do we allow those limitations to control our lives, or can we become more than others think us capable of? And from my own personal experience, the happily ever after comes by surrounding ourselves with people who see more than the disabilities that we are burdened with. And maybe, if we are lucky, finding someone to stand by us through it all. A person that is not a crutch, but a partner who supports us in what we do.

I introduced the future Green Lady in one of my earlier short stories, "The Burden of Her Gifts." I really have no idea why I needed the little girl, Annah Treemain, to be blind. I only knew at the time that she would be important someday. And she was and will be more so in the future. As I did, Annah had to decide whether blindness would define her life or whether she would live a life better than many people ever do. She had to choose to be more than just a poor little blind girl.

And then there is Shorty. My lovable ogre had to overcome his own limitations. No bery smart is a tough way to go through life. His great strength and his heart could only take him so far. He had to learn that not every situation could be controlled. And more importantly, he had to learn that he was not to blame for everyone else's choices. Responsibility was a burden that everyone had to bear. And harder still was the idea that sometimes, he had to let others choose for themselves and maybe even for him.

And so, both the hero and heroine had to fight their own battles with self so that each of them could come together to achieve what neither of them could achieve on their own. They had to learn to trust themselves and each other. It is a love story of sorts. But to love each other, they had to learn to love themselves first.

I am blind. I have a hereditary eye disease called Retinitis Pigmentosa. I have no vision in my right eye and I see through a pinhole in my left. Please do not feel sorry for me. I don't. I have visited six continents and someday I will get to Antarctica, too. I have had two fantastic careers, one in the Air Force and another as a teacher. I had two children and adopted six others. And, although it took me half a century, I met and married a woman that is the partner I always wanted in life. As a blind man, I have written six books so far. I think I have had a good run of things.

My question is, can you do the same? I hope so. But in the end, it's up to you. As my very blind great grandfather once told a very naïve six-year-old boy, "You can cry about the bad things that happen and people will laugh at you. Or, you can laugh about the times you stumble and people will laugh with you. It's your choice."

Becoming Da Mama was written before the fight over whether a man could be a mother or not became one of the world's biggest political and social battlegrounds. Shorty became a parent with all the responsibilities that entails. The idea that the big ogre, a no bery smart warrior, could be called Mama was supposed to be amusing. What it is not is a political statement of any kind. It is a tale of a lonely man and an orphan finding family with each other. After adopting six times, I know just how hard and important that is.

And finally, there is Cat. For those that know me, I am NOT a cat person. But the big sabretooth called to me. Was she just a plaything or something more? I just had to bring her to life. I would like to say her amusing personality was my idea, but I think she took a much greater role in writing this story than I did. She is the Prime after all. She is Cat and no male, not even the author, was going to tell her who she was or what she would become.

CONTENTS

The Green Lady

Preface

The unstoppable foe had been beaten back. But that unexpected victory had not saved the land or the things that grew within it. The invaders called their plan "Scorched Earth" while those that lived here just called it evil. How their enemy had poisoned the land was still a mystery. Plants just withered away, and the soil had died leaving little more than dust in its wake. The warriors they had fought had been bad enough, but this new assailant was one that the people of Arcturus had no way to fight. The end of their world had seemed inevitable.

The High Druid and his new Green Knight had refused to accept that fate. They fought on, unwilling to yield the land to this implacable foe. Their stubborn refusal led to a most surprising solution – a tiny insect-like creature that the people of Arcturus considered little more than a pest. The bane that their enemy had loosed upon the land could be defeated by the almost comical Armadillo Bug. Swarms of the unseeming heroes had answered the call of the High Druid. Like soldiers preparing for battle, the tiny creatures had unrolled their armored bodies and burrowed into the heart of a dying world. The people could only watch and pray.

And then it happened. The incoming tide of dust began to slow its advance as Arcturus's many-legged warriors dug in to battle it. Hopes began to rise as the dust reached its high mark and faltered. The people cheered when the dust finally began to ebb. Arcturus's smallest army was winning. The slow process of reclaiming the territory lost in the war began in earnest. The restoration would not be quick or easy. The final outcome would require the mortal races above the ground to stand united with the gray army below.

Eyes that had seen too much devastation, surveyed the vast sea of dust and barren soil that was all that remained of the land surrounding Stormhold Keep. A ribbon of silver meandered into the distance connecting the half dozen small farmhouses that dotted the plain. Long before his arrival in this land, that trickle of water had been a mighty river that had nourished this land from the mountains to the distant sea. The once proud river had been an early victim of the invaders.

Small patches of green and gold seemed insignificant in the vast emptiness. Before the war, this entire region had been covered by old-growth forest. At least, that was the tale he had been told over a mug of that watery swill the locals called ale. He knew that he was being more than a little unkind. The lousy ale really was not the old innkeeper's fault. Where, in what was left of this land, could anyone get enough grain to brew a decent ale? Sadly, that situation was not likely to improve any time soon. "Beans and corn," the High Druid had recommended. "That is the only way to feed people and rejuvenate the soil." He would not be seeing a good ale out of either of those crops, Rankin groused. But, he thought, he knew a recipe for corn whiskey that would curl even a dwarf's beard. For that to happen though, the people of Stormhold needed a place to store the meager fruits of their labor. They needed a barn. More importantly, they needed a Pebblestone to build it right.

The old dwarf turned his back on the sea of dust. He spread his sketches and diagrams out on the table near the construction site. Looking from the diagrams to the site, he grunted in disgust. He grasped the table in his strong hands and dragged it several feet to the right. The alignment still did not satisfy him, so he slid the left corner of the table just a touch closer to himself until the angles were identical. Now he was ready to get to work.

This would be the first barn that he had ever built. It would be the best barn in this or any other realm or his name was not Rankin Pebblestone. He walked around the table and marched toward the line of holes that had been dug into the hilltop. He pulled a weighted chain from his pocket and lowered it into the first hole.

Half an hour later, he had verified that each hole measured exactly fifteen links deep from the layer of crushed stone to the lip of the hole. The bottom layer of each hole had two links of heavy clay covered by three links of crushed stone. A compression post had been used to compact both layers. The beams of his barn would not settle with the passing of the seasons. This barn would still be serving the people of Stormhold a thousand years from this day. House Pebblestone had engineered some of the finest castles in his own realm, he would deliver no less on this project.

Rankin pulled out a spool of string and several stakes. Pushing the first stake in by hole number one, he ran a line of string to the center of the next hole. When he was sure the angles were correct, he staked the string in place and moved on. It took another hour to get all the strings lined up. The strings would ensure that the support beams were properly aligned. They would also guide his teams in the placement of the cross beams. He had checked the angles of each string twice as was proper when doing good engineering. Finally satisfied, Rankin stepped back to admire the precision of his work.

There had been a time when designing a barn would have been beneath his dignity. Funny how a trip to the Gates of Hell in slave chains shifted a dwarf's view of the world. Rankin turned and stared down the hill at the pile of support beams waiting to be carried up to the construction site. A muscular ogre stood talking to a group of human farmers. That ogre had forced him to re-examine his beliefs and values even more than the slave collar had. If any of his kinfolk still lived, would he even be able to explain working with one of the ogre-kin? Most likely, his kin would banish him from clan and family for what he was doing. He doubted even that threat would deter him from helping the ogre anymore.

Rankin shrugged. It was not like he was the only one who felt that way. He was not sure anyone living on this side of the mountains could explain the individual chatting so happily with the farmers. The Lord was a half-breed. How, by the Dwarven gods' hairy chins, had a human woman birthed an ogre brat? And why would she even try? Most women would have killed themselves first. The insanity did not stop there either. This particular half-blood was some kind of holy knight sworn to serve a forest goddess of the far north. The thought of it made Rankin's head throb. To top it all off, the ogre was the Lord of Stormhold Keep, something like a Baron in Rankin's world. The Keep and title were supposed to be a reward for saving the entire realm from an invasion by followers of the evil god Set. Every dwarf knew that ogres ravaged kingdoms, not saved them.

Rankin would have thought the tale nothing more than the aftereffects of a night with too much bad ale. But he could not dismiss the story so easily. His kin had been all but wiped out by an army of giants. That army had also been led by minions of Set. Rankin had been one of the few survivors. And that was only if you counted being drugged and left to rot in a slave pen in the Gates of Hell as surviving. Rankin would have preferred death.

His own fate had looked grim until a certain half-ogre had appeared in the slave market with two monstrous swords sticking up over his shoulders. The proud warrior had not even bothered to bargain with the devil that held the key to Rankin's collar. "How muches fer all dem?" was the only question that the ogre had asked. The ogre had then purchased each and every person held there that day. Twenty-two slaves, including three children, had been purchased for the outrageous sum of sixty thousand gold pieces. He did not buy them to serve him or even to be served as his next meal. He bought every dwarf, elf, and human in that nightmare reality to free them. He did it so he could bring them to a place of safety.

Rankin still had trouble accepting the events of that day. He had been raised to believe that all ogres were evil. He had never had a reason to question that belief. And yet, this ogre had freed him. Had freed all of them. The monster that should have been his new master made it clear that Rankin's freedom came without obligation. There would be no debt of honor or coin. Nothing had been demanded of any of the former slaves. That act alone was like something out of a fairy tale. But the ogre had gone one step further. He had offered each of them a home and a dream to share. It was a dream that might take a dwarven lifetime to bring about, but the ogre intended to work at their sides to make it a reality. Who did things like that? No one, as far as Rankin had ever known. At least, not until he met an eight-foot-tall ogre named Shorty.

Some of the former slaves had taken their freedom and left. No one had tried to stop them. Those that left did so with coin in their pockets to help them find their way home. Rankin doubted that any of those homes still existed. Wars seldom ended well for the losers and none of the slaves had been on the winning side of the battles. His own home was proof enough of that. The ogre and his friends had never questioned why any of the slaves left, but that did not stop Rankin from wondering. Had those that left done so because they could not see past the ogre in the person who had saved them? If so, it was a sad thing indeed. Prejudice was truly a double-bladed axe. It was as likely to cut its wielder as it was its intended victim.

Others, like him, had nowhere else to go. They had come to see if the home and the future the ogre had spoken of really existed. Those that had come here had gotten more than just a home. They found a place worth fighting for. Their new leader freely gave them the tools to build a new life and defend it. The land and its people had been hurt by the war, but its spirit had not been broken. Nothing had been lost that time and hard work could not replace. In time, this land would be green again and its people would successfully stand against any foe, even the followers of Set.

The Green Knight was generous beyond anything Rankin could understand. Rankin stared down at the magic ring on his own left hand. Shorty, the Green Knight, had given him that ring on his first day here. The other settlers, warriors not engineers like him, had received armor and weapons. Shorty handed out magic, weapons, and tools like gold had no value to him at all. The ogre never asked for repayment. Rankin was not even sure the Knight remembered half the gifts he gave. All the Knight seemed to want in return for his gifts was friendship. Rankin frequently questioned the sanity of the Knight. Only a fool kept giving without thought of a return on his investment. In the end, Rankin was an even bigger fool. He had pledged himself to the ogre without hesitation. Shorty might not be the brightest Lord that Rankin had ever served, but he had the biggest heart and he truly believed in the dream he shared with everyone.

Rankin found he was not the only believer. The people of Stormhold were building the dream day by day. These people would stand against the minions of Set or any other evil that came against them.

The people of Stormhold would heal the land and live in harmony with it. Rankin liked that vision. And truth be told, he liked building barns and farmhouses too. They served honest people in a way that the castles never had.

Rankin watched the Knight strip off his shirt and begin to stretch. He made an impression on people wearing his armor with all those weapons strapped every which way. Apparently, he inspired just as much confidence in nothing more than boots and pants with his great sword at his waist. He might be small for an ogre, but he had heart and strength to spare.

Rankin raised a hand and the Lord of Stormhold turned to the pile of beams. He bent to lift the end of one up into the air. Each beam was two rods long and the square ends measured two links in each direction. They weighed more than a pair of drunken dwarves.

Shorty handled them like they were little more than twigs. He was a sight handier than a team of oxen. His Lord quickly settled the first beam across his shoulders and began to walk up the hill. Rankin shook his head. Who had ever heard of a Baron stripping down to build a barn like a common laborer? His Lord actually seemed to enjoy sweaty work.

Rankin's musings were interrupted when the beam was lowered into hole number one. Shorty held the beam upright as Rankin twisted it to adjust its facing. Rankin barked, "Now!" and several workers rushed from the side to fill the hole around the beam. The beam was locked into place by a 480-pound ogre stomping his boots down to compact the heavy clay. Eleven beams later, the main supports were all in place.

Rankin watched as Shorty, Lord of Stormhold and Green Knight of Arcturus, walked back down the hill humming happily as he headed home. The sound of hammering filled the air as the rest of Rankin's team ran braces between the beams. Rankin watched the figure walk away with a silent prayer for the survival of his new liege lord. He wanted the Lord of Stormhold to live long enough to see that dream become reality. It was a lot to ask of the gods. Shorty was as head-strong and arrogant as an ogre could get. Rankin supposed that was what it took to stand against an evil god and his many minions. The old dwarf knew that this Lord would not just sit and wait for the next attack. The Green Knight would seek out those that had attacked his home. Shorty would do all that was ogrely possible to ensure that no other realm suffered the same fate as Arcturus had.

Part 1

Worlds Apart

"Sum a da times gots ta break tings. Mo betterer ta make new tings."

Chapter 1

The Knight

The midday sun beat down on the tall figure standing at the base of the hill. His body glistened with accumulated sweat as he watched the bustle of activity up on the hilltop. He raised the mostly clean shirt gripped in his left hand and casually wiped away the sweat running down his face. Shorty, Lord of Stormhold Keep, smiled at the dull ache in his arms and shoulders. It had felt good to work hard. It felt even better when that work was to build things people needed. "Muches mo betterer den jus killin tings," he whispered to himself.

He wiped more sweat from his chest as he watched the figures scurrying around the partially built structure. They looked like squirrels chasing after the last nuts before a long winter. Dwarves, elves, and humans worked side by side to make their home a better place. This was why he fought the battles that he did, to help people and protect them the way that Mama taught him to do. People working to help each other was the only way to survive in a world nearly destroyed by war. Seeing so many people excited and happy helped to ease his guilt over those he had failed to protect. Too many friends had died along the way because he had failed. Too many times he had not been strong enough to keep the bad things from hurting those he cared about. Never again. He would not let anyone else get hurt because of him. That was his promise to himself, and he always kept his promises.

There was an enthusiastic cry from one of the groups up above. Shorty watched as a small section of wall was pushed upright and hammered into place between two of the beams he had hauled up the hill that morning. As he watched, another was lifted up beside it. He wondered if they would finish today. This barn, whatever a barn was, was a really big building. He was not sure why a big house with no rooms inside was so important, but he was glad everyone was so happy about building it.

Shorty turned away with a smile. He had done his part. He had carried twelve beams up the hill. He could count real gooder now. He had finally learned all the numbers up to twenty. Know Man said he was the smartest ogre he had ever teached. Shorty was not sure Know Man had ever teached any other ogres, but it was a nice thing to say.

The sun was shining, he could count, and he had learned how to build a barn. Shorty felt pretty good about his day. Even the old fuzzface, Rankin, had said something nice to him. Shorty was "Better den two ox." It had been a very good day.

Shorty's thoughts wandered as he walked back to Stormhold Keep. Why did the big building called barn make all the farmers so happy? None of them were going to live in it after all. The building had no windows and there was not even a stove to keep the inside warm or to cook on. Shorty shrugged. Barn was just another strange thing that smart people liked to have.

After a mile or so, Shorty came to the edge of the stream. Stormhold was close enough now that he could see people up on the walls of the Keep. Shorty crouched down to scoop water into his hands. He splashed the water on his face to cool himself off. Then he took another handful to drink. The water was cold and clean. It tasted really good. When Shorty had first come to Stormhold, this stream had been little more than a trickle of water. Now it was wider than he was tall, and it came up past his ankles in the middle of the stream. This, too, was a good thing.

Alano's magic had brought the rain back to the mountains. Someday this would be a large river again. Then the forests would all return and this home would be a land full of life. Shorty would not allow the Bad Cloud named Set or anyone else to harm this land again. He would protect his home and his people. Protecting was all that he really knew how to do well.

Shorty was hot and the cold water felt good. He debated taking a cold bath here or a warm bath back at the Keep. Or maybeso baths? Shorty liked to bathe. He did not like to smell like an ogre anymore. Two baths, he decided. Shorty sat and pulled off his boots and socks. He removed his sword belt and lay it on the bank of the stream. Even this close to the Keep, he made sure he could reach the hilt from the water's edge.

Then he rose and stomped into the stream. He played for a time, splashing water like a small child. But it was not as much fun without his friend Ride. There was no one to splash water back at him. The mammoth would have filled its great trunk with water and sprayed it all over him. It would have been a great game. With no one to play with, Shorty lay down near the bank and just let the cold water wash over his body. He used the sweat-stained shirt to scrub some of the dirt away. Then he closed his eyes and let his problems be carried away by the gently running water.

He was not sure how long he lay there with the water pulling the sun's heat from his body. It was peaceful. That peace was shattered by a muffled sound on the grassy bank above his head. Shorty's hand was already on the hilt of his sword when a shadow fell across his face and upper body. Shorty opened his eyes unsure if he faced a friend or an enemy. He was unprepared for the two creatures that stared down at his prone form.

A horse, black except for its charcoal-colored mane, stood on the bank above him. Jutting from its forehead was a long golden horn. It took him a moment to remember the word for the horses with horns. Unicorn. He had met unicorns before, but never one with a squirrel riding on top of its head. The squirrel was perched right behind the horn.

He released the hilt of his sword and rose slowly to stand barefoot in the stream. The squirrel began to chatter excitedly. It sounded very bossy. Shorty raised his hand and shook a finger at it. "No posed ta talks mean ta me dat way. Better says sorry or me no gonna cracks nuts fer youse."

The squirrel crossed its arms over its chest and made a rude noise. The noise sounded like the squirrel had gas except the sound came from its mouth. He shook his head and ignored the small creature. He turned his attention to the unicorn. He had never seen a black one before. And, all the unicorns he knew had white horns, not ones made of gold. Shorty locked stares with the unicorn and asked, "Him all a da times bees no bery nice?"

There was a soft nicker as the unicorn's head moved up and down. The squirrel grabbed for the horn to keep from falling into the stream. More angry chittering erupted from it.

Shorty hesitantly reached out. The urge to caress the black fur was almost irresistible. The unicorn came slowly down the bank and pressed its muzzle into Shorty's palm. Shorty's other hand came up to rub its neck. Its fur was so soft. They stood like that for a time as the chattering squirrel climbed slowly down the unicorn's neck to sit upon its broad back.

Shorty asked hopefully, "Him no bees da boss?"

The unicorn shook its head from side to side as another rude noise came from the direction of the squirrel. The unicorn began to nicker. Shorty listened carefully as the great beast told him what the Forest Lady wanted him to do.

Shorty nodded, "Finds Hicks, den go in ta magic door. Protect peoples dere. Bery portent ta keeps dem lady safe."

The squirrel chattered again. Shorty shook another finger at it. "Dat bees muches portent word. Youse need learns ta bees mo nicer." Then he nodded to the unicorn, "Me ken do dis fer da Lady."

The squirrel began to complain again, but the unicorn turned its head and blew softly at it. The squirrel threw its arms over its head and then went silent. It sat with its arms crossed, glaring at Shorty.

Shorty stretched his arms around the unicorn's neck and gave it a soft squeeze. As he leaned against it, he whispered, "Tank youse fer come ta me. Me do gooder job. Protects like Lady say ta do. Me bery sorry youse stuck wid only mean squirrel in whole world."

The unicorn rubbed its cheek against his before it turned, heading back up the bank. There was a sound strangely like laughter as it walked away. The squirrel continued to glare at Shorty. Shorty scratched his head as the two seemed to fade from view. There were no trees here to hide in. The unicorn and squirrel just disappeared.

Shorty picked up his sword and boots and began to walk home. Stormhold Keep awaited him. It took most of the evening to make sure everyone knew what needed doing while he was gone. Know Man and Relin always ran things while he was on missions for the goddess Mielikki. More often than not, they knew more about what needed doing than he did. His final stop was a visit with his son, Arlon, and Birdie Max. He needed to say goodbye again. Arlon was getting too used to his mother being gone. Shorty was not sure that was a good thing. He gave him a big hug and scratched his sensitive neck scales while his son chatted happily. Arlon promised once again that he would help Shorty protect Arcturus when he was bigger. Shorty intended to kill all the bad things before his son was old enough to keep that promise. That was what Mama's did, right?

Tired, Shorty began the long walk back through the tunnel that led to his son's lair. He needed to sleep. But first, he was going to get that hot bath he had promised himself many hours ago.

Shorty woke well before dawn. He donned his armor and placed each of his weapons in the right place. There were a lot of weapons. It was always hard to know which ones he might need, so he just brought them all. He made sure each was ready to use. Protecting usually meant fighting. He needed to be ready for anything and everything the Bad Cloud, Set, might send at him. This was why he was the Green Knight after all.

When everything was arranged to his satisfaction, he headed down to the dining room. Althea was already there. She had prepared a large platter of meat rolls. Shorty thanked her before sitting down to polish them off. Sausage, egg, and crispy pig meat with lots of garlic and onion. Althea always took good care of him.

Ez'ard wandered into the room while he was eating. His friend did not look very happy to be awake. "Tell me again why all of your missions mean that I have to get out of bed and watch the sun come up. What is wrong with leaving after lunch?"

Shorty just grinned at his friend and offered him the last meat roll. Ez'ard shook his head looking a bit ill. "It is too early to eat, especially one of those."

Shorty shrugged and popped the last meat roll into his mouth. He picked up the pitcher of juice and poured a large glass that disappeared faster than his food had. He winked at Ez'ard as he placed the glass back on the table. "Youse ken goes backs ta bed soon as youse opens magic door ta Hicks. Or, ken maybeso comes wid me gets in muches big fight. Maybeso finds treasure. Maybeso jus gets hurted. Dat bees muches mo fun den sleepin."

The sour look on the elf's face made Shorty laugh. Ez'ard motioned to the door and the two walked quietly down the hall to the main door. Once in the courtyard, Ez'ard reached into his belt pouch and pulled out a scroll. "I miss my arch, Shorty. I hate asking Know Man for portal scrolls." Ez'ard unrolled the scroll and stared down at it. He whispered as he read, "shAH At." Shorty tried to remember the word, but it slid from his thoughts and was gone.

A silver oval four feet wide and ten feet tall shimmered into existence. Ez'ard motioned for Shorty to approach the light. When Shorty stood before the portal, the elf muttered softly, "Do not to get yourself killed, Shorty. You do not have the team to back you up this time. So, do not act like an ogre."

Shorty grinned and patted his friend on the shoulder. "Me bees ogre, Ez'ard. No ken bees sumtin else." Shorty's attention shifted to the oval before him. On the far side was a grove of trees. One of the trees shifted position, stepping forward. It must be his friend Hicks. With a wave goodbye, Shorty stepped through the oval.

The ground on the far side of the oval was not smooth like the courtyard's. The boot on Shorty's bad leg struck a rock which bounced across the ground in front of him. He took a deep breath. The air here smelled of trees and grass and other plants. The Grove of the Tree People had recovered much faster than Stormhold had. Plants grew everywhere here.

Shorty turned to greet his friend Hicks, but the tree person standing by the trees was not Hicks. This tree person was much smaller than Hicks. He, no, she, was covered in white and pink flowers. In some places, small red fruit hung from her branches. Shorty had to think for a moment before he remembered her name. "Hullo, Cherry. Me no see you fer long time. All bees kay?"

Cherry took several long steps and stood before Shorty. "I am well, Green Knight. Thank you for asking. It is good to see you once more. Would you mind sitting and talking with me before the Hickory takes you to the gate between worlds?"

Shorty shrugged. He checked behind him before sitting, but the magic door to his home was gone. He dropped to the grass and looked up at Cherry. "Me likes ta talks. What wants ta talks bout?"

Cherry's root-like toes wiggled and sank into the soil. Shorty watched them in fascination. They had completely disappeared before he remembered that he was supposed to be listening to Cherry not watching her feet. He grinned up at her sheepishly. "Oopses!" he muttered when he saw she was waiting for him to pay attention.

The tree shivered as a merry chuckle escaped from her lips. "It is okay, Shorty. Sometimes, I forget how easily distracted you are. I will keep my feet in the soil so you can concentrate." Cherry waited until Shorty was focused on her before she continued. "The Grove needs your help."

Shorty thought for a moment before answering. "Me wants ta helps tree friends, but me posed ta do sumtin fer Lady of Forest. Ken do when me comes back?"

A branch lowered to gently caress Shorty's cheek. "The help we need, my friend, would be part of the journey Mielikki has asked you to take. This task may even help you to accomplish what she has asked you to do. Will you listen carefully?"

Shorty nodded and did his best to pay attention. Cherry continued, "The place you are going to has long been a place of safety for those that the Goddess needs to protect. Treants used to thrive there. They were the guardians of Sanctuary. But even our kind do not live forever. Only three of the tree folk still survive in Sanctuary. If Sanctuary is to continue being a place of safety, then my kind must flourish there once more."

Shorty was puzzled. Only a few of her words had made sense to him. "No knowed what me ken do ta helps. Me jus bees ogre. No bees drud ta makes tree growed up."

Cherry's laughter came again, softer this time. Several blossoms floated down to land near Shorty's feet. "You will never be just an ogre, Shorty. What we ask is simple. We have seeds for our children. We ask that you carry them with you and plant them around Sanctuary. Nothing more than that is needed."

Excitement washed over Shorty. "Ken makes mo friend ifn puts seed in ground?"

Cherry's voice is regretful. "I am sorry Shorty. Our children take a long, long time to grow. Far longer that the life of an ogre. Even an ogre that is the Green Knight."

Shorty considered her answer and then asked, "Maybeso bees friend fer Arlon when him growed up?"

Cherry nodded; her branches all shook in time with her head. "Yes, Shorty. If Arlon is patient and a very good boy, these seeds might give him many new friends."

Shorty stood. "Den me do ifn no bees fightin all da times."

Another taller form entered the clearing carrying a cloth sack. Shorty looked up and waved. "Hullo, Hicks."

The tall hickory Treant walked closer. "Hello to you, my very short friend."

One of Cherry's limbs gestured towards the sack hanging from Hick's branch-like hand. "That is an enchanted seed bag, Shorty. It contains twenty seed pods. There are two for each type of Treant that lives in this Grove. The seeds are… uhm… asleep as long as they are in the sack. Once you take one out, it must be planted right away."

Shorty chimed in, "Den gibs seed water."

Hicks' laugher joined with Cherry's. "That would be a wonderful thing to do for the seed, Shorty. Can you remember all this?"

Shorty began to touch a different finger for each step as he replied, "No open bag cept fer ta plant seed. Take seed out an puts in da ground fast. Den gib water."

Hicks nodded. Cherry added one more instruction, "Do not plant them close together. They need a lot of room to grow strong."

Shorty nodded and held out his hand. Hicks lowered his branch and Shorty took the seed bag. It did not feel heavy, so he tied it to his belt.

The hickory Treant turned and began to walk north. "Time to go, my short friend. I will take you to the portal."

Shorty began to run after Hicks. Then he paused and turned. "Me sees youse when done protect an plant friends fer Arlon. Bye, Cherry. Me do good job."

Cherry waved a limb. "So long, Shorty. I know you will do your best."

Shorty turned and ran to catch up with Hicks.

Hicks led Shorty past a great many trees. As it had the other times they had come this way, a thick mist rose from the ground. Soon it was hard to tell where he was going. Hicks did not seem to notice the mist at all.

An unexpected gust of wind cleared the area before them, revealing the familiar sight of the gateway. Two purplish-brown trees leaned together, their upper branches intwined to form an arch that shimmered with silver light. Shorty knew touching that pool of light would leave him wet and strangely refreshed.

The deep, slow rumble of Hicks' voice sent him on his way, "Be well, Green Knight. The Lady's blessing be upon you."

Shorty patted his friend's trunk before plunging into the silver light.

Chapter 2

The Lady

Voices bombarded her from every direction. There was no place she could go to escape them. "Attack… Mage… Flee… Priest… Fire… Knight… Ogre… Save you… Trust… Hell… Faith…" The voices swirled and clashed. Their messages eluded her as each voice attempted to be heard over the others. All of them seemed convinced that their message was more important than any of the others.

She wanted to scream. It was all so overwhelming. Just as she felt she could take no more, a new sound cut through the chaos. A deep, melodious voice began to hum. The song was beautiful, and it brought her a measure of peace. But the song was somehow incomplete as if some important piece of the melody was missing.

The chaos receded leaving Annah alone in that place between sleep and waking. Part of her wanted to remain asleep so she could listen to that deep voice and the song that made her feel so safe. She wanted to hear the missing notes that would complete the song and her understanding of the world she lived in. Another part of her yearned to awaken before the voices she feared resumed their assault on her mind. In the end, the choice was not hers to make. Her eyes fluttered open to darkness. It was not the darkness of night though. It was the darkness of her prison, a prison she would never be able to escape. There was, after all, no way to escape one's own body.

Annah lay quietly in her bed. She tried to remember the song, but it was already slipping away from her. It took with it the sense of peace she had felt. All that was left of the dream were voices, so jarring and loud that she could still feel their vibrations on her skin. The hair on her arms was standing up straight. Air flowing across the upright hair made her shiver.

She stroked her arms to calm her nerves and force the hair to lay flat once more. What had the voices been trying to warn her about? Was there a threat to the Grove or was it all just a silly nightmare? Had the warnings been a manifestation of her magic or were they just a figment of her overactive imagination? The only thing she was certain of was that she did not want the voices to come again.

Annah rolled to her stomach and buried her face in her pillow. She wanted to have normal dreams. Dreams like other people did. Her sister, Meerah, would sit at breakfast and describe the wonderous things she saw and did in her dreams. Annah wanted dreams like those, but she would never have that kind of dream. Those were the kind of dreams that people who could see had. Blind people like her did not see images in their heads. Their minds could not create dream pictures of things they had never seen. Maybe if she had been able to see when she was little, but Annah had been born blind. Her mind had nothing to build that kind of dream from.

All Annah had in her head were the auras she could see when she looked at other people. Sometimes there were auras in her dreams, but auras were little more than light or dark spots in the haze of nothingness. Those spots could be frightening or make her feel safe. Real or dream, the auras did not make for exciting tales to tell at breakfast. Even the visions that the Goddess sometimes sent contained only sound. Why were they called visions if she could not see in them? Annah wanted so much more. Was a beautiful dream too much to ask for? Life was so unfair.

Annah sighed. Self-pity would change nothing in her life. She rose and stood beside the bed. She used the edge of the mattress to check her angle before she walked carefully away from the bed. One... two... three steps and stop. Reach out with her right hand. The small bone comb was not there. Her steps had been a little too small. She edged forward a little and reached again. Her fingers closed around the handle sticking out from the lone shelf where she kept all her worldly possessions, the comb, a spare shirt, several sets of socks. It was not much, but she was grateful for what she had.

Annah ran the comb through her hair. It was a mess. She pulled several hairs out before she just gave up. What did the tangles matter? The only people that might see her were her mother and sister and the three Treants. Mama would fuss at her, but the Treants would not care if she had brushed her hair or not. She placed the comb back on the shelf and spun towards the door to her room. She swung her right foot forward and felt pain as her foot slammed into the wooden leg of her bed. The sharp pain in her two smallest toes brought tears to her eyes.

Annah took a deep breath. She was the only one who would pay the price if she let herself get angry. She bent carefully, making sure that she did not hit her head too. A lump on her forehead would just make things worse. Her fingers felt along the ends of her toes. Both toes were dry which meant they were not bleeding. The bad news was that she had shattered one of the nails. Annah picked away the broken pieces. This was her own fault. She knew better than to charge around the bed that way.

Shaking her head, she felt her way back around the bed to the small stool that sat on the floor near the head of the bed. Annah sat down and reached under the bed. Her socks were carefully tucked in her boots. The socks and boots were the only protection her feet had from the many hazards she could not see. She felt a little safer once they were on.

Rising from the stool, Annah felt her way around the bed to the door. She took a deep breath before opening it.

Her mother's too cheerful voice greeted her as she stepped into the common room. "Good morning, Annah. I was wondering if you were ever going to get out of bed. The sun has been up for several hours now."

Annah held her breath to keep from screaming. She wanted to yell that there was no daytime for a blind person. But she knew she was still feeling sorry for herself. The dream had upset her. It was not fair to take that frustration out on her mother. She placed her hand on the wall that would lead her to the table. "Good morning, Mama. I had a bad dream last night. Sorry to be so late."

"It is all right, child. I saved you a glass of cider and some acorn cakes for breakfast. They are on the table with a bowl of strawberry jam."

Annah counted seven steps along the wall. Her fingers sought and found the hook that Mama hung her apron on. She reached out with her right hand and found the back of the chair, thankfully, where it was supposed to be. "Thank you, Mama."

She sat down and slowly slid her hands across the table making sure where everything was. Each piece was where she expected it to be. Her sister, Meerah, never put things back when she ate. Guilt stretched out its sharp claws for Annah. She really had stayed in bed too long if Mama had already cleaned up the kitchen.

Annah used a spoon to spread some of the jam on her acorn cakes. She spread a second spoonful of jam before she began to eat. The jam was sweet and it hid the bitter aftertaste of the acorn meal. They had not had real flour since their arrival in the Grove. The thought of real pancakes or even real bread made her mouth water. Annah jumped when she felt her mother begin to brush her long hair. Her mother gently worked out the tangles Annah had been too angry to deal with.

Annah relaxed into the rhythm of her mother's brush strokes. Normally, she hated it when Mama fussed over her like this. It made her feel like a child who could not care for herself. She was almost nineteen years old now. She did not need her mother brushing her hair. But today, the love in her mother's touch was soothing. Annah sat eating quietly as her mother finished by twisting her hair into a loose braid.

"That looks better, child. You can be so beautiful with just a little effort. Now you will not be embarrassed if someone sees you."

Annah could not help the sarcasm in her voice, "Who, Mama? The Treants? We are trapped in a Grove that no one even knows exists."

Her mother patted her on the shoulder and turned away. "I need you to work in the garden this morning. The old plants are near played out. We will need more cucumbers and tomatoes and, I think, carrots. A little of your magic to get them started would be a nice touch.”

“Meerah was supposed to work in the garden today. Where did she disappear to this time?” Annah grumbled.

“Be nice, child. Your sister is working too. I am running low on meal, so I sent her out to the oaks to gather acorns. We can crack them tonight and I will grind them up tomorrow while you girls are studying.”

Annah swallowed her complaint. Searching for acorns on the ground was not something she could do. It was a back-breaking chore that required working eyes. Gathering enough food for the three of them was a lot of work even with the magic of the Grove. Crops grew surprisingly well here. More importantly, they grew all year long because there was no winter in the Grove. They would never have been able to store up enough food to get through a winter.

In addition to what they grew in their small garden, the Treants brought them a regular supply of apples, cherries, and pears. With the Treants help, they ate fairly well. But Annah did miss the wheat and corn that Papa had grown on their farm. And, truth be told, she missed the milk from the cows and the bacon from the boars Papa had hunted.

Annah put the spoon back into the jam. She had planned to spend the day with the Treants today. Ashley had promised to take her to the pond for a swim. But Mama was right, her magic would help the new plants grow faster. “I will be happy to work in the gardens this morning, Mama. Would you mind getting me to the right rows? Is there anything else you want me to plant?”

“Those are the things I need right now. But we can always use more lettuce and potatoes. But only if you have time.”

Annah finished her breakfast and made her way to the privy. Then she returned to the kitchen to get the cuttings and seeds she would need. It was looking to be another very boring day.

Part 2

The Knight's Quest

*"Neber knowed what youse gonna finds when opens new
door."*

Chapter 3

First Impressions

Moisture soaked into his skin and clothing. The world went cold and dark for an instant before bursting into light and warmth. His mind was suddenly clear and alert. His sore muscles from the day before moved without a hint of pain. He wondered if this was what if felt like to be borned all over again. The portal was good magic, a wonderful gift from the Goddess.

The buzzing sounds of many tiny wings filled the air. The sun, filtered through the trees, warmed his skin and armor. He inhaled deeply. The smell of life, of a woodland in bloom, welcomed him. The Balance was strong here. The scents of this place were different from those he had left on the other side of the portal. The plants and trees were not the same as those in Arcturus, but their smells were just as inviting. His mission seemed to be starting well.

He stood in the center of a small clearing surrounded by thick, older trees. These trees had been here for a long, long time. Shorty stared up at the sun that filtered through the trees. It felt good now, but it would not take long for his armor to become uncomfortably warm under that blazing orb. He was already growing thirsty.

Shorty licked the moisture of the portal from his lips. It tasted like a mix of fruits or maybeso some kind of nut. He could never quite decide which. As always though, that moisture satisfied his thirst completely. "Bery muches good," he murmured as he looked around the clearing.

Shorty squatted and dug his fingers into the ground beneath the tall grasses. The soil he raised to his nose was heavy and black. It smelled good. This clearing seemed a safe place and he had made a promise to Cherry. Shorty sank to his knees. He drew his dagger and used it to cut away a square in the soft grass. As the tuft of grass came loose, Shorty shook the dirt from its roots. Then used his hands to scoop out a hole about half the length of his dagger.

Opening the seed sack, he reached inside. He did not recognize the small nut that he pulled out of the sack. He wondered if squirrels would like this kind of nut. Shorty had a strange thought. Moisture from the portal still beaded on his armor. Would it help the seed the way it helped him? He rubbed the seed in those drops until the nut was damp. The nut pulsed in his hand. It was strange to feel a nut move by itself. Shorty placed the nut carefully in the hole.

The breeze seemed to hold its breath as Shorty scooped dirt back into the hole. The rustling of leaves and the calls of the birds died away as he smoothed the ground over the seed. Then, even the insects paused their activity as Shorty poured some of his own drinking water onto the resting place of the strange seed. Only after Shorty gave the ground a loving pat, did the sounds of the forest return to normal. He sheathed his dagger and stood once more. The first of Arlon's new friends had been planted. He had done everything he knew how to do.

Now it was time to do what the Lady had asked him to do. The problem was, he had no idea where to go next. The trees looked the same in every direction. He had expected to arrive near the women he was supposed to protect. He was trying to decide which way to go when the ground began to tremble beneath his feet. The sound of something large crashing through the forest came suddenly to his ears. Whatever was coming was big. Really big. Would he be forced to fight his first battle before he even found those he was to protect? His mission was not going the way he had expected. His fingers twitched with the need to grasp his sword's hilt, but he resisted that urge. Better to learn if this really was an enemy before drawing a weapon.

The crack of branches hitting each other was very close now. Then, one of the tree people charged into the clearing. The huge figure ignored Shorty. It made its way directly to the place where Shorty had buried the seed. It had many small branches that hung low like the long braid his mother had had. Shorty knew this type of tree was called willow. The hanging branches swung wildly as the willow rushed across the clearing. It came to a stop and its large eyes stared in shock at the resting place of the nut Shorty had just planted.

The willow's tall form loomed over Shorty, but it did not seem to notice him at all. The willow's large eyes were totally focused on the small square of bare dirt between its root-like feet. A low whisper that sounded like a breeze blowing through its branches filled the clearing. "Magic. Powerful, wonderful magic. Creation magic that we have not felt in many, many seasons. A new cycle of life begins. I must tell Ashley and Corey."

The Treant's eyes slowly rose from the ground. It blinked in surprise as it became aware of the ogre standing quietly before it. It leaned closer to Shorty as if trying to understand how Shorty had appeared in front of it. "You are a stranger to Sanctuary. The wards let you in, but they did not tell us of your coming. That should not have happened. This, too, I must tell Ashley."

Shorty watched as the willow straightened and began to turn away. It paused and a long rope-like limb pointed towards the bare spot on the ground. "Did you bring this gift?"

Shorty smiled as he stared down at his work. "Me plant seed. But no bees me idea. Friends, Cherry an Hicks, tells me ta plants new friend in dis place. Gib me da seeds. Me jus puts one in dat hole."

The Willow's soft whisper became agitated, "Seeds? You have more such gifts?"

Shorty nodded as his hand touched thc sack at his waist. "Gots muches. Hicks an Cherry say no ta puts dem bery close ta eaches udder."

The Willow shivered in excitement. It turned and began to move back the way it had come. Shorty heard it mutter to itself as it practically ran away, "I must tell Ashley and Corey. Sanctuary can live again. They must hear the good news."

The willow rushed towards a gap between two large pine trees. Shorty quickly considered his options. He did not have any. The willow at least had some idea where it was going. Shorty followed it. Maybeso the Ashley or Corey it was heading for would know where to find the ladies he was supposed to protect. Shorty could only hope.

The willow was fast. It had an almost magical ability to avoid tree trunks and the many large roots that stuck up above the ground. Shorty was not so lucky. Even with what the portal had done for him, Shorty's bad leg ached as he tried to keep up with the fast-moving tree. His left leg did not always clear the roots, causing him to crash into tree trunks as he tried to run after his prey. Shorty had never felt this clumsy in a forest before. Would the leg also hinder him in battle? For the sake of the ladies, he prayed it would not.

Shorty quickly realized that he could not keep up. The willow was simply too fast. Shorty slowed to a walk. Before long, he did not even have swaying branches to show him where the willow had gone. Shorty checked for tracks but found none. It was hard to believe that anything that big could move through the forest without leaving any signs. Not even the fallen leaves had been disturbed by the willow's passing. He had lost his guide. With no other options, he continued to walk in the same direction.

Shorty moved quietly through the trees. His attention was split between the underbrush before him and the branches above him. Maybeso he could find a squirrel or a bird that would give him directions. But there were none. The small creatures must have fled as the willow ran past. Shorty was about to admit he was lost when he heard voices to the left of his chosen path. The voices were too soft to hear clearly and Shorty could not make out any of their words.

Again, he wondered if these were friends or enemies. There were just so many things that the unicorn and squirrel had not told him about this place. He was not happy. He was positive it was the mean squirrel's fault. Shorty moved slowly from tree to tree, using all of his ranger skills to remain undetected. For once, even his bad leg cooperated. He listened at each tree, hoping for more information about whoever was ahead.

His patience was eventually rewarded. The voices became clearer and the words more distinct. What he had assumed to be a conversation was only a single voice, that of a woman. The woman was not talking though, she was singing. Although Shorty did not recognize the song she sang, it was very similar to the teaching songs that Mama had sung to him when he was small.

The sunlight grew brighter as he approached the voice. The woman appeared to be in a large clearing just ahead. Shorty slipped from shadow to shadow as he searched for the source of the song. He wanted to see the person singing before they saw him. He worried that the singer would run in fear at the sudden appearance of an ogre like him. His approach to the edge of the clearing went unnoticed, his footsteps lost in the simple rhythm of the song. He stood behind a large, double-trunked tree on the edge of the clearing. The words of the song were finally understandable.

"Plant tomatoes and cucumbers far apart,

They will need more space once they start.

Carrots grow best in straight lines,

Give lettuce more room and it will be fine.

Potatoes and onions grow under the ground,

Mark where you put them so they can be found."

Shorty leaned closer to the narrow opening between the twin trunks. The small gap revealed rows of plants growing in the clearing. A stream marked the far edge of what could only be a garden. The words of the song faded away, but the voice continued to hum to the sound of a shovel digging in the soil.

The woman with the pretty voice was hidden behind the larger of the two trunks. The only way to satisfy his curiosity about her would be to move. Staying close to the tree, Shorty began to shift left as quietly as he could. He lifted and carefully settled each foot before moving the next one. He made no sound as he came out from behind the twin trunks.

Row after row of plants became visible as he slipped out of his hiding place. This garden was like the one Althea grew, only much bigger. A path ran through the center of the garden, continuing into the forest on the far side of the clearing. The path did not matter though. One more step to the left brought a small form into view. A young woman knelt in the dirt with a tiny shovel in one hand. Her attention was on the seedlings she was planting in an empty row.

The shovel sank into the soil, creating a small hole. Shorty watched as she lifted something green from a pot and settled it into the hole. Then her dirt-covered hands packed the loose soil around the tiny plant. Her actions captivated him. She began to sing a new verse about beans and peas. Her voice reminded him of Mama. He still remembered the songs Mama had sung to him as a child.

He watched her for a long time as she dug, planted, and patted down the soil much as Althea did. But the young woman added an extra step. Before moving to the next plant, the woman cupped her hands around the seedling. The plants between her hands shivered and reached for her fingers. Shorty was sure the plants looked bigger when she pulled her hands away. How could that be? Plants took time to grow. He was certain nothing in Althea's garden grew that fast.

Shorty was fascinated by what he saw. He wanted a closer look at one of the plants as it rested between her hands. Without thinking, he shifted his left foot forward, hoping to see more of what she did to make the plants grow. A small twig cracked under his boot. It was a soft sound, but the woman noticed and sat up straighter. Her head came up, but she did not turn to look at where he stood. Instead, she turned one ear towards him as if listening.

"Who is there? Mama? Meerah, is that you?" The woman placed her small shovel on the ground in front of her. Anger tinged her voice as she called again, "Meerah, please do not play around today. I had a bad night, and I am not in the mood for silly games. If you are done collecting acorns, please help me finish in the garden."

The woman sat as if waiting for a response. Shorty watched as her anger was replaced by uncertainty. "Meerah? Mama?"

Shorty shook his head. She was already afraid and she had not even seen him. He could not frighten her any more than he already had. He spoke softly as he stepped fully into the clearing, "No bees youse Mama or dis Meer Ah. Youse no knowed me, but me no gonna hurts youse. Me promise."

The young woman twisted around on her knees to face him. Shorty saw shock on her face. What else could he expect? Ogres were scary to the small peoples. Her eyes locked on him, but there was something strange about her stare. She did not blink. And, instead of looking up at his face, her gaze was focused on his chest. Shorty did not understand, but he was relieved not to see fear in her eyes. She seemed more curious about him than afraid of him. Almost of its own accord, her right hand came up and reached towards him.

Confusion tinged her voice as she spoke, "Your aura. I have never seen one like it before. Why is your aura so different?" Her head tilted to one side as she studied him. "Are those what Mama and Meerah call colors? You aura is… green. But how do I know what green is? And there is blue in it too. This is so strange."

Shorty looked down at himself in confusion. He had no idea what she was talking about. "What bees Ora? Me posed ta hab one a dem?"

The young woman continued to stare, but Shorty did not mind. He stared at her too. She was purty. He liked the way her feelings showed clearly on her face. She seemed like someone he could trust. But he did not understand why she still had not looked up at his face. Her eyes remained locked on his chest. Shorty shrugged, at least she did not seem to be afraid of him. Maybeso, she did not know how dangerous ogres were.

The woman drew in a deep steadying breath. "I am sorry. It has been a very long time since I met anyone new. Seeing you here is somewhat of a shock. No one new ever comes to Sanctuary, at least not in all the years that we have been here. And yes, you do have an aura. Everyone does. Yours is the most beautiful one I have ever seen."

Shorty looked down at himself still trying to figure out where the Ora was on him. "Lady bees kay? Youse talks bery strange."

The young woman began to giggle. "I am not the only one that talks strange. I have never heard anyone pronounce words the way you do. And I am not a lady. I am just an ordinary girl. My name is Annah."

Shorty felt embarrassed at her words. "Sorry, Ann Ah. Me no talks bery gooder. People talk bery hard ta dos some a da times."

The woman smiled at him. "It is alright. I like the way you talk. It is different and different is very exciting. Who are you? Are you here to hide in Sanctuary too?"

Shorty shook his head, but the woman was still looking at his chest. So, he tried words instead, "No come ta hides in dis place. Here ta protect. Me bees Shorty. Me da Green Knight. Forest Lady send me ta keeps youse safe."

The woman's eyes opened wider. "Forest Lady? Mielikki? You serve her too?"

Shorty nodded, but the woman still seemed to be waiting for him to answer her. After an awkward silence, Shorty again resorted to words. "Yes. Serbe her."

Ann Ah slowly rose to her feet, bent her knees and did something strange. "It is so nice to meet you, Green Knight."

Shorty tried to imitate her actions, but his bad leg did not like bending that way. He stumbled and almost fell. Ann Ah cocked her head to the side listening. "Are you alright Sir Knight?"

Shorty straitened back up. "Try ta do dat funny ting youse do. Bery hard. Almosted fall down."

The young woman giggled again. Shorty really liked that sound. "Men do not curtsey, Sir Knight. They bow like this." Shorty watched as Ann Ah bent forward at the waist keeping her head high as she did it.

Shorty nodded, "Dat bees ting me get teached ta do fer king. Posed ta makes king feels muches portent."

Ann Ah sucked in a breath. "You have met a king?"

Shorty considered her question carefully. He had met many kings. Should he tell her about all of them? Maybeso it would be better if he did not tell her about the salamander king he had killed. "Knowed two king. One fer peoples an one fer da fuzzface. No bees knowing hows come ebrybody make muches fuss bout king. Dem no bery good at fightin."

The woman's face grew puzzled. "What is a fuzzface?"

"Dem bery small peoples wid muches hair on dem face. Me Tribe call dem fuzzface," Shorty answered.

Ann ah became more excited at his explanation. "You have met dwarves too? I would love to hear your stories. Life here is pretty dull. Can you tell me more about your world while I finish planting the vegetables?"

Shorty glanced around the clearing. "No bees good idea. Me posed ta protect youse an yer Mama and maybeso Meer Ah. Three lady me posed to finds an keeps safe."

Ann Ah pointed off behind her. "Mama is back at the cabin cooking. Meerah is off collecting acorns."

A broad grin came over Shorty's face. "Nuts bees fer squirrel?"

Ann Ah shook her head. "No silly, for us. We need the acorns to make flour."

Shorty scratched his head. "Bees good magics ta makes purty flower from nut. Nut grow tree. Tiny seed make flower."

Ann Ah laughed once more. "That is a good joke." But her voice trailed off as she realized he was not joking.

Shorty took a step closer. "Ken usn finds youse Mama an Meer Ah? Ken no protect ifn no in da same place."

Ann Ah knelt back down and felt around until she found the tiny shovel. "We do not need to be protected, Sir Knight. Sanctuary is hidden by powerful magic. Even if someone found it, they could not get past the wards. There really is nothing to worry about."

Ann Ah continued talking as she began to dig another hole. "My family depends on this garden for most of our food. I need to finish the planting or we will go hungry in a month or so when these vegetables should be ready. Now that you are here, we have another mouth to feed. The new plants are even more important than ever."

Even to Shorty, it was obvious that she did not believe that any danger could reach her here. But he knew better. The Lady of the Forest would not have sent him if the danger was not real. He just did not have the words to convince Ann Ah. The only way he was going to get Ann Ahh to leave her garden was to help her finish what she was doing. The problem was that he really did not know much about gardens. Althea never wanted help. Her garden was like Shorty's marbles, something fun to play with.

Shorty eased around Ann Ah, making sure he did not step on any of her plants. Then he knelt on the ground facing her. He watched her cup her hands around one of the new plants. The plant really did move. Ann Ah had magic. The plant did not grow much, but it was definitely bigger when she moved her hands away. This was a magic even Shorty liked.

Ann Ah picked up her shovel and dug another hole. Shorty studied that hole carefully. It was about the length of his finger deep. One quick scoop with her small shovel and the hole was ready for a plant. Shorty did not have a small shovel, but he was not afraid to get his hands dirty either. While Ann Ah used her magic again, Shorty scooped out the next hole with his fingers. He was pretty sure it was about the right size. He waited to see if Ann Ah liked his hole.

Ann Ah picked up her shovel and scooted closer to Shorty. He watched in surprise as she sank the small tool into the ground right beside the hole he had created. The two holes looked the same. Shorty did not understand what was wrong with the hole he had made for her. He must have done something wrong. He pointed at his own hole and asked, "Why Ann Ah digs nudder hole in same place? Hole me makes no bees gooder nuf?"

Ann Ah stared down at the tool in her hand. Her face turned a strange shade of red. "I cannot see the hole you made, Sir Knight. I am blind. I thought you understood that."

But Shorty did not understand and that bothered him. Somehow, he had missed something important. "What bees blind? Not knowed dat word."

Ann Ah looked up in surprise. Her eyes centered on his chest again. "How can you not know?" She stopped then and the anger left her face and her voice, "You really do not know. There is only truth in your aura." Her hand came up and she wiggled her dirt-stained fingers in front of her eyes. "Blind is when your eyes do not work. Blind is a world filled with darkness that never ends." Her hand came down sweeping in a half circle in front of her. "I cannot see the ground or the holes. I cannot see the shovel or the seedlings or even the garden. And, I cannot see you, Sir Knight."

Sadness and pain marred her beauty for a brief instant. And then both were gone as if they had never been. Shorty had only seen that kind of pain once before, in a slave market filled with people that were now his friends. He felt her pain as he had felt the pain of those slaves. But he could not free her as he had freed the slaves. Shorty reached out and patted her hand. "Youse eyes no makes youse broke, Ann Ah. No eber bees broke long as keeps try hard."

Her face hardened and she almost growled at him, "How would you know? You have never been blind!"

Shorty tried to find the words to let her know he really did understand. "Me no bery smart. Head no work berry gooder. Makes muches big mess a tings. Muches mistake me make an me ken sees."

Ann Ah stared at his chest for long time. Shorty wondered what she saw there. Could she see his heart beating? When she finally broke the silence, her words were so soft that he could barely understand them. "I thought you were being cruel, but there is no darkness in your aura. I see only truth in your words." She paused, lost in thought. "Does it bother you that I am blind, Sir Knight?"

Shorty shook his head and then remembered that she did not see him. "No bees portent ifn youse eye no work. No bees portent ifn me head no all da times work. Portent ting bees hab good heart. Me tink Ann Ah gots bery good heart."

The sadness on her face eased, but did not disappear completely. She stared at his chest as she replied, "Thank you for the kind words, Sir Knight."

Shorty leaned forward and whispered, "Ann Ah maybeso calls me Shorty? Needs do dat afore me fergets who Sir Knight bees." She smiled then and Shorty felt better. At her smile, he knew they could work together. He rushed on, "Me wants ta helps. Maybeso me dig hole and Ann Ah puts little plant in hole? Maybeso yes?"

Ann Ah nodded and placed the shovel next to the row of new plants. Shorty began to make holes. Ann Ah ran her fingers across the row until she found his first hole. Her own fingers slid inside the hole. "Not quite so deep please, Shorty. Only the roots go into the hole, not the whole seedling."

Shorty nodded his agreement and made another hole. But he leaned forward to watch as Ann Ah cupped her hands around the next plant. The plant did move and reach out for her fingers. The plant was more than a seedling when Ann Ah pulled her fingers away. Shorty asked her, "Ann Ah gots magics?"

She hesitated for a long moment before answering, "Only a little, Shorty."

"Bery nice magics. Ann Ah makes magics like drud do." Shorty stuck his finger in the ground to make another hole.

Ann Ah lifted the next plant from the pot of seedlings. "Tell me about yourself please, Shorty."

They continued to plant while he told her about the Tribe where he grew up. When he finished, she told him about her father's farm and about her family. He understood the pain she felt when her father died. Before either realized it, they reached the end of the row.

When the last of the seedlings had been planted, Ann Ah retrieved the shovel and moved carefully back up the row of new plants. A thin staff lay at the ground at the end of the row. Shorty watched with interest as Ann Ah located the staff with her foot. She bent and grasped one end of the staff in her right hand. She began to tap the other end of the staff against the ground as she walked toward the center of the garden. Shorty followed a short distance behind trying to understand what she was doing.

Ann Ah moved the staff in a strange pattern. She seemed to be searching for something. When Ann Ah reached the path, the staff made a sharp click as it struck the ground. Shorty moved closer to see what she had found. A flat stone had been set into the ground in the center of the path. Shorty studied the path as it ran through the garden and into the trees. A line of similar stones marked the middle of the entire path.

Shorty was still trying to understand why anyone would spend the time to bury so many stones when Ann Ah began to follow the path. When her staff struck stone, it made another sharp click. When the staff strayed from the center of the path, there was almost no sound at all. The stones suddenly made sense. Ann Ah could not see, but she could hear well enough to follow the path.

Ann Ah walked through the garden with Shorty right behind her. When she reached the tree line, she turned to him. "Shorty, I can follow the path by tapping for stones, but it will take longer to return home. It would be much faster if you led the way. Then I can just follow your aura. Please? I want to introduce you to Mama and Meerah."

Shorty still did not understand what an "ora" was, but he could see the path and she could not. He moved past Ann Ah and began to walk slowly along the stone-lined path.

Chapter 4

Fear and Friendship

Shorty followed the winding path. The steam gurgled pleasantly just out of sight among the trees. The steady tapping of the staff on the rocks told him that Ann Ah was close behind. He glanced back to check on her. The staff continued to sweep from side to side, but Ann Ah's attention was on him. Whatever an ora was, Ann Ah seemed able to follow it without any problems.

The path they followed was a good one, but it was not without hazards for someone who could not see. The stones and dirt of the path had been worn smooth by frequent use. It was the trees to either side of the path that made their route more dangerous. Roots stuck up in many places, often between the stones that Ann Ah followed. Shorty marveled at the way the staff seemed to seek out and mark each obstacle. It was as if the staff were magic. His new friend never stumbled as she followed him.

They came around a final curve into another large clearing. Shorty stopped on the last of the smooth stone. A stone building rested in the center of the cleared space. This must be where Ann Ah and her family lived. It was a nice house if a bit small for someone his size. The building was old, very old. The stone corners were beginning to look almost round with age. Shorty wondered how long this place had been here. How many people had come here to escape the evil in the world? Had any of them ever been able to go back to their lives after coming here?

The clearing was mostly bare, hard ground. No grass grew within the circle formed by the trees. The clearing was not lifeless though. Beds of flowers had been planted around the house. Each bed contained a different color pattern. Pink and white in one bed, red with yellows and oranges in another, blues and purples in a third. Someone had worked hard to bring beauty to this place. Shorty felt sad that his new friend could not enjoy the view. The mingled scents of the flowers filled the clearing where his new friend lived. At least Ann Ah could enjoy the smells.

Shorty turned his attention to the building. Could he use it to protect the three ladies? The home was made of large stone blocks. A heavy wooden door was centered in the front wall. There was a small window to the right of the door and another window on the side of the building. Neither window had glass, but both had good wooden shutters. The house appeared sturdy enough to handle an attack. Unless the attackers had magic. Either way, he would have to protect them from outside. He was not sure if he could even fit through the door.

Ann Ah moved quickly past him; her staff leading the way. She headed straight towards the door as if she knew right where it was. Her voice was filled with excitement as she called out, "Mama, Meerah. Someone new has come to the Grove. Come meet my new friend. His name is Shorty."

Shorty moved further into the clearing where he could be seen, but he did not get any closer to the door. Ann Ah had made it clear that her family was not used to strangers, let alone an ogre coming to visit.

Before Ann Ah reached the house, the door flew open. A young girl about half the size of Ann Ah rushed out. She had dark hair and brown eyes just like Ann Ah. The young girl's mouth fell open as she got her first look at Shorty. Instead of the fear he expected, the young girl became excited. Shorty smiled encouragingly at her.

Shorty almost panicked as words began to pour from the child's mouth. "He is so big Annah. I thought you said he was short? And what are those things sticking up from his bottom lip? Is he going to be staying here in the Grove with us? I do not think he will fit through the door. He might need to live with the tree people. He could stay with Willie or Corey. No, that will not work, neither of them has a house."

The onslaught of words became a jumble in Shorty's head. He could not process even half of what erupted from the child's mouth. She seemed to be able to answer her own questions before anyone else could speak. He would have said hullo to the girl, but she hardly stopped talking long enough to breathe. There was no gap big enough for that one word. She finally paused and Shorty prepared himself for the next barrage of words. Before the young girl could continue, a second figure stepped from the house.

Shorty's heart sank. He knew trouble when he saw it. An older version of Ann Ah stood in the doorway. She turned slowly to face him. This woman's face had tiny wrinkles and her hair was the color of steel. The woman's eyes widened when she saw Shorty. Her face went pale. He could smell her fear from across the clearing. The older woman's hands shot out and grabbed the young girl, pulling her close. "Get inside, Meerah! Now!"

The young girl tried to twist away. "But Mama. I want to…"

The older woman backed through the doorway, pulling the child behind her. "Do not argue with me, Meerah. That thing is an ogre."

The child looked confused, "What is an ogre, Mama? Why do I have to come back inside, Annah said he was her friend?"

Ann Ah started to protest as well, "Mama, Shorty is not going to hurt us. He is a knight."

The young girl disappeared from view. The woman stepped out and grabbed Ann Ah's arm and yanked her towards the door. "Do not be a fool, Annah. Ogres are not knights. They are monsters. Ogres eat children. Get in here before he tries to eat you or Meerah."

Ann Ah allowed herself to be pulled through the door. The door closed with a loud thud. Shorty heard a bar slide into place. The shudders were slammed shut next even though he would never fit through the small windows. He heard Ann Ah arguing with her mother inside the locked building. It did not sound like Ann Ah was winning the argument.

Shorty had finally gotten the three ladies together in one place, but that was all that he had accomplished. The rest of his mission was not going well at all. Shorty stared at the closed door. Maybeso he could keep them safe if they stayed inside the house. But that meant not being allowed to talk to Ann Ah anymore. He did not like that idea very much.

Somehow, he needed to fix this. He needed the three women to believe that something dangerous was coming, but how could he convince Ann Ah's Mama that he was not the one they needed to be afraid of? Shorty was not sure how he had messed up the Lady's instructions so quickly, but he had. Keeping his promise was going to be very hard now.

Shorty considered what he should do next. He knew it would do no good to stand outside Ann Ah's home. Ann Ah's Mama would be even more afraid if she saw him waiting for them to come out. Shorty headed back to the garden. It was as good a place to wait as any. He would be close enough to help if anything attacked. And, if he stayed out of sight, maybeso Ann Ah would come back to work in her garden.

The walk back to the garden seemed longer without Ann Ah's company. Shorty stood on the edge of the garden wondering what he should do next. The rows of vegetables did not take up all of the space within the clearing. There was an open area along the edge of the stream. He might not be able to keep his promise to the Lady today, but perhaps he could do more of what Cherry had asked him to do.

Shorty crossed the garden to a spot beside the stream where a collection of dead plants had been piled. He knelt and pushed aside the pile. The dirt beneath was soft and moist. Shorty scooped out a hole like the ones he had made for Ann Ah. The sack opened easily, and Shorty pulled out a nut that he recognized. This one was from the same kind of tree as his friend Hicks. With a grin, he placed it in the hole and scooped dirt back on top of it. The forest around him went still as it had when he planted the first tree friend.

He had just sealed the sack when he heard movement behind him. Heavy footsteps approached down the path from Ann Ah's house. The sound of wood striking stone repeated over and over, but it was not the sound of Ann Ah's staff. These strikes were more solid. Shorty had expected company this time. The tree people somehow sensed the magic of the seeds. A familiar voice that reminded Shorty of rustling leaves exclaimed, "He is doing it again!"

Shorty did not turn to face the voice. He patted the soil one last time as he asked the Goddess to help the little nut grow. Then he rose and brushed the loose dirt from his armor. He stood with his back to his visitors, waiting until the rustling branches stilled. He turned to find three tree people watching him intently. The willow was at the back of the group pointing a branch-like hand at him. "He has gifted Sanctuary with another guardian. Can you feel it bonding with the Grove?"

Two more of the tree people stood beside the willow, an ash to its right and a hickory to its left. Shorty studied each of them in turn as they shifted their attention to the place where he had planted the nut. What he saw disturbed him. These tree people did not seem as vibrant as his friends in Arcturus. They looked worn out. Mold grew on their bark. Were they sick or just very old? He had never actually met an old tree person before. As weak as they appeared to be, Shorty guessed that they would be in as much danger as the three women when the attack finally came.

The ash tree stepped closer to Shorty. He realized that this tree person was a female. He recognized the tone of authority in her voice when she spoke to him, "Thank you, stranger, for what you have done here. Our strength returns as your gifts become a part of this Grove. I am Ashley. We are the last Guardians of this refuge. It is our duty to defend Sanctuary and all who seek to shelter here. I do not know who you are or why you have done this wonderous thing, but we welcome you. Your gifts may give us a little more time to save our home."

Shorty bowed. As his head came back up, he met her gaze. "No bees me gift. Arcturus send seed ta helps youse be strong gin."

The hickory stepped up beside Ashley. "I am Corey and my friend who you met earlier is Willie. Who or what is Arcturus? Although two seeds will not save us, we shall treasure them and nurture them to be best of our ability."

"Arcturus be me home. It bees far from dis place." Shorty's hand went to the sack tied to his belt. "Dere no bees jus two seed. Bees many mo. Arcturus want dis place bees bery strong."

The branches and leaves of all three Trees began to rustle and move. At first, Shorty thought that they were just excited. Then he realized that they were talking amongst themselves. He waited patiently until the Trees settled down again. The one called Ashley leaned forward in what Shorty assumed was a bow. "We do not understand why this land, Arcturus, would make such a sacrifice, but we offer our thanks for their gift."

Shorty returned the bow and Ashley straightened. Corey stepped forward and asked, "Who are you and why were you chosen to carry the gifts to us?"

Shorty smiled his best smile. "Me bees Shorty. Me da Green Knight a Arcturus. Me serbe da Forest Lady."

Corey swayed in Shorty's direction. His branches hovered just over Shorty's head. It was as if the hickory was trying to take in his scent, but tree people did not have noses. Corey slowly returned to a vertical position. "He speaks the truth. He is imbued with the power of a Green Knight. Sanctuary has not been blessed with the presence of a Knight since before I sprouted. The goddess Mielikki has answered our plea."

Willie creaked in the background as he swayed from side to side. The noise almost sounded like a giggle. His voice was soft as he spoke, "See, I told you he was a Green Knight."

Ashley waved a branch at the willow as if to silence him. Then she turned her attention back to Shorty. "Sanctuary welcomes you, Knight, for as long as you choose to stay among us. Be at peace here."

Shorty shook his head. "No gonna becs peace in dis place. Da Lady send me ta protect da peoples dat lib wid youse. Sum ting bad come fer dem lady. Muches danger."

The rustling noise began once more. After a time, Corey spoke, "We are old and have not the power we once did, but we have always kept those who shelter here safe. Few can see through the ancient spells that hide this place and none can break our wards. This will remain a place of safety. We will not fail at our sacred duty."

What was he to do if not even the tree peoples took his warning seriously. The hickory's words made it clear that Shorty now had six innocents to protect instead of just the three he had been charged with. Their faith in the magic of this place would get them all kilt unless he did much better than he ever had before. There could be no mistakes in the battle to come. Everything would depend on him.

Shorty watched as Willie and Corey wandered into the trees. It was clear that they had no concerns about the future. Ashley started to follow, but turned back to face Shorty. "If there is anything we can do to aid you in the planting, please ask. We will assist you in any way that we can."

Shorty gazed down the path that led to Ann Ah's home. A longing that he did not understand made him ask, "Ken youse telled da Mama dat me no bees monster? No gonna eats her kid."

Ashley nodded slowly, but her reply did not sound very hopeful. "I will speak to her, but that one's roots do not move easily once she has sunk them into the soil. The young saplings will hear my words, but their will is bound by she whose fruit they are." Then the ash turned and followed the other two trees into the forest.

Shorty spread his bedroll just outside the clearing that held the garden. He wanted to be close if anything went wrong. The night was a restless one for Shorty. He woke many times. The need to check on the small house and the women inside it drove him back up the path over and over again. Each time, the door was closed and the windows shuttered. Dawn found him pacing up and down the stone lined path. He greeted the sun with tired eyes and a sense of helplessness.

He did not like the way things were going, but there was little he could do here except worry and wait. And that waiting would be hard. Perhaps his time would be better spent planting more of the tree people seeds. His only hope was that the magic of those seeds could somehow strengthen the defenses that protected Ann Ah and her family.

This Grove was not so small like those of Arcturus. That was because it had not been through a war with the Bad Cloud named Set. Not yet at least. Shorty had a feeling that part of why he was here was to prevent such a war. He would do his best. A Grove this size must have many, many clearings that would be perfect for the seeds he carried. He just needed to find them. The tree people had offered to help, but Shorty preferred someone else's help. What he needed was a squirrel. His little friends would know all the best clearings to play in. With a last look at the locked door, he followed the stream away from the garden.

Shorty left the stone-lined path far behind. He wandered slowly through the trees, looking and, more importantly, listening for the sounds made by small creatures that could help his in his search. Unlike the day before, the air was filled with the voices of the tiny creatures who knew the hidden ways of the forest. One song in particular made him smile. The cheerful chirping of the birdie with the red belly was close by.

Shorty paused to study the nearby trees. He examined the trunk of each tree until he found the crevice with the nest hidden inside. Shorty moved closer to the nest. The happy song became a harsh scolding. Shorty looked up to see a male birdie perched on a nearby branch.

Shorty took two steps back when the female came out of the nest to join her mate. Both birds began to complain loudly. Shorty raised his hands in surrender. He pitched his voice low as he tried to reassure them, "No wants youse egg. Jus wants ta asks fer help. Please?"

The birds seemed surprised that they could understand him. He was not. This was the magic of being a Green Knight. Shorty waited for them to calm down before he asked where to find squirrels. The female began to chirp angrily. Apparently, she did not like squirrels very much. She complained that the pesky squirrels liked to hide nuts among her eggs. She did not like sitting on hard nuts. Shorty had to listen politely as the female told him the entire tale of her suffering. Thankfully, the male told him how to find the squirrels when she finished complaining. The female returned to her eggs and Shorty moved away as quickly as he could.

The direction that the male had indicated led through a bramble that left him with several nasty scratches. This path might be a good one for a bird, but it was not a lot of fun for ogres. Shorty considered the landmarks he had been given. They made very little sense to him. If this was how birds thought, maybeso ogres were not the no bery smartest things around. Only time would tell if birdies or ogres were smarter. As a second bramble came into view, Shorty wished again that the male had been willing to show him the way. But the birdie had refused. He would not travel far from the nest until the eggs hatched.

Traveling in a straight line like the birdie had told him to do was just not possible. Shorty had to dodge around trees, a small pond, and even a grumpy badger's den. It did not help that he had no idea what the place where the beetles swarmed even looked like. It was only by chance that he found the old pine where it had fallen in the tall grasses. Its wood was soft with rot and the trunk had more small holes in it than Shorty could count. Not only did several varieties of what Shorty assumed were 'delicious' beetles scurrying across it, many of the beetles' worm-like children were eating what was left of the old tree.

If this was in fact the right place, Shorty was getting close to where he wanted to be. He turned right and began to walk once more. According to the bird, the meadow filled with grasshoppers should be very close. The far side of the meadow was supposed to be where the squirrels made their homes.

It really was not a long walk to the place where the trees fell away on both sides of his path. A large meadow filled with tall grass stood before him. Shorty began to move through the sea of grass. Swarms of grasshoppers leapt from his path to disappear into the waist deep sea of gold. The trees on the far side of the meadow were all giants. He could see walnut and oak and even a few hickory trees. Many, many nuts for his little friends to eat. It was no wonder that the squirrels all lived nearby. Now he just needed to find a friend to help him. Squirrels were so much easier to talk to than birds.

Shorty paused out among the noisy grasshoppers to examine the trees. Somewhere in their branches, small balls of fur would be running from place to place. The squirrels would be playing hide and find or chase from tree to tree. All he had to do was crack a few nuts and he could have all the friends he wanted. Squirrels did not need a lot of encouragement to be friendly.

He scanned the upper branches searching for movement. A small brown form darted out across a broad limb. It paused in the middle of the branch and stood on its hind legs. Shorty imagined that it was checking for danger. Then it dropped to all four legs and darted towards the far end of the branch.

Shorty's breath caught in his chest. The branch that the squirrel was racing down stuck out over the meadow. There were no other trees nearby for the squirrel to leap to. The squirrel did not slow as it headed for the end of a branch. The branch bent low as the squirrel neared the end. Then it gathered itself and leapt.

The end of the branch sprang back up and the tiny brown body arced through the air. Tears came to Shorty's eyes as he imagined the end of the squirrel's leap. He refused to turn away. He watched as the squirrel spread its four legs wide as if reaching for a branch that was not there. Shorty blinked in confusion. The tears had to be blurring his vision. But no, tiny wings stretched between the squirrel's front and rear legs. It began to fly.

The squirrel was as amazing as it was beautiful. Before this moment, he could not have imagined such a thing as a flying squirrel. The squirrel did not beat its wings like the birds with the red bellies. It soared like a hunting bird high in the air. He watched it tip to one side, its path curving towards one of the large nut trees. Just before it crashed into the large walnut tree, it pulled its tiny legs back in close to its body. The legs scrambled furiously as it reached for a hold. And then it disappeared into the leaves of the walnut. Shorty let out a sigh of relief.

Longing gripped him like the squirrels did their nuts. He wanted very much to make friends with the flying squirrel. He would crack all of his nuts for such a friend. Could there be more than one such wonder in this Grove? Maybeso he could invite them to come home with him to Stormhold. In his mind, he saw squirrels flying from the trees and walls of the Keep to his bedroom window. They would eat nuts and tell each other stories. What could possibly be better than squirrels flying all around the Keep?

Then his happy dream met the unbreakable walls of reality. He had made a promise. He could not break it or the rules that Alano had given him. He had promised to never bring home any of the plants or animals that he made friends with as he traveled between worlds. He had no idea how the little squirrels could be dangerous, but Alano had assured him that it would turn out very, very badly. The druid's rules seemed very silly to him, but he had promised. So, there would be no flying squirrels at Stormhold.

Shorty continued across the meadow. He might not be able to bring a flying squirrel home with him, but he could still make friends with it. And he had never promised not to crack nuts for them. Shorty searched around the base of the trees for the best nuts he could find. There was quite a selection. He could see why the squirrels liked this place. When he had a large pile of nuts, Shorty found a comfortable tree to lean against. He began to crack the nuts, setting the nut meat on his leg and tossing away the shells.

While he worked, Shorty talked about squirrel things like playing chase, hiding nuts, and enjoying the sunshine on a high branch. He spoke of the squirrels that he had known before and how much he loved them. Mostly he talked about sharing all the lovely nut meat sitting in his lap. Shorty was patient. He moved slowly so as not to frighten those he knew were watching him. Eventually, he heard the sound of tiny claws sinking into the bark of the tree above him. Shorty kept the flow of his words soft and steady.

When a small hand reached up and grabbed a piece of nut meat, Shorty just smiled. The claws ran back up the tree behind him, but he did not even turn his head to look. The squirrel would come back. They always did. It was not long before he had several visitors scattered around him eating the pieces of nut he tossed their way. The squirrels chittered to each other. Only once did he interrupt their conversation. He made sure to correct that voice. "Ogres no eats squirrel. Me jus scratch dem ear bery gooder."

Soon the squirrel was perched on his knee eating and chattering at him. A second squirrel joined the first. By the time he ran out of nuts that he could reach, he had six squirrels playing chase around him. When they wanted more to eat, they brought him new nuts to crack.

He lost track of time as he visited with the squirrels. One of them even let him touch its wings. The wings did not have feathers, but they were very soft. Shorty was startled when the squirrels all scurried into his lap to hide. Ann Ah's voice spoke from behind him, "What are all the small lights around you, Shorty? I have never seen such tiny auras before."

That voice made the world seem a brighter and happier place. He looked up to see Ann Ah sitting in the crook of one of Ashley's sturdy limbs. Shorty grinned at her before looking down to reassure his new friends. "Bees kay," he whispered to them. "Me keeps youse safe." Shorty watched as Ashley lowered Ann Ah to the ground. Then, without a word, Ashley just walked away. Shorty was so happy to have Ann Ah back with him that he forgot to thank Ashley.

Shorty began to tell the squirrels how nice and friendly Ann Ah was. One by one they crawled up on his lap to watch her. Ann Ah waited patiently as Shorty asked the squirrels if she could join them. When they agreed, he looked at Ann Ah and said, "Dese bees me friends, da squirrels. Ann Ah come close bery slow. No makes dem scairt please."

Ann Ah laid her staff on the ground before approaching him one careful step at a time. Shorty continued to reassure the squirrels as she came closer, "Dat bees Ann Ah. Her no gots many friend. Her needs squirrel mo dem eben Shorty. Maybeso youse bees her friend too?"

When she reached his side, she eased herself to the ground. Shorty was glad to see that she kept her hands folded in her lap. The squirrels watched her even more closely than Shorty did. Their attitude was more curious than aft raid. Ann Ah's eyes darted from side to side as the squirrels began to chatter once more. Her voice was filled with awe as she told Shorty, "Their auras grow brighter when you talk to them. It is like they are becoming more than they were. This is all so strange and a little scary."

Shorty stared at the squirrels; not sure what Ann Ah saw that he did not. "Squirrel got dem ora ting too? Maybeso it jus bees dem nuts."

"All living things have an aura, Shorty. Some are just brighter than others," she explained.

One of the squirrels climbed out of Shorty's lap to sniff at Ann Ah. She did not move, so it grew bolder. It reached out a small hand to touch her fingers. Ann Ah smiled down at it. "What does it want?" she asked.

Shorty reached out and placed a small piece of nut meat in her palm. "Wants nut ta eats. No bees fraid Ann Ah." Shorty withdrew his own hand.

The brave squirrel climbed onto Ann Ah's leg. It sniffed at the nut in her hand before standing on her fingers to reach the tiny treat.

Ann Ah's smile grew. "They are soft and so warm." Then the squirrel ran up her arm to rest on her shoulder. Ann Ah giggled, "it's feet tickle."

Shorty placed another piece of nut meat in her hand. "Her want mo nut. Gib her ta eats."

Ann Ah slowly raised the nut to the squirrel on her shoulder. Tiny paws took the treat and shoved the whole piece into its mouth. It leaned over and gently patted Ann Ah' on her cheek before leaping to the ground. Shorty watched it run into the sunshine. The nut came back out of its mouth, and it began to nibble at the treat.

Ann Ah raised her eyes towards Shorty. "How do you get them to come to you this way? Wild animals are normally afraid of people."

"Me feed dem. Me talk wid dem. Talk muches cuz squirrel listen gooderer. Dem no care ifn me no talks bery good."

Ann Ah smiled and shook her head. "I hear you chattering to them. But I think they just like the sound of your voice. It is not like they can understand you."

Shorty looked down at the squirrels climbing in his lap. "Dem knowed what me say. Me talks dem listen. Sum a da times eben tells me da answer ta me question."

Ann Ah sounded incredulous, "How is that possible, Shorty? They are just animals."

Shorty cracked several more nuts and handed them to Ann Ah. "Afore me bees Green Knight, me talk but me not knowed what dem told me. Now me knowed what dem say and dem knowed what me say. Maybeso bees magics."

He began to speak with the squirrels. He asked them to help him watch over Ann Ah. As he chattered with them, Ann Ah seemed to stare at him. Then she sucked in a breath and whispered, "Magic. It is so faint that I almost missed it. Forest magic. Did you cast a spell to speak with them?"

Shorty shook his head. "No bees spell. No eben bees me magic. Arcturus put da magics in me when makes me Green Knight."

Ann Ah stared down at her arm. "I wonder, can my magic do that as well? Maybe. Shorty, please talk with them again."

He did as she asked. Shorty began to chatter with the squirrels. He told them of his need to plant the special seeds. But the squirrels only wanted to eat his seeds. Burying nuts was only for the cold time and there was no cold time here. The squirrels began to lose interest until Shorty explained that planting the seeds was a new game.

Shorty looked up when Ann Ah suddenly interrupted, "I can do it, Shorty! I can understand them! I have to concentrate, but their words are there." Ann Ah stared at the squirrels as they continued to chatter in Shorty's lap. "Do they ever talk about anything except nuts and games?"

Shorty considered his answer. "Some dem bring message from Forest Lady. Udders jus talks bout hab fun. Ken helps ifn no ask hard tings." Shorty held out his hand and one of the squirrels climbed up onto it. He asked it to help him with his special game. He needed a good place to plant one of the seeds. The squirrel tilted its head to one side as it considered his request, then ran up his arm to sit on hiss shoulder. A tiny squirrel hand pointed into the forest.

The other squirrels scampered up the tree and were soon out of sight. Shorty stood and helped Ann Ah to rise. Then he picked up her staff. She seemed puzzled. "What seeds do you need to plant? This is too far from our home to gather food."

Shorty placed her staff in her hands and began to walk in the direction the squirrel had pointed. He walked slowly as he had the day before. "No plant fer food. Plant friend. Dem takes bery long time ta growed."

Ann Ah laughed, "How can you plant friends? Do you have a stash of magic people seeds?"

Shorty paused to wait for her. "Come, me show youse." Ann Ah's staff began its strange dance as she followed him.

The squirrel led them to a small grass filled clearing. Sunlight bathed the center of the clearing. Ann Ah joined Shorty as he knelt in the sunlight. It took but a moment to cut away a small square of grass and dig a shallow hole. Shorty opened the sack and reached inside. The seed he pulled out was a walnut like the ones he had fed the squirrels.

The squirrel on his shoulder leaned forward, suddenly interested in this new game. Shorty whispered to it, "Dis one no fer youse. Dis one make new tree fer ta grow many mo nut. No digs it up." The squirrel chirruped its agreement. Reaching up, Shorty tugged Ann Ah's fingers until she knelt beside him. He placed the walnut in her hand.

Ann Ah's mouth fell open as her fingers wrapped around the hard surface of the nut. "Shorty, do you know what this is?"

Shorty smiled at her, "Tree peoples seed. Bery porten!"

She hugged the seed to her chest. "I feel the magic inside it. It calls to me. I thought you were just teasing me when you said you were going to plant a friend. Is this why Willie is so happy you are here?"

Shorty did not answer, he could not. He did not understand the strange willow. Instead, he simply moved her hand to the hole he had dug. He waited for her to place the seed in the hole. When she did, he poured water into the hole. Together, they pushed the dirt over the seed and patted it down. Then Shorty sat back as Ann Ah cupped her hands over the mound of dirt. The squirrel chittered excitedly. When Ann Ah pulled her hands back, a small green shoot protruded from the soil.

Ann Ah found his hand and squeezed it. "Thank you for sharing that with me. Planting a Treant seed is not something I ever expected to do."

Shorty smiled. "Ken do mo ifn youse wants. Meer Ah ken comes too ifn youse Mama no bees fraid no mo."

Ann Ah slowly shook her head. "I would love to do more Shorty. But not Meerah, not yet at least. Changing Mama's mind is going to take some time. She is so afraid of you. I do not understand it. Mama would not listen to Ashley. I am sorry," she smiled for a moment. "Ashley told her you definitely do not eat children."

Shorty grunted in disgust. "Peoples no taste bery gooder. Ifn me eats da peoples den gots no bodies fer bees me friends. Better ta eats horse. Dat berry yummy. Eben eats bread bees betterer den peoples."

When he spoke of bread, Ann Ah's stomach began to growl. Shorty laughed, "Me do dat lots time. Ann Ah wants ta eat?"

"Are there any fruit trees nearby? I snacked on enough nuts for one day when we were with the squirrels."

Shorty looked around. "No see no apple tree. It bees kay. Me ken get lotta food ifn Ann Ah bee hungry."

Ann Ah brushed the dirt from her hand and asked, "How are you going to make food? Do you have a kitchen hidden somewhere around here?"

Shorty replied proudly, "Muches betterer. Me gots magics sword."

Ann Ah sounded doubtful, "Are you going to hunt for food? I am not sure the Treants will approve of that."

Shorty shook his head. "Huntin take muches time. Den gots to cooks meat." Shorty could see she was confused by his response, but he was not sure how to explain it to her.

 What other kind of food can you get from a sword?" she finally asked him.

"Da bestus kinds!" Shorty exclaimed. Shorty rose and moved to a shady spot on the edge of the clearing. As he spread his cloak on the ground, the squirrel leapt from his shoulder and scurried up a tree. Shorty led Ann Ah to the cloak and helped her to sit on it. He could tell she wanted to ask questions, but he did not give her a chance. He wanted this to be a surprise.

Shorty reached over his shoulder and drew his sword, New Horizons, from its scabbard before sitting on the cloak across from Ann Ah. Shorty settled the blade across his lap with the edge facing his own stomach. It was not the safe way to hold the sword, but he did not want to risk Ann Ah getting cut. The cloak suddenly shifted beneath him. Shorty looked up to see Ann Ah pulling away. He realized that he should have warned her but now it was too late. "Bees Kay, Ann Ah! No bodies gonna hurts youse."

Ann Ah seemed to stare at the sword resting on Shorty's knees. "That aura… What is it? It just appeared between us. It is too bright to be one of the squirrels."

Shorty looked around in confusion. "No bodies bees wid us. Eben squirrel gone. Jus youse an me an New Horizons."

Ann Ah's eyes stared blankly down at Shorty's lap. For the first time, he could see that there were golden flecks in the deep brown of her eyes. She blinked and raised her head. "Who or what is New Horizons?"

Shorty lifted the sword into the air before her. "Bees me sword. Bery smart sword. It knowed muches. Ken do magics. Telled me portent tings when me no unnerstan what me posed ta do."

Ann Ah smiled at him. "You are just teasing me now." Then the smile was replaced by a look Shorty did not recognize. "But the squirrels did talk to you, I just did not understand them. Your sword can really talk to you? Does it talk like the squirrels do or like you and I do?"

Shorty shook his head, forgetting that Ann Ah could not see him. "No da same. Squirrel an peoples make noise when talk. Hear dem wid me ear. Sword gots no mouth. It just make word in me head."

"The things you tell me are so strange," Ann Ah replied with a small shake of her head. "Sometimes they are difficult to understand or even believe."

Shorty tried to reassure her, "All da times me telled Ann Ah da truth. Me promise."

Ann Ah smiled at him. "Thank you for your honesty, Shorty. Your sword sounds exciting. I have never spoken to a sword before."

Shorty lowered the sword to his knees again. He took a moment to think before speaking. "New Horizon, dis bees me new friend, Ann Ah. Her tinks youse got nice ora. Not knowed what dat bees. Her neber talks ta sword afore. Maybeso youse ken says hullo ta her?"

New Horizons did not answer him immediately as it normally did. But then its familiar presence filled his mind. *An aura is the good or bad that lives inside of each person, Shorty. It is a rare gift to see auras the way she does. And yes, I will speak with your Annah. She intrigues me. Help her to place her hand on to my hilt.*

Shorty was not sure how to take New Horizons' explanation. "Ann Ah eyes no work. Hows ken her sees in da side a me?"

There are many ways to sense things, Shorty. You see, but you also use your nose and your ears. Your friend can sense what kind of person you are on the inside. She is very special.

Shorty wondered what part of her Ann Ah used to sense the oras, but he was not sure it would be nice to ask.

Ann Ah interrupted the one-sided conversation, "Is the sword talking to you right now?"

Shorty did not answer. Instead, he crawled closer to Ann Ah. He sat with his knees almost touching hers. New Horizons' hilt hung in the air before Ann Ah. In his excitement to introduce his friends to each other, Shorty reached for Ann Ah's hand. But he paused and asked, "Ken me touches youse hand? No wants youse ta touches sharp part a da sword."

At her nod, he took Ann Ah's right hand in his. He laid her palm carefully on the hilt. Her fingers curled around it. Shorty then grasped the hilt just below her tentative grip.

Hello Annah, friend of Shorty. My name is Tainkintana. And I am the sword of the Green Knight.

Shorty felt Ann Ah tense as the sword's mental voice reached out to her. He felt her surprise as the sword's words merged with their thoughts. He realized she had not known whether to believe him. Shorty smiled as he felt her surprise turn to delight at the new experience. He heard her reply in his head the same way the sword spoke to him. *Hello, Tainkintana. I am a little confused by all this. I thought your name was New Horizons?*

Those who forged me from the star stone named me Tainkintana. When the star stone fell from the sky, it landed where the sky and the land appeared to come together. For that reason, some also call me New Horizons. Shorty finds New Horizons an easier name to pronounce.

The flow of thoughts paused. Shorty felt New Horizons' examination of his friend. The sword studied Ann Ah as it had studied him the first time he touched its hilt. He relaxed when New Horizons continued, *It is a great pleasure to meet you, Chosen of the goddess Mielikki.*

Ann Ah's thoughts were a gentle caress as they filled Shorty's head, *It is a pleasure to meet you as well Tainkintana. I had no idea that swords could be alive, let alone talk like this.*

Shorty sat and listened to the conversation between his two friends. The expression on Ann Ah's face told him that he had made her happy. Their thoughts flowed swiftly back and forth. Ann Ah asked many questions of New Horizons, and the sword told her of its journey through the stars before it came to Arcturus.

Shorty let them talk until he heard Ann Ah's stomach grumble again. He was hungry too. At the next pause between questions, Shorty interrupted, "Ann Ah bees hungry. Me hungry too. Please ta makes food fer us? Sumtin Ann Ah like."

Of course, Shorty. What would you like Annah?

Shorty watched as a hopeful smile broke across Ann Ah's lips. *Real bread. The kind made from wheat and real flour. Not the acorn bread we have here. And maybe some cheese?*

Seven round loaves of bread and two small rounds of yellow cheese appeared on the cloak in front of them. As the smell of the bread rose into the air, Ann Ah's nose began to twitch. *Thank you, Tainkintana. It smells wonderful.*

You are most welcome Annah. Enjoy your meal. Perhaps we can talk again some time. Goodbye for now Green Lady.

Ann Ah slowly lifted her hand from the hilt and Shorty returned the sword to its scabbard. Then he handed her a loaf of the bread. Annah held it to her nose and just took in the scent of it. "It is warm like it just came out of the oven."

Shorty cut several slices of cheese that he placed on Ann Ah's knee. Then he took another loaf and began to eat. Both ate well, but Ann ah's appetite could not keep up with Shorty. When Shorty finally finished, a single loaf of bread and half a round of cheese were all that remained.

Ann Ah asked him. "Would it be alright if I take the rest to Mama and Meerah? They would be very grateful."

Shorty dug around in his backpack until he found an old canvas sack. He placed the last loaf and the remaining cheese in the sack. Then he handed the sack to Ann Ah. "Take. Me eated nuf. Gibs to youse Mama and Meer Ah. Maybeso den her no bees fraid me sum day?"

Ann Ah held on to his hand as she took the sack of food. "Maybe, but I cannot promise she will change. I am sorry, Shorty. I do not understand why she is so afraid."

Shorty gave her fingers a light squeeze. "Bees kay, Ann Ah. Me knowed why she fraid a ogre."

They rose to their feet and Shorty handed Ann Ah her staff. He carried the food for her as they turned back to her home.

Shorty walked silently through the trees with Ann Ah just behind him. He led her through the forest and the garden, but stopped before entering the clearing with the small house. Shorty was not sure what to say as he turned and handed her the sack.

Ann Ah took the sack and gave him a beautiful smile. "I had a wonderful time today. Will you be here tomorrow? Can I meet you in the garden tomorrow morning?"

Shorty let out a breath he had not realized he was holding. "Ann Ah really want to do gin?" Shorty pointed back the way they had come. "Follow squirrel an plant mo friends?"

Ann Ah nodded eagerly. "Oh, yes. That would be a perfect way to spend the day. Could we have more bread too?"

Shorty nodded and Ann Ah turned towards her home. She practically ran to the door yelling. "Mama! Meerah! Real bread and cheese. Are you hungry?"

Shorty watched the door close behind Ann Ah. He heard the locking bar slide back into place. He turned back towards the garden, but his heart was not as heavy this time.

The next several days were spent visiting the squirrels and planting the seeds around the Grove. Each afternoon, New Horizons created more bread and cheese and other foods that Ann Ah remembered from when she was young.

Thoughts of the danger he had come here to fight slipped from his mind. He had Ann Ah and the squirrels. There was no room in Shorty's head for thoughts of battle and danger.

Chapter 5

Sanctuary Lost

The small red fruit pulsed in his hand. Even he could sense the magic in the seed. "Cherry," he murmured. Shorty wondered if it would grow up and look like his friend Cherry, or would this be a male tree person?

Shorty smiled as a woman's voice spoke from beside him, "A second cherry tree? That is wonderful Shorty. I think your friends sent us two of each kind of tree."

He gently lowered the fruit into the small hole he had dug earlier. Reaching over, he tapped the water bag Ann Ah held in her hands. She felt around for the hole and poured water into it. Shorty folded the now empty seed sack while he watched her. "Dat bees last friend ta plant."

Ann Ah closed the waterskin and set it by her leg. "It is hard to believe that someday there will be twenty young Treants living here in the Grove. Ashley says that she can already feel Sanctuary growing stronger. We owe you a great debt."

"Me jus carry da bag. Gifts bees from Arcturus." He scooped the loose soil back into the hole until the surface was level once more. Then he sat back to let Ann Ah use her magic. Shorty chuckled as he watched the small cherry sprout burst from the soil between her cupped hands. "Hicks say gonna takes muches long time fer dem ta growed up, but him not knows dere bees Ann Ah in dis place."

Ann Ah grinned at his complement, "The Treants do not notice the passage of time. What do a few seasons mean when you live for a thousand years?

Shorty held out his hand to help Ann Ah stand. When she did not take it, he remembered again that she could not see. Shorty touched her hand with his. Ann Ah wrapped her fingers around his and pulled herself up. He hardly noticed her weight as she pulled against his hand. Shorty rose to stand beside her.

Ann Ah let go of his hand and spun once in a circle. "The sun feels good today. What should we do next? Mama said she did not need my help today."

"Go ta sees da squirrel?" Shorty suggested cheerfully.

Ann Ah laughed at his suggestion. Shorty liked that sound bery muches. "I swear, Sir Knight, sometimes I think you like those little fur balls more than you like me. We visit them every day."

Shorty shook his head in protest, "Likes Ann Ah lots mo. But Ann Ah wid da squirrel make bestus day eber. Maybeso eats lunches wid dem?"

Ann Ah laughed again as she took hold of his arm. "Are you trying to bribe me with food? If so, be assured that I will not eat nuts for lunch today. You will have to do much better than that to impress me. Maybe some bacon and eggs and, of course, warm bread and cheese," she paused for a moment, lost in thought. "And some fresh milk, I think, to wash it all down." Ann Ah began to tug as his arm as if to hurry him up.

"Kay, kay. Ann Ah win. Nut only bees fer squirrel dis time," he replied with a grin. Shorty did not argue. It was not hard to keep up with Ann Ah's shorter legs. Besides, the lunch she wanted did sound good. Well, everything except the milk. He still did not understand why she liked to drink that stuff. Shorty's stomach growled at the thought of a big lunch.

At the sound, Ann Ah gave his arm a gentle slap. "Remember what I taught you, Sir Knight, you must share with the Lady. No eating most of the food yourself." They both laughed as they hurried towards the trees where the squirrels nested.

Shorty began to walk faster. He really was hungry today. But Ann Ah pulled back against his arm. He turned to see her shaking a finger at him, but there was a smile on her lips. "Smaller steps, Sir Knight. The lady has shorter legs than you do. And no, you may not carry me so we can get there sooner."

Shorty walked slower, listening to Ann Ah talk about things she wanted to do if she ever got to leave the Grove called Sang ta Air. He wanted to take her to Arcturus and introduce her to all of his friends and his family. Or maybeso to Delith and the market there. He would not promise her anything until he was sure that she would be safe outside the Grove.

Squirrels began to race through the trees over their heads. He listened to their happy chatter. They were excited to see Ann Ah too. His small friends were coming to trust Ann Ah too. He knew that they would continue to watch over her and visit her even if he had to leave her here. Shorty did not like that idea, but he knew it was a possibility. He could not stay here forever. Arcturus needed him and so did his friends in Delith.

They came to a small stream. Shorty bent to lift Ann Ah over the water, but she stiffened in his arms. Not knowing what he had done wrong, Shorty set her down and stepped back. A look of horror crossed Ann Ah's face. Shorty came and knelt in front of her. "Ann Ah bees kay?" he asjed. "Not wants youse ta falls in da water."

Her left hand came to rest on his shoulder. "Goddess help us! Something just shattered the wards." Her fingernails clutched at his armor as tears ran down her cheeks. There was fear in her voice as she told him, "Evil walks in Sanctuary."

Shorty growled in frustration. He had forgotten why he came to this place. He had not been sent here to play with squirrels and spend time with Ann Ah. He had known an attack was coming and he had done nothing to prepare. Even ogres were smarter than that. He did not even have the three women in one place. How would he keep his promise to the Lady of the Forest now?

Ann Ah leaned into him. He could feel her trembling as she begged, "Please, we have to save Mama and Meerah!"

Shorty suddenly sensed trees crying out in pain. Something was burning the Grove. What should he do? If he took Ann Ah to find her Mama and Meer Ah, he might get her hurt, or worse, killed. He knelt there, frozen, while his heart and his head could not agree.

Ann Ah took the decision away from him. She began to stumble towards home.

"No bery gooder place fer Ann Ah. Danger dere," Shorty grumbled.

Ann Ah's stinging reply made him wince, "Then run away, Knight. I will save them myself."

Shorty surged to his feet and ran. He caught the woman in three strides and scooped her up in his arms. Despite his better judgement, he ran towards her home and family. He wove through the trees, moving as quickly as his bad leg would allow. He did his best to keep Ann Ah safe from branches that she could not see coming her way.

He was almost to the family's garden when he saw a large form moving his way. It was one of the tree people. Ashley carried two forms in her branches. He could see Ann Ah's mother's and sister's arms wrapped around the ash's trunk. Small branches swarmed around their bodies to hold them in place. Ashley did not slow as she ran past him. The words she spoke were a command that Shorty did not want to argue with, "Run, Green Knight! Take the Chosen to safety!"

Shorty turned and ran. Ann Ah's weight went unnoticed as he strove the catch up to Ashley. It was a futile attempt. Even with two good legs, he would never have kept up with her in the forest. As he had on that first day when he chased after Willie, Shorty fell behind quickly. And that was before Ann Ah began to struggle in his arms. She thrashed and beat her small fists against his chest, demanding that he put her down.

Shorty tried to calm her fears, "Youse Mama and Meer Ah bees safe. Ashley hab dem." His words did not help. Ann Ah continued to struggle. Shorty kept running. Her anger was not as important as keeping her safe.

But then she began to cry. That was something he was not prepared for. He could just make out her words through her sobs, "The trees are dying! Corey and Willie are hurt! I can save them if you just put me down. My magic, I can make it rain."

Anger, he could handle. Tears though, were more than he could bear. Shorty stumbled to a stop. But he did not put Ann Ah down right away. He checked for any threats first and looked for a defensible position. The only thing he could find was a nearby dogwood thicket. Shorty pushed his way to the center of the thicket and lowered Ann Ah to the ground. As she glared at him with tear-streaked cheeks, Shorty knelt and apologized. "Bery sorry Ann Ah. Me posed ta keeps youse safe. No wants youse gets hurted."

She sighed heavily and placed a hand on his cheek. "I know Shorty, but you cannot always choose for other people. Our lives are our own to live as we choose. Do you understand?"

Shorty nodded slowly. "Me no want bees da boss a youse. Dat bees wrong. But not knowed ifn me can lets youse get hurted." He sensed that this was not exactly the answer she had wanted so he asked, "What Ann Ah want me ta do?"

Ann Ah turned from him. He knew she was still angry by her harsh tone. "If you are really sorry, you should prove it. Go help Willie and Corey. They are in trouble. There are two strangers using magic against them. Save my friends, Knight."

Shorty stared at her back, knowing she would not forgive him if he did not go. But doing so would be hard. He was not afraid of dying if it came to that, but he was very afraid that she would try to follow him. "Me go. Only ask dat Ann Ah stay here. Hide till killin bees done."

"Fine!" she snapped angrily. "I must call the rain, or the Grove will burn."

Shorty backed from the thicket as Ann Ah knelt on the ground. He could feel her begin to draw on her magic. She did not even look at him when he told her, "Me go fer Ann Ah. No likes it. No bees what me promise da Lady. Sum day, maybeso youse bees me friend gin."

Shorty turned from her and began to walk back the way he had come. After a few steps, he paused to take off his backpack. He rummaged around inside until he found the white marble of his beloved figurine. He placed the cat-shaped figurine on the ground before him. He placed a loving hand on its feline back and called out in a low voice, "Friend Cat, me needs youse help. Bery hard game ta plays. No ken lose dis one."

Mist began to rise from the figurine. A cloud billowed out until it obscured the area around the figurine. Then the mist faded away to reveal a large feline form. Its yellowish-brown body stood well over four feet at the shoulders. Cat rumbled a greeting as her intelligent eyes moved from Shorty to Ann Ah and back again. A long pink tongue shot out from between seven-inch canines to lick Shorty on the cheek.

Ann Ah gave a startled squeak as Cat studied her. Shorty expected a question, but Ann Ah stayed focused on whatever she was doing with her magic. Maybeso, he thought, Cat did not have one of those ora things.

Shorty pulled his shield from his back and slid his left arm into the straps. He slid the backpack on again before he drew New Horizons. Then the two hunters began to run, side by side. Cat did not need words to know what to do. She was an expert at the Great Game.

As the two ran towards the fire and smoke, Shorty watched clouds beginning to gather in the sky over the Grove. Ann Ah would have her rain soon. He needed to make sure that the fires did not get started again. He would deal with the intruders. He would protect Ann Ah.

Cat paused and turned to stare at him. She growled softly. Shorty nodded, "Two dem bees what Ann Ah say. Whiches one youse want?" Cat turned and sniffed at the forest. Then she turned to the left and disappeared into the trees and the smoke.

Shorty accepted her answer and continued on. The garden was straight ahead and beyond that was the house. He paused at the entrance to the garden clearing. Something had changed. His eyes scanned the garden. They came to rest on the smoldering tree that leaned far to one side. It was Willie.

Most of Willie's small hanging branches had been burned away. Bare, blackened branches obscured by smoke was all that remained of his once beautiful hanging tendrils. It was not a pretty sight. There was also a large dent low in the willow's trunk that oozed a lot of sap. The wound was strange. The dent was a perfect circle with many deeper circles within its depths. Shorty only knew of one kind of weapon that made wounds like that. "Mace wid spike hurts Willie bery bad."

Shorty rushed across the garden not worrying about Ann Ah's plants this time. He leaned his sword against Willie's trunk and dug into his belt pouch. It took longer to remove the vial's wax seal than it did to find the vial in his pouch. Shorty had no idea if the healing potion would work as well on tree people as it did on ogres. But it was all he had. Shorty poured the potion into the dent.

The dent did not fill in like Shorty's own skin would have, but it did stop leaking sap. Shorty dropped the vial to grab his sword as Willie tried to stand up straight.

Shorty helped to steady Willie. "Where bad people bees?" Shorty asked once Willie could stand on his own.

A burnt branch pointed towards the stone lined path. "I will take you there," Willie managed to creak out in a harsh, pain-filled voice.

"No!" Shorty said with more force than he intended. "Willie bad hurted. Go now. Bees safe. Time fer da Green Knights to do him job."

The willow did not argue. It turned and disappeared into the trees, leaving only the smell of burnt wood in the garden.

Shorty felt the anger of his kind begin to rise to the surface. He must not let the rage take him. He must use what little brains he had if he was to keep those who lived in the Grove safe. Shorty began to walk along the path to Ann Ah's house. His prey lay somewhere ahead.

It did not take long to find his prey. Standing in front of the stone house was a thin man wearing black plate and a helm. The helm's visor was lowered, so Shorty could not see his face. The shield on the man's right arm was also black. In its center was a golden rod. Shorty thought the rod looked like the rod the King of Delith held when he sat on his big stone chair.

The figure gave a slight bow as Shorty entered the clearing. His foe carried a large mace in his left hand. It was an unusual weapon. The mace had a three-foot-long metal haft instead of one made of wood. There were spikes all around the head of the mace, but each had a flat top instead of points. This was the weapon that had hurt Willie.

Shorty watched as the man brought the mace up high over his right shoulder. The mace slashed in a hard diagonal swing down across his foe's body. With no apparent effort, the man halted the motion of the heavy weapon so that it pointed directly at Shorty's chest. The display did not impress Shorty. The warrior was strong, but so was he. He continued to advance on his foe. "Youse no posed ta bees dis place. Leave afore me kills youse. No shoulda hurted me friend. No bery nice."

A harsh and very confident laugh came from within the helm. "My Master, Set, was right. He thought the Green Knight would be here. They make such a fuss about you. Why, I wonder? You are little more than a low born simpleton who can barely speak the common tongue. What threat could you possibly pose to mighty Set's plans?"

The warrior's words had a much bigger effect than the fancy trick with the mace. The man was a follower of Set. This was no simple threat. Shorty paused to study the man more carefully. His task had become much more complicated. "What Bad Cloud want in dis place? No bees fer him."

"It is not the place that matters. Useless trees to burn down like in your Arcturus." The figure gestured with his mace. "My Master wants the girl with the tree-shaped birthmark on her arm. Your little Goddess has been hiding her for far too long. Set grows impatient. The power he will grant me when I bring her to him is beyond your understanding. Let me have her and I will spare your precious trees. I might even let you live."

Shorty stiffened. There was a flash of fear for Ann Ah, but it was quickly replaced by anger. Set would not take Ann Ah. He would protect her. He needed to kill this warrior, and then he needed to help Cat find the other intruder that had come with this man. The one that was making the fire.

Shorty pulled his shield tight against his body. His fingers slid along his belt until he felt the round ball tucked into the pouch on that side. He squeezed it quickly three times. The magic of the ball rose within him. He smiled as he felt its power seep into his arms and legs. The tip of New Horizons rose till it aligned with the eye slits of the warrior's helm. Then he attacked.

Cat slipped between the trees and into the thick smoke. She really did not like the smoke. It was not so much that she could not see, she was used to hunting without her vision. The real problem was that the smoke stank. She hated being nose blind. As the smoke invaded her nose, her natural instincts screamed "Flee!" Smoke meant fire and death. She dismissed the urge to run. She was Cat and she did not run from anything. Such fear was beneath her. She would use the smoke as a tool to hunt those who invaded this place that her ogre had claimed.

She considered her advantages in this hunt. The coloring of her pelt made her almost undetectable in the ever-changing clouds of smoke. She would be even harder to detect than the two-leg she was hunting. Although she was now nose blind, so was her quarry. The loss of sight and scent would not keep her from tracking her prey. She was Cat and she hunted with all of her senses. Her ears twitched as Cat listened. Her head turned to the left. Her prey was there.

The two-leg she hunted was clumsy. It seemed unaware of the brittle twigs and old leaves that carpeted the forest floor. Each step it took told her where it was and where it was headed. Her ogre was very large and heavy, but he did not reveal himself this way. This one must be a human from one of the places called city.

Cat sighed softly. This prey was not worthy of her skills. It could not even control its breathing. It panted as it ran, sucking in deep breaths that made it cough in the heavy smoke. Everything it did was loud. The game she had hoped to play in the ogre's world would be a disappointment. She had wanted a challenge, and this would be too easy.

Cat listened as her quarry moved through the trees. Her ears did not detect the sound of branches rubbing against metal. The prey did not wear one of the hard shells to protect its soft flesh. Would it even be able to fight back? Playing with helpless prey was for kits. Cat wanted a real challenge. She should have chosen the other two-leg as her prey. Cat's whiskers twitched in irritation. This hunt did not look to be much fun. She needed to find a way to amuse herself.

Cat contemplated her options, then her lips pulled back to reveal all of her very sharp teeth. She could always steal the ogre's prey from him. She liked the one called Shorty. For a male, he hunted and fought well. But he could not be allowed to think that he was her equal. The idea of proving her superiority as both hunter and warrior appealed to Cat. If her prey was indeed weak, she would show the ogre why she was a Prime. She would claim both kills as was her right.

The prey continued to stumble around among the trees. Was it really that clumsy? Or, was it just trying to draw her in? Perhaps the two-leg was smarter than she had given it credit for. It was not smart enough though. She chuffed. Two could play the game of Traps and Bait. And when her prey came for her, she would enjoy its reaction when it realized she had outsmarted it. Cat changed course and ran through the trees, no longer concerned if she made noise or not. Let the prey think her a fool. It would make the eventual victory that much sweeter when she sprung her own trap.

It did not take her long to find the perfect place for what she had in mind. The clearing was not large. On one of its edges, there as a thicket to hide in. Cat settled on her haunches and listened. Her prey was already trying to follow the sounds of her run through the trees. But it was already off course. Why start so many fires if you could not track your prey through your own smoke? Two-legs only thought they were good predators. In reality, they were not even very smart prey. Rabbits were stupid but they had more sense than this prey did.

She would have to help the two-leg find its way to her. A low moan issued from deep within Cat. She chose the sound because it would carry well through the trees. Then Cat moved around the clearing and settled into the thicket. She lay there with her head resting on her front paws. She did not need to see the prey. She would hear it enter the clearing.

The smoke in the clearing continue to swirl around. The light breeze was not enough to clear the air. Cat heard her prey approach. It was making even more noise as it hurried towards her. The two-leg stopped just outside the clearing. She could still hear it breathing, but its feet were still.

Cat was patient. She did not move when she heard it take its first step into the clearing. It was not yet time to spring. Then it took several more steps forward. In her mind, she could see the two-leg standing near the center of the clearing, staring blindly around as it searched for her. But it would not see her until she struck. When the shuffling steps reached the center of the clearing, Cat raised her head just enough to see her foe.

A dark form, shrouded by smoke, stood exactly where she had imagined it would be. Its head turned from side to side as it searched for danger. As its head turned away from her, Cat's sharp eyes noted the pointed tip at the top of its ear. Her prey was an elf. She had known elves before, but never one that would willingly destroy the forest. And why would one of the forest people be so inept among the trees. Killing this one would be like slaying a wounded deer. It would be a mercy killing.

Cat tensed her leg muscles and sprang. It was not a long leap, less than three body lengths. When she reached the top of her spring, Cat released her hunting cry. She expected to see the elf panic and freeze. But the elf was tricky. It disappeared. A wave of magic caused the fur at her nape to stand up. She landed gracefully in the spot where her prey had been. Without hesitating, Cat sprang again. Her second leap took her between the two trees where the elf had entered the clearing. Sadly, her prey was not there either.

A melodious voice rang out from the far side of the small clearing, "Baw-rAWk!" Cat leapt again. There was a flash of light in the clearing and the sharp crackling sound like that of the fury of a summer storm. Cat felt a burning pain on her left flank near her haunches. Her pelt on that side rose to stand on end. Cat slipped deeper into the smoke as soon as her paws touched the forest floor. Cat purred happily. This would be a good hunt after all.

Shorty studied the figure standing before him. His opponent was not tall, nor did he appear to be very muscular. Looks did not always tell the truth though and his foe had little trouble swinging the heavy mace. Shorty sniffed the air. The smell of old sweat came to him from the armor. This was a human. But there was something in the scent that bothered Shorty. It smelled like corruption.

He considered how to end the fight quickly. Was the man strong enough to stand against the magic that made Shorty as strong as a giant? If he could drive his opponent to his knees, he could end this fight and get back to Ann Ah. Shorty watched as the human continued to swing the mace. It was almost like the man was daring Shorty to attack. He waited until the mace was already in a downward arc before he stepped forward. Raising New Horizons over his head.

Shorty brought the great sword down in a hard slash. He grinned as he felt the magic sword slice towards his opponent's head. The black shield came up over his foe's head to meet New Horizons. Shorty felt as much as he heard the clash of metal on metal. To his surprise, the human did not even stagger from the blow.

The man danced back a step, flourishing the mace once more. Mocking laughter came from within the helm. The man's smug voice called to him, "Ah, the look on your face, Sir Knight. So entertaining! Did you think we would not be ready for you? My Master knows what you are capable of. He gave me the tools to withstand even your blows. I had hoped you would be a little more of a challenge than you appear to be. And why are you not using both of your swords?"

Shorty also took a step back. As he had expected, this would not be an easy fight. "Talks to muches. Time fer fightin."

The figure raised his mace and pointed it at Shorty. "As much as I would enjoy playing with you Green Knight, I need to find that girl and take her to my Master. I apologize for killing you this way."

Light burst from two of the mace's spikes. Two blood-red bolts of energy shot towards Shorty's chest. Shorty shifted his right leg back, bringing his shield forward. The path of both bolts abruptly changed as they dove into the shield. The shield shimmered and the magic bolts were gone. Shorty heard the man muttering to himself, "Unexpected and most unfortunate. It worked so well against the Treant." The dark opening of the visor stared into Shorty's face and the man's voice became more determined, "I guess we will have to do this the hard way, Sir Knight."

Shorty began to circle left. He needed to learn more about this enemy. How well did the human move in his heavy armor? Anyone who followed the Bad Cloud name Set was dangerous. Shorty had to find a weakness so he could kill this man. He had to make sure the other intruder did not get to Ann Ah.

Shorty felt the first drops of rain begin to fall. He welcomed them. Maybe the rain would make the metal armor even heavier. As they circled, the plated warrior continued to talk to himself, "I told him fire would not be enough to put the guardians out of action. He had better finish them and join me. Diavol, be ready."

Shorty had never faced a foe that talked to himself like this. He drove forward with a flurry of swings trying to take advantage of his longer reach. The smaller fighter was quick as well as strong. The man parried or blocked most of Shorty's swings. The two blows that did get past the shield and mace bounced harmlessly off the armor. Neither blow even dented the black plate.

Shorty moved constantly to keep his foe from getting in close. It was harder with only one sword. He was used to the rhythm of his two blades. The other problem he was having was that the mace seemed to move much faster than it should. Openings disappeared before he could take advantage of them.

Shorty gambled and lunged, driving the tip of New Horizons at his opponent's neck. The mace swatted the strike aside. Before Shorty could recover, the mace punched straight into his stomach. The magical armor of the Green Knight absorbed most of the force of the blow. But light again flashed from the head of the mace. Twin points of burning pain bit at him. Shorty pulled back feeling both marks rub painfully under his armor.

Shorty could not find a way through the man's defenses. He took a step back. Should he drop the shield and pull his other sword? If he did that, the man could use the magic of the mace to hurt him. Shorty cocked his head to one side as the man began to mutter to himself once more. With the added space between them, the man raised the mace and pointed it at Shorty. "Now, Diavol! Take him!"

Light flashed again as another pair of magical bolts erupted from the end of the mace. Shorty lifted the shield to catch the bolts. The voice of New Horizons crashed into his mind, *Roll right, Shorty!*

Shorty's faith in his sword was absolute. His shield came up high to the left and the great sword went down and to the left. Then he launched himself into a roll over his right shoulder. As the shield came across the top of his body, he felt something slam against its upper edge. That blow was followed quickly by the impact of the two energy bolts. One went into the shield and the second sank into his right thigh.

The roll was clumsy, but Shorty had at least avoided cutting himself on his own blade. The Elf Lord who had been his teacher would have come back to his feet. The best Shorty could manage was to come up on one knee. His leg burned where the bolt had hit, and he could feel blisters forming under his leg armor. But he was alive. He lowered the shield to find the human he was fighting.

Shorty blinked as he took in the figure that seemed to float in the air between him and his foe. He had never seen anything like this new enemy. Red leathery skin was stretched tight over its small body. The skin reminded him of blood, only the small bat-shaped wings and its long tail were different. They were a black that seemed to absorb the sunlight.

His eyes were drawn to the long whip-like tail that lashed the air around the creature. The tail ended in a sharp spike that gleamed wetly. The creature hissed at him in anger, revealing a mouth full of tiny fangs below a piggy nose. As Shorty studied it, the creature faded from view. It was then that he noticed the thick, oily-looking fluid that ran down the back of the shield. Some of that fluid dripped on the hand holding the shield strap. His fingers burned and then went numb. He could not feel the strap or tell if his grip was solid. Shorty knew that was bad.

He would have to end this fight quickly before he lost the use of his shield. Shorty rose to his feet. He understood now that the man had not been talking to himself. He had been talking to the flying thing.

The warrior in the black plate gave a small bow. "Impressive, Knight. Lacking grace, but you still live, for the moment."

Shorty grimaced. He was outnumbered now and one of his foes could not be seen. And it could fly. No bery good.

Cat sat licking the rain from her pelt. She was rather pleased with herself. She had spent her time getting the elf so worked up that he was using his magic every time the leaves rustled in the breeze. She could not smell it over the stink of burnt wood, but she knew that he was scared.

His magic had only caught her twice more as she played with him. The second storm magic had done little more than make her fur stand on end. She had been well protected by the large tree she had used for cover. The fire blast had singed her pelt and curled the whiskers on one side of her face. She would make the elf pay for that insult.

Another explosion of fire went off in the distance. Cat chuffed happily. The elf must be attacking shadows now. Soon he would run out of magic. Then he would be hers. The game was more exciting than she had expected it to be. Despite her misgivings, the elf was turning out to be a moderate challenge. She was really enjoying this hunt.

Cat sniffed the air. The smoke was mostly gone, but everything still had a burnt smell. That would fade soon if the rain continued. The trees were wet enough that the elf's magic could not start more fires. That was good. She did not want to rush the game, but she knew her ogre would be unhappy if more trees were damaged while she played with her prey.

Cat listened to see where the elf was headed next. The only sound was the rain falling gently on the trees. The prey had finally gone silent. What was the tricky elf up to now? Cat wondered if his magic was gone. Or, was the elf setting another trap for her? It did not matter either way. She was ready to win the game while it was still exciting. The elf was just doing the same things over and over. If he was going to make the game boring, then there was no reason to continue playing.

Cat turned to stare in the direction of the last blast she had heard. She had been building a map of the forest in her mind as she game progressed. That last loud magic had been in the direction of the setting sun. There was a small clearing in that direction. It would be the perfect spot for her own trap. She rose to her feet and began to walk. She would circle around to the far side of the clearing.

The elf continued to be silent as she moved through the trees. He had finally stopped breathing so loud. Cat reached the clearing without seeing or hearing the elf. If she was lucky, the elf might have one more new trick he could show her. She could only hope so.

Cat crouched just outside the clearing. Something about the clearing bothered her. Her instincts warned her there was danger. Cat drew in another breath through her nose. She did not smell the elf, but there was another very faint scent that did not belong. It tickled her nose, but she did not recognize it.

Cat was not sure what made her distrust the clearing, but she did. She could not sense any danger here, but she was not about to ignore her instincts. She slowly came around the tree, placing one paw into the clearing. She froze. Something soft lay beneath the leaves scattered across the ground. Even with the rain, the ground here should be firm, not squishy. Whatever this was, she knew it was the elf's doing.

Slowly, Cat lifted her paw from the ground. Something long and white was stuck to the pads of that paw. She lifted the paw even higher to study the elf's trap. The thing attached to her pad was like a long white vine. Cat attempted to shake her paw free. That motion revealed more of the white vines laid out in a pattern across the clearing. And not just any pattern, she realized. She had stepped onto a web, but one spun by a spider far larger than any she had ever seen. Tricky elf, Cat told herself with a smile.

Her adversary had gone to a great deal of trouble to leave this gift for her. It would be cruel to disappoint him. But first, she needed to free herself from his web. Cat lowered her paw to the ground, making contact but not placing any weight on the white strand. Slowly, she began to rock the paw forward and then back. The strand began to pick up pits of leaf and dirt. Bit by bit, the webs grip loosened as the strand became coated with dirt and debris. Cat resisted the urge to pull back. She just continued the rocking motion until the strand released her.

Cat stared at the bits of web now visible through the leaves. She decided the elf had made a good trap. The trap deserved to be used. If it was not going to catch her, she should at least let it catch the elf. And what better way to show the elf that she was the better predator. She was Cat and she would have his respect. He was not even a good elf. He needed to learn respect for the forest and for those that lived within it.

Cat extended her senses until she once again found her prey. One of the many small puddles on the forest floor had been disturbed. The disturbance was not the steady drip of water from the trees. It was the splash of a foot moving carelessly. The elf was getting impatient.

Cat carefully skirted the clearing until she was roughly between the elf and his own trap. As she moved, she evaluated all of the places she could hide from the elf. There was a leaf filled depression that would serve her needs.

Cat stepped carefully into the depression. She used one paw to sweep the leaves to one side so she could use them as cover. The she lowered herself to her belly. It was time to call the elf to her. Cat gave a mewling cry of surprise. She began to thrash in the leaves, making sure that many of them landed on her back and haunches. Cat growled in anger as she crushed some of the leaves with her paws. Cat thought the sounds were quite entertaining. Then she lowered her head to her front paws and waited.

Feet began to pound through the trees as the elf ran towards his trap. He was a fool. He was coming fast with little caution. The stupid elf must be sure that he had caught her in his trap. He would soon learn who was the superior hunter. She listened as he came to a stop on the edge of the clearing. She wished she could see his face when he saw there was nothing in the trap to use his magic on. She almost pitied the poor elf.

Cat rose silently. The elf faced the clearing with his back to her. A menacing growl came from deep in Cat's chest. The elf jumped like a frightened deer. He spun and raised his hands. Cat did not give him time to release his magic. She sprang. She could have taken him with that leap. Her rear claws would have opened his belly, but that would not have been as much fun. Instead, she leapt just to the side of the elf.

The smell of urine filled the air. The elf stumbled backwards with a cry of fear. First one foot and then the other tangled in the strands of the elf's own web. His body tumbled backward and he landed hard. Cat watched as the elf tried to push himself up. His arm caught on another of the strands. Panic set in and the elf began to thrash. Cat nodded to herself. It was indeed a very good trap. In moments, the elf was wrapped by many of the strands. Her prey could not move.

Cat chuffed once more as the elf began to threaten her. His master would destroy her and all her kind. Cat did not fear his master. She did not even know what a god was. If this Set hunted her, she would teach him why she was the Prime. The threats turned to pleas and offers of vast riches. But what could the elf give her that she could not get with her own skills? When she hungered, she would hunt. She could always find enough prey to feed herself. When she was tired, she slept. The treasures that he offered were just things. She had as much use for things as she did his other empty promises.

Instead of listening to him mewl like a kit, she studied the placement of the remaining strands. She carefully placed her paws as she moved to stand over the elf. Cat would not bite the elf. The blood of all two-legs was foul to the taste. That would ruin the game. Cat raised her paw over the elf. She let him watch as she extended her claws. When she was sure he understood his fate, she ended the game with a quick slash across his throat.

At the death of the elf, the strands began to melt into the earth. The elf's magic died with him. She studied the body for a moment. There were many things strapped to the corpse. Cat did not need things. If the ogre wanted the elf's things, he would have to come get them himself.

Cat turned from the dead elf and began to move towards the distant sound of combat. The clang of metal striking metal now rang through the forest. She wondered if she could still steal the ogre's kill. That would be a fun game. Cat began to run. There might be time to best the ogre, but only if she hurried.

A growl of frustration began to build deep inside Shorty. Ann Ah needed him to protect her home. He needed to protect her. To do both of those things, he needed to defeat this one small human standing before him. But he did not know how. Now he also had the flying thing to fight. If that tail hit him, he would let Ann Ah down. How was he supposed to fight them both? "No bery gooder," he told to himself, "needs too muches."

The calm voice of New Horizons spoke in his mind, *That creature is an imp, Shorty. It is from the Abyss. They are very dangerous but, like undead, my touch is deadly to it.*

Like his foe, Shorty began to mutter to himself as he watched the fighter come closer. "Dat no gonna helps ifn me no ken sees it. How me posed ta hit what me no ken sees?"

I know exactly where the imp is Shorty. If you trust me, we can hurt them both badly. Do you need my healing or can you take another solid hit from the mace?

Shorty did not hesitate, "Trust youse muches. Mace burn but no hurted bery bad. Armor protect me."

Then fight hard like you did before. The imp is a coward. It will strike from behind. When I tell you, spin and strike above your head. I will help guide your swing.

Shorty nodded to himself. This fight had gone on too long. Ann Ah might need him. He had to hope that Cat had dealt with the other intruder. Shorty stopped thinking and worrying. It was time to fight.

Fighting like an ogre had not gotten him very far. Maybe it was time to fight like a fuzzface. Maybe it was time to use one of Thorn's tricks. Shorty stepped forward, bringing New Horizons up as he had in his first attack. The heavy sword came down with all of his strength. The human raised his own shield and once again deflected the blow easily.

The power if the block sent New Horizons wide to the right. Shorty allowed the force of the rebound to turn his body to the side. His own shield came across in time to intercept the mace. The blow was hard, and Shorty felt the shield shift on his arm. He knew that he would not be able to control the shield much longer.

His sword arm was extended far to the right. Shorty brought his blade back across in a horizontal slash at the human's left arm. Shorty bared his tusks as the mace swung out to parry his blade. Shorty waited until the mace was committed to the block. That was when he made his real attack. Shorty stepped in close and drove his shield at the human.

The man's reflexes were incredible. His own shield shifted to meet Shorty's. The two came together in a loud clang. But this time, it was not a question of strength or skill. The shield bash was a question of weight and balance. It was not a move his foe had expected.

Shorty felt his smaller opponent bounce back as their bodies collided. The man did not fall as Shorty had hoped, but he did lose his balance and stumble backwards. Shorty squeezed New Horizons' hilt as he prepared to press the small advantage he had gained.

That was when New Horizons shouted a warning, *Behind you, Knight. Strike now! High to the right!*

Shorty twisted around, his sword moving with the force of the spin. He felt the sword's desire to strike a bit higher and wider. He did not fight the gentle tug of the blade. His sword was almost where it wanted to be when the blood red creature appeared above his head. Shorty felt its hate filled eyes staring at him as its tail went back to strike. That attack never came as New Horizons cut deep into its body.

The sword emitted a brilliant white light and the flying pig-bat squealed in pain and hatred. Shorty's world shrank until all he saw was the creatures flat, piggy nose. Then the nose and the rest of the creature were reduced to a cloud of dust.

Before Shorty could savor his first real success in the fight, pain erupted in his right shoulder. The solid impact of the mace on his shoulder blade was quickly followed by the burning pain of the twin bolts of energy. The burns seemed much deeper this time. The force of the blow caused Shorty to stagger forward several steps. He needed to turn and face the human before he got hit in the back again. He needed to raise his sword, but the muscles in his shoulder were not responding properly.

A strange cry came from behind Shorty. It was not a cry of pain so much as one of loss and regret. Shorty turned to face the human. The battle he was expecting was over. The warrior now knelt on the ground, the mace and shield lay untouched beside him. Trembling hands rose to loosen the strap holding the helm in place. The man struggled for long moments before the helm fell to the ground behind him.

Shorty stared in amazement as the man's dark hair began to turn gray. Wrinkles formed and spread across the man's face. The warrior's powerful arms withered and shrank. The armor that had fit so well now hung loosely on the man's body. It took Shorty a moment to understand that the man was growing old. How strange, he thought, as the grey hair turned white and the man's cheeks began to sag. Tears slid down those cheeks as fingers came up to explore what he had become.

The now old man glared at Shorty, hatred evident on his face. "That is not the sword you carried in the battle for Arcturus. The Master did not mention that your sword could destroy my Diavol." Then he sighed with resignation, "Or, perhaps he just chose not to tell me."

Shorty did not understand what was happening to the powerful warrior he had fought. "What happen to youse?"

The man just shook his head. "Defeated by a mere fool. I am shamed."

New Horizons' explanation was a strange as what had happened to the warrior, *He made a deal with the powers of Hell. The imp gave him strength and youth in exchange for access to this world. The death of the imp broke that contract. The magic that kept him young is gone. Now he is what he was meant to be, an old man. Such are the risks when one bargains with evil.*

Shorty stared down at the feeble old man. There was nothing left
of the powerful warrior that had almost defeated him. Even the old
man's voice sounded weak, but he still managed to growl at Shorty,
"Your pity is an insult, Green Knight. It is most unwelcome. Know
this, I will regain what I have lost no matter what price the Master
asks of me. Then, I will return and destroy this place. I will take the
girl and there will be nothing you can do to stop me."

The man's words left Shorty little choice. He did not want to kill an
old man, but it was the only way to protect Ann An and her Grove. If
she was ever going to be safe, this evil man must die. Shorty stepped
before the kneeling figure and raised the tip of New Horizons.

The old man smiled bitterly. "So, the great Green Knight will kill a
helpless old man? What of your honor, Sir Knight?"

Shorty shook his head as he looked down on the man he was about
to kill. "No fight fer honor. Fights ta protect. Protect forest. Protects
world. Protect Ann Ah. No ken lets youse hurts dem." The man
seemed to accept that and he nodded once.

The old warrior kept his eyes locked on Shorty's. There was no
regret in his angry gaze. Shorty thrust and the tip of his sword went
completely through the man's neck. Evil or not, Shorty would not
allow the man to suffer at his hands. A tear ran down Shorty's cheek
as the old man's body slumped to the ground. His death seemed such
a waste.

Shorty turned away from the dead warrior. not even bothering to
search the body. New toys were not important right now. It was time
for him to do his job keeping Ann Ah safe. That would probably
mean more fighting, and that might be a problem after his last battle.

"Me arm no work bery gooder. Maybeso bees mo fightin. Helps,
please?" Shorty asked his sword. Instantly, a wave of healing flowed
up his arm as he began to follow the path back to the garden. His
shoulder was not perfect, but he could swing his sword now, and that
was all that mattered.

Cat stood on the stone lined path just outside the garden, her golden
eyes watching him. He met her gaze solemnly. Was that approval
that he saw in her eyes? He did not ask. Somethings were better not

known. Shorty pointed down the garden trail. "Needs ta find Ann Ah. Protect her."

Cat turned and ran. Shorty followed her. Pain of his injuries, both old and new, clouded his thoughts and tried to slow him down. He ignored the pain and just focused on following Cat. She would know the way back. He did not need to think, only run.

Cat studied her ogre. He had defeated the other two-leg before she could steal his prey. The smell of human blood told her the prey was indeed dead. But her senses also told her that he had fought something else too. The faint scent of venom clung to the ogre. Did one of his many injuries carry that taint within it? She could not be sure. What she was sure of was that he had done well, not that she would ever tell him so. Males were impossible when their egos became too large. It would have to be enough for him that she did not criticize his performance.

Now, despite his injuries, he desired the female he had claimed. Males were so predictable. Cat turned to lead the way. She would do that much for him at least. Cat began to lope through the trees. She kept her pace down though. Two-legs were never fast to begin with and with so many injuries, her ogre was much slower than normal.

The place where they had left the female was not hard to find. Her own scent was more than enough to mark the way back. Cat knew well before they arrived that something was wrong. The female's scent was much fainter than it should have been. The ogre's female had been rather noisy. Now, Cat heard only the sound of the forest ahead. When the thicket came into view, there was no one inside it. The female was gone.

Her ogre stumbled into the thicket; she could see that he was not well. Something more than his obvious injuries was bothering him. The venom? The ogre still had enough wits about him to stoop and check for tracks. Let him use his eyes, Cat began to move around the thicket searching for clues with her nose. It took only a moment to find what she was looking for. She growled then, knowing how this was going to turn out. The woman's scent was strong here. But so was the scent of another male. She knew her ogre would challenge this male for the female. She just was not sure if he could survive another battle like the one he had just fought.

The ogre was suddenly at her side. His fingers traced both sets of tracks, the smaller set that smelled of his female and the larger set that stank of the offending male. The ogre rose and began to track the new prey. Cat surged ahead. In his pride, he would not allow her to challenge this new male, but he could hardly complain about her help in tracking the prey.

The trail was not long or difficult to follow. It led a short distance to a clearing. There it ended suddenly. The stink of powerful magic washed away the scent of both two-legs. Beyond the magic, there was no trace of the prey. Cat moaned in explanation. Her ogre understood, even if he could not smell the magic. Then her ogre did something she would never have expected of him. He dropped to his knees, lowering his head in defeat.

Cat grew angry then. He would not shame her so. Even if venom was coursing through his body, he would not give up and die here. She did not like losing this game either, but she was still Cat and he was her kit. They would continue the game somehow. In her anger, Cat lashed out. She did not extend her claws; one did not do that with kits. But the blow she landed on his chest would have sent most within the Pride tumbling back, head over haunches.

He had failed her. Now Ann Ah was gone, taken by a magic that left no tracks or scent that he could follow. He would never know her fate. He would never be able to rescue her. The pain in his heart overwhelmed even the pain in his body. He just wanted to give up. Maybeso he could just go to sleep and never wake up.

The blow to his chest was enough to knock the breath from his lungs. He had not even seen it coming. He did not let that powerful strike knock him over. Instead, he leaned into it, baring his tusks. Being hit like that made him angry and that anger cut through the fog in his head. Shorty blinked as he stared into Cat's golden eyes. She was angry too. He deserved her anger and the swat that she had given him. He understood and the part of him that was not angry was thankful that she had gotten his attention. He would not give up. Not until Ann Ah was safe once more and maybeso not even then.

Shorty rose. He did not know anything about magic. Did it need something with the prey's scent to work with? If so, he knew where to find it. Again, he began to retrace his steps. This time back towards the small stone house. He ran, but his pace was slower. He was injured and his leg hurt. But he had a plan.

The clearing outside the home was as he had left it. The body still lay there, a grim reminder of his battle. Shorty ignored the body and headed for the front door of Ann Ah's home. The door was closed but not locked. It swung open easily at his touch. But the door was small. Much too small for an ogre to walk through. In the end, he crawled into the home.

The inside of the home was not much larger. Even on his knees, his head almost touched the ceiling. The main area of the house was one large room. The kitchen and dining area were on the far side of the room. A sitting area was near the main door. Shorty saw three more small doors on the left wall. He guessed that those were the bedrooms.

He began to crawl across the room to the first door. He opened it and sniffed. The scent here was that of Ann Ah's Mama. Shorty closed the door and moved to the middle door. He did not need to open this one. Meer Ah's scent was strong. Shorty opened the door closest to the kitchen area. The scent he had searched for was here. This was Ann Ah's room.

Shorty could not fit fully into the room without breaking the bed that sat just inside the door. Sticking his head through the opening, he looked for something that belonged to Ann Ah. There were not many things in the room. Ann Ah did not have many toys or even clothes. A tiny shelf sat on the wall beside the door. On it sat a comb with several hairs caught on it. On the floor below the shelf was a small basket with a few dirty clothes inside.

Shorty reached into the basket and grabbed the first thing his fingers touched. It was a sock and it smelled of Ann Ah. As an afterthought, Shorty stretched his arm towards the shelf. He took the comb as well.

Both treasures went into the pouch on his belt. He hoped they would be enough to allow Dualis to find Ann Ah.

Moments later, Shorty had worked his way back out of the women's home without breaking anything. Cat waited patiently for him. Shorty rose and Cat came to stand at his side. He placed a large hand on her head and gently rubbed her ears. The feel of her soft fur comforted him. Cat allowed his touch, and he was thankful.

Shorty reached into his armor with his left hand. His numb fingers fumbled but finally drew out the leather cord that hung around his neck. At the end of the cord was the metal circle that allowed him to travel to Dualis's home. It was time to ask for help. He gripped the amulet in his hand as best he could. Then he willed himself and Cat to the Keep.

Only the injured Willie saw the two disappear.

Chapter 6

Asking for Help

Shorty and Cat appeared on the slope of a grassy knoll surrounded on all sides by snow-topped mountains. Sunlight reflected off a small lake down in the valley below. A glittering ribbon of water followed a winding path from the mountains into the right side of the lake. Its twin emerged from the far side of the lake, disappearing into the forest that covered the valley floor. A blue expanse of sky stretched from horizon to horizon.

The view was breath taking. Shorty had often spent hours just staring at it. But today, he could not afford to be distracted by such beauty. He scratched the base of Cat's ears before turning to face the large structure resting at the top of the knoll. Shorty's gaze swept across the stone exterior of the Arch Mage's home. The rectangular central building was nearly fifty feet high. Two towers rose high above the rectangular building. Each stood like a sentry on opposite ends of the central structure.

Shorty shook his head. He could not imagine living in such a place. He preferred his own home. Stormhold was not built for show. It existed solely to protect the border of Arcturus. Stormhold was meant to serve warriors like him.

But Dualis was a mage and not a warrior. Maybeso mages needed homes like this. To his eyes, none of the pieces of this place belonged together. It was like the Arch Mage took pieces of different worlds and forced them together. More importantly, none of the pieces really fit in the peaceful valley where they had been built.

The tower on the left was built with a strange black stone that did not reflect the sunlight the way normal stone did. In contrast, the tower on the left was wrapped in flames that never went out. The flames were so bright that he could not tell what material lay beneath them. Whatever lay beneath those flames absorbed the heat of those fires because the interior of that tower was always cool.

The central structure was the only part of the building that Shorty approved of. It had been built of real stone like that found in the mountains of his birth. But even this part of the Keep had its oddities. Shorty had seen many castles and keeps. He had even seen one being built. Each was constructed of heavy blocks, linked together to provide strength. This building did not have blocks of stone. It was as if the entire structure had been carved from a single immense block. Wherever the stone had come from, it was not the same color stone as found in the mountains nearby. It did not belong here.

Shorty stared at the blank walls of the building and towers. There were no windows or doors to be seen anywhere. At least not on the outside of the building. There were many windows to look out when you were inside. There was a door that you could walk out. But from outside, there were no breaks in the stone. He shook his head as he muttered, "Too muches magics in dis place. Sum day it gonna jus go boom."

Shorty began to walk towards the center of the rectangular building. Cat kept pace at his side. The lack of a door did not bother Shorty. Someone always let him in when he came. He was still a dozen paces away when he raised his voice to yell, "Somebodies ken please ta opens door. Me comes ta talks wid Dualis!" Shorty's determined stride did not slow as he approached the wall.

When the door did not appear right away, Shorty glared at the wall. He raised a fist to pound on the wall, but the spot before him began to shimmer. An ogre sized door appeared before him. The door was forged of a black metal that looked like iron except for the large gold ring to one side. Shorty reached out and tugged on the ring. The door moved towards him with very little effort.

A miniature dragon hung in the air just inside the door. Its tiny wings flapped slowly, too slow, Shorty thought, to keep even its small body in the air. "Mo magics," he thought. Tiny iridescent scales covered the dragon's body. Shorty liked the way the dragon's color seemed to change as its body moved. The scales seemed to glow except for the darker scales on its belly and wings.

The tiny dragon was normally a bit grumpy, but Shorty could tell that this was not one of his "good" days. "What is the problem Shorty? Did you forget how to use the amulet to tell us you were coming? I cannot just drop my research to open the door every time you decide to drop in unannounced."

Shorty shrugged, "No getted drop. Go pop ta comes."

Apparently, that was the wrong answer. The tiny dragon began to lecture him about being an idiom.

Shorty ignored the lecture. He was no bery smart, but he was not an idiot. Especially not when the little dragon could not even say the word right. He decided not to get angry with Celestron. This was not the first time Celestron had gotten mad at him. He had a talent for saying or doing the wrong thing around Celestron. "No times fer talkin, Celestron. Where bees da Mage? Needs ta talk. Bery portent."

The dragon opened his mouth to speak. Shorty braced himself for the outburst he knew was coming. But the tiny dragon paused. For the first time he really looked at Shorty's disheveled appearance. His eyes seemed to take in each of Shorty's injuries even though they were hidden under his armor. His gaze moved on to Cat. His neck craned to one side to study the singed fur on her flank.

Celestron's voice had more patience when he continued speaking. "You have obviously gotten into trouble again, but the Arch Mage is busy at the moment. He is with several very important dignitaries. Perhaps I can help you instead?"

Shorty smiled at the dragon as he shook his head. "Tank youse, but me tinks need Dualis fer dis. Muches portent. No ken waits."

The tiny dragon shook its head. "As I said, Dualis cannot see you until his meeting is over. He will be available this evening. Why not wait in the library. I will send word up to the conference room that you are waiting…."

"No!" Shorty stepped through the door moving closer to Celestron. Cat followed him in.

Celestron's face hardened as he floated backwards to give Shorty space. The anger returned to his voice. "You are acting like… well, like an ogre. Even you normally have better manners than this, Shorty. Please use them."

Before Celestron could continue, Shorty patted Cat on the back. Cat looked up at him with a feline grin. A contented rumbling sound came from deep within Cat's chest as she stepped forward. One of her large paws came up to bat playfully at the tiny dragon. Shorty noted thankfully that her claws were not visible.

Celestron's eyes narrowed. The tiny dragon bared his many sharp teeth as it hissed, "She would not dare!"

Cat purred even louder. Her tongue slid out between her two large canines. She seemed to lick her lips. Then she raised her paw and took another friendly swipe at the dragon.

Celestron spun and flew away, disappearing into the Keep. His voice echoed from somewhere down the hall, "You are both impossible to deal with when you are like this. I do not understand what use Dualis has for either of you. You deserve whatever the Arch Mage does to you. Maybe he will turn you into lizards and I can have a snack before I go to bed tonight."

Cat mewled a question. Shorty could only shrug, "Maybeso. Neber bees a lizard afore." Shorty knelt by his friend. "Tank youse Cat. No could hab stop dem ifn no hab youse help." Cat ran a rough tongue along Shorty's cheek. "Goes home me friend. Lick ouches. Gets all betterer. Maybeso needs youse help bery soon."

At his words, a mist began to form around Cat. It thickened until she could no longer be seen. The mist began to draw in upon itself, thickening and shrinking into a small sphere. Then the sphere faded leaving the ivory figurine in its place. Shorty tucked the figurine into his pouch before rising to his feet. He headed down the hall towards the stairs. The large door slammed shut behind him. He winced at the thought of how mad he had made Celestron, but his mission could not be delayed.

Shorty turned right and stepped into a large chamber. A circular stairwell waited for him in the center of the room. The stairs rose up through the ceiling well over his head. Shorty remembered just how far up they went. He reached out and placed his large right hand on the handrail. The leg the devil had injured did not like stairs. The pain he was about to endure was necessary. He began to climb, one step at a time.

The climb seemed to go on far longer than it should have. Shorty was not sure if the stairs were punishing him or if somehow Celestron was responsible. Either way, the answer was the same. "Mo magics!" He would not let the stairs or the little dragon keep him from Dualis. He set his mind on making it to the top and continued to climb.

To distract himself, Shorty hummed the strange melody that the tree in Alano's grove had sung to him. The melody was still not right, but the song distracted him from the stairs. As the first part of the song came to an end, so did the stairs. Shorty found himself standing on the upper landing and he sighed with relief.

Shorty stepped away from the stairs. He wanted no more of them today. To his right was an open area with a number of soft chairs. The chairs were in a rough circle around a large picture on the floor. The picture was made of many small tiles. The floor picture made Shorty uncomfortable. Sometimes the tiny people in the picture moved around and fought battles. He did like to watch the picture move, but he always worried about stepping on the little people. He really did not want to hurt any of them.

Just past the circle of chairs were two large wooden doors. The doors were very purty with many shapes carved into them. Beyond the doors was the meeting room where he and his friends met to discuss the missions they would go on. Shorty liked the room. One whole side of the room opened up onto something Dualis called a Ball Conny. It was really a ledge and it looked out over the mountains. It had lots of fresh air. The mountains gave him something to look at when Dualis talked too long about what they needed to do.

He hesitated as he approached the door. He did not know who the Arch Mage was meeting with or why. He could only hope that he did not make too big a mess of things for Dualis. But waiting would just make it that much harder to find Ann Ah. Shorty stepped past the chairs and the picture on the floor until only the door stood between him and the help he needed.

He reached for the door handles. It would not turn. It was locked. Thoughts of trying to break the lock flashed through his mind. It was an ogre thought. Was he strong enough to do it? He pushed the thought aside. It would be a very bad idea. He did not want to make Dualis any madder than he already would be. He was here to ask for help after all.

Shorty decided to be polite. Althea had been teaching him about polite. He reached out and knocked. The sound of his hand on the door was like that of a giant drum being beaten. He had not intended to hit it that hard. Shorty stepped away from the door so he could not be blamed. He realized that would not help. He was the only one here.

The left door moved inward about the width of his hand. Through the opening, Shorty could see the back of a tall man in black robes. At least the man was tall for a human. His long red hair was woven into an intricate braid that hung almost to the man's waist. Dualis's voice was very precise and formal. That was not good, but Shorty did not have anyone else to turn to. "Please excuse the interruption. I can only assume that the world has stopped spinning, or someone has an overwhelming desire to be turned into a lizard. Please help yourselves to refreshments. I will return in a moment."

Dualis eased out of the room and closed the door before turning to face Shorty. Shorty's eyes dropped briefly to the two swords belted at Dualis's waist, a longsword and a short sword. Mages did not normally carry swords. Shorty wondered how good Dualis really was with them. He looked up to see Dualis studying him with a stern expression on his face.

The Arch Mage's piercing green eyes assessed Shorty, moving slowly from Shorty's boots to the top of his head. Dualis was not angry, Shorty had never really seen him angry before. But it was obvious that he was not happy about the interruption. At the look in Dualis's eyes, Shorty almost forgot what he wanted to ask. Shorty prepared for the worse, but the immediate reprimand he expected did not come.

An expression of curiosity slowly replaced the stern lines on Dualis's face as he studied Shorty's appearance. One eyebrow rose as he noted the scorch marks on Shorty's shield and armor. He seemed to study each injury, even the burn marks hidden below the heavy leather armor. Then his eyes locked on Shorty's face and the look of desperation stamped there.

There was concern in the Arch Mage's voice when he spoke, something that Shorty had not expected. "I assume that you have a very good reason for interrupting this meeting. And an even better reason for allowing your cat to insult Celestron the way you did. I expect better of someone I sponsored to become the Green Knight. Now, what is it that you feel is more important than the treaty negotiations that I am hosting?"

The Arch Mage's eyes grew wide as Shorty dropped to one knee. "Needs youse help please. Dem takes her. Takes her wid magics. No let dem hurts her, Dualis. Me not knowed any bodies else ta asks."

Dualis stared at the form kneeling before him and blew out his breath in disgust. "Get up Shorty! You do not need to beg for my help. Surprisingly, I think I prefer your normal disrespect to this groveling. Now who is this her and who is the them that took her."

Shorty rose slowly to his feet. "Ann Ah. Forest Lady tells me ta protect her. Too manys a da Bad Cloud peoples come. Me sabe Grove but dem get Ann Ah. Go pop. Now me no ken finds dem."

Dualis stared into Shorty's eyes as he processed the outburst. Then he raised a hand into the air. "Wait, please, Shorty. This is not a discussion that I want my guests to overhear. I ask you to go to the library. I will be there very soon. Trinny will have to finish the negotiations. There will be several healing potions waiting for you in the library. Please use them. I promise not to keep you waiting long."

Shorty bowed his head and turned for the stairs. As he headed down the stairs he heard Dualis mutter, "No more bowing and scraping. It is unnerving coming from you."

A short time later, Shorty was seated in an oversized chair in the library's reading area. Two empty vials sat on a small table to his right. The pain of his burns began to fade.

Without the distraction of his other injuries, he became more aware of the growing numbness in his left hand. Shorty was not even sure he could close that hand around the hilt of his sword anymore. The finger of his right hand rubbed at the place where the liquid on his shield had dripped. His left hand did not even feel the touch of those fingers. Whatever was wrong with his hand, the healing potions had not helped at all. Shorty continued to rub at the hand as he leaned back and closed his eyes.

Shorty sat up quickly when the sound of leather slapping against the floor tiles approached his chair. He looked up to see Dualis heading towards him. A large, metal owl sat upon his shoulder. Man and bird came to a stop in front of Shorty's chair. He began to rise, but Dualis shook his head. "Sit Shorty. You look exhausted."

The owl turned its head so that its left eye focused on Shorty. The eye seemed to spin and then lock into place. "He has been poisoned, Dualis. I can see it eating at the fingers of his left hand. I do not recognize the poison, but it is dangerous."

Dualis nodded in response, "Thank you, Wisdom." Then he looked at Shorty, "What happened to your hand, Shorty?"

Shorty held the hand before his face. "Get drip on. Little red ting wid wing try ta kills me. It hitted shield wid long tail. Sumtin wet dripped on me hand."

Dualis glanced at the shield leaning against Shorty's chair. "Red thing?"

Shorty lifted the shoulder of his uninjured arm. "Gots face like bat but nose like piggy. It help warrior in black plate. Bad Cloud peoples."

Dualis nodded, "Sounds like an Imp."

The metal bird concurred, "I agree, Arch Mage."

Dualis held out his left hand, making a complicated gesture. "Servant, please go to the infirmary and bring me a salve for poisons. You should bring the greenish one on the top shelf just in case."

Shorty looked around, but there was no one else there. Dualis appeared to be talking to himself. Shorty was about to ask if Dualis was okay when he heard the pattering of tiny feet running from the room.

Dualis slid a padded chair from a nearby table and set it before Shorty. With an exaggerated sigh, he sat down. The bird Wisdom flapped its wings and flew to a high-backed chair where it landed. Without turning its body, it rotated its head so that one eye faced each of the rooms occupants. Dualis leaned forward. "We will heal your hand soon Shorty. Now tell me what kind of trouble you have stirred up this time?"

Shorty continued to rub at his fingers. He tried to organize his thoughts, but they were spinning in too many directions for him to control them. He knew he would have to speak slow and careful. Dualis did not always understand the important things. Despite his good intentions, once he began to talk, the words were impossible to stop.

"No me fault. Me no start da fight. Forest Lady hab portent job fer da Green Knight. Sends me ta protect. No telled me bout Bad Cloud peoples. Jus sayed me no posed to let three lady gets hurted. Go ta Grove an finds Ann Ah an her Mama an Meer Ah. Try bery hard ta do what Lady say. Bad Cloud peoples come. Me only kills two a den. Not knowed orc bees dere too. Him takes Ann Ah. Needs ta find Ann Ah. Youse maybeso use magic fer me? Please? Unnerstan now?"

Shorty paused to breathe and Dualis winced at the onslaught of words. His hands rose up to rub his temples. A look of pain crossed his face. "Wisdom, did you get any of that?"

The metal owls head swung back and forth. "I can replay the words but most of it is still a jumble. I am only sure of the part about the mission for the Forest Lady who I assume to be Mielikki."

Dualis's hands returned to his lap. "Let us try this a different way Shorty. Let me ask questions and you just give me simple answers."

Shorty nodded and Dualis asked, "This Grove you mentioned, is it in Arcturus?"

Shorty shook his head. "No, it bees secret place. Dis Grove belong ta tree peoples. No bery many dem dere. Three tree peoples an three lady me posed ta protect."

Dualis sighed. "Shorty, please slow down. Simple answers till we understand a little more."

Shorty looked at him puzzled. "No use big word. Me not knowed big word."

Dualis reached up to squeeze the bridge of his nose. "My head is beginning to hurt already' and we are just getting started."

Shorty lifted the two empty vials. "Sorry, drinked dem all gone."

A small green pottery bowl with a lid floated into the room. Dualis reached out and took it. "Thank you, servant." He opened the container and held it out to Shorty. "Take a small amount of this, and rub it into your fingers."

Shorty reached into the bowl with the first two fingers of his right hand. They came out covered with a green cream. He began to rub the cream into the numb fingers on his left hand. The numb fingers became slippery, but they also began to tingle.

As Shorty focused on his hand, Dualis asked, "Do you know where this Grove is, Shorty or what it is called?"

Shorty shook his head, "Secret place." He paused for a second watching the cream disappear into his skin. "Ann Ah call it funny name. She say sang ta air. Why tree peoples wants ta sing ta air? Bery silly."

Dualis stiffened in his chair. "Shorty, this is important. Did she perhaps say Sanctuary?"

Shorty looked at the Arch Mage with the normal look of sympathy he used when the man asked a silly question. "Dat what me jus say, sang ta air."

Dualis ignored the look Shorty gave him. "Tell me about the followers of Set that attacked Sanctuary."

Shorty looked up from his hands to meet Dualis gaze. "Bees mage. Muches fire magics. Bees warrior in plate wid no bery nice spike mace. Bees little red monkey bat pig dat fly. New Horizons calls it…" Shorty paused as he considered the word. "Imp. It tail bery bad. An dere bees da orc dat me neber sees. Him takes Ann Ah. Gots ta finds her, Dualis."

Wisdom spoke first, "How do you know it was an orc that took her if you did not see it?"

Shorty raised a greasy finger to his nose. "Smells it." He paused and sniffed the finger near his nose. "Dis smell bery nice. Straw berry in dat stuff. Maybeso make soap dat smell like dis?"

Dualis cut off Shorty's rambling. "So, the orc got away and took this Ann Ah. What happened to the mage, the priest, and the imp?"

Shorty replied with a grin, "Bery dead!"

Dualis gave Shorty a curious look before carefully asking, "You killed a Priest of Set, a mage, and an imp all by yourself? That is impressive even for you."

Shorty shook his head, "No, me hunt wid Cat. Cat kill da mage. New Horizons help me ta kills monkey bat pig dat fly."

"And the warrior priest?" Dualis asked.

Shorty scratched his head in puzzlement. "Dat bery no makes sense. Him no look so good when da monkey bat pig die. Him get bery old bery fast. Him say gonna comes back ta hurts mo tree. Me kill but no bees fight. No could lets him hurted mo peoples or tree."

Dualis relaxed in the chair as the story began to come together. "What happened to the other two Ladies?"

Shorty shrugged. "Ashley run way wid dem. Safe in Grove sum place. No look fer dem. Needs ta find Ann Ah."

The owl's voice sounded confused when it asked, "Who is Ashley?"

"Her bees tree lady. Lib in Grove wid Corey and Willie. Dey all dat bees left dere."

Dualis sat thinking and Shorty waited patiently for him to figure things out. "I am not sure how to help you track your Ann Ah. If I had met her or had some other link to her this would be fairly simple. Even my magic needs something to work with."

Shorty grinned as he reached inside his belt pouch and pulled out a dirty sock wrapped carefully around a bone comb. He held them out to Dualis.

The Arch Mage stared at Shorty's offering. "Those are her hairs in the comb?"

Shorty sniffed at the comb and then nodded once. "Tink so. Bees from Ann Ah room. Smell like Ann Ah. Maybeso youse ken gets da scent? Ken finds her fer me?"

Dualis reached out and plucked the hairs from the comb. "I cannot promise you Shorty, but I will try. This hair may be enough to find her. Rest here or in your room. I will come for you if I learn more."

Dualis turned to leave the room. "Wisdom, please contact Kaine. He needs to know about this. Tell him Sanctuary was breached."

Shorty watched the owl flap its wings and sail off in one direction. The Arch Mage rushed off in a different direction. He wished that he had something to eat, but it would have to wait. Shorty moved to one of the large couches. It was not big enough for him to lay down on, but he thought he could take a nap there. He leaned back on the couch and worried about Ann Ah. His eyes drifted closed. A low-pitched snore echoed through the library.

Shorty sat up suddenly. A noise that had not been there before intruded in his dream. Something or someone was moving through the library. It should not have bothered him, but he was still on edge from the recent battle. He listened. Footsteps echoed from somewhere back among the many shelves in the library. The murmur of voices accompanied the approaching steps. Shorty glanced up at one of the windows in the ceiling above him. Night had fallen while he slept.

His need to do something, anything, drove him to stand. He desperately wanted to know where Ann Ah had been taken. Perhaps the answer was coming. If not, he had already wasted too much time sleeping. His hopes soared when Dualis came around the shelf that held books filled with pictures of animals and plants. Those were his favorite books in the whole library.

Another man that Shorty recognized was walking just behind Dualis. The druid, Kaine, had come. Shorty liked Kaine even if he asked very hard questions. Like Dualis, he seemed to want Shorty to have big answers to questions that Shorty believed had easy answers.

Shorty started to rise to greet them, but Dualis pointed back at the couch. "Sit down please. We have things to discuss before I answer your question."

Shorty stood there stubbornly. "Ann Ah?" he demanded.

Kaine chuckled. "I told you it would not be that easy."

Dualis grunted in acknowledgement, "Fine. I know where your Annah is. Rescuing her will be, shall we say, complicated. Before we try to figure out how to get her back, Kaine needs to ask you some questions."

His concern for Ann Ah's safety ate at him, but Dualis had at least found her. He sat as he had been asked. Besides, Dualis had used the voice that told him the Arch Mage was not happy about something. Shorty looked at Kaine as the druid pulled up a chair and sat. "Mo hard question?"

Kaine smiled. "Hello, Shorty. I hope these are not hard questions. Nothing like when you wanted to become the Green Knight."

Shorty did not return the smile. "Hullo, Kaine. What wants ta asks me? Needs ta hurry. Friend in troubles. Dis fer da Forest Lady."

Kaine tried to give a reassuring smile. Shorty did not believe it. "I will try to make this quick my friend. Your Lady has work for me as well." Kaine leaned forward with an intense look in his eyes. " I went to Sanctuary while you rested. It has changed and not just the destruction of the wards. I need to understand what happened there. Will you help me?"

Shorty tilted his head to one side. "Me telled Dualis. Bad Cloud peoples come. Us fights. Now ken talk bout Ann Ah?"

Kaine shook his head. "I am sorry Shorty. Please give me a little more of your time."

Shorty signed in frustration but did not argue. Kaine asked gently, "The wards were brought down by powerful magic. I have repaired some of them. But it will take time to fix it all. Were the wards up when you arrived?"

Shorty gave him a puzzled look. "Not knowed dat word. What bees ward? Lady sends me dere. Me tries ta protect when da bad peoples come."

Kaine glanced over at Dualis and then back to Shorty. "Sanctuary is a secret place. How did you find it?"

Shorty puzzlement grew. "No hab ta finds it. Lady say go. Hicks send me dere. No bery hard."

Kaine looked puzzled now too. "Hicks, your Treant from Arcturus?" At Shorty's nod, Kaine continued, asking, "How did he send you there?"

Shorty did not understand why it mattered, but he answered anyway. "Him takes me ta tree door. Same ting ebry time Lady gib me job."

Kaine's tone grew suddenly serious, "You used druidic magic to walk between trees into Sanctuary?"

Shorty shook his head again, "No dat. Bees magic door. Two tree touch at top. Bees water in atween dem. Go in da water. Pop. Bees place da Lady want me bees."

Kaine spun to face Dualis. "Is there a portal in Arcturus?"

Dualis's face was thoughtful. "Not that I know of. That is not something Alano would have hidden from me. But if there is a portal…"

Kaine finished the statement for him, "It would explain why Set wants Arcturus so badly."

Kaine turned back to Shorty. "Only the Treants, the tree people know about this magic doorway?"

Shorty just shrugged. "Not knowin who knowed bout it. Lady gib ta tree peoples."

Kaine sat back and laced his fingers together. "What did you do while you were in Sanctuary? Despite the damage, Sanctuary is stronger than I can remember it ever being. Ashley would not let me look around in the Grove. Do you know why?"

"Me protect. But no do bery good."

Kaine prompted Shorty again, "Anything else?"

Shorty thought for a moment. "Meet Ann Ah. Play wid squirrel. Me plant lots."

Kaine leaned close again. "What did you plant Shorty?"

Shorty smiled for the first time as he thought of all the seeds he had planted with Ann Ah. "Plant friend. Many friends."

Kaine stared at him. "Friends? How do you plant friends Shorty?"

Shorty's smile grew broader. "Tree Friend. Many seed. Plants dem all ober dat place."

Kaine's mouth dropped open for a time. "You planted Treants? Are you sure? Where did the seeds come from? Treant seedlings are so rare."

Shorty reached across and patted Kaine on the knee. "Bees kay Kaine. Hicks an Cherry say seed bees gift. Arcturus want dat place bees strong."

Kaine rose and bowed to Shorty. "Thank you, Green Knight. Thank you for your answers and mostly thank you for planting those seeds.

Sanctuary was dying. Now it might live. I must get all of the wards back up."

Kaine turned to Dualis. "Sorry, old friend, but you will have to do the next part without me. This is important."

Dualis just nodded, "I understand Kaine. What comes next is best between Shorty and I anyway. Good luck. If you need my help, call on me."

As Kaine rushed from the room, Dualis came and sat in the chair that Kaine had just vacated. "I do not know of an easy way to tell you this Shorty. They have taken your Annah to the Gates of Hell. She is in the slave market there."

Shorty blinked in surprise. This was even worse than he had expected. He thought about his last trip to the Ba Zaar and shuddered. All of the people he had been able to save from that place bore scars from their time in Hell. Shorty looked hopefully at Dualis. Maybeso he could buy Ann Ah and bring her back. It was not much of a plan, but it was all he had so he asked, "Ken youse comes? Helps me get Ann Ah back?"

Dualis's face was expressionless as he replied, "I am still not allowed to go there, Shorty. If I do, it will start a war and we might never get your Ann Ah back."

Shorty tried to think of another way. Could he do this on his own? "Me hab muches dem metal circle here. Da ones youse keep fer me." At Dualis's nod, he continued, "Youse gibs me paper afore ta buys peoples. Ken makes nudder one. Me go gets Ann Ah. No so hard ta trade paper fer friend."

The look on the Arch Mage's face was not hopeful and Shorty knew that he was about to hear all of the problems with his simple plan. Dualis's hands came together in his lap. "The letter to guarantee the funds is easy Shorty. And yes, you have a great deal of gold stored here. But I am not sure that it will be enough. Annah is very important to someone. They went to a great deal of effort to capture her. I suspect the price of her freedom will be more than you can afford."

Shorty's face became set with ogrish determination, "Me gots ta tries!"

Dualis's hands rose to make a calming motion. "You cannot rush off and do this by yourself Shorty. It will not work."

Shorty scowled at Dualis. "Hows come?"

Dualis's face tightened in frustration. "Shorty, think about this carefully. You have learned so much since you became the Knight. You are starting to read. You know many more numbers than you used to. Your Annah is going to cost a lot. A really big number. Who will help you with those big numbers?"

Shorty finally understood the problem. "Friends helps me like afore. Team bees strong nuf ta do?"

Dualis shook his head, "They are, but the team is missing, Shorty. Even Ez'ard. I have not been able to find them."

Shorty's frustration grew. He had counted on his friends help. Now they were missing too. There were too many people to save. "Gots ta sabe Ann Ah now. How me find team ta helps?"

"I cannot answer that Shorty. Something is blocking my spells. I will find them, but I cannot say how long it will take. Even Zargon is not available. He is out searching for the team. This is why I told you it was complicated."

Shorty got up and began to pace. He was not going to be able to save Ann Ah by himself. He wanted to, but if he tried, he would make a mess of things. He could not fail her again. But he also did not want to put other friends in danger. He needed at least two people to help him. One for the numbers and one to watch his back. But who?

He thought about who was left at Stormhold. Relin could fight well enough, but Shorty could not ask his friend to go back to that place. Relin would agree to help him, but Althea and the kids needed him safe.

Without the team, he only knew of one other place he could get the help he needed. Could he face his old friends after sneaking away like he had? Could he find the courage to ask them for help?

Especially in such a dangerous place? But he really did not have many choices left if he was to save Ann Ah.

He turned to face the Arch Mage. Dualis's voice was very firm. "I will not allow you to go there alone Shorty. Neither you nor your friend would return."

Shorty walked back to the couch and sat. "No jus me. Hab friend. Strong one dat ken helps. But needs da paper ta pays fer Ann Ah. Den me need ta go ta me old home."

Dualis studied Shorty with skepticism. "Are you sure about these friends of yours? I do not doubt they will help you, but are they strong enough?"

Shorty remained quiet as he weighed the risks that he was about to ask his old friends to take. "Dem ken do dis. Dwarf an Knight. Thorn ken do da number. Roiland bees like Zargon. Dey helps ifn me ask."

Dualis considered Shorty's words. "You must promise not to go without them Shorty. I insist on that. I really wish you had a mage to bring along. But the only other mage available is Know Man and he is needed at Stormhold."

Dualis rose as a tray filled with food floated into the room. "Eat, Shorty. I will return in a bit with the things you need."

The tray was filled with breads and cheeses and a plate full of thick ham slices. Shorty did not hesitate. He ate it all.

The Arch Mage returned soon after Shorty finished eating with two rolled parchments in his hand. He extended the first one to Shorty. "This will guarantee payment for 125,000 gold. That is everything that you have left."

Shorty thanked Dualis and placed the parchment in his backpack where it would be safe. "Little metal tings no do nuttin. Me no care ifn all gone."

Dualis shook his head. "Those coins accomplish many things, Shorty. Look at all you have done for Stormhold and Arcturus. That money has paid for many things that your people need. People who had nothing left in the world now have homes and, for some, their freedom thanks to your generosity."

Shorty opened his backpack and placed the parchment inside it. "Nees mo metal tings in da world ifn need dem."

"You risk your life every time you go on a mission," Dualis pointed out. "Remember what happened to your leg under the hill, my friend? One day you may not come back from trying to save the world."

Shorty just shrugged and began to close the backpack. Dualis extended the second roll of parchment. "Take this one too. I do not think you will have enough for your friend without it. Trust me, Shorty."

Shorty shook his head. "Me mistake. No shoulda lets Ann Ah gets took. Me pay fer her bees free, no youse."

Dualis asked simply, "Are you willing to leave her there if you do not have enough?"

Doubt warred with stubbornness on Shorty's face. "No wants ta owes youse. No fer dis. No ken all time lets udder peoples fix me problem."

Dualis smiled knowingly. "There would be no debt Shorty. But if it makes you feel better. If you use the second parchment, I will keep the things you left behind in Sanctuary. The priest and the mage had several very powerful magic items. Would you consider that a fair trade?"

Shorty bowed his head. "Tank youse, Dualis. Me no ferget dis." Shorty stood and held out his hand.

The Arch mage rose and took Shorty's hand. "I wish you the best of luck, Shorty. Where do you need to go next?"

Shorty squeezed Dualis' hand lightly and released it. "Gots ta sees Hicks. Him ken sends me ta home me hab long time go. Says sorry an asks fer help dere."

Shorty turned and walked from the library. He hoped he would see this place again. He walked swiftly to the exit and out onto the grassy knoll. The moon hung over the mountains as he drew New Horizons. He whispered softly to the sword, "Takes ta Arcturus, please. Needs ta talk ta Hicks."

There was a small woosh of displaced air and the knoll was empty except for the sound of insects.

Chapter 7

A Homecoming of Sorts

He stood in near darkness; leaves fluttered in the breeze all around him. His friend Hicks watched him from across the clearing. Despite Hick's company, Shorty felt very alone. Going back was hard.

The liquid surface of the portal glowed in the moonlight. Everything was ready for him to return to his old home. Everything except him. He was not even sure what he was waiting for. All it took to go back was a single step forward.

Shorty stared at his own image shimmering on the surface of the portal. His normal smile was missing tonight. He looked as tired as he felt. His clothes were torn and stained. Worse, he had not bathed in a long time. He smelled of blood and ogre sweat. It was not a good smell.

The dirt and the smell were not who he was or who he wanted to be. They were a part of someone he did not know. If he did not recognize himself tonight, would his old friends even know him? He knew that he was not the ogre that had left them so long ago. He had changed. Would they welcome this Shorty back? He was not sure.

Had they been angry when he disappeared that night? He told himself that he had left to keep them safe. Now he was going back to ask them to go to a bad place with him. He did not want to do this to them. Then he remembered that it did not matter what he wanted. He needed their help. He had no place left to turn.

Shorty closed his eyes and took a step forward. The cool water of the portal closed around him. It accepted him even if he did not accept himself.

He opened his eyes to a deeper darkness. There was no moon here and the sound of the leaves was gone. The air passing in and out through his nose was all that disturbed the silence of this place. Cold stone walls now surrounded him on three sides. The only direction open to him was to his left. The emptiness of that long hallway stretched farther than he could see.

He was back. The corridor had changed as much as he had. Gone were the magic lights that had once lined its walls. Were the many traps gone as well? He hoped so. Once, long ago, he had worked so hard to get to this very spot. He had opened a door, seeking a future he had not understood. And now that future had brought him face to face with his past.

He turned to stare down the dark passageway. Fire and lightening had ruled this place the last time he had been here. Somehow, those traps seemed less frightening than facing the people he had left behind. Shorty began to walk. For bad or good, it was time to face his old friends.

He walked in silence, unable to even hum to himself. It was cold and wet this far below the castle. The hot dry air from the fire traps was long gone. The cold sank into his heart and the dampness seeped into his bad leg. His steps grew slow and hesitant, but he could not blame the cold or the wet for that. He also could not blame the traps either. They were gone too. As always, he only had himself to blame.

Long before he reached the end of the hallway, he saw the warm, red glow on the ramp ahead. Someone was waiting for him there. How had they known he was coming? He had not known himself until a short time ago. The gruff voice that shattered the silence was not angry like he expected it to be. A voice he had never forgotten called to him across the years, "It is about time you came home, Lad."

Shorty flinched as the words stroked the guilt he felt. "Hullo, Thorn. Bees good ta sees youse gin."

There was a long silence before the voice continued, "Six years since you left us Shorty. Not a word from you in all that time. Are you running back here with your tail between your legs?"

Shorty shook his head. "No gots tail. No ken run bery good no mo."

The gruff voice chuckled. "Some things have not changed at least. Are you running from trouble again, Lad?"

The question hurt. He was not sure why it bothered him so much. "Youse knowed me no bees fraid ta fights. No den. No now."

The warmth of his old friend came closer. "Then why are you here?"

Now it was Shorty's turn to be silent. His words, when he finally got them out, came easier than he expected them to. "Me need helps. Needs go ta bad place. Muches danger. Gots no bodies else ken ask."

A strong hand grasped Shorty by the wrist. He instinctively returned the gesture in a warrior greeting. Thorn's voice seemed almost cheerful as he replied, "At least you were smart enough to come home to ask. Took you long enough, Lad. Welcome home, my friend."

Shorty held his friend's wrist, not wanting to let go. "Hows youse knowed me gonna bees dis place?"

The dwarf made a sound of disgust. "Roiland and his Moon Lady. Said he had a mission but could not figure out where to go. Kisa started casting spells to talk to her Goddess. Between them they figured it out. Too damned much magic if you ask me."

He did not quite understand the part about Roiland, but Shorty could accept the answer of magic. "Kisa sleepin now?"

Thorn tugged him towards the ramp. "No, the ladies are sitting in the kitchen waiting for you."

Shorty fell into step beside the dwarf. It felt like old times. "More den one lady?"

Thorn chuckled. "Yes, Shorty. I am married now."

"Ranger Lady?" Shorty asked.

Thorn paused and turned to stare up at Shorty. "How did you know that? You been keeping tabs on us?"

Shorty shook his head. "Youse always likes when her fights wid you. Fights bout silly tings all da times. No bodies else youse likes ta fights wid."

His old friend shook his head, laughing heartily. "You are smarter than I was. Maybe ogres are smarter than dwarves about some things. Took me a long time to figure that out fer meself."

Shorty touched the circlet around his forehead. "Dis helps muches. Good magics."

Thorn turned and continued up the long ramp. Shorty was glad that the dwarf had short legs. His leg hurt. Thankfully it got warmer as they climbed up from the foundations of the castle. Thorn did not comment when Shorty ran his hand along the wall as they climbed. After the ramp, there were several sets of stairs to reach the main level of the castle.

The sound of laughter greeted him when they reached the top of the final flight of stairs. Shorty froze at the sound. Two female voices carried clearly down the short hallway from the kitchen. He did not catch their words, but both women began laughing again. Thorn nudged him forward. "Go on Shorty. You have made her wait long enough already."

Shorty eased forward and stepped around the corner into the kitchen. It was a large space with multiple ovens and cooking surfaces. Sitting along one wall was an old oak table with four chairs. A beautiful woman with long blond hair and striking blue eyes sat on the far side of the table. Shorty noticed that while most of her body was slim and fit as it had been when they fought the orcs, her stomach was now large and swollen. Her eyes seemed to glitter happily as she saw him standing there.

A second woman sat with her back to him. A long dark braid hung down her back. Her voice was very animated as she spoke, "He stood in the middle of that inn with three of them around him. It was insane…" Her voice trailed off as Anjelique raised a finger and pointed it at Shorty.

The second woman turned to face him. Shorty struggled for words. "Kisa Lady. Me bees sorry. No wants ta bodder…"

That was as far as he got before she rose from the chair and rushed towards him. Her words surprised him almost as much as her tears. "Thank the Goddess you are home!" Then she leapt into the air and wrapped her arms around his neck. Shorty caught her small form easily, allowing himself to relax into her hug.

When she released her grip on him, he lowered her to her feet. "Kisa Lady no bees mad me?"

She slapped a hand against his chest. "Not tonight, but when this is over, you are in so much trouble."

Thorn appeared behind him with the large chair Shorty had used long ago. Shorty sat slowly. Kisa shoved a bowl of stew in front of him. It was still warm and filled the air with a wonderful smell. The bowl was filled with lots of meat, potatoes, and gravy. Shorty even ate the small orange things, but only because he knew Kisa would fuss at him if he left them in the bowl.

Shorty watched as Anjelique rose and walked over to Thorn. She tugged gently on his red beard and whispered, "Thorn, please go up and get Roiland. He is checking on the children."

Shorty's spoon clattered into the bowl. He looked up at Kisa with a broad smiled. "Kids? Youse gots mo den one?"

Kisa helped Anjelique to sit back down and then slid her chair up next to Shorty. "Yes, Shorty. Two boys that are five and a daughter that is about nine-months-old."

"Ken me sees dem? Play wid dem? Me ken teaches dem ta plays marbles." The hopeful look on his face made Anjelique giggle.

Kisa sat back in her chair with a stern look on her face. "Not this time Shorty. If we survive this misadventure, I will introduce you to them when we get home."

Shorty stared down at the empty bowl on the table. He was not sure how to say what he needed to say without hurting his friend again. His eyes roamed the room that had once been his favorite place in the castle. He noticed that Roiland and Thorn had come in to stand near the ovens. Thorn's voice was reassuring as he spoke, "Be an ogre and tell her the truth Shorty. I think she is the only one that has not figured it out."

Shorty met Kisa's intense gaze. "Kisa Lady, dis no bees me home no mo. Gots new home. Me home bees Stormhold an dere bees peoples me protect. Me da Green Knight. Muches work me posed ta do."

He began to fidget with the bowl as Kisa studied him. After a bit she nodded, "I think I wanted you to come home so badly that I did not think it through. You have been gone a long time. I should have realized you would have a home of your own by now. Where is your home Shorty? And what is a Green Knight?"

"Me home bees bery far way," he began. Shorty finished off two more bowls of stew as he told them of Arcturus and Stormhold Keep. He told briefly of his battles with the followers of Set in both Delith and Arcturus. And he told them of being accepted by the Land of Arcturus. Last of all, he told her of his own son, Arlon.

Kisa looked at him in surprise. "You adopted a dragon? A red? I am not sure what to say."

Thorn muttered something about "Of all the foo…" He sputtered to an abrupt stop, though, when Anjelique gave his beard a hard tug.

Shorty assured her that Arlon was a good boy and that he played well with the other children in the Keep.

When the stories and the laughter died down, Roiland rose and spoke, "You have fought many battles against evil, Shorty, and you have grown much. You came here to ask for help. My Lady of Silences bids me to go with you. How can I help you?"

Kisa reached up and took his hand. "We, Husband. How can WE help him?"

This story was harder to tell, but somehow, he found the words to tell them of his mission to protect the three women in the tree people's grove. He spoke of Ann Ah and their time planting new friends. And then he told of the attack, the fighting, and his failure to protect Ann Ah. "Must sabe her. Brings her back."

Roiland's bow now lay across his lap and his hand was moving restlessly along the wood. "Bring her back from where, Shorty?"

Shorty could not meet his eyes. "Bad place Roiland. It bees call da Gate a Hell. She bees in slabe market. Must buys her. Me no smart nuf do all lone. Needs help."

Kisa reached across and took Shorty's hand. "Then we will help you bring her back Shorty. That is what a family does. We help each other."

Shorty shook his head desperately. "No wants youse bees hurted. Bery muches danger dere."

Kisa's expression grew firm, but Roiland intervened before she could speak. "Kisa is coming with us. She has spoken to Akka and the Goddess agrees that she must be a part of this."

Shorty uttered one last protest, "Kids need dem Mama!"

A smile grew on Kisa's face. "Then you best make sure we get back Green Knight. The children will be fine here with Thorn and Anjelique."

Shorty glanced sadly at Thorn. "Me tinked youse come wid Roiland."

Thorn stood and came to stand beside Shorty. He placed a callused hand on Shorty's shoulder. "I would like to stand at your side once more Shorty. But Anjelique will bring our child into this world soon. Someone has to protect this…"

Shorty's head snapped around at the ranger's quiet reprimand, "Careful, Husband. My bow can still take off pieces of your beard even while delivering our child."

Thorn winked at Shorty before turning to stare at Anjelique. "My pardon, Lady Wife. I need to be here to greet our child at its birth."

Anjelique relaxed in her chair. "Better answer, Husband."

Shorty shook his head and muttered, "Still likes ta fights."

Thorn laughed, "Keeps life interesting, my large friend."

Kisa rose. "Shorty, go take a bath. You smell of blood and death. I need to sleep a few hours and speak once more with Akka. You need some sleep too before we go."

Shorty rose from the chair. "No time fer sleepin."

Roiland rose as well. "Listen to her Shorty. You asked for our help. Let us make sure we are ready."

Shorty sighed and agreed. Kisa came and took his arm. "We will leave at noon tomorrow. For now, your old room is waiting for you. You know where to bathe."

Shorty turned and headed for the stairs. As much as he wanted to get started, the thought of being clean and not smelling himself sounded bery, bery good.

Roiland pulled the back side of the chainmail shirt down over Kisa's quilted padding. The mail had seemed almost delicate, but Roiland knew it could take a great deal of punishment. The links made very little noise as they sank to Kisa's knees. "I would prefer that your first time in the new armor be somewhere safer than a trip to Hell."

Kisa turned to face him. She smiled as she leaned in to lay her head against his chest. "Akka said together my love. And for what you paid the Elves for this chain, it had better keep me safe. Now get your own armor on while I grab a few things."

Roiland reached for another set of older looking armor hanging on a rack below his bow. He watched his wife as he donned his own chainmail.

Kisa tightened a belt about her waist and hung her mace from it. The mace was old, but he knew the dweomer was still strong. That mace had served her well over the years. He watched in curiosity as his wife went to her dresser and opened a drawer. She pulled out a small, ornate wooden box and set it on top of the dresser. "I thought you hated those."

Kisa opened the box and removed a string of pale white and golden pearls. "Worse than hate. I loathe them actually. My parents only sent them to ingratiate themselves. They want to curry favor now that they think we are powerful and influential."

Roiland came up behind her. He reached up to place his hands on her shoulders. "Then why bring them out now?"

Kisa lifted the pearls over her head and set them around her neck. She tucked them under her armor, checking in the mirror to make sure they were not visible. "We are headed to a slave market to free slaves. I know Shorty thinks he has this covered, but a little insurance cannot hurt, right?"

Roiland began to laugh softly, "Somehow, I do not think your parents will be pleased with your use of their gift. But I for one approve."

She turned and kissed him before heading for the door. "I go to speak with Akka. I will meet you in the kitchen."

Shorty was waiting in the courtyard well before noon. He had not been able to sit patiently inside, so he came out to pace as he waited. He was clean and he no longer smelled like an ogre. He had taken a second bath early that morning after cleaning his armor and weapons. He was ready to go find Ann Ah.

Thorn and Anjelique were the first to join him outside. Thorn helped his wife to sit on a wooden bench near a large apple tree. Shorty was surprised to see large red apples hanging on the tree. It was too early for apples. The bushes around the tree were also covered in small blueberries. It was strange.

Thorn came to stand beside Shorty. He was glad that his friend did not try to talk. Shorty went back to staring at the tree. It was easier to think about apples than about rescuing Ann Ah.

Shorty's attention turned from the apple tree to the door into the kitchen. Roiland came out followed by Kisa. Both were armed and armored. Shorty hoped that they would not need their weapons and armor. As the two came to stand beside him, Thorn grunted and walked to stand beside his wife.

There was a long moment of silence. Shorty did not know what to say. Kisa smiled up at him. "It is going to be alright, Shorty. Now tell me, how do we get there?"

"Magics," was all he said as he reached out a hand to each of them. Shorty focused on the amulet lying against his chest. He remembered his first view of the place called the Gates of Hell. The air had been so dry.

There was the sudden sound of rushing air. Thorn stood staring at the place where his three friends had been. His gruff voice complained loudly, "Bah! Too much damn magic in this world."

The very pregnant woman sitting beside him reached out a hand to stroke his beard. "They will be fine without you. You just want a piece of the fighting. Now help me back inside. Our child is coming."

Chapter 8

The Market of Souls

Two ten-foot-tall forms stood guard on a vast plain of reddish sand and black gravel. A harsh light beat down on them from the haze-filled sky. Despite the intense heat and bright light, no sun was visible through the haze. The light just seemed to emanate from everywhere. The ground was dry and parched. Nothing grew as far as the eye could see.

The two bone devils did not seem to notice the heat or the lack of moisture. Their dry, translucent skin was stretched tightly over their massive skeletal frames. The outlines of individual bones could be seen through their skin, but not a single blood vessel was visible. It was as if the essence of life did not flow within them.

Neither devil carried a weapon in their hands. They did not need them. Their bodies were weapon enough to defeat almost any foe. Long claws of serrated bone protruded from the end of each arm. Curled up over their heads was a segmented tail with a twelve-inch stinger at its tip. An oily substance coating the end of the stinger was the only sign of moisture visible on the plain.

Far behind the two sentries was a large collection of colorful tents. Banners hung before many of the tents. Each banner offered delicacies and delights beyond the imagination. Barely visible beyond those tents, the masts of great sailing ships pointed into the sky like boney fingers. The few sails visible hung limp and lifeless. No breeze blew in this place to disturb the sails or provide relief from the burning heat coming off the endless sand.

A soft pop announced the arrival of something new. Neither sentry reacted when three figures appeared on the sand before them. Visitors to this place were a common enough occurrence. Many desired the wonders and the horrors that could be purchased at the Bazaar of Souls. Those who came to buy were welcomed. Those who did not come to buy were themselves sold in one form or another.

The first of the three figures was tall, but not quite as tall as either of the two devils. His bulk stood in contrast to their emaciated forms. The hilt of a large sword rose above each of his shoulders. The armor-clad ogre ignored the two devils. His attention was focused on the tents of the Bazaar.

Standing beside the ogre was a small human woman wearing chainmail and carrying a shield. A mace hung from her belt. Around her neck was a gold chain. Hanging from the chain was the wooded symbol carved and painted in the shape of a sheaf of wheat. The symbol seemed out of place in a land so devoid of life.

The final figure was hidden in a heavy cloak that also seemed out of place considering the intense heat. The figure was a mystery except for one detail that was impossible to miss. A beautifully fashioned longbow was clasped tightly in the figures left hand. The outer curve of the bow contained silver symbols representing the different phases of the moon.

The orangish eyes of the two devils examined the large figure as he began to walk between them. First one and then the other released a raspy hiss of warning. Dry skin creaked in protest as both suddenly shifted positions. Their clawed forearms came up defensively.

The ogre warrior looked from one to the other. "Me comes ta buy, no ta fight. Me no hab bery gooder day dis day. Maybeso me feels betterer ifn breaks all your bones. Youse wants ta fights?" The warrior gave a low, menacing growl that revealed two tusks in his lower jaw.

Both devils shifted nervously on the sand. Then the jaws of the devil to the left opened slowly as if had not been used in a long time. A dry, somewhat abrasive voice issued from its throat. "We were warned that you might come again, Green Knight. If you truly come to buy, then pass freely into the Bazaar of Souls. But know that if you cause problems, you will pay for it in blood instead of coin. So the Master has spoken, so shall it be done."

The two devils resumed their bored stances.

The Green Knight stepped between them with no apparent signs of concern. He paused briefly to fan a hand before his face. "Should takes mo bath. Smell like been dead fer long, long times." Neither devil responded to the taunt and the Knight and his companions continued past them. The three headed directly towards the tents.

The human woman moved closer to the ogre and hissed, "Was it wise to try and pick a fight with them? Especially that last crack about needing a bath. I thought the plan was to get in and out without getting into trouble?"

Shorty did not look down at her. "It no bery smart. But bees betterer den looks like bees fraid. Only safe in dis place ifn bees strong. Udders jus bees meat."

The cloaked figure swore softly, "That was almost as much fun as returning to my homeland. Remind me never to return here either."

Shorty shook his head. "Dis bees muches badderer place. Dem two bees da easy part."

Kisa whispered, "Where do you think they are holding her?"

Shorty gestured towards the masts far ahead. "Slabe market bees close ta dirty riber. Boats bring dem fer sellin. Tents bee fer udder tings."

"What things?" the woman asked.

Shorty stared straight ahead. "Bad tings. Youse no wants to knowed."

The anger in his voice made Kisa shiver. She dropped back beside her husband. "Are you going to scout ahead?"

The hooded figure murmured in reply, "No, our big friend knows as much about this place as I am likely to learn. I think it best if I fade back into the crowd. Better that no one notices me unless you need me."

Kisa nodded and moved to walk one pace behind and to the left of Shorty, doing her best to stay out of the way if he had to draw one or both of his large swords. Shorty led her down street after street. Kisa had never seen such a variety of creatures. Maybe her lack of experience was not a bad thing. Most of those they passed smelled of death and corruption. Just being in this place was like an assault on her soul. She would be glad to be away from this place. Kisa glanced back to check on her husband. He was gone and she was not even sure when he had disappeared.

Shorty led the way past colorful tents and banners. Beings of various races approached with offers of power and pleasure. Most backed away at the ogre's glare. Only twice did he resort to reaching up to place a hand on the hilt of his sword. Both vendors smiled as they backed away.

Shorty could tell by the smell that they were nearing the docks and the slave pens. He glanced over to Kisa. Her face was pale and drawn. Shorty moved to the side of the street to check on her. Placing a large hand on her shoulder he asked, "Youse kay?"

Kisa looked up at him. "I lived near the docks of Boat Town for years. The boats there stank, but nothing like this. No Captain I knew would have allowed his boat to be this foul."

Shorty looked at her with sympathy. His own nose was overwhelmed with the stink of the Bazaar. "Water in da riber bery dirty. Bad. Men on boat no care bout smell. Slabe boat neber bees clean. Smell muches bad when peoples no bees free."

Kisa reached up to squeeze his hand. "I will be okay. This is a bit more than I expected. The Goddess warned me it would be bad. But it was something she wanted me to see for myself." Her eyes scanned the slave market just ahead. "Words would never have been enough. I needed to experience this to truly understand what I was fighting to prevent."

Shorty pointed to a large red and gold tent not far ahead. His finger trailed from the tent to an area to the left of the tent. There were cages and pens. Some were empty and some were not. Shorty felt Kisa grow tense, but he also saw the determination on her face. He knew now that she could do what needed to be done to save Ann Ah.

Shorty shifted his gaze upwards to a spot above the cages and pens. "Looks an sees. Sees what dere. Try bery hard ta no sees what him wants youse ta sees."

Kisa followed Shorty's gaze up to the top of a large marble pillar that rose above the slave pens. The pillar was thirty feet tall and at least ten feet across. A desk sat perched atop the pillar. Something large sat behind the desk. Kisa stared at the creature. It was a frost giant. A strange thing to see in this heat. Then it seemed to blur before her eyes and a gold dragon crouched behind the desk. The figure blurred again. Kisa started to sway from side to side as her mind fought to understand.

Then Shorty's body blocked her view of the pillar and the ever-changing form at its peak. The hands on her shoulders shook her gently. Shorty released her shoulder and wagged a large finger in her face. "No looks at him eye."

Kisa drew in a sharp breath and nodded. Shorty moved to the side and this time he pointed out many small forms darting to and from the desk. Each either carried parchment or other objects to drop upon the desk. The desk never seemed to grow cluttered.

Shorty took her arm and turned her away from the pillar. He muttered "Fiend" before leading her on. He kept a gentle grip on her arm as he turned towards the red and gold tent. He whispered to her as they entered the silk tent, "Dis bees place fer special peoples an tings ta gets selled."

The tent was relatively empty. It had been almost full the last time he was here. This time, only three creatures were chained within. Shorty stared at the two almost human creatures collared near the far side of the tent. One of the pair looked up at him with hungry eyes. Shorty stared back at it with interest. Where its mouth should have been was a nest of tiny tentacles that seemed to be in constant motion. The creatures were not Ann Ah and neither seemed interested in being saved so he turned to look at the remaining occupant of the tent.

The final occupant of the tent made Shorty give a soft whistle of excitement. A beautiful black stallion stood in the center of the tent. There were chains about its neck and chains with manacles around all four of its legs. Shorty hated to see such a beautiful creature trapped in this place. He moved close and raised a hand to touch its mane. The horse lunched at him. The chains snapped taut. Wicked sharp teeth closed just inches from his fingers. Shorty stared into eyes that glowed red with hatred. A chill ran through him.

A voice barked from somewhere in the tent, "Damage it and you will pay for it. I do not have enough stock to lose something so valuable as a nightmare. If you are not interested in what you see, come back after midnight. I will have another shipment of oddities by then."

Shorty turned and led Kisa from the tent. "She no bees dis place."

Outside, they crossed the street to the area with the slave pens. The place was the same as he remembered it. A table, empty except for a wooden box, stood at the entrance to the pens. It was here that the creature Zargon called an Ulug Ulu had taken his payment and placed it into the box. The Ulug was not behind the table this time. That was good. Shorty had not liked the creature, not even a little. Shorty turned to examine the pens, looking for Ann Ah or anyone else trapped here.

The first pen held five dwarves. The dwarves sat motionless, staring with dead eyes at the ground before them. Collars were bolted around their necks. Chains led from the collars to large posts driven deep into the ground. Shorty heard Kisa muttering to herself. Her voice held a mixture of anger and confusion, "They do not fight to be free. Why? Would death not be better than this?"

Shorty's answer was hardly more than a whisper, "Magics steal dem heart an poisons steal dem strength. Bees no hope in dis place."

He led her closer to the dwarves so he could get a better look at what he would be purchasing. All five of the dwarves had bruises and scrapes, but otherwise seemed healthy enough. They should all recover if he could get them out of the Bazaar. But for the moment, they were not who he had come to find.

He turned from the dwarves to scan the rest of the pens. Like the tent, this area was much emptier than the last time he had been here. Only one other pen was occupied. Three cages on the far side of the auction area held prisoners. Seven humans stood listlessly in the cages. From where Shorty stood, none of them appeared to be young. He was glad there were no children this time. He was not sure he could handle the sight of caged children again. There were also only two women, standing almost motionless in a cage by themselves. Both were older. Neither was his Ann Ah.

Kisa reached out to rest a hand on Shorty's arm. "There are no young women here, Shorty. Are you sure she is still here?"

He wanted to scream, "Her hab ta bees dis place!" Any other answer would mean he had failed Ann Ah again. But even he knew how desperate that answer would sound. Instead, Shorty nodded and replied, "Arch Mage say she in dis place."

Thankfully, Kisa did not argue. She merely asked, "Then what do we do next?"

Shorty turned back towards the table and raised his voice without looking around, "How muches fer all dem?"

A familiar form with yellowish skin and long dark hair just appeared behind the table with the box. He had not been there before; Shorty would have heard him breathing if he had been. Shorty prepared himself for the insults that he knew were about to be rained on him. This Ulug was no bery nice. But he would accept the abuse if it would get Ann Ah back.

The Ulug had a sour look on its face, more so that the last time Shorty had dealt with it. There was anger in its voice as it told him, "I had hoped never to see you again, ogre." The Ulug held out its left hand. Shorty could see only three black-nailed fingers and a thumb on that hand. Where the smallest finger had been, only a tiny nub remained. "This is what you cost me the last time you were here. My Master was not pleased with our deal. Take your business somewhere else."

Shorty felt no sympathy for the evil creature. It lived off the suffering of others and Shorty did not like it. Shorty ignored the missing finger and asked again, "Hows muches?"

The Ulug growled, but answered, "The prices have not changed since your last visit, idiot. Three thousand gold for each dwarf and two thousand each for the humans." Then the Ulug noticed Kisa standing slightly behind Shorty. The Ulug gave her an appraising stare. "I could offer you a good discount, ogre, if you include the woman as part of your payment.

A dangerous sounding rumble began low in Shorty's chest. The thought of the Ulug touching Kisa made the beast he kept locked deep inside him rattle its cage. It was hard, but he controlled the rage that wanted to burst free. "No fer sale!" was all he let slip out.

The Ulug just grinned knowingly at Shorty's response. "Then keep your little bed warmer. That is the only deal I will offer you. I will not lose any more fingers because of you." The Ulug scanned the crowd out on the street. "No Zargon to back your play this time, ogre? Without that paladin at your side, we have nothing further to discuss. Pay up or leave!" The Ulug turned its back on Shorty and began to walk away.

Shorty's hand shot out and locked around the Ulug's arm. The Ulug was large and powerful, but Shorty's grip did not loosen when it tried to pull away. Shorty did not need to raise his voice to make his meaning clear, "Me no need Zargon help fer little fish like youse. Time fer youse ta bees nice. Unnerstan?"

The Ulug hissed angrily and tried once more to jerk its arm free. Shorty just smiled at its futile effort. The Ulug glanced down at the iron grip holding it in place, its confidence obviously shaken. The creature recovered quickly though. When it looked back up at Shorty, there was a slight smile on its lips as it asked, "Would you break the peace of the Bazaar, ogre?"

Shorty returned its smile. "Youse bees safe little Ulug. No gonna hurts youse. Tells me gin, how muches fer all?"

Shorty released his grip and the Ulug stumbled out of reach. Anger tinged its response, "My pardon, Patron of the Bazaar. I forgot that you are too stupid to do the math by yourself. For all twelve, the price is 29,000 gold."

The Ulug's grin grew even bigger then. "But, as is my right, I am imposing a penalty because you dare to place your hand on me. Since this is your first offense, we shall set the price of your apology at another thousand gold. Your total for the lot is 30,000 gold pieces or their equivalent in gems and jewelry."

Kisa gave his arm a squeeze. Shorty understood her meaning. He had enough to cover that amount. But he also knew that the real cost was still to come. Could he do this without messing it up? He waited until the Ulug had taken its place behind the table where it waited to take his money. Then Shorty gestured to the empty cages. "Want nudder female. Young an purtty one."

The Ulug grinned and waved its hand towards Kisa. "That one is not enough to satisfy you, Oh Mighty Ogre? Too bad. In case it was not clear to your keen powers of observation, you are already buying all of my remaining stock. The next shipment of slaves is not due in until midnight. There might be a female in the lot to warm you bed in that batch, but I make no promises."

Shorty turned back around and gave a warning growl in response to the Ulug's accusations. The Ulug just laughed and continued, "If you do not want to wait that long Knight, there are a few tents that I could direct you to. For a fee, I am sure that they have someone that would meet your needs."

Shorty's face grew hot. He had allowed the Ulug to get the upper hand and he was not even sure how. All he could think of to say in reply was, "No dat!"

The Ulug shrugged, "Then I cannot help you."

Shorty decided he had had enough of the Ulug's insults. He bared his tusks as he took a menacing step forward. "No mo tells lie. Me knowed her bees in dis place. Wants da one dem stealed from da Grove. Gives back. Me pay."

The Ulug began to back further away. "I told you, ogre, there are no other slaves for sale at the moment. If you want these wretches, pay for them and leave! If you do not want them, then just leave."

Shorty large hands clenched into fists. He matched the Ulug step for step, not letting him escape. The set of his face promised death. "Girl wid picture a tree on arm. She bees here. Brings so me ken buy. Do now!"

The merchant pursed his lips and whistled three sharp tones. Shorty felt magic pulse in the air around him. The entire Bazaar went silent, even the vendors ceased their cries. A voice boomed from somewhere over Shorty's head, "Do you violate the hospitality of the Bazaar, Green Knight? There will be consequences if you do."

Shorty looked up and matched gazes with the one who sat atop the pillar. The figure blurred as they stared into each other's eyes. Magic reached for his mind, but in his anger, Shorty slapped those probing tendrils aside. This time, he saw the master of the slave market for what it was. This demon, for that was what he assumed it was, had skin so dark it seemed to absorb the light around it. It had large bat wings and a long, spiked tail. It reminded Shorty of the imp he had fought, only this creature was much, much bigger.

Shorty continued to meet its gaze, showing no respect or fear for the creature that ruled the market. "Insolent fool!" it roared at him. One of its large hands reached out, snatching an imp messenger from the air. The imp trembled in its grip. The demon's other hand pulled a piece of parchment from the desk. "This is a Writ of Banishment from the Gates of Hell. Deliver it." The demonic form then threw the imp at Shorty.

The tiny imp tumbled several times before it managed to control its flight. It beat its wings, racing towards Shorty and Kisa. The small form never saw the pair of arrows headed its way. Howls of pain and anger rose from many of the denizens of the Bazaar as bright flashes of pure white light marked the impacts of both arrows. When the light faded, the imp was gone.

A hooded figure carrying a longbow stepped from the crowd. Those near the archer began to back away, many of them pushing and shoving to distance themselves from the one what had challenged the Master of the Market. Apparently, no one wanted to be close enough to share his fate.

Shorty watched as the small scrap of parchment floated to the ground accompanied by the dust and ash that were all that remained of the imp. Roiland's bow would have been quite useful in the battle at the Grove. Shorty turned to face the Ulug once more. He would have his answer now or the Ulug would die too. "Where bees girl wid tree picture on arm?" Shorty demanded.

The Ulug's deep-set eyes darted towards an iron box that sat near where the dwarves were chained. His gaze rested on the box for no more than a heartbeat, but that instinctive flicker of the Ulug's eyes was more than enough to answer Shorty's question.

Shorty turned to examine the box. He did not like what he saw. The box was less than half of Shorty's height. The heavy metal plates it was constructed from were painted black to absorb what passed for sunlight in this place. Shorty could only imagine how hot it was inside that box. The only air that could reach the occupant of that prison came from a few vertical slots down near the base of the box. They were making Ann Ah suffer and that made him even angrier.

Shorty turned back towards the Ulug. His hand came up slightly. His fingers twitched with an almost unbearable need to wrap themselves around the Ulug's yellow neck. He wondered if he could snap its neck with just one squeeze. His words came out low and deadly, "How muches fer da girl?"

Surprisingly, the Ulug turned its back on Shorty as it looked up to the top of the pillar. Shorty's eyes followed the Ulug's. The thing with the large bat wings stood there with a long deadly-looking whip in its hand. Shorty understood then that the Ulug was trapped with death to his front and rear. Shorty had little sympathy for the Ulug.

"No, please, Master!" the Ulug begged as it backed away from the pillar. Its escape was blocked by the table that had stood between it and Shorty. When the Ulug hit the table, it tilted to one side and the wooden box clattered to the ground. Sensing how close Shorty was now, the Ulug spun to face Shorty. There was fear in its eyes as it shook its head from side to side. "I cannot sell her. She is promised to..."

The crack of a whip was as sharp as it was unexpected. The Ulug's response was cut off in a cry of pain as the tip of a long strand of braided leather struck the back of its shoulder. Jagged shards of metal embedded in the whip dug deep into the Ulug's flesh. As quickly as it had struck, the whip was pulled back. The Ulug fell to its knees. Black blood oozed from where the metal bits had torn free from its back.

Shorty's gaze followed the retreating whip back up to the top of the pillar. A booming voice filled with authority proclaimed, "Your companions will not change the facts, Knight. The woman is not for sale. Make your other purchases and begone or I will summon the Legions of Hell to destroy you. Know that you and your irritating friends are banished from the Bazaar. You should not have slain my servant."

From somewhere within the crowd, a male voice rang out in sharp rebuke, "You accuse the Knight of violating the sanctity of the Bazaar. And yet, you would set aside the Bazaar's most unbreakable rule."

The crowd began to mutter at those words. The magic that had silenced them had been dispelled by the unknown speaker's voice. Every face in the crowd turned towards the pillar as they waited for a response to that unexpected challenge.

The fiend's eyes seemed to burn as it searched the crowd for its accuser. The crowd shifted nervously under its demonic gaze, but no one stepped forward. Obviously frustrated, it roared in anger before replying, "What law do you accuse me of breaking, mortal who hides behind others?"

The same voice rang out again from a different location in the crowd, "The laws of the Bazaar are very clear. Everything within its boundaries is for sale, even you. Therefore, everything in the Bazaar may be purchased for a price. There are no exceptions. Before all present here, you have denied the Knight the right to buy the slave he desires."

The demon seemed to consider the voice's words as it continued to search for the individual who mocked it. Its laughter boomed out over the crowd as it answered, "Foolish mortal, you actually expect there to be rules in Hell?"

The voice came again from a third spot in the milling crowd, this one much closer to the archer. "Even the lawless must have rules or a place like the Bazaar cannot exist. If you forswear all rules, there can be no trade within the markets of the Bazaar. For none can do business where anarchy reigns. Would you bring about the end of the Bazaar, Ancient One? And if you do, where else can one such as you play godling?"

The crowd began to mutter at his words. Many heads in the crowd began to nod in agreement. The fiend, truly angered now, raised its head to the sunless sky and roared once more. Despite the lack of clouds, lightning flashed, and the sound of thunder filled the air. The whip lashed out again. This time its tip struck one of the passing imps. The tiny creature exploded in a spray of black blood.

The fiend calmed at the destruction of the imp and its eyes once more turned to searching the crowd. Its harsh voice demanded, "Who is it that thinks they know the laws of the Gates of Hell better than He Who Rules here?"

A slim figure in a light brown cowl stepped into the open space beside the archer. His face was hidden in the deep hood of his robe. "Do not reach for power that has been denied you for centuries, Ancient One. I know well what truly rules here and those powers would take great offense at your words. Those who truly rule the Nine Hells merely allow you to administer this place and nothing more."

Kisa stared in astonishment at the figure standing beside her husband. How had he come to be here? Her lips began to move as she asked herself, "What are you doing here, F…"

Shorty quickly clamped his large hand over her mouth, preventing her from finishing that question. Kisa's eyes widened in surprise, but Shorty just leaned in close to whisper, "No say name, Lady! Neber say in dis place. Muches danger!"

The fiend on the pedestal pointed a finger at the hooded figure. "Whoever you are, your interference is not welcome here. Begone before I deal with you in my own way." The fiend gestured and two bone devils appeared at the base of the pillar. The fiend smiled as it waited for its command to be obeyed.

The crowd watch in anticipation as the owner of that voice reached up and drew back his hood. The elf that stood revealed had the white-blond hair of an elven noble. His striking features were beautiful by the standards of the mortal world, with the possible exception of the arrogant smile on his lips. But even his smile was not uncommon for a high-born elf.

The elf ignored the two bone devils, almost as if they were of no concern to him at all. Instead, he raised his eyes to meet those of the fiend. "Would YOU now break the peace of the Bazaar, Ancient One?" he asked with more than a trace of sarcasm in his voice. "Would you set aside another of the Bazaar's rules to cover for your own mistake? I have come here unarmed to browse the wonders available in the markets here. I have cast no spells." The elf raised his thumb and forefinger up to stroke his chin and asked, "Would you deny a customer the right to spend gold here? How will you explain that decision to those who are your masters?"

Voices began to mutter more loudly. Patrons gestured towards the elf who stood against the Master of the Bazaar. No one else challenged the figure atop the pillar, but the concern of those watching was very clear.

Hate filled eyes studied the elf. An imp darted in to drop a scrap of parchment on the desk. The fiend glanced down at the note and then smiled. Understanding flashed across his face as his gaze returned to the elf. "You risk much coming here Seeker. There are many within Hell who are tired of your meddling ways. You can add my name to the list of those who would like to see your head on the dinner platter. Your interference here will not be forgotten."

The Master of the Market turned from the elf to stare at Shorty. "Knight, you have demanded a price for the woman. You shall have it. Her price is a half million gold pieces of standard weight, or, of course, its equivalent in gems and jewelry." With a soft chuckle, it added, "I have named a price, Seeker. Your complaint is no longer valid."

The elf smiled, but there was no humor in his reply. "The going price of a human slave is only 2,000 gold. What you ask for her is unreasonable. It is more than the cost of opening a shop in the Bazaar."

The fiend's laughter reverberated from every corner of the slave market. "Tell me, Seeker, where in the laws of the Bazaar am I required to set a reasonable price? This is, as humans are fond of saying, a seller's market. But, if it makes you feel any better, I have another buyer for that particular slave. Your Knight must exceed my current offer."

The elf nodded sagely. "If that is your best offer, then I suspect I will need to help the Knight raise enough money to pay your price." The elf drew himself up, somehow seeming taller than he had before. His voice grew much louder, although he did not appear to be yelling. His voice echoed almost as much as the fiends as he announced, "I am the Seeker. I deal in information. I have information of great value to all who work within the Bazaar of Souls."

"Pathetic," the fiend countered, "What could you possibly know that would be of any value here?"

"Perhaps a small preview of the information is in order," the elf replied with a grin. With a theatrical bow, the elf met the fiend's gaze once more. Power s gathered around him as he began to chant, "Aenon B'MaN OeAK, LeT…"

A scream of outrage cut off the rest of the elf's words. The desk fell from the pillar to land on one of the two bone devils. The desk shattered as it flattened the devil beneath its great weight. The second devil ignored its kin's fate as its eyes darted from the fiend that had summoned it to the Seeker. For the first time since it had been summoned, it appeared interested in what was going on around it.

The voice of the fiend held a note of desperation when it commanded, "Desist!"

The crowd retreated even further from the elf and the archer. Some even left the slave market all together, heading for the safety of the tents and pavilions. Neither the Seeker nor the Archer retreated from the angry fiend, one stood with an arrow notched and the other with a look of satisfaction on his face.

"You will pay for that!" the Master of the Bazaar began, but the Seeker cut him off.

"What can you ever do to me, Ancient One?" he asked, "I know your true name. I can speak it in the common tongue, or I can recite it in the Old Tongue. With it I can bind you. Or, for the right price, I can share what I know with any and all here."

"What is the price of your silence, Seeker?" the Master demanded.

The one known as the Seeker appeared to ponder that question, but his answer was not long in coming. "I only ask that you give a reasonable price to the Knight. In exchange for that, I agree not to share what I know with any other, here or in the mortal world."

The fiend dropped its whip and intoned, "So it is agreed, so let it be done," It recited formally.

Shorty watched his brother go from picking a fight they could not win to ending the battle before it even began. What were those strange words that F'lar had spoken? And why had the thing on the pillar been so afraid of them? He would have to ask his brother when this was all over. Shorty looked up again as the demon thing spoke to him.

"The woman you seek is very valuable, Knight. She cost me a great deal to procure. My price for her is 250,000 gold. I can go no lower."

Shorty turned to see Kisa digging the two parchments that Dualis had given him from a pouch on her belt. She unrolled them both, checking them for what he assumed were the big numbers written on them. He knew from the look on her face that they were not enough. Dualis had been right. Kisa stepped closer to him. "You are close, but it is not enough. I can help."

Shorty shook his head. He took the two parchments from Kisa and dropped them on the counting table. Then he reached into his own belt pouch and pulled out his precious bag of marbles. He loosened the strings holding the bag closed. Then he dumped the marbles on the table beside the parchments. Blue and red fire mingled with greens, yellows, and white flashes of brilliance. Each marble glittered as it rolled towards the Ulug. He pulled a second smaller bag out and dumped several rings and a bracelet beside the marbles. Strangely, there was no sense of loss as he gave up his treasured playthings.

Everyone in the crowd watched as the Ulug struggled to its feet. The arm below its injured shoulder hung limp. Shorty had to help it return the box back on the table. With its precious box back in place, the Ulug first examined the two parchments. He shook his head when he reached the places where Dualis had signed his name, but he did not argue about that signature as it had the last time Shorty had been here. Then, one by one, the Ulug examined each of Shorty's marbles. Its black nails rolled each gem on the table, examining them for flaws.

When it was finished, it turned to face the pillar. But it did not raise its eyes to meet those of its master.

"Well?" its master demanded.

Still without looking up, the Ulug replied, "The Knight has the purchase price for the female slave and the penalty that he was assessed for his insolence."

"And for the other slaves?" the Master asked.

Shorty had a sinking feeling as a broad grin spread across the Ulug's face. "No, Master. He can barely afford the female he desires so greatly."

The figure on the pillar laughed at that pronouncement. It spoke first to his brother saying, "I have kept my end of the bargain, Seeker. Now, you must keep yours as well."

Then it turned to face Shorty with an almost joyful expression on its face. "You have enough for the woman Knight, but not enough for the other slaves. Will your honor allow you to sacrifice twelve souls to save just one?"

Shorty was lost. He did not know what else to do. He had no way to pay for them all. He looked pleadingly at his brother.

F'lar shook his head. "I am sorry Knight. I have done all that I am allowed to do. Even I have rules that I must obey. You must choose."

Shorty's fingers twitched. His hand began to move towards the hilt rising above his shoulder. An eager gleam lit the fiend's eyes. The Archer sighed and lifted his bow.

Kisa reached out before Shorty could draw his sword. Her fingers tightened on his arm. "No, Sir Knight, that is what they want you to do."

Shorty looked down at her. He had the right to sacrifice his own life to save Ann Ah and the others. Did he have the right to sacrifice her life as well? She had children waiting for her at home. Then Kisa reached inside her armor and pulled out a string of white and gold marbles. They were smooth and perfectly round like no marble Shorty had ever seen before. She lifted them over her head and allowed them to dangle from her index finger.

Shorty wanted to protest that this was his responsibility, but those words would not come. He could see no other way out of the mess he had gotten himself into.

Kisa leaned against him. "I know you wanted to do this yourself, but it is time for you to learn that you are not the only one who gets to save those that need saving. You are also not the only one who gets to make sacrifices for the sake of others. This is my choice to make, not yours. Remember, old friend, that you asked for my help. This is how I choose to give it. Now hush." Then Kisa tossed the necklace at the Ulug. "That will cover the cost of the others."

A yellow hand shot out to snatch the pearls from the air. Raising them before its eyes, the Ulug studied the prize grasped in its claws. The Ulug's eyes widened with its obvious excitement. It sniffed at the necklace and even licked one of the white marbles. Kisa's offering disappeared into the box so quickly that Shorty almost did not see the Ulug's hand move. Then its smug voice announced, "I do not give change, human."

At Kisa's dismissive wave, the Ulug used the one good hand it still had to scoop Shorty's marbles into the box. Shorty did not hear any of them clatter against the bottom of the box. He wondered why. The last to be placed in the box were the two pieces of parchment.

The fiend on the pillar spoke once more, "The bargain is struck and the contract is complete. The slaves are yours. Take your property and leave my realm. Your banishment from the Bazaar still stands." Then the fiend turned its attention back to the elf. "You have made many enemies this day, Seeker. Do not consider this a victory. Your actions here today will not be forgotten. Each of you will regret taking this prize from him to whom she was promised."

Shorty's nostrils flared at the threat. He met the fiend's glare with one of his own. He slowly raised a fist towards the figure standing above him. Then he extended his index finger to point at the fiend. "No! No gonna bees dat way. Youse tells Bad Cloud dat Shorty do. No udder. Him knowed where ta finds me."

Kisa sucked in a breath as Shorty spoke his own name. F'lar simply shook his head and lowered his eyes. He muttered softly, "No bery smart brother. Damnably brave, but definitely no bery smart."

Darkness wrapped itself around the fiend and then the pillar was empty. The Ulug brought out a single key and two small key rings. Shorty tossed the rings to Roiland and kept the single key for himself. He walked swiftly to the iron box. He desperately needed to get Ann Ah safely out of that box. After that, he wanted to leave this place forever.

Shorty ran his hand over the box. There was a small hole the size of the key just below the cover. He stared down at the small key in his hand. He had no idea how to use it. He did not use locks at Stormhold. Everyone there was his friend. Why would he need to lock things? Shorty tried to put the key into the hole, but it did not fit. He was getting angry. Then Kisa's hand reached out and took the key from him.

Shorty watched as Kisa fit the smaller end into the hole and twisted. She stepped back and Shorty lifted the heavy lid and threw it open. Ann Ah lay in a heap at the bottom of the box. Shorty's heart sank. He bent and carefully lifted her out of the box. She lay limp in his arms.

He turned once more to Kisa. "Helps her?"

Kisa ran her hands over the young woman's face and neck. "She is alive Shorty. I can heal her, but not here. My connection to Akka is too weak here."

Shorty held Ann Ah in his arms as he watched his brother and Roiland unchain the other slaves and move them into a circle near the now empty table. F'lar looked at him. "I can use magic to leave this place, but I am not sure where you want to go."

Shorty reluctantly handed Ann Ah to his brother. "Me takes us out a dis bad place."

Shorty knew that what he was about to do was against the rules of the Bazaar. But he did not care anymore. He reached up over his shoulder and pulled New Horizons from its scabbard. It felt good to hold his sword in his hand once more. Hatred and distrust emanated from many of the beings that watched them. Shorty bared his tusks in challenge. Then he asked his sword to take them home, all of them.

Shorty could feel New Horizons' desire for battle. It had been forged to fight and vanquish the beings that ruled here. Shorty would have welcomed that battle. He hated this place. But Ann Ah lay in his brother's arms. Kisa and Roiland stood watch over the rest of the former slaves. All of them needed to get away. It was his duty to make sure none of them died in this place.

"Home, please, Tainkintana." There was a flash of pure white light and the world shifted around him. Screams of anger were cut off as the Bazaar was just gone. Sunlight and the smells of home replaced those screams. Then voices Shorty knew and loved cried out in greeting. He was home and Ann Ah was finally safe.

Chapter 9

Darkness Comes

Shorty wandered out of the dining room; he had learned everything he could in the meeting. If he asked any more questions, his friends would figure out that he was up to something. He knew he was not smart enough to fool them for long. If they had not been arguing with each other about how to defend Stormhold, his plans would already have been discovered. Sometimes, the best way to fool the smart peoples was to let them do most of the talking.

Shorty knew that none of his friends would like his plan. When they finally found out what he had done, they would all be angry. But by then, it would be too late. He would not be here to be "spoken to". "Spoken to" was smart people talk for getting yelled at again. They could all be mad at him if they wanted to. All that mattered to him was that his home and the people who depended on him would be safe.

 He stood outside the door for a moment longer, listening to the voices of the people he loved. Forks banged on plates and his friends kept interrupting each other. Things were almost back to the way they were supposed to be. Even Ez'ard had returned from wherever he had been lost. He wished he had time to hear the story about the sea monster, but the evil would be here very soon. When it arrived, he would begin his final battle as the Green Knight. He would save them all, even Dualis, whether they liked it or not.

He smiled as the arguments started up again. Each of his friends had their own idea about how to stop what was coming. The argument would keep them distracted and that was all he cared about. The evil was much closer than any of them realized. He was not sure how he knew it was close, but he did. He must be ready for it before it got here.

Maybeso he knew because the evil was coming for him and not for Stormhold. He had made sure of that when he challenged the pit fiend atop the pillar. His brother had taught him what the creature was called. It was a very bad thing and F'lar told him just how no bery smart that challenge had been. Shorty did not agree though. If he did this his way, he would not lose any more friends. He had lost enough of them over the years.

Shorty began to walk the halls of his home one last time. He liked Stormhold and he loved the people that now lived here. Most were people he had managed to rescue. If he allowed them to fight the battle they were planning, how many would die? Even one was too many. No, his way was better. Besides, it had been his mistake that allowed Ann Ah to be captured. It had probably been an even bigger mistake to take her back from the Gates of Hell. But he would willingly make that mistake again. He could never have left her there. If his plan worked, she would be free to live a better life here among his friends.

He walked slowly past each door on the first floor. He knew who or what was in each of those rooms. The squires and Rankin lived in this hall. The kitchen where Althea cooked for him and the library with his books were here too. He even knew what was in each storage room he passed. This was his home, and he would protect it. At least, he would try to.

Everything depended on that strange thing his brother called a soul. Souls were very confusing. F'lar said that souls were very important, but Shorty could not see them. Even Know Man had agreed that everyone had one. Shorty wondered if the souls were the same as the ora things that Ann Ah saw. If that were true, then maybeso he really had one. Having a soul was an important part of his plan. And if things went badly tonight, he might lose his soul to the evil. But that was okay. He would trade something he could not see or touch to save his friends.

Shorty came to a stop outside the largest of Stormhold's storage rooms. The supplies had all been removed. In their place, a small hospital had been set up for the people Kisa had rescued from the slave market. The room was filled with cots, each holding a now free person. He hoped that these people would want to join Stormhold's growing family. Shorty knew his home needed many more good people. He only regretted that he would not be able to make friends with each of them.

He quietly opened the door and stepped inside. The room was filled with the sound of people sleeping. Know Man had used his magic to ensure that they slept without dreams. Tomorrow they could deal with what had been done to them. Tonight, they deserved some peace. Seeing that his guests were as comfortable as he could make them, he slipped back into the hallway.

It was time to prepare for the night ahead. Shorty headed back towards the dining room and the stairs to the upper level. As he turned to climb the stairs, he could tell the argument was still going on. The Arch Mage was giving one of the long, boring explanations that Shorty hated. Dualis liked to tell people things, even if those people did not really want to listen. Shorty hurried up the steps before someone decided he needed to listen too. The voices faded as he climbed the stairs. The darkness and silence were just what Shorty needed.

When he reached the second floor, he turned down the long hallway to his room. His eyes had not yet adjusted to the darkness, but Shorty sensed someone up ahead. He drew a shallow breath in through his nose and he relaxed. It was Relin. Shorty waited until he could see the warmth of the man's body.

The Captain of his Guard stood before the last guest room door. Shorty smiled. "Hullo Relin. How's come youse bees guard? Captain a da Guard ken hab sum bodies else do dis."

Relin chuckled in the darkness. "Because my Lord Shorty, you told me that she was important, and you asked me to make sure she was safe. Watching over her myself is the least I can do for you."

Shorty walked down the hall until he stood beside his friend. He placed a hand on the Guard Captain's shoulder. Relin was wearing his black chain mail. Shorty knew his friend was prepared to protect Ann Ah. "Youse bery good friend Relin. Muches tanks. All bees safe bery soon."

Shorty could hear the relief in the man's voice. "Have your friends come up with a plan? I thought they expected this to be a difficult battle."

He patted Relin's shoulder before lowering his hand. He could not look Relin in the eye as he answered, "Dere bees new plan. Bees big secret. Youse kids gonna bees safe. Me promise."

Shorty felt the tension drain from his friend's body. "That is very good news Shorty. I do not remember much of our time in the slave market, but I have no desire to end up there again."

"Me no gonna lets dat happens," Shorty reassured the former slave. Relin nodded solemnly, the faith he had in Shorty was clear on his face. Shorty just wished that he believed in himself as much as Relin seemed to.

Shorty headed for his own room. It was where he had chosen to meet his most unwelcome guest. His door was just a few steps beyond Ann Ah's room. But he could not bring himself to meet his fate without seeing her one more time. He needed to say goodbye even if she never knew he had been there. He spun to face Relin and the door his friend guarded.

Relin grinned at him and stepped to the side. Shorty opened the door. Moonlight drew him in, and he closed the door behind him. Shorty looked across the room. The shutters had been opened to allow the light of the moon to bathe the entire room. He could see Ann Ah's form resting beneath one of Althea's quilts. His breath caught in his throat when he saw her lying there motionless. Then he heard her breathe and the fear left him. She was still alive. Somehow, he would make sure she stayed that way.

Shorty walked to the side of the bed. He stared down at her face, wishing that he could see her smile at him one last time. At least the bruises that had marred her face and neck when he had taken her from the Bazaar were gone. Kisa had been able to heal her. Shorty was glad. His gaze traveled down from her face to her right arm where it lay atop the quilt. The image of a tree glowed in the moonlight, stretching from her wrist to her elbow. Shorty knelt to study it.

The tree was perfect from its roots to the many branches covered in leaves. As he watched, moonlight seemed to gather on the trees leaves, outlining each individual leaf. This was more than just a painting, but he did not know what it was. Unbidden, Shorty's fingers touched the tree just above Ann Ah's inner wrist. He could actually feel the texture of the bark. His fingers traced the trunk up to where the branches spread out to encircle Ann Ah's arm. The leaves seemed to shiver beneath his fingers. Shorty knew then that Ann Ah had been marked by Mielikki. But for what purpose, he did not know.

Ann Ah was special. He did not need the tree on her arm to know that. He wondered what the Forest Goddess had in mind for her. Whatever those plans were, Shorty hoped Ann Ah would live a good life here in Arcturus. "Bees well, Ann Ah," he whispered to her before rising to his feet.

"She will be fine, Shorty," a feminine voice said from the darkness behind him. Shorty turned towards the voice, his hand reaching instinctively for New Horizons. Shorty released his grip on the hilt when Kisa stepped out of the dark corner. The Priestess of Akka stepped past him to examine her patient. "Her physical injuries are healed. Akka has also removed the magic they used to bind her. The rest will take time and courage on her part."

Shorty stared down at the woman who had been like a second mother to him. Ann Ah would be safe with her. Kisa had always taken good care of him. He knew she would do the same for Ann Ah. He just needed to win this one last battle and everyone would be safe. But before that battle began, he needed to thank Kisa for her help rescuing Ann Ah and a great deal more. "Youse all da times bees good ta me, Lady. Tank Youse fer bees me friend. Youse bees in muches danger fer help me dis day. Me gonna fix dat bery sooner."

She leaned against him then, her warm cheek resting against his arm and her fingers sliding into his hand. "I told you, Shorty. We are family. Taking care of each other is what we do." Then her voice grew stern like Mama's used to do. "Does Dualis have a plan or are you about to do something that I will not be happy about?"

Shorty almost sighed, but he stopped himself. He had to be careful now. Kisa would know if he lied just like Mama had when he was small. Shorty chose his words carefully, "Smart peoples argue bout whats ta do. Gonna talks bout all da night. Me need ta go me room. Rest. Bees bery long day." That had all been true as far as it went, but he could not stop himself from adding, "Me gots ta fix what bees broke, Lady."

Kisa's voice sounded tired as she asked, "Why is fixing what is broke always your job Shorty?"

He gently squeezed her hand. "Cause me da ogre. Ogre bery muches bigger den all. Posed ta do da hard tings. Bees what Mama makes me promise ta do. Me all da times keep me promise. Youse knowed dat."

Kisa released his hand and turned to face him. There was an edge to her voice that he had never heard before. She would not be disobeyed. "Not alone, Shorty. Do you understand me? You will not sneak out of this Keep to face that thing alone. I will not have it! Now, promise me you will not leave Stormhold without us."

He thought hard about what she was asking him to do. This was a promise he could make and still do what he needed to do. So, he nodded, "Me promise Kisa, Lady. No leabe Stormhold widout youse. Shorty neber break him promise."

Kisa relaxed, "I know you keep your promises Shorty. Thank you." Then she pointed to the door. "Go get some sleep. I will watch over her tonight."

He gave her a hug and turned back to the bed. He tried very hard to remember how Ann Ah looked lying there. Win or lose, this would be the last time he ever saw her. He could not even tell her goodbye. If he did, Kisa would know he was up to something. Shorty turned and left the room, once more closing the door behind him.

Relin stepped aside as Shorty came through the door. Shorty stood in silence outside the door. Relin asked, "Is she well?"

Shorty nodded, "Bees sleepin now." He turned right and entered his own room. He paused as the door clicked shut behind him. Turning back to face the door, he studied the small knob that Ez'ard called lock. He had never used it before. It seemed a silly thing to even have. None of his friends would ever come here to take his toys. And even if they did, they would always bring them back.

This night would be very different. He needed the lock. Not to protect his things but to protect his friends from the evil thing that would be in his room. He did not want anyone coming in until it was safe. Knowing Ez'ard, his friend could open the lock in the morning when he and the evil were done with their battle. He reached out and slid the knob towards the door frame. It seemed such a small thing to protect all those he loved. Shorty turned his back on the door and the thing called lock.

A light breeze from the open windows stirred the hair hanging loose at his shoulders. Shorty drew the fresh scent of growing things into his lungs. Both of his trees were growing well now. He could also smell the flowers that bloomed around the base of both trees. The smell of home soothed him. Someday there would be many more trees around Stormhold, but only if his plan worked this night.

Shorty turned to the small table where his favorite toys rested when he was home. He placed Ride and Cat on their pedestals. He knew the new Lord of Stormhold would need their help. He just hoped that Relin or the squires would play with the cat and mammoth when he was gone. Next, he placed the bag of magic marbles below Cat and the two balls in front of Ride. Someone would know what to do with them.

Shorty reached up to his head. He thought about taking off the circlet that made him smarter, but he would need its help keeping his thoughts straight if his plan was going to work. Thinking was not something he was good at. What else did he need to do? He understood normal battle. He was good at that. But how did one fight for souls? Certainly not with a sword or even two swords. There were to many things that he just did not know.

He crossed the room to the rack where his armor hung. He ran his fingers across the thick leather. He traced each of the green oak leaves that crossed his chest when he wore the armor. He did not really need armor, but it would feel wrong to be without it. This armor had become a part of who he was. In it, he was the Green Knight. He wanted to be that powerful knight when the evil got here. As with any battle, believing in one's self was important. Shorty pulled the reddish leather from the rack and began to dress for whichever bad thing was coming.

His fingers checked that each piece of armor was in place. He had everything except his shield. A shield would look foolish with him sitting in his chair. His thought briefly about all the wonderful things scattered around his room. Things he had collected in a lifetime of battle. Tomorrow they would belong to someone else. He was not sure how he felt about that.

He walked over to stand before the windows. A bowl of nuts sat on the window's wide ledge. Would the new Lord of Stormhold ever open these windows? Would anyone ever feed his small friends when he was gone? He hoped so. He would miss the squirrels. He did not want them to be lonely. Shorty took three steps backwards to the large rocking chair. He sat and began to rock slowly, his left hand caressing the smooth wood of the chair's arm.

The lcft window was right in front of his chair. An oak tree grew tall outside that window. Its thick trunk and branches blocked all but one corner of the window. But in that corner, he could see a scattering of stars and a small piece of the moon. The stars and moon did not give off enough light to see the nests that his friends had built in the tree. But that was okay, he did not need to see them to know where each nest was located. With Alano's help, the trees were growing strong. Strong trees had brought the squirrels.

Like the trees, Stormhold was growing stronger. He had started with a few friends and the two squires. More good people had come after he had freed the first group of slaves from the Bazaar. Now, people fleeing other wars were coming to Stormhold too. And today he had freed more slaves. People, like the squirrels would be drawn to a strong land. Stormhold and Arcturus would continue to grow. But only if he was very, very good tonight.

He looked up as a chittering noise came from the windowsill. Shorty's hand reached to the bowl of nuts sitting on the table beside his chair. He squeezed two of them, cracking them easily. Opening his hand, he began to pick out the nut meat, dropping the shells fragments into another basket on the floor.

The squirrel hopped down from the window. It raced across the floor and clambered up his leg to perch on his knee. Its tiny arms began to gesture, and its chittering sounded quite angry. When it finished its lecture, it glared at him.

Shorty smiled down at the squirrel and ran a gentle finger along its back. "Me knowed dis no bery smart. No ken sees nudder way. Protect bees all me know." The squirrel crossed its arms and stamped a small foot on his leg.

Shorty chuckled at its obvious displeasure. "Youse no bees only one dat gonna gets mad me. Kisa Lady gonna yells muches. Youse tells her me no breaks promise. Keeps promise ta Mama. No breaks promise to Arcturus. Me protect real gooder."

The squirrel shook its tiny head at the mention of his promise to Kisa. Shorty frowned thoughtfully. "No, Kisa Lady say no sneaks outside ta fights by self. Shorty fight in him room. No bees da same."

The squirrel's shoulders seemed to slump in defeat. It sat down in his lap and curled its bushy tail around itself. Shorty lowered the hand with the nut meat and the squirrel picked up a piece of nut and began to nibble at it. It chattered unhappily as it ate. When it finished the nut, Shorty gestured towards the window. "Time fer little friend ta goes. No gonna bees safe till me fix what broke."

The squirrel clambered up to his shoulder and nuzzled its small head against his neck. Then it patted his cheek with one small hand before it scampered to the floor. The small ball of fur ran across the floor and leapt to the windowsill. There, it turned to look back at him one last time. It gave a questioning chirp.

Shorty nodded, "Me sure. Go now afore trouble come."

It turned and sprang into the darkness. Shorty smiled as he heard it moving rapidly through the leaves. It would be safe now too.

The squirrel was right. This probably was no bery smart. Shorty reached up to run a finger along the circlet. It was supposed to make him smarter, but he had not done many smart things lately. What

he was about to do might be one of his worst ideas ever. But all of
the other plans put his friends in danger. Smart or not, this was his
choice.

Shorty reached over his shoulder and drew the great sword, New
Horizons, from its scabbard. The mind of the intelligent sword
reached out and merged with him. New Horizons at least did not
argue with him. It simply offered its support. Shorty lay the sword
across his lap. His hand slid from the hilt to rest against the cool
metal of the blade. There was nothing left to do but wait.

He lost track of time as he rocked in the chair watching the moon
through the branches of the oak. The soft breeze coming in the
window calmed his nerves. The sound of the leaves fluttering in the
breeze made him feel less alone. His world was peaceful for a time.
All was as it should be. Shorty knew that was about to change.

He almost missed the first sign of the coming danger. It was such a
small thing, easy to overlook. A single star went dark in Arcturus's
sky. Then a second and a third disappeared too. The darkness spread
as he watched, eventually eating even the moon. Something large
was coming. It was coming for him. The waiting game was almost
done.

He felt the evil long before it arrived. There was a sense of
wrongness that grew stronger as the dark spot grew. The breeze no
longer refreshed him. It carried the scent of decay into the room. He
felt dirty and oily. He wanted to take another bath. Shorty understood
that no amount of scrubbing could wash away the stain of what was
coming.

His head turned to the side as a new sound reached his ears. The
steady beating of wings. The sound was growing louder. This was
not his son, Arlon. The wingbeats came to close together for it to be
a dragon. Shorty turned his head back to face the window just as it
went black. There was a thump as something hit the outer wall of
the Keep. Dark talons sank into the window's wide ledge. Stormhold
cried out at the assault.

A dark shadow climbed through the window and into the room. As
that shadow stepped away from the window, a moon reappeared in
the sky. But it was not the moon that Shorty knew. Gone was the

silver orb and its pure, white light. The thing that had replaced it pulsed with a red glow that made Shorty feel ill. The Balance that Shorty had sworn to defend, cried out against the change.

The blood moon's light was enough to reveal a tall figure standing beside Shorty's bed. The intruder was human in form, but that was where the similarities ended. Its skin was golden in color. Its eyes were solid silver. It wore midnight black robes. Somehow Shorty knew that they were of the finest quality. Protruding from each of its elbows were large, curved spikes. They looked deadly. He turned his eyes to its face. It was not human. His instincts said wolf, except for the black horns on its forehead.

His unwelcome guest finished its own appraisal of him. It nodded and moved to sit on the edge of the windowsill. It moved with confidence as if there was no doubt how this meeting would end. Shorty smiled an ogrish smile. He would win this battle. His foe just did not know it yet.

A cultured voice spoke to him, "I see that you were expecting me. I hope I have not kept you waiting long."

Shorty shrugged. His voice was strong and clear when he spoke. He had practiced these words in his head several times since speaking to F'lar. There were words he must say if this was going to work. "Youse no welcome in me home. Comed in wid no ask permission. Yes, me knowed youse comin eben ifn no bodies call fer youse. So, me waits. Now tells youse ta leabe an neber comes back ta me home."

The figure seemed to consider the demand. "Most interesting. The stubbornness of the ogre and the manners of the Knight. I had expected only the ogre to be waiting for me. So be it. I believe that my response should be to introduce myself and announce my intentions. I am called Avarice, Lord and Master of the Third Hell. You have taken something valuable from me. My reputation has been compromised and that must be rectified. I am here to settle my grievance with you and with your friends. Each of you must pay for the affront to my honor."

Shorty continued to rock in his chair, seemingly unconcerned with the words of his visitor. "Friends no part a dis. Shorty takes her back from youse. Me an no bodies else."

Avarice chuckled softly. "It does not work that way Knight. You do not dictate how I repay the insult given me. As for the woman, she was to be delivered to my Master. He will have his prize despite your interference. This night will bring me much pleasure as I destroy each of those who meddled in my affairs."

Shorty bared his tusks in a mock growl. "Me Chief dis Tribe. Me make da rules no youse. Me telled dem whats ta do. Now me tells youse. No ken hurted me friend. Dat bees rule Chief makes. No like what Chief say den youse knowed what ta do. Dat bees Tribe law."

The dark shape stiffened. "That is another insult you will pay for little ogre. I am not of your lowly breed, nor am I bound by your foolish rules." His silver eyes flashed with anger as the creature stared at Shorty and the blade across his lap. Then it smiled, revealing sharp canine teeth.

Their eyes locked on each other for a long time, neither willing or able to back down. Finally, the golden form began to laugh. "Few on this plain or any other have dared to speak to me as you have. Fewer still have dared to meet my gaze. I might almost be tempted to thank you for the rare bit of entertainment you offer. But my Master waits for the woman. To move things along, I will humor you. I believe my next line is…"

The golden figure stood up. Shorty realized its horns almost scraped the ceiling of his room. It was taller than he was. Then it spoke the ritual words he had been waiting for, "I challenge you, Chieftain. for rule of your Tribe and the right to decide the fate of all the little playthings in your insignificant little realm."

Shorty grinned. "Talks too muches. Takes too long. Time fer dis ta bees over. Ifn lose, youse bees banish. Ken neber comes back. Ken neber hurts me people eber gin."

"I do not lose little ogre." Shorty locked gazes with his foe once more. This time he felt magic infuse its gaze. A part of him wanted to fall on his knees before the golden form and worship it. The part of him that cared about his friends fought that urge. Power flowed from New Horizons and he pushed aside the magical attack. Avarice grunted in surprise. "Again, unexpected." Then he asked, "What are the rules, little ogre?"

Shorty kept his eyes locked on the two silver orbs. "No rule. Youse no follow rule eben ifn hab dem. Both fights, one lose. One dat win bees Chief."

The dark presence began to laugh once more as it loomed over him. Shorty continued to rock. His hand lay still on the blade of New Horizons. As the laughter died away, cold, harsh words flowed into Shorty's mind, *Excellent. As you say, I do not believe in rules. So many fools think they can hide behind them. Sadly, you will feel no pain when I rip your soul from your body. The pain will come later when I have you in my realm. There I will torture you for a millennium. I will take great pleasure in describing the fate of your friends to you as I make you scream.*

Shorty growled softly in reply, "No bees prey fer youse. Come feel me bite."

The golden form stepped forward. Shorty could see the shadowy outline of large leathery wings folded against its back. A large hand reached out towards his chest. Shorty felt something reach deep within him. He bid his friends a silent farewell.

Shorty broke his connection to New Horizons. He felt its cry of protest, but he did not want even the sword to be harmed by this foe. Then he began his retreat deep into the recesses of his own mind. Memories flowed past him as he ran before the golden form. He passed the place where he kept "the ogre" captive, and still he ran on. As proper prey should, he kept the predator, his golden enemy, close enough to follow him. He did not want Avar Ice to fall too far behind. He would keep his enemy close.

At long last, he came to Stormhold. Not the Stormhold of the outside world, it was filled with those he must protect. This was a Stormhold that he had built stone by stone from the magic Arturus had placed within him. It lived deep within him, past even the place that Arcturus had given him as a gift the day he became the Green Knight. This Stormhold was empty as the original had been the day he arrived. This one was a prison for him and his enemy. Here, he would defend his world against the evil of Avar Ice.

But reaching this Stormhold was not enough. He needed his enemy within its walls. Shorty ran through its gate, closely pursued by a foe that found the whole chase amusing. It would learn, soon enough, that Shorty was no novice in the Great Game. He had been taught to play to win by none other than Cat.

Shorty flowed through the halls of the other Stormhold. Up the stairs he scampered and down the hall to his room, leaving each door open for his pursuer. Finally, Shorty reached the rocking chair. He turned it to face the door and sat, waiting as he had in the real world.

Avar Ice appeared at the door to Shorty's room. The beast had a smile on its face as it walked towards him. "There is nowhere left to run, little ogre. I have played your stupid game. Now, you will be mine for eternity."

This time it was Shorty who laughed, "Youse lose da game."

His unwelcome guest paused as the sound of the front gate slamming closed echoed through the room. The outer door to the Keep and Shorty's windows closed next. Other doors throughout the Keep banged shut, one by one, as Shorty closed his mind. So many times, Dualis had told him he was closed-minded. Shorty wondered what the Arch Mage would think of how he used that skill to protect even Dualis himself. Shorty grinned at Avar Ice as he released the ogre from its cage and called it to him. Let his foe learn just how stubborn an ogre could be.

The tapestry hanging over the bed fluttered as the breeze came through the windows once more. The smell of wrongness dissipated as the smell of the trees and flowers flowed through the window. The rocking of the chair slowly ceased, and silence reined in the room. The Green Knight sat, unmoving except for the slight rise and fall of his chest.

A small form leapt from the oak to the windowsill. It gave a mournful cry as it stared at the ogre that was its friend. It chittered unhappily at him for a moment before returning to the shelter of the oak tree.

Part 3

Annah's Path

"Neber easy ta finds da place youse belong."

Chapter 10

A Vision of Darkness

Annah felt herself rising through layers of sleep and nightmare. Reality seemed far too close. If it were possible, she would choose to sleep forever. The horrors of the waking world were much worse than those in her nightmares. Her mind fled from the memory of where she had been taken. She did not want to go back to that terrible place even in her thoughts. Despite her objections, the world around her chased away her dreams.

The pain she expected did not come to torment her. Even the unyielding surface of the iron box was missing. She lay upon something warm and inviting. Her hands traveled across the softness, exploring its texture. She lay upon a bed. The bed was covered by a quilt, one that was worn with age. The feel of it soothed her fears. Her fingers traced the squares and stitching. It might be old, but the needlework was much better than even Mama could do.

Her eyes fluttered open to reveal a dimly lit room. She wondered where she was. She turned her head to the side to examine her surroundings. There was a window across from the bed. Silvery tendrils of light reached across the room to caress her skin. It was not the light of daytime that warmed her. It was a softer light that wrapped itself around her, calming her fears. The word moonlight passed through her scattered thoughts.

She rose and sat on the edge of the bed facing the window. The room was filled with beautiful things. Her fingers stretched out to trace the design on a wooden chest resting against the wall beside the bed. The urge to follow each whorl carved into the wood was almost irresistible. Her fingers could have spent hours following the patterns and imprinting them in her memory.

How had she come to a place of such beauty? Had she died? Her last memories had been of the slave market. The spells they had cast to control her mind had failed so they had thrown her into a box to bake in the heat. But the box had not insulated her from the evil that surrounded it. Even in the box, she could hear screams and smell the fear. The laughter of the damned and the cries of their victims still assaulted her soul.

She stood and walked slowly to the window with her hands outstretched before her. She moved her feet carefully so she would not stub her bare toes. Her fingertips found the cool glass of the window. She stared out into the night. What lay before her took her breath away. More than anything, she wanted to be a part of this place.

Never in her life, not even on the farm with Papa, had she felt such a sense of belonging. Not even the Grove called to her as this room did. It was strange and unsettling to feel such longing for a place. She had never been anywhere for long. As a child, her family had moved from place to place to keep her safe. Was this what a home was supposed to feel like? All of her memories paled in comparison to this place. The feeling was frightening.

As she traveled the roads of memory, tears began to flow from her eyes. Sadness overwhelmed her. She realized that none of this was real. It could not be real because she could see it. She was blind and blind people did not see moonlight reflecting off a castle wall. They could not see the alternating pattern of light and shadow among the leaves of a tree. Blind people could not know the shape of tall mountains or perceive moonlight reflecting off snowy peaks. And, they certainly could not stare at a moon that lay nestled within a field of twinkling stars. So very, very many stars. She could never count them all if she lived a hundred years. The view filled her with joy and it broke her heart. She would never see this with her own eyes. This could only exist in a vision.

Her hands reached out and touched the latch holding the window closed. Her eyes made no sense of it, so she closed them. Her fingers finally deciphered how the latch worked. They lifted the handle and she swung the window open. In the vision, there was a soft breeze that tried to dry her tears. It felt good. She could smell leaves and flowers. The scent was faint compared to that of the Grove. Plants and trees must be less abundant here.

Annah sat down on the wide sill and opened her eyes once more. So many things to see but she could not turn her eyes away from the moon and stars. She wanted to burn them into her memory. Maybe in the future she could dream about stars, now that she had seen them.

She tried to think as she stared into the night sky. Fresh tears rolled down her cheeks. This vision was more powerful than any she had ever had. In the past, her visions had been limited to sound and occasional glimpses of an aura she had seen, little more than flashes of light or a deeper darkness. This time, she could really see and, somehow, she knew the names of the things she saw. Where did the knowledge come from? It was a bit much to take in. The world she knew was one she could feel with her fingertips or sometimes smell with her nose. For the first time in her life, she wondered if Mama was right. Her magic might be a gift.

Her fingers searched for the birthmark on her right arm. It was here even in the vision. Her fingers followed the patterns she knew so well. Then she looked at it for the very first time. Her eyes struggled to comprehend the symbol that marked her as the Goddess's chosen. Her fingers knew it as a tree, but her eyes had to learn what a tree looked like. Mama had called it a hickory tree. It was just like Corey.

Annah studied the mark. She would not forget what it looked like. It was important that she to remember it. She knew the birthmark was the sign of the Goddess. Mielikki had selected her before she was even born. Her magic, her blindness, the auras, and even the visions were all a part of being a Chosen. But what was the purpose of it all? She wished she knew. Her fingers continued to trace the leaves of her mark as her eyes turned back to the moon and the stars.

She was not sure how she felt about the birthmark anymore. She had hated it for most of her life. Mama said it made her special, but life had taught her a different lesson. Special meant that people wanted to control her so they could use her magic. People wanted her magic, but why? It was not like it was powerful or even useful. What good was the magic if it had let Papa die? She would have given up the magic just to save him.

The gift had also brought the slavers. Her family had run but not far enough. She and her mother and sister had been captured. If not for the bear that had not been a bear, they would have ended up as things to be used and discarded. Mama and Meerah might have ended up in the slave market too. All because of magic she hardly knew how to use.

She had begun to learn about her magic in the Grove. But only a little. The Treants used magic to make plants grow, but that was all they could teach her. Then the Green Knight had arrived. So much had changed then. His aura had contained color. After meeting Shorty, every aura she saw contained color. She had quickly learned that the colors had meaning. She just needed time to understand them all.

The changes had not stopped there. The Knight had spoken to the squirrels, and she had learned to speak with animals too. The squirrels had become her friends. It was not like having someone her own age to talk to, but it was a wonderous ability for a lonely young woman. Shorty had shared so much with her, with them. But her family had not been kind to him, not even her.

Mama had treated the Knight badly from the start. She had been afraid, and she wanted Annah and Meerah to be afraid too. She warned the girls that the Knight was an ogre and ogres ate people, especially little girls. Annah was not sure what an ogre was, but the Knight had not tried to eat her. Instead, he had helped her in the garden. So she did what young people often do, she snuck away seeking excitement.

The Green Knight was not at all what she had expected. He was not interested in power or in her magic. He did not look for monsters to slay or lands to conquer. He played with squirrels and fed them nuts. He planted Treant seeds around the grove. He did not care what others thought about him. And he listened to her. Not just listened, he heard her. He never told her how she should feel or how she should act. He made her believe that her feelings mattered.

Despite all that, Annah could not bring herself to believe in the Knight. When he said he wanted to be her friend, she had doubted him. Why would a Knight want to be friends with a peasant girl? She had not believed him when he said, "Neber ken hab nuf friend." So, she had held a part of herself back. And now he was gone.

She had seen his aura, but she had not really seen him. And then the Grove had been attacked. Shorty had tried to save her, and she had called him a coward. There had been no fear in his aura, but she had accused him anyway. She had even demanded he fight for her home. He had gone without complaint. That was when she finally trusted him, but that trust had come too late. Annah vowed to tell him she was sorry, that she would be his friend. She had not been able to keep that vow. Fate or the gods had denied her that opportunity.

Annah had waited in the thicket where Shorty had left her. She waited and hoped for his return. Then a hand closed roughly around her arm. She was pulled backwards and another arm wrapped around her neck. She tried to scream but the arm was too tight. Her captor lifted her and carried her from the thicket. She was dropped to her feet and shoved forward. She stumbled ahead of him as she was herded through the trees.

Her captor pulled her to a stop and magic like nothing she had ever felt before pulsed around her and through her. The rain and the smell of smoke were suddenly gone. Her connection to the Grove was severed. The hand grabbed her arm again and spun her around. An aura devoid of light floated before her.

Annah drew in a ragged breath. Her captor leaned in close. His breath was hot against her cheek. Fear made her stomach clench. His voice was harsh as he whispered in her ear, "Do not make me hurt you, girl. I will enjoy it."

His name was Undaur. She was going to make him the riches half-orc in all the realms. He would be even richer if the ogre and the Treants managed to kill his two associates. She could not believe he was excited about the prospect of his own friends being killed. It made no sense to her.

He had tied her arms together with rope, leaving one end long so he could drag her behind him. She had spent what felt like days stumbling over rocks or slipping in sand before they reached his destination. Along the way, Undaur boasted about the reward the god Set had offered for her capture. She would spend eternity as Set's slave.

Undaur led her on, not telling her where they were going. Annah sensed the magic of the portal before they reached it. She had been too tired at that point to even care. Her legs were scraped and bleeding. She was so hungry it was hard to think. That had been the easiest part of her captivity. Annah shuddered as she remembered stepping through the portal.

On its far side was a place Undaur called the Bazaar. He told her it was located in a place called the Gates to Hell. She was actually thankful that she could not see the place. The auras had been terrifying enough. So many auras filled with blackness. The rest were filled with despair and hopelessness. She tried to close her eyes to the auras, but they were always before her.

She felt magic attack her. It tried to take her will. Power had risen from deep within her to fight it. She had been slapped for resisting. She fell and bled again. Something with a dark aura had lifted her. She had been placed in the iron box. Heat and pain wrapped themselves around her. At some point, her awareness had faded and she knew no more.

Now she was in this vision. Was her body still trapped in that box? It was one of many questions that might never be answered. What had happened to Mama and Meerah? And the Treants? Had the Green Knight survived? Had he saved the Grove? She wanted to know, and she feared the answers to those questions. But those were small fears. Her greatest fear was what came after the vision ended.

Annah's gaze returned to the moon and the stars. She could not control the world outside the vision, so she might as well enjoy it while it lasted. She could only pray to the Goddess that some part of this vision was in her future. If there was a way to live in a place like this, even without sight, then she wanted it. Annah smiled and began to count the stars.

The stars flickered as she counted them. She wondered why they did that. Then a star to the left of the moon stayed dark. Did stars do that too? She waited for it to come back, but it remained dark. A second star disappeared beside the first. Then a third. Annah began to be afraid. Darkness grew in the sky and even the stars could not stand against it.

Annah tried to stand. Maybe she could run. But her vision body would not obey her mind. She could not even turn her head from the growing darkness. It spread as more of the stars died. The edge of the darkness came nearer to the moon. Would it go out as well? She sensed movement in the center of the darkness. It was an aura.

Annah's lungs froze in her chest. Such evil. Beyond anything she had experienced in the Bazaar. She had never imagined anything so vile existed. And it was coming. It was coming to this place. It was coming for her. She could not escape it. She could not even breathe.

The moon flared with brightness. The stars returned as if nothing had happened. Air rushed into her lungs and Annah screamed.

Chapter 11

The World of Her Dreams

Annah jerked upright. Her throat hurt. Had she screamed here too? Her heart was racing and the terror she had felt in the vision still filled her mind. Her eyes opened to darkness. It was not the darkness of the evil that she had seen in the vision. This was the perpetual darkness she had known her whole life. Disappointment washed away some of the terror. She knew it was foolish, but a tiny part of her had hoped her blindness was cured.

She forced herself to put aside both fear and disappointment. It was hard, but she needed to understand what had happened to her. She knew immediately that she was no longer in the iron box. The hard metal and the heat had been replaced by a cool breeze and a softness beneath her. She rejoiced in that much of a reprieve.

Her fists were clenched in that softness. Annah forced her hands to relax. The material she had gripped so tightly fell from her fingers. Trembling hands reached down to smooth the material until it lay flat. A sense of wonder grew as her fingers caressed the worn quilt that covered her legs. The stitching was as intricate as it had been in the vision. Somehow, she had come to the place she longed for.

As her mind struggled to accept the reality of the room, Annah remembered the end of the vision. Had the evil she had seen already come? Or was it on its way? She had to find out. More importantly, she had to warn someone about the danger. But who?

Annah tried desperately to remember everything she could about the room around her. There had been a chest next to the bed and then the window. The far wall had a chair resting against it. But she did not remember seeing a door. Annah turned her head away from the windows. She had never examined this side of the room. Surely there was a door here.

The pale golden glow of an aura hovered in the air not far from the bed she lay on. She was not alone. Annah held her breath. As her own body stilled, Annah could hear the steady breathing of the room's other occupant. Whoever was there was asleep. Annah relaxed and, she had time to study the person's aura.

The aura was not tainted by evil. At least, no more so than anyone's would be. The golden color seemed to wash away any darkness it touched. Annah sensed a connection between the aura and something beyond the bounds of the mortal world. It was like her connection to Mielikki and yet it was different. This was a cleric. He or she served goodness and life. Instinctively, Annah knew this was someone that she could trust.

Annah called out, her voice little more than a harsh whisper, "Hello. Can you help me, please?"

There was a loud yawn as whoever was there came awake. The aura blazed to life. Streaks of blue and tendrils of pink ran through the golden glow. Both colors were ones she had seen in Shorty's aura. Peace and concern for others.

The aura rose and floated closer. Despite what the colors told her, Annah tensed and drew away from the aura. There had been so much pain since her capture, she was afraid of being hurt by this person. The owner of the aura seemed to sense her fear and stepped back.

The tendrils of pink in the aura spread to replace the blue streaks. The calm voice of a young woman spoke from the darkness, "Hello Ann Ah. Or is it pronounced Annah? My name is Kisa. I am a Priestess of Akka, the Earth Mother. I was asked to watch over you.

I am sorry that I dozed off like that. How do you feel? Shorty will be so glad to know you are awake."

The mention of Shorty was a balm that soothed her nerves. "Hello, Kisa, it is pronounced Annah. I am okay, I think. At least, I feel much better than I did. But this is all a bit confusing. I do not know where I am or how I got here. And, I am blind, so new places are difficult."

Kisa smiled reassuringly. Then she shook her head at her own foolishness. Her patient could not see her face. "Shorty mentioned that you could not see. That is why I have been sitting with you. As for where you are, this is Stormhold Keep. It is Shorty's home. He brought you here after we rescued you."

Annah felt overwhelmed by the information. She had known that Shorty was a knight, but she had never thought about what that might mean. Did all knights have castles like this? "He, Shorty, had never mentioned owning a castle. I just thought he wandered from place to place doing knight things."

Kisa began to laugh. "No, telling you about his home would not occur to him, Annah. Friends and family are what makes this home for Shorty. It is not the buildings that he cares about, it is the people."

Annah nodded as she remembered Shorty's words about not ever having enough friends. Kisa's voice interrupted her thoughts, "May I come closer and sit beside you? With your permission, I would like to check your wounds."

Annah hesitated but then curled her legs up next to her and gestured towards the bed. "How did I get here Kisa? The last thing I remember I was…" Annah could not say the words. Her voice trailed off into silence.

The bed shifted as the golden aura settled in front of her. A warm hand came to rest on Annah's forehead and another touched her cheek. Both hands were rough like her own. Kisa was not a soft city person. Annah suspected she worked as hard as Annah and her family did. Kisa's voice muttered, "Good, the fever is gone."

The hands withdrew from her face. One of them patted Annah lightly on her knee. "There is no need to speak of that place or what they did to you until you are ready. What little I saw of the Bazaar will haunt me for the rest of my life. If you ever want someone to talk to about what happened there, let me know. I will come and listen."

Annah squeezed her eyes shut for a moment. She did not want to cry. Not now. Maybe not ever. "How did I get here Kisa?"

Kisa's callused hand took hers and squeezed. "Shorty came to us, his friends, seeking help rescuing you. I do not know how he knew you were there, but he was not willing to let them have you. I have never seen him that angry before. He was able to purchase your freedom, but I think he would have fought them all if it came to that. We also rescued a number of other slaves. That seems to be what Shorty does. Then he brought all of you here to his home. Akka healed your wounds and removed the geas that was placed on you."

"You all went to that terrible place just for me?" Annah asked.

There was a pause before Kisa responded, "Yes, you were the reason for going. Shorty does not like to lose his friends. He was rather determined to get you back."

Annah's voice trembled as she asked, "And the rest of you? Why did you go?"

Kisa's voice was solemn as she answered, "Shorty is family. We would never have let him go alone."

A single tear rolled down Annah's cheek. She wiped it away quickly hoping Kisa had not seen it. "You all took such a terrible risk for someone you do not even know. Shorty just met me a few days ago. What he did… What you all did was crazy."

Kisa chuckled. "Do not try to tell Shorty that. Our large friend is rather stubborn about protecting his friends. He knew the risk. I understand that this is not his first trip to the Bazaar. Last time he and his friends rescued a great many humans, dwarves, and elves. Some of them are still here at Stormhold. Our Green Knight has some unusual ideas about how to find new friends."

Annah's fears began to return. "Does he really understand the danger of that place? Unspeakable evil dwells there."

There was a trace of concern in the priestess' voice, "We know Annah. We took precautions. Or we tried to, at least. The powers that rule the Bazaar were not happy about your rescue. It appears that you are more important to them than any of us realized."

Annah began to shiver. She felt Kisa's hands close around hers. Annah finally released the tight hold she had on her emotions. "This was not the first time slaver's have come for me, Kisa. I spent years hiding in Sanctuary. But I brought evil there too. It is not safe to be around me. Whoever it is that wants me, they will come for me again. You must send me away before it is too late."

Kisa drew Annah into her arms and hugged her. "It is alright, Annah. We know something is coming for you and Shorty. We are preparing a welcome for it. As for sending you away, Shorty would never allow it. The Green Knight does not abandon those he cares about. You are under his protection now. These are his lands and all here are his friends. He will not let any of them be taken."

Panic blossomed within Annah . "I think it is already here. I saw it in a vision. The darkness, it came from the stars."

Kisa paused as if weighing the panic in Annah's voice. Then she called out, "Relin! Annah is awake now, and she thinks we may already have a problem."

Annah heard a door open and another aura became visible. This one was also filled with light. But within it, she could see shadowy scars that she recognized from her own aura. The aura's scars were fading, maybe hers would too someday.

A male voice came from the doorway, "What is the danger, Lady Kisa?" The aura began to turn red. There was confidence in that voice. Both reassured her.

 "Wake Shorty up now." Kisa order. "Then get Roiland up here and probably Dualis too. Our enemy might already be here."

"Yes, Ma'am." And the door closed.

Kisa rose from the bed. "I am going to light a lamp. I am neither blind nor blessed with the ability to see in the dark. Besides, I do not want to get in Shorty's way when he sees that you are awake." Soft laughter suddenly filled the room. "Prepare yourself. He has been very worried about you."

Annah scooted back against the headboard. She found a pillow there. It was filled with soft down. Annah pulled it into her lap and held it tight. It felt like more security that it really was. "Mama and my sister? Are they here too?"

Kisa was doing something in what Annah guesses was the far corner of the room. Annah caught the faint scent of burning oil. "Shorty believes that they are safe. Someone called Ashley apparently took them deep into your Grove. He and that cat killed the other two intruders. We have not had time to find them yet. But I believe Shorty has asked for help bringing them here."

Annah sighed in relief. It was enough to know they were safe. She listened as feet ran back and forth outside the door. She heard knocking somewhere and the voice of the man named Relin calling, "Shorty? She is awake. Kisa would like to speak to you." There was silence for a moment and then the knocking resumed, only louder. "Lord Knight?"

New voices rose on the far side of the door. Annah did not recognize any of them. People called out to each other, some asking questions and others answering them. It was almost as if preparing for evil to descend on them was a daily occurrence. She listened, hoping to learn what she could about the people of Stormhold.

A new voice called out, "Relin, why are you pounding on Shorty's door?"

The voice of the man who had opened her door replied, "He is not answering me."

The new voice responded, "Maybe he is sleeping. He has had a rough couple of days."

Relin sounded concerned. "Think Roiland. You know how he reacts when there is danger. When has he ever slept through this much noise?"

A third voice joined the others, this man sounded older and calmer. "Just open the door and go in Relin. Shorty will not mind. Just stay out of reach of that sword of his."

"I tried, Know Man. His door is locked," Relin replied.

Another voice sputtered, "What? Shorty does not use locks. He does not even close his windows."

There was more arguing as each voice seemed to have a different opinion about what to do next. Annah raised a hand tentatively in the darkness. "Please? I want… I need to go to him. I want to know what happened to Shorty. Will you take me, Kisa?"

Kisa's aura moved closer and she felt fingers grasp her own. "Are you sure you want to go out there? There are a lot of people you do not know. It is just a hallway. They mean no harm, but people will get close to you. It is your choice. I will lead you if you want to go."

Annah squeezed the fingers that held hers. "I think it will be okay. Please?"

Those strong hands helped Annah to get out of the bed and stand. She was weaker than she had realized, but she refused to let that stop her. "I can do this," she muttered as much to herself as to Kisa.

Kisa did not argue with her, she only asked, "What is the best way to lead you?"

In response, Annah released her grip on Kisa's hand. Her own fingers trailed up Kisa's arm until they found her shoulder. "This works best in tight places. Just walk normally and I will follow you."

Kisa turned slowly to face the door. She gently patted Annah's hand. "Hang on then. I will get you to him."

They walked a few steps and paused. Annah heard the door open. Auras seemed to dance before her, but she did not take the time to study them. A new, deeper voice cut through the confusion. The others fell silent. This new voice carried the authority of one used to being obeyed. "Stand ready. I will use magic to open his door."

A voice she had heard already replied, this time it rang with amused disrespect, "Really, Dualis? That is almost insulting. I put that lock on his door. What kind of thief would I be if I could not open my own lock?"

One of the auras pushed past as the deeper voice replied, "Fine, Ez'ard. Just get it…" His words were interrupted by a loud click. A door to Annah's right creaked as it opened.

The voice of Relin hissed, "There is nothing moving inside."

The deep voice ordered, "Then let me through."

Annah pleaded, "Please?"

Kisa's voice rose sharply, cutting off everyone else, "No, Dualis. Not yet. Let us though first."

Several voices rose in protest. Annah felt Kisa tense beneath her hand. The protests were cut off when the deeper voice spoke again, "Alright, Priestess. Relin, stay right behind them, just in case."

Another voice contradicted the deeper voice, "No, I will guard my wife's back."

An exasperated sigh came from her left. "Fine, Archer. Anyone else want to argue with the All-Powerful Arch Mage? You are all in a nice line for a lightning bolt."

The kind voice she had heard earlier remarked dryly, "Did you really expect them to just follow your orders, Dualis? They are all Shorty's friends after all."

If there was a reply, Annah did not hear it. Kisa began to move. They turned to the right and walked forward. Her left hand clenched Kisa's shoulder while her right trailed along a wall. "Careful now," Kisa warmed. "We are at the entrance to his room. The door is on the left side and it opens into the room." A hand grasped her right hand and moved it to the doorframe. Past the door, the wall to her right disappeared.

Kisa turned to the right and led her three steps forward. Annah heard her ask, "Shorty are you okay? Why are you just sitting there?" There was no response. Kisa took another two steps forward.

Annah's hand slid down Kisa's arm as she moved up to stand shoulder to shoulder with the cleric. There was mostly darkness in front of her. The aura she knew as Shorty was not there. All she could see was a glowing green line that she recognized as the sword, Tainkintana. There was no sign of the Knight himself.

Kisa leaned into her as she quietly described the room, "Shorty is sitting in a chair before you. He is breathing so I know he is still alive. He is just staring out the window. He does not even blink. I am not sure what is wrong with him ."

Annah understood why there was no response. She felt a lump form in her throat as a sense of loss overcame her. She had to force her words past it, "He is not there, Kisa. That which is truly Shorty is gone. He has no aura. What you see is only an empty shell."

Kisa stepped in front of her. The golden aura came between her and the green line of the sword. "No! I will not accept that he is gone. Not after all we have been through. His body still lives. As long as there is life, we have hope. If his soul was taken, we will find it and bring him back Annah. And we will make them regret what they have done."

Annah heard more people enter the room. Voices were discussing options for saving Shorty. He was gone and yet they seemed certain they would save him? What kind of people were Shorty's friends? She was not sure, but their confidence gave her hope too. Still. She could not stop the questions that bubbled out of her, "His soul was taken? That thing was evil, Kisa. How can you fight something that steals souls?"

The deep voice spoke from just behind her, "Anything that has been stolen can be recovered, young lady. We have faced this problem before and we will do it again. Our first step is to determine where they took him. Then we come up with a plan."

The kind voice she had heard in the hall spoke next, "What would you have the rest of us do while we search for him, Dualis?"

The deep voice replied, "Make sure this Keep is safe from further attacks. And someone get Alano up here. These are his lands. We will need his help."

A new voice spoke from the doorway, "I am already here, Dualis."

A breeze tickled the hair hanging across her shoulders. Annah raised a hand towards the source of the breeze. "Is that a window? Can anyone see the stars? Are any of them missing?"

The newest voice replied with certainty, "The stars are all where they should be. Why do you ask?"

Kisa answered for her, "She had a vision earlier this evening."

Annah searched her memory of the vision for clues. But she found none.

A small light appeared in the darkness before her. Not a light, but a tiny aura. It came closer in short bursts of speed. It appeared to bounce from place to place. Annah recognized the shape of the aura if not the individual. It was a squirrel. Probably one of Shorty's many friends.

Kisa sucked in her breath. "The squirrels still come to him?"

Annah heard the squirrel begin to chatter. Without thinking, she cast the spell that allowed her to speak with it. She listened carefully as it delivered its message. She thanked it as it disappeared back the way it had come.

The voice named Dualis spoke from beside her, "Alano, what did the little rodent say?"

Annah answered without turning from where the squirrel had been, "It said it was sent to warn Shorty. Shorty was not supposed to do whatever he did. He was not supposed to face it alone. It was too dangerous. Shorty did not listen. He sent the squirrel away so that it would be safe. It is not mad at him for not listening. He fed it some nuts." Annah's voice trailed off.

The new voice by the door spoke again, "Well done, Lady. Few besides my Knight understand the small ones. Later, I would like to speak with you about your gift."

Annah remained silent, lost in her own thoughts. Dualis spoke again, this time he was clearly angry, "What was the damn fool thinking? We had a plan. If he knew it was coming, he should have told us."

Kisa's sharp rebuke was almost immediate, "I do not know you very well, mage, but I do know Shorty. The DAMN FOOL OGRE was thinking as he always does. He was protecting everyone, even you, mighty Arch Mage. And that is something every one of us should have predicted. He only knows one way to protect his friends and his people. He faces the monsters by himself. The world was broken and he had to fix it. I think the damn fools are the ones standing here now."

A long silence filled the room. Then an aura moved past Annah to stand in front of Kisa. This aura was filled with light, but the light was veiled somehow. The deep voice of Dualis came from that strangely muted aura, "Forgive my frustration, Kisa. I did not mean to belittle his sacrifice. But it was probably not necessary."

She could hear the pain in Kisa's reply, "Find him for me and I will forgive you."

The cold determination in Dualis's hiss of anger made Annah shiver, "Oh, I will find him and whoever took him. Then someone will answer to me." Then his aura moved back towards the door. "Most of us have work to do tonight. We will find Shorty. This all started with the Bazaar. Once we know who is responsible, we will take him back and make them pay for what they have done."

Many voices began to speak behind Annah. So many who would risk going back to the place of her nightmares to save their friend. Some of them had suffered there already and they would willingly go back again. She had doubted his friendship and these people would risk everything for that friendship. Could she find the courage to go back there too? Annah hoped so.

Annah felt Kisa squeeze her hand. "Do not worry, Annah. We will find him."

Dualis spoke again, "We need information. Know Man, I need your help in that spell chamber of yours. Alano, I could use your help as well."

The voice that had asked to speak about her gifts replied, "I will have better luck working in my Grove, Arch Mage. When do we reconvene?"

There was a moment of hesitation. "After breakfast. It will take that long to summon those that I intend to question. Gentlemen, if possible, please get the Knight into his bed. I find it disturbing to see him staring out the window like that. Then get some sleep. Tomorrow will be a long day."

Chapter 12

A Knight without Sleep

Annah sat in the Keep's dining room. It was also the place where meetings were held. Apparently, Shorty believed that food was an important part of any long discussion. After tasting some of Althea's cooking, Annah could see why. But now she was just tired. Sleep had not been possible after they had found Shorty. She did not think anyone else had gotten much sleep that night. The room was filled with tired but very determined people. For now, they waited for the Druid, Alano, to return. Then the rescue planning would start.

Annah scanned the room with her gift. So many auras and not one tainted with darkness. Throughout the long night they had come to her. Some sought her opinions and others simply wanted to meet Shorty's new friend. So many people, all bustling around. After years living with just her family, the crowd had taken some getting used to.

As people had come to talk to her, Annah had studied each aura. Despite the loss of the Green Knight, they were all filled with hope. It was obvious that the people of Stormhold were more than just friends. They were a family. The bonds between Shorty and his friends seemed stronger than those she shared with Mama and Meerah. How was that even possible? What surprised her even more was how each of them made her feel like a part of that family. Shorty had chosen his friends well.

She had spent most of her time talking with Kisa. Kisa was not much older than Annah was, but she had a husband and three children already. She and Roiland ruled a land far away. Shorty had helped to free their land from followers of the god Set. Annah smiled as Kisa spoke of Shorty with the same loving tones that she used to describe her own children. Kisa's love for their friend shone bright in her aura.

The druid Alano had stopped to speak with her before he left to search for Shorty. Alano was not a follower of the goddess Mielikki. He did not pray to a god or goddess at all. Instead, he served something he called the Living Land. He preserved the harmony of the land and all that lived in and on it. His aura was unusual. It was like a giant spider web with cables that ran in every direction, connecting him to so many places within this land. Some seemed to nourish him. Others seemed to draw his life force away. She thought that he gave much more than he received. How could anyone give so much of themselves and still live?

Alano had also told her of the battle that Shorty and his friends had fought to save the land of Arcturus. Set had struck here as well. It made Annah wonder, why would a deity that wanted to conquer so many worlds want her? And why did Shorty always seem to be the one to stand against Set? Alano had left her with more questions than answers.

The wonderful woman who had introduced herself as Althea brought her a plate of food and a glass of cold milk. Annah smelled fresh bread on the plate, as well as eggs and bacon. She thanked Althea for the rare treat. Althea hugged her and told her to eat up. Annah could see the familiar scars of the Bazaar in Althea's aura. But like Relin, those scars were fading away.

Annah ate as her sight moved around the room reviewing all of the people she had met during that long night. Two auras seemed to bounce around the room. They were like the young puppies her father had brought home long ago. Their auras were fresh and eager. They were the squires Pat and Robert. Both were young Knights-in-Training. She liked the two boys.

An aura she now knew as Ez'ard sat on the far side of the table. There was a bright core to his aura. But that core was hidden behind shields and other distractions. The elf was a good person despite being a thief. He used his thieving to mask what lay within. Ez'ard was complicated and did not let many people see the person he really was. There were two obvious exceptions, the small aura that sat on Ez'ard's shoulder and Shorty. Someday she would like to learn how Ez'ard and Shorty came to be friends.

Beside Ez'ard was an aura she had learned was the elf, F'lar. She recognized his strong connection to Mielikki. A second bright aura flittered around him, but no one else seemed to notice it. F'lar had introduced himself as Shorty's brother. She did not understand how an ogre and an elf could be brothers. F'lar had promised to explain it to her one day.

Annah glanced to her right. Sitting next to her were Kisa and Roiland. In many ways, they were the two most interesting auras to watch. The golden yellow of Kisa's aura floating so close to the bright silver glow that was Roiland. At times, the two auras seemed to swirl and mingle with each other, becoming almost one without losing their individuality. Annah wondered what it would be like to be so connected to another person.

The last two people in the room were standing at the far end of the table from her. The one she recognized as Know Man stood still. Peace and calm emanated from him. Near him, in constant motion, was the aura of the Arch Mage Dualis. Dualis's aura moved back and forth, sometimes moving fast and at others slow. She could hear him muttering as he moved about. The bright red streaks in his aura combined with his frustrated tones indicated that his own search for Shorty had not gone well.

Know Man was the Arch Mage's counterpoint. While Dualis's aura swirled, Know Man's aura was tranquil. The turmoil raging around him did not disturb who or what he was. His aura was connected to other aura's within the room by lines of blue light. She could see where the peace he emanated comforted many of the occupants of the room.

Somewhere, a large door slammed shut. Moments later, Alano's aura entered the room. His connections to the land of Arcturus seemed to have grown thicker since he had left the Keep a few hours ago. As she stared at him, she realized that his own aura was shrinking slowly over time. He was giving of himself to restore the land around him. What would happen when he had no more to give to this land? Would he become a part of the land itself? Annah realized she wanted to know him better before he was gone.

The druid came around the table to sit on the other side of her. She felt him place a reassuring hand on her arm. Then he murmured softly, "Your Treant friends are doing well. They are very focused right now on repairing the damage to Sanctuary. Your mother and sister are well too. I have sent an emissary to invite them to join you here at Stormhold. If they agree, it will take some time to pack their things and move them here."

Annah dropped her fork in surprise. "They are coming here? I, I do not know what to say. Thank you, Alano."

Alano gave her forearm a gentle squeeze before letting go. "Thank Shorty when we find him. He was quite insistent that we bring them to you."

"Oh," was the only thing she could think to say.

"All right everyone, please take a seat so we can discuss our next move." Annah looked up to see that Dualis's aura now hovered near where the head of the table should be. Everyone except F'lar gathered around the table.

Dualis continued, "My own sources of information were not as useful as I would have liked. I would like to know what the rest of you learned last night. Maybe your information will bring some clarity to what I have learned. This is your land Alano, would you like to begin?"

The old druid did not move from beside her. His voice sounded tired, "Something powerful entered Arcturus last night. It was not of this world and its very presence is an anathema to this land and everything that lives within it. I have not been able to identify it. I only know that it is no longer in Arcturus."

As Alano sat back, Dualis seemed pleased with something the Druid had said, "Then it is gone. Do you have any sense of where it went or how it departed?"

"You misunderstood me, Dualis. I did not say it left Arcturus. I only said it was here and now it was gone."

Dualis grumbled, "It is gone but it did not leave? How did it manage that?"

Know Man's quiet words ended Dualis's complaint, "It makes as little sense as the answers we got from those creatures you summoned. The lower plains seem to be as confused about what happened as we are."

A snort of amusement came from the corner where F'lar sat. Dualis's voice grew angrier and he snapped, "Do you have something useful to offer, Seeker? I see little reason for humor at this juncture."

A somewhat irreverent voice replied, "I might, Dualis. But I prefer to hear the rest of the facts before I hazard an opinion. I defer to the Arch Mage of Delith, for now."

Annah heard a chair scrape again. The agitated aura churned as it moved around the room. "There is nothing to defer to, F'lar. Know Man and I cast a dozen summonings. Under geas, not one of the denizens I questioned could tell us where Shorty is or, for that matter, where the Great One that came for him went. Every location spell I cast points right back at this Keep!"

Dualis's frustration got the better of him again. Annah heard the sharp slap of his hand striking the table. "The Evil is gone but it never left. Shorty's soul is missing but he is here in Stormhold. Contradiction after contradiction!"

Kisa asked from beside her, "Then all your magic can locate is his physical form? Did you try to magically shield his room?"

Know Man responded this time. "His body, his room, and the entire keep. Everything still led right back here. It is as if his soul was hidden like a child's play toy instead of stolen."

Annah felt her heart sink at the pronouncement. Shorty was gone. Or was he? One aura in the room shone brighter at the Arch Mage's tirade. Annah stared at the corner where F'lar's aura pulsed bright blue.

Dualis hit the table again, his voice even more agitated this time, "F'lar, are you aware of just how annoying that smirk of yours is? They call you the Seeker. If you have discovered something then out with it before I lose my temper."

Annah studied F'lar's aura. Streaks of bright yellow shot through its brilliant blue. Annah could almost feel F'lar's excitement from across the room. She waited for his response, as did everyone else. "I learned several things that by themselves made little sense. But with what you and Alano have added, I have a pretty good idea where my brother is."

"A pretty good idea F'lar?" came Dualis's sarcastic response. "Is that all?"

"Maybe more than just an Idea. And, a very, very important piece of information. But that tidbit is not for your ears, Arch Mage."

Annah could almost hear Dualis's teeth grind at those words. "And why not for my ears? What could you possibly know that I cannot be trusted with?"

"It is not about trust, Dualis. It is more a question of the repercussions from the Arch Mage of Delith acting on what I know. There will be consequences that I prefer not to risk. This world is not ready for another war such as you might cause."

Dualis cut off his own angry response. After a moment, he continued in a calmer tone, "What makes you immune to those same consequences Seeker? Are you that powerful?"

"No, Dualis. I am safer because I am not an Arch Mage. More importantly, I am not even interested in being an Arch Mage. I am content protecting a tiny kingdom in the middle of nowhere. I also have no desire to be on the mage or druid councils. I have my family and my lands and that is enough. You are The Arch Mage of Delith. Our enemies would never believe that you would not use what I know."

Dualis sat back down. Annah watched as the agitation disappeared from his aura. "Then what good is this information of yours?"

F'lar chuckled. "It will save my brother and whoever goes to retrieve him."

Dualis grumbled. "Since I cannot find him, it is going to be difficult for anyone to go after him."

All traces of mockery left F'lar's voice, "Dualis, your spells told me exactly where to find my brother. And Alano's information tells me exactly what my brother did. This is Shorty we are talking about. The answer is not as complicated as you are trying to make it."

Dualis aura rose back up and began to pace. "What is your idea it F'lar? What is it that you think the rest of us have missed? I am at a loss."

"That, Dualis, is because you think like an Arch Mage and not like an ogre. Or more precisely, like an ogre chief. A pretty good ogre chieftain in my opinion. I do not think you ever truly understood my brother despite all the times you worked with him."

Dualis sighed, "He is stubborn, intractable and refuses to think or use his head. Even that circlet did not change that. What more is there to understand?"

F'lar's aura grew even brighter. "Exactly, Arch Mage. He does not use his head. He is ruled by his heart and that irritates you to no end."

Annah watched colors begin to swirl in Dualis's aura, but F'lar continued on. "Please, I am not trying to insult you. Let me come at this a different way. I want to see if anyone else reaches the same conclusion I did."

Dualis remained silent. F'lar's aura floated closer to the table. "Kisa, if there was real danger and Shorty believed his friends might get hurt, what would he do?"

Kisa's response was almost immediate, "He would have gone after the threat on his own. He would try to shield us all from whatever he thought would hurt us."

Roiland spoke next as if continuing Kisa's thought, "He challenged the orc-troll to personal combat. He went into that ancient black dragon's lair by himself."

Ez'ard joined in next, "He went after Bone Man on his own too. He does things like that all the time."

Annah cringed at the mockery in the Arch Mage's voice, "Are you suggesting he challenged Hell itself and fought them in his room? That is ridiculous, even for Shorty."

F'lar disagreed, "But he did challenge Hell. He told that pit fiend that he and he alone was responsible for that rescue mission. He told them who he was and practically dared the God, Set, to do something about it. Something answered that challenge. That something is what Alano detected entering Arcturus."

Dualis's voice was puzzled. "Shorty is a fine warrior, but even as the Green Knight… what could he possibly do against something that powerful?"

F'lar grinned at the simplicity of his answer, "He could be Shorty. You just described him, Dualis. What did you say his most annoying trait was?"

"Stubbornness," Dualis replied. :But what does that have to do with anything?"

Kisa suddenly sat up straighter. "Oh, Goddess!" she blurted out. "Think about it, Dualis.. Whatever Hell sent to steal his soul, it would have had to reach inside Shorty to take it, right? For that instant in time, it would be on a battleground of Shorty's choosing. If he got his hands on it, he would not have let it go."

"Like that dire wolf he fought in the orc war," Roiland murmured. He shoved his hand down its throat while it literally chewed on his arm."

Know Man spoke with a trace of awe in his voice, "It makes a strange kind of sense, Dualis. You constantly complain that he is closed minded. What if he actually closed his mind with that thing still inside?"

Alano sounded like a proud father as he asked. "What you are suggesting is that a Hellborn entered this land, and that the reason we cannot find it is because my Green Knight imprisoned it inside his own mind? He sacrificed himself to protect Arcturus?" There was a long pause as Alano rose and moved to stand beside Dualis. "We chose well when we selected him. Now the question is how do we save him from himself?"

F'lar clapped his hands. "Then we are agreed."

Dualis began to move again. His aura seemed to swirl within itself. The internal motion grew faster and faster and then it stilled. "If an entity from Hell cannot breach his defenses, how do we get in without destroying his mind? Or, worse yet, freeing whatever he has locked in there?"

F'lar's aura flickered and faded. "That is the part I have not worked out yet."

Annah heard her own voice cut through the muttering in the room, "His sword. Tainkintana. It can enter Shorty's mind. Maybe it can help us rescue him."

There was silence at her words. Then Alano spoke sadly, "It is a wonderful idea, child, but it will not work. Tainkintana is the Green Knight's sword. It will not allow another to hold it. We would have to select a new Green Knight and the Land will not accept another as long as Shorty lives."

Annah shook her head. "That cannot be true."

"I wish that it was otherwise, but even I cannot take up Tainkintana. It is bonded to the Green Knight and will accept no other. Its magic will attack anyone else who grasps the hilt."

Annah continued to argue with him, "Then why did it let me hold it? Tainkintana did not hurt me."

Annah felt Kisa take her hand as Alano's aura came much closer. "You held his sword, Annah? Tainkintana let you hold its hilt in your hands? How did this happen?"

Annah felt her face flush as her words just gushed out. She wanted to sound knowledgeable, but what came out sounded more like a child caught stealing fresh baked cookies from the kitchen. "I held the hilt of the sword, well sort of. Not like Shorty does I mean. He made it sound like the sword was alive. It sounded so exciting to talk to a sword so I asked if I could try. He asked the sword if it would be okay. I think it must have said yes."

Before she could continue on, Alano gently demanded, "Tell me about when you held the hilt, Annah."

Annah took a deep breath before continuing, "Shorty sat beside me. He put my hand on the hilt beside his. It was too heavy to hold by myself. And then it spoke to me."

Again, Alano focused her tale. "It spoke to you?"

Annah excitement grew. "No. Yes. I mean not with words like we are speaking now. I could hear it in my head. Like someone was thinking at me. It called me the Green Lady. It said we could talk again some time." Annah's voice trailed off.

At first, no one spoke, the silence was almost painful. Auras around the room seemed to draw in on themselves as each person considered her words. Finally, it was F'lar who spoke, "It would appear that we have only one solution to our problem. The question is, Annah, would you be willing to go inside Shorty's mind to save him?"

Kisa pulled her hand from Annah's as she stood and faced F'lar. "We just rescued her from the Gates of Hell. Akka only knows what they did to her there. You helped bring her out of that place. Now you want to pit her up against Hell again? Your brother would kill you for suggesting it."

F'lar's response was cold and toneless, "If my brother survived this, he is welcome to try. Right now, it appears that Annah is the only one that can get to him."

Angry voices erupted around the table. The argument continued in the background as Annah's attention was drawn inward. She could feel her magic swelling inside her, encouraging her to take the risk. Her magic was ready to grow and it wanted her to grow with it. Did she have the courage to try?

Her hand went to the intricate patterns of her birthmark. Her fingers moved from the rough bark of the tree to the winding branches and leaves. As she reached the outer edges of the tree, she felt new leaves sprout upon her arm. She could be so much more if she dared. Annah's hand fell away from the mark. She realized that she was tired of being the poor little blind girl. She would not be led around anymore; she would make her own way in life. Starting now.

Annah stood and waited. No one in the room seemed to notice, their arguments raged on. She was filled with a sense of conviction that she had never felt before. It felt good to know exactly what she wanted to do for a change. Then she raised her voice so that everyone would hear her, "Stop!" The room was suddenly silent. Annah continued, "You all act like this is your decision to make. Well, it is NOT! I may be blind, but it is still my life. I choose my path, not any of you. So far only one person has bothered to ask me what I want to do. Thank you for that, F'lar. The rest of you should have waited for my answer."

Kisa's voice softened as she turned to apologize, "I am sorry, Annah. You are right, it was and still is your decision. We were just trying to protect you. Maybe Shorty has rubbed off on us over time. What is your choice in this?"

Annah turned her back on the rest of the room as she stared into the golden glow that was Kisa. "I am going to find my friend. I have things that I need to say to him. I choose to save him as he saved me."

Kisa's next question came as a surprise, "May I hug you, Annah?"

Annah was not sure how to answer. Mama had never been big on hugs. Was this how normal families did things? Her uncertainty made her words sound clumsy, "I… I guess."

Kisa's arms came around her and squeezed gently. "Thank you for trying to save my friend." Annah relaxed and returned the hug. She wondered briefly if this was what it was like to have a friend.

Dualis's words were an unwelcome interruption, "Are you certain, Annah? None of us will think less of you if you walk away from this."

Annah released Kisa and turned towards the Arch Mage. "Yes, Dualis. This is what I want."

This time when the voices exploded around the room, it was with excitement, not anger. Annah checked the position of her chair before sitting back down. It would not do to miss the chair and land on the floor. She did not want to look foolish after standing up for herself the way she had.

The excitement seems to grow in the room. Shorty's friends had hope now. There was no need for them to just sit and wait. Annah listened for a while but she realized she was stalling. There was nothing anyone could do or say that impacted what she needed to do next. She leaned towards Kisa and whispered, "Please lead me to Shorty again. I want to get started."

She felt Kisa rise. Annah stood and reached once again for Kisa's shoulder. The room went still as the two women walked from the room. Kisa led her a short way and then warned, "Stairs." Annah found a hand rail and began to climb. It was easier moving towards the danger than it had been sitting in that room thinking about it.

When the handrail ended, Annah once more reached for Kisa. Footsteps hurried up the stairs behind her. A male voice called her name from below.

Annah recognized F'lar's voice. She waited as he came up to stand beside her. The man who had baited an arch mage seemed hesitant as he spoke to her. "Annah. That thing that Shorty has locked in his head is pure evil. It will lie and deceive you at every opportunity. Assume every offer it makes is a trap. You must be cunning."

Annah shook her head. "You are asking me to be someone that I am not, F'lar. My whole life has been spent hiding from those who would hurt me. Every time evil has come for me in the past, someone like Shorty showed up to keep me safe. The only people I have ever spent much time with are my family. And the only one I ever matched wits with was my little sister. How am I supposed to outsmart the creature you describe?"

"Do not underestimate yourself." F'lar touched a finger to her birthmark. "Do not take the gifts of the Goddess lightly Annah. You are more than you believe and she will be within you."

Kisa's voice came from behind Annah. "How is she to defeat this thing F'lar? Give her something more to work with than your vague assurances."

There was a long pause before he continued. "Annah, you must understand that there are rules that even the powers of Hell must obey. Rules that bind good and the evil alike. To break those rules is to forfeit power and more importantly prestige."

His words made everything sound so simple. Annah could not accept that so she argued, "You make it sound like a children's game."

"That is not a bad way to see it. Some of the greater powers are little more than spoiled children. Children who would win at almost any cost. But this game has rules that cannot be broken without penalty. Those are the rules that you must use against them."

Annah shook her head and turned to go. "I do not know the rules for this game and I doubt that I will have time to learn them."

F'lar placed his hand on her shoulder before she could walk away. "The most important rules is that names give you power. Especially true names."

Annah turn back to face him. "How does that help me? We do not know who or what came here. And how does knowing its name give me power over this thing from Hell?"

"Names define who and what we are, Annah. One's true name defines the very essence of what we are. It is powerful magic." He paused for a moment and his aura was suddenly streaked with reds and oranges. "You heard me called the Seeker. That name is the essence of what I am. As a mage, I will never be Dualis equal in power, but he will never match my ability to find lost knowledge. That is what I excel at. It has often been said that I have a talent for sticking my nose in places that it does not belong."

Kisa chuckled softly. "I have noticed that over the years, F'lar. Now what can you tell Annah that might help her?"

F'lar's voice dropped to a whisper that only Annah could hear, "I am sorry that I cannot tell you when or how to use what I know. I only know that you must use it wisely, Annah. One time, and one time only, you can bind the being you must face with its true name."

Annah leaned closer, unwilling to miss this one hope he had to offer her. His words held a magic that was his and his alone as he told her, "He is Mammon. That name is everything that he is or ever will be. He cannot deny that naming. Remember it or you and Shorty will be lost."

Annah reached out her hand and found the elf's face. Her fingers traced it lightly. There was sincerity there and concern. "I will remember. I can only promise to do my best."

She felt him nod. "Please, save my brother. And come back to us as well. My brother will never forgive me if something happens to you. I might not forgive myself either." Then he turned away and she heard him hurry down the stairs.

Annah followed Kisa again. Before them, she saw two auras that she did not know. They blocked the hallway. Both moved aside silently and Kisa kept walking. Annah heard a door open and she felt the touch of a breeze on her face and in her hair. The smell of oak and flowers told her where she was.

Kisa took Annah's hand from her shoulder. "Shorty is still sitting in his chair. They could not get him out of it. If you give me a moment, I will move the other chair closer to Shorty."

Annah watched Kisa's aura as she moved around the room. Its golden glow chased away some of the fear that threatened to overwhelm her. Kisa returned and took her hand, leading her forward. Kisa placed Annah's hand on something smooth. It was a curved piece of wood. Her fingers explored, finding spindles and the rounded back of a rocking chair. The wood was worn, but well cared for. Her fingers traced an intricate design along the upper edge of the chair back. It was a flower of some kind. Annah wished she could see it.

She moved carefully around the chair. Her fingers sliding down the wood until she found the thick arms of the chair. There were designs along the edges of the chair arms, but they were so worn with age that Annah could not tell what they had been. How many generations had used and loved this rocker? Annah held the chair steady as she lowered herself onto the seat. She felt a soft cushion on beneath her.

Kisa's voice whispered in her ear, "Before you do this, Annah, there is something I want you to hear. Sometimes, the things we want and need most in life come from places or people we least expect."

"I do not understand, Kisa."

Kisa chuckled softly. "That is okay, Annah. It took me time to understand it too. I am a Priestess of Akka. I serve a Goddess of Life and Goodness. The man I chose as my husband is a Drow, a Dark Elf. His kind are known for evil and wickedness. Our relationship is a paradox beyond the understanding of most people. I can only tell you that we are more together than either of us could have been on our own. He is the best choice that I ever made."

Annah sounded confused, "I still do not understand what this has to do with me."

Kisa squeezed her shoulder. "My friend is an ogre with all of his kinds power and ferocity. And he is one of the gentlest souls that I know. A time will come when you see the ogre in him. Do not lose sight of who he really is when that happens."

Annah still did not understand, but she murmured, "Okay."

Kisa's hand slid down to her left wrist. She lifted Annah's hand, moving it up and to the left. "The sword's hilt is right below your hand. Be well Annah and go with Akka's blessing."

Annah whispered her thanks as she searched within herself for the courage to lower her hand. It had not seemed as frightening when Shorty's hand had rested alongside hers on the hilt. With a prayer to Mielikki, Annah let her hand drop. Instead of cold metal, the hilt felt alive and warm, almost welcoming.

Chapter 13

A Knight of Memories

As her fingers wrapped around the hilt, emotions that were not her own surged into her mind. Excitement at her coming warred with anger at the attack on Shorty. Both emotions gave way to determination to free Shorty from his self-imposed prison. Then, as they had the first time she held the sword's hilt, words formed in her mind, *Welcome, Green Lady!*

Annah was not sure if she should speak out loud as Shorty did or just think in her head.

*Either or both, Lady. Whichever is more natural for you. *

Annah took a moment to compose her thoughts then asked, *Why do you call me Green Lady? My name is Annah and I am just a girl from nowhere. No one would ever mistake me for a Lady.*

There was humor in the sword's response, *You are not now, nor have you ever been just a girl from nowhere. The Green Lady is what you are or, at least, that is who you may become if we win this battle. The choice will be yours then.*

Annah considered the sword's words carefully. She could not imagine a future where she would be a Lady. But now was not the time to argue possible futures. She was here to find out if the sword could help her to save her friend. *Tainkintana…* Annah's thoughts began to race. *I am here because of the Knight. Shorty, is lost. I need your help finding him.*

Strength and comfort seemed to wrap themselves around her. Tainkintana's thoughts grew serious. *He is not lost, Lady. He is where he chose to be.*

Then why can none of us locate him?

Frustration suffused the sword's response. *Because the Knight has closed every door into and out of that part of his mind. Even I have been barred from entry. I cannot reach him or aide him. Shorty made certain the abomination had no path to escape its prison.*

Tainkintana's words extinguished the hope that had been kindled in her heart. Was all their planning for nothing? *Then he is lost to us forever?*

There was a long pause. It seemed to last an eternity, or was it no more than a single heartbeat? Did time have any meaning in a world of thoughts? Tainkintana finally responded, *There may be a way, Lady, that Shorty did not consider. A door may exist in his mind that is hidden even from him.*

Where, or maybe how, would I find this door? she asked.

She sensed the swords thoughts race as it considered her question. *Shorty did more than just close the paths in and out of his mind. Somehow, he cut off access to his most cherished memories. It was almost as if there was something there that he needed to protect from the abomination. Those memories exist like an island outside the fortress of his mind*

Annah did not understand how any of this helped her. *If he cut off access to these memories, how do I get from this island to Shorty?*

Tainkintana gave what Annah interpreted as a mental shrug. *They may not. But there is something there that Shorty was desperate to protect. If there is a way to reach the Green Knight, it is hidden there. Find out what Shorty tried to hide from this minion of Hell and then search it. The key to his mind has to be there somewhere.*

The idea was so strange. Searching through another person's memories. How would she do it? But if it was the only way to reach her friend then she really had no other choice. *So, I would have to find my own way from Shorty's memories to the place he has imprisoned himself. Are there any risks?*

Was there a note of anxiety in Tainkintana's reply? *I can get you in Lady, but I cannot bring you back out again. Only Shorty can release you from his thoughts.*

Trapped in another person's mind. It was a frightening thought. What would she find there? Her own nightmares were bad enough. What horrors were hidden in Shorty's mind? Then she considered what Shorty had risked to save her. Could his mind be any worse than the Gates of Hell? He had not hesitated to go into that nightmare to save her. Could she risk any less for him?

The sword must have been listening to her thoughts because it warned her, *His life has not been pleasant, Lady. He has experienced a great deal of evil for one so young. He has seen things you might find disturbing.*

But he has seen. A rush of shame washed over her. Annah was not sure where that bitter response had come from. Tainkintana did not deserve it and neither did Shorty. Thankfully, the sword did not answer her. It gave her time to come to her own decision.

Annah realized she was just stalling. She had made her decision down in the dining room. Her thoughts carried that decision to the sword, *I have to try, Tainkintana. Not just for Shorty, but for myself and everyone else that depends on him. I am his only hope as he was mine.*

This is but a part of my reason for naming you the Green Lady, the sword said as much to itself as to her. Then, Annah felt something cold and heavy around her neck. Mental fingers rose to examine what now hung down between her breasts. There was a chain and something heavier below it. A picture appeared in her mind of a tiny sword dangling from the chain. *What?* she asked in surprise.

I have faith that you will find a way to reach him Lady. The Knight will have need of me if you are both to win through this. When you can, place this chain around his neck.

Annah wanted to hug the sword as Kisa had hugged her, but that seemed both dangerous and impractical. Instead, she willed her hand to grip the hilt more tightly. But she was not sure if her hand obeyed. The connection to her body seemed so distant. Words would just have to do, *Thank you, Tainkintana. You are a good friend to us both.*

You are only the second to name me friend in all of my existence, Lady. Shorty was the first. Stay safe and come back to me. I find that I like having friends. It would appear that Shorty was correct all along, one can never have enough friends.

Shorty's words, repeated by his sword, were just one of the reasons that she could not fail. She had to make things right with Shorty. Was she ready to go? She was not sure. Annah could only think of one other question to ask, *Is there anything else I should know?*

When you face evil like this, have faith. Faith in your Goddess and in each other. Faith is the bane of your foe.

Before she could ask about the being they faced, Annah felt her consciousness swirl away into a place filled with light and sound.

Annah's eyes opened on a world filled with trees. She could see! She realized that she had not even considered her blindness when she agreed to come into Shorty's mind. She took a moment to simply enjoy the gift.

Trees looked more imposing than they felt to her fingers. She had never truly understood how tall they were. She felt small as she was forced to look up and up. She stood on the edge of a clearing beside an immense tree. A scattering of small objects lay on the ground. Annah bent and picked one up. Her fingers recognized the shape. It was a walnut. That meant these were walnut trees. Annah stared at one of the trees, wanting to remember its beauty for the rest of her life. Finally, Annah had to force herself to look away. She had a door to find and a Knight to rescue.

The open expanse of the clearing was surrounded by more walnut trees. Each tree stretched up into a clear blue sky. Sunlight filtered through the trees weaving patterns of shadow and light. The world was a much bigger place than she had ever imagined. A breeze caressed her face and arms. The air was filled with the scent of life and the sound of rustling leaves. It was beautiful, but it was also too much.

Annah closed her eyes as her mind tried to absorb it all. She placed a hand against the walnut tree to steady herself. The feel of the bark soothed her. The smell of life, the sounds of the forest, and the texture of the tree were things she was familiar with. Open space, sky, and colors so vibrant that they were almost painful to see were new to her. How could so many details exist in the memories of one person?

Her vision the day before had been a shock. But that vision had been at night. The colors had been muted. The sense of space and distance had been limited by the darkness. The world in Shorty's mind stunned her senses. Was this what it was like to see? Or did this only exist in the mind of her friend? Annah realized sadly that she would never know for sure.

Opening her eyes once more, Annah turned and began to walk through the trees. Her hands and arms before her. She did not know if she could trust what her eyes told her about the forest around her. Trees hurt and she did not want to walk into one. Her feet slid just above the surface of the ground, feeling for obstacles. She missed her staff and the sense of safety it gave her. Walking this way was frightening and it was wonderful.

Annah began to move with more confidence. Her new sight had not betrayed her yet. Annah walked on without any idea where she was headed. She came upon a tree filled with bright red shapes. She approached it and picked one. Annah closed her eyes as her fingers explored the shape. Her nose recognized the scent of apple. Annah took a bite and felt the juice run down her chin.

Without the distraction of sight, Annah realized that she was not alone. Chirps and the songs of birds came from all around her. She heard the rhythmic beat of a woodpecker from somewhere to her right. This forest felt like the Grove. It felt like home. A friendly chitter came from just over her head.

Annah opened her eyes to see a small reddish-brown form standing on the side of a tree. She knew that sound. It was a squirrel. The squirrel had paused on its way down the tree. Its head tilted back as it stared at Annah. She could see that one cheek was stretched tight over something round. Probably a nut she decided. The squirrel chittered again as it stared into Annah's eyes expectantly.

She smiled at it. "Do you have any idea where I am, little one?"

The squirrel gave a soft chirrup and turned its eyes to stare at the ground at her feet. She laughed, "Yes, I suppose I am right here. Would you like some help with that nut?"

Annah held her hand out to the squirrel. To her surprise, the small creature leapt to her hand and scrambled up to sit upon her shoulder. From the corner of her eye, she saw it remove the nut from its mouth and hold it out to her.

Annah took the nut from its tiny paws. Her fingers told her that this was an acorn. The acorn was surprisingly easy to crack. Annah picked out the nut meat and handed it to the squirrel. It took the proffered gift and began to nibble at it. Annah turned her eyes up into the trees. Every tree around her seemed to have nuts of one kind or another. Dozens of squirrels chased each other along the branches of the trees. She smiled again. Of course, Shorty's memories would be filled with images of his small friends.

The squirrel finished its treat and leaned against her cheek. The soft fur of it tiny head was warm as it showered her with affection. "I am glad you enjoyed the acorn, Small One. But I am lost here in your home. Do you have any idea where I need to go?"

A tiny hand patted her on the cheek and then wound itself into her hair. The squirrel leaned forward and pointed off to the left. Annah muttered to herself, "I hope you are not taking me on a nut gathering expedition." The tiny hand in her hair tugged twice and the squirrel pointed again.

She shrugged and began to walk. Her passenger crooned happily as she followed its pointing finger. Annah lost track of time as she followed the squirrel's directions. The sounds of the forest grew fainter as Annah trudged on. A new sound came from somewhere ahead. Annah paused and asked the squirrel, "Do you know what that is?"

The squirrel stomped its tiny foot on her shoulder and gestured towards the sound. "Fine," Annah muttered, "but if its hungry, I am going to let it eat you first."

The sound grew louder until Annah no longer needed the squirrel to show her the way. The sound became her guide. The noise was not some random forest sound. It had a melody and it was familiar somehow. She just could not place where she had heard it. Annah tried to hum along and that was when she recognized the song. It was something Shorty had hummed as they had traveled through the Grove planting Treant seeds.

The song drew her closer. The version that Shorty had hummed did not do the song justice. This version was richer. There were undertones that Shorty had missed. Annah tried to mimic the song as she moved through the trees. She was no more successful than Shorty had been. It would take multiple voices in perfect harmony to replicate the song.

A clearing opened up before her. Annah paused at the outer ring of trees to study the scene before her. A single small tree, little more than a sapling really, sat in the center of the clearing. The tree was the source of the song. The melody drew her forward. Annah entered the clearing and walked into the song. She knelt before the tree and opened herself to the music.

The branches and leaves confused her. Needles and leaves of various types grew from each of its many branches. Her minds could not process what her eyes told her. Annah closed them and reached out to the tree. She found a maple leaf growing on a branch beside pine needles. Another branch held spruce needles intermixed with the leaves of a willow. Some branches even found a cherry growing beside an apple. By touch, Annah identified parts of at least a dozen trees all growing from the same trunk.

Annah struggled to understand how this could be. Was this the result of some misguided magical experiment? Annah reached out to the tree with her own magic. Its song swelled in her mind. The name One Tree came to her. No, this was not a magical creation. This tree was part of creation itself. Annah felt the squirrel curl up on her shoulder. Annah's own thoughts drifted away and she rested.

Her spirit soared in a place of peace and harmony. But it was not her time to stay here. Duties and obligations called her back to the world below. Annah selected a beam of sunlight and rode it back to the world that Shorty had created in his mind. Annah roused from the perfection of that other place, unsure of how much time had passed. She felt more rested than she ever had before. The horrors of her time in the Bazaar were still there, but they were no longer sharp and painful. Annah knew her spirit had been healed while she knelt before the tree.

She opened her eyes to stare at the tree. Its many leaves, needles, fruit and nuts no longer seemed so strange. It was beautiful, but it was also forbidden. She could look, but she must not eat of its fruit. Annah rose to her feet. The squirrel scrambled to keep its position on her shoulder. Something soft and pleasing slid down her legs as she stood. Annah's fingers and eyes moved to investigate what it was.

The simple homespun dress that she had been wearing was gone. In its place was a dark green gown with lighter greens woven throughout the corset. The gown fell to her ankles where soft leather boots now covered her once bare feet. The sleeves of the gown reached to her elbows, leaving her birthmark fully visible. The dress was beautiful. It was far too fine for a peasant girl like her. She curtsied to the tree. "Thank you."

Her small guide patted her cheek once more to get her attention. Annah laughed, "Now what small one?" The squirrel pointed past the One Tree into the forest behind it. Annah reached up and gently caressed its head, "Yes, your Majesty. Right away." Then she followed the directions of her guide.

The trees closed in around her once more. She wove her way between their trunks following the directions of the tiny pointing arm. It no longer bothered her that she did not know where she was going. The encounter with the strange tree had given her hope that she was on the right path.

The trees began to thin out once more. Annah wondered what she would find this time. She was startled when her guide leapt from her shoulder to the trunk of an oak tree. It clung to the side of the tree with three legs. It chattered excitedly as it gestured with one front leg for her to continue on. Annah turned and bowed her head to the squirrel. "Thank you for your help, Small One." The squirrel chirped happily and scrambled up the tree.

There was a smile on Annah's face as she continued on. She would have to thank Shorty for introducing her to squirrels. She was beginning to understand why he loved them so much. Annah was still musing over the squirrels when the trees pulled back on both sides. A stone pathway ran between the trees to her left and right, disappearing around curves in both directions. Annah stopped to stare at the strange road that she had been led to.

Each of the square stones was as long as she was tall. The path, two stones across, was a strange sight to behold. Stones of pure white alternated in both directions with stones of a dark green material. It was like a child's game board twisting and turning as it meandered through the trees. The path called to her, urging her to join the game and frolic among the trees. Annah moved forward and knelt beside one of the white stones. She slid her fingers across its surface. Smooth but not slippery. And it was level with the ground on the outside edge. There was no lip for her to trip on.

The urge to walk the path was so strong. Annah stood, lifting her right foot to begin her journey of exploration. But her foot returned to its place as she considered how to travel this road. Were there rules to this game? She could move diagonally, following either white or green. Neither of those options appealed to her. The Treants had always stressed the Balance in their lessons. Her journey through life must honor that Balance in all things.

Annah stepped onto the white stone and turned right to follow the path. Green and then another white stone. It felt right. Trees continued to line both sides of the path. The sun filtered through the trees to light the way and warm her skin. The path curved gently as she walked its surface. She lost count of the tiles as she followed the alternating colors of the stepping stones.

The pattern of the stones was mesmerizing. Green, white, green, white. She almost did not notice when the path did change. Annah was already three stones into the clearing when her brain processed that the path had widened out to each side. The pattern of the tones remained the same as it opened into a space the size of her garden in the Grove. The alternating colors stretched from one side of the open area to the other. All except for a perfect square of four stones missing in the center of the clearing.

In the place where the four stones should have been was a single large oak tree. Annah almost cried out in anger when she saw the damage that had been done to the trunk of the tree. Someone or something had carved a large rectangular opening in the center of the tree. Standing within that opening was a man-shaped figure. The figure faced away from her so she could not tell who or what it was.

Annah stepped closer as she studied the tree. The leaves and branches of the tree seemed healthy and vibrant despite the damage to the trunk. Who would harm such an ancient tree by cutting away its core? And why would Shorty keep such a travesty among so many beautiful memories. When she reached the last stone before the tree, she stared at the figure standing in the center. It had pointed ears and wore armor. It was an elf. Her confusion grew. No elf would willingly harm a tree this way.

Annah followed the stones around the tree. The damage to the tree disturbed her, but she had to admit that the carving was exquisite. She could see the individual links in the elf's chain mail. It was like staring at a perfect replica of a living elf. She came around to the front of the tree and paused.

This was not one of the peaceful forest folk of Papa's stories. The carving showed a warrior in battle. A sword was gripped in his left hand, but it was his right hand that drew her attention. Something jagged erupted from the palm of that hand. It took her a moment to recognize it as lightning. The elf was a battle mage. Papa had sometimes told exciting tales of such heroes. The beauty of the figure almost made Annah forget about the desecration of the tree.

Annah moved to stand beside the outstretched right hand. She wanted a better look at the expression on the elf's face. His handsome face showed neither fear nor anger. Annah studied the hard line formed by his lips; it was a look of determination. She wondered what evil the elf had faced. It had to be evil he was fighting. No one this beautiful could themselves be evil, could they?

Annah stretched out her hand. Her fingers trailed lightly down the elf's arm. The wood was warm and it pulse beneath her fingers. She pulled back, surprised. The part of the tree that formed the elf was as alive and vibrant as the rest of the tree. The elf was formed of living wood. How could such a thing be done? Was this Shorty's doing?

It was a puzzle that could only be answered by finding Shorty. She had to assume that this was her road to the Green Knight. Annah turned from the elf and walked on. The opening narrowed once more to two stones wide as it had been before the elf. This time, Annah did not allow the pattern of the stones to distract her.

She saw a second open area far ahead. Curiosity made her hurry forward. What would this new opening reveal? Again, the open area was covered by stones except for a two-by-two square in the center of the clearing. This time the tree growing there was a willow. The trunk of the willow had a hole similar to the oak's. Within, a figure stood facing away from her.

Annah approached the willow. Something stuck out from the back of the figure standing in the tree. Wings grew there, thin and delicate looking. Annah could almost see through them. She walked slowly around the willow studying the small figure. She did not know what it was until a word was whispered on the breeze, "Sprite." Annah spun around, but there was no one there. Slowly, she turned to face the tree once more.

The 'sprite' also appeared to be in battle. It gripped something blue in its right hand. Annah leaned in closer. It was a tiny, blue sword. It was little more than a small knife to Annah, but it was huge in the 'sprite's' tiny hand. This figure was also a warrior. The sprite's face held a look of satisfaction. Annah wondered what made these two warriors so important. What role had they played in Shorty's life?

Annah continued on and soon a third area opened up before her. This time a walnut tree grew in the center of the open space. Annah circled to see the form of an old man standing proud in the center of the tree. In one hand the old man held a stringed instrument that she did not have a name for. His other hand held a sword-like weapon. Instead of a flat blade, this sword had a rounded blade with a sharp point.

Each of the people she had seen in the images had been fighting. Was that important? Annah stepped back from the living image. She looked up into the blue sky and asked, "What do these all mean, Shorty? Why are they here?"

Annah almost screamed when a pleasant female voice replied from behind her, "They are living memorials honoring those Shorty believes he let down. He holds them safe in his heart so that he can never forget the price of failures."

Annah spun around. Her heart was racing. Had the evil Shorty kept in his mind found her so quickly? A woman stood there watching her. "You are safe, child. The one you fear is barred from this place. Shorty would never allow these memories to be desecrated by it."

She studied the woman standing on the path she had not yet traveled. The woman was tall. Annah guessed her to be over six feet. Her dark hair was long and tied into an intricate braid that fell over her right shoulder. A sprig of mistletoe had been worked into the braid. Despite the simple gown she wore, Annah understood this woman was powerful. Annah's magic spoke to her then, "Priestess."

The woman smiled at her and continued, "I apologize if I startled you, Ann Ah. My name is Alauriel."

Annah stammered, "How do you know my name? Or at least the way Shorty says it?"

Alauriel gestured to the woods around them. "Our Goddess whispered your name to me. But even if she had not, the name Ann Ah echoes through this place. I believe that everyone who lives in Shorty's memories knows your name by now. You are very important to Shorty."

Annah shook her head. "But we only met a week ago." She looked away then, unsure if she wanted to continue this discussion or not. Looking back at Alauriel, Annah tried to focus on what she needed to accomplish and not the past. "I need to find Shorty. I, well we, want to save him."

Compassion filled the older woman's eyes. "There is much that you need to know if you are to succeed in your quest. Walk with me, please? And I will explain what I can." The woman turned and began to walk up the path.

Annah had too many questions to resist the offer of an explanation. She wanted to understand this place that Shorty had created in his mind. And, she needed to know how to get from his memories to where he had trapped his foe. She hurried to catch up. As she fell into step with the woman, Annah gestured at the path and the surrounding trees. "This place is not what I expected. It is beautiful. It seems more a place for druids than a warrior like Shorty."

A smile came to Alauriel's lips and quickly disappeared. She did not turn to look at Annah. "He is a ranger now. At heart, I think he always was. His love for the outside and small animals was so different from the attitudes of the other ogre children. He was so much happier once he escaped from under the mountain."

Annah wondered if she could steer the conversation to get the information she needed. She had to try. "And now he is trapped inside once more. This time he cannot escape unless someone helps him."

There was anger in the woman's sharp reply, "He has sacrificed everything to imprison that thing in his mind. He allows it to torture him. He tries to protect the whole world so there will be no more shrines here on the Path."

 "Tortured?" Annah felt a stab of pain at Alauriel's words. She could still remember her time in the Bazaar.

The woman's anger seemed to swell. "It thinks it can force him to let it go, but it has no idea just how stubborn he is."

A deep male voice growled within the trees, "Him do whats youse teaches him ta do. Protects all dat bees small. Youse no gib him nudder way. No bees bery smart."

Annah spun around staring into the trees. Nothing moved in the shadows cast by their thick canopies. Where had the voice come from? Alauriel just kept walking as if she had not heard the voice. Had it been real or was it just another of the voices in her head?

Annah had to run to catch up with her guide. Ahead the next open area was already visible. In its center, she could already see the massive walnut that marked the next memorial.

This area was both longer and wider than the previous ones. The opening for the tree was four stones by four stones and the walnut filled the entire space. She had never seen or felt a tree that big before. Not only was the walnut much bigger than the other memorial trees, so to was the hole in its trunk. The figure that filled almost every bit of that opening was enormous too.

Annah practically ran around the tree to see the image's face. Somehow, she knew this memorial was more important to her than the others had been. She was well ahead of her guide when the image came into view. Annah came to a halt, staring up to see the image growing in the center of the tree. Only this image was not of a single person. This was a memorial for two people and, based on the image, the man and woman portrayed there were a couple.

These images were even more detailed than the first three had been. It depicted a large male, standing tall in the center of the tree. His right hand held a massive sword. The determined look on the male's face was frightening. The huge male's left arm cradled a beautiful woman. His grip on her was protective and he did not seem bothered by her weight. It reminded her of how easily Shorty had scooped her up to flee the attack at Sanctuary.

Annah's eyes were drawn to the woman. She was slender. Despite being dwarfed by the man that held her, she had been tall. Much taller than Annah. Annah noticed that the woman's left leg was bent in places it should not have been. Annah doubted the woman would have been able to walk. Her gaze moved to meet the eyes of the female figure. Those eyes were intent and focused. They were… Annah paused and glanced over at Alauriel. They were the eyes of the woman who was staring at her now.

The woman nodded and Annah looked back at the figure before her. Now she studied the face of the muscular male. There were details here that she had almost missed. The male had pale green eyes. His features were broad but handsome. There was something strange about his mouth though. There were two tusk-like teeth protruding from his lower lip. The teeth and his great size told Annah that he was not human.

Annah's first question came out a little more blunt than she had intended. Her second was not much kinder. "What is he? And what happened to your leg?"

Alauriel laughed, "You sound like a member of the Tribe. Ogres are not known for their tact either." Then she gestured at the memorial, "He is an ogre. As for my leg, I was injured when his Tribe attacked the caravan I was traveling with. I should have died in that attack, but he spared me and nursed me back to health."

Annah stared down at the woman's leg looking for some sign of her injury. Alauriel stretched out her leg so Annah could see it clearly. "My injuries did not follow me here and I am not sure why. Shorty only knew me as I am in that image, broken in body. Perhaps the Goddess had pity on me. Someday I hope to ask her that question and many more."

The woman walked forward and placed a hand on the sword arm of the large male. "This is Hunter, the Chief of our Tribe. He is also my husband."

The same male voice came from among the trees. It was more insistent this time, "Bees me mate!"

"Yes, my love. My mate," Alauriel corrected herself. Then the woman waved a hand towards the trees. "Please forgive my mate. Ogres do not like magic. He refuses to step upon the Path."

The implications of Alauriel's words began to sink in. This was an ogre. The thing that Mama had feared. If this was what Shorty looked like, then Mama might have had good reason for her fears. But Annah did not have that excuse. She had only seen Shorty's aura and still she had not trusted him.

Annah was silent, lost in her own regrets. Alauriel gave her time. There was no right way to ask Annah's next question. But there was something here that she needed to understand. She asked as tactfully as she could, "You said that each of these shrines is for someone Shorty thought he let down. How did Shorty fail you and your mate?"

Alauriel's face flushed with anger. With an icy glare, she rebuked Annah, "Our son has never failed anyone, let alone us! I do not know how that crazy idea got into his head."

The male immediately chided her, "Youse teached him dat. Tells him all da times ta protect. No him fault"

Alauriel turned her anger towards the trees. "I did not want our son to be like the others, always hurting those weaker than themselves."

Annah's mind went blank at that revelation. She lost track of their argument as she struggled to accept that these were Shorty's parents. "How? I mean you are a human. How could Shorty be your son? I am sorry. I know that sounds rude, but this is coming too quickly for me to understand it all." Annah reached up to absently rub at her temples.

Alauriel's voice calmed considerably, "Forgive me. My frustration is with my son and myself. I wanted so much for him. He took things farther than I ever intended. He tries to take responsibility for the whole world."

The male snickered loudly. "Like him Mama."

Alauriel turned to face the trees. "Like you taught him any different my Chief? The Tribe always came first, right?"

There was no response to her question.

Annah was truly curious. "If Shorty was not to blame, what did happen to the two of you?"

Angry words spewed from the trees, "Cowards! Dem cheats!"

Alauriel turned back to face Annah. "My husb... mate was ambushed by two members of the Tribe. A father and son. The father wanted to be Chief, but he was afraid to challenge my mate. Hunter would have crushed him. Instead, the two of them lured Hunter into a trap down in the deep tunnels. Hunter died with a boy's spear in his back."

Annah winced at the description. "And you?"

Alauriel gave her a grin that was frightening. "My mate's murderer came looking to kill our son."

The male voice chuckled as he interjected, "No bery smart, dat one."

Alauriel eyes narrowed, but there was pride in her voice as she went on, "I made sure he never killed anyone ever again. I released my final spell just before he laid his hands on me. He died without ever being named Chief by the Elders. My son lived."

Hunter's voice was filled with pride, "Fierce little warrior!"

"What happened to Shorty after you both died?"

Alauriel's smile grew even broader. "He took care of the boy that put that spear in his father's back. The boy came with two older youth to kill Shorty. Things did not go as they planned."

 "Did he kill them?" Annah asked, remembering Tainkintana's warning about the evil that Shorty had experienced.

Alauriel shook her head. "Worse, he let them live. The smallest male ogre in the Tribe beat the three of them badly. Then he left them to tell the tale of their humiliation. It is never a good thing to be seen as weak in an ogre tribe."

Somehow knowing that Shorty had not killed the three boys made her feel better. But none of this explained why Shorty thought he was to blame for his parents' deaths. His guilt made no sense. "Then why does Shorty feel responsible for your deaths? Or for any of the others who line this path?

Alauriel's eyes dropped to her feet. "That is probably my fault. I never thought he would take it this far. How could it have gone so wrong?" her voice became fainter as she spoke.

"I do not understand. What did you do?" Annah asked.

Alauriel looked up to meet Annah's questioning gaze. "As I said, I did not want him to be like the other ogres. So I drilled it into him that he needed to protect those who were smaller than he was. He was such a small ogre. It should have been easy."

The woman gestured towards the trees. "First it was the squirrels. He was their protector. His ideas seemed harmless enough. But I was also smaller than he was. He blamed himself for my death. A death I chose. Then he went outside. Suddenly everyone was smaller than he was. In his mind he became responsible for protecting everyone he knew. He was the only one allowed to make sacrifices. People died and Shorty lived. To him, that meant he failed them."

Annah blurted out, "That is ridiculous. He has to be smarter than that."

Alauriel shook her head. "He was so young when Hunter and I died. He took my lesson literally. He was too young to understand. Shorty was thrust from our small world into a larger one filled with evil. He lost friends and blamed himself for their deaths too. It is a part of who he is now."

Annah looked back down the path towards the other shrines she had seen. "It does not make sense. There has to be more to their deaths. No one blames themselves for other people's choices."

The voice of the male ogre boomed from somewhere in the trees. This time it demanded compliance, "Shows ta her!"

Alauriel spun towards the trees, arguing, "She is not ready, Hunter. Not for that, not yet."

There was no give in Hunter's voice, It was filled with command, "Shows!"

Annah watched as Shorty's mother bowed her head. "Yes, my Chief." Alauriel stared between two trees on the inside edge of the curved path. Annah could tell that she did not want to do what her mate had ordered, "Please come with me, Annah. The Path does not yet go where I must take you."

Annah was puzzled but she followed Shorty's mother through the trees. Alauriel walked in silence and Annah was left to wonder what it was that she needed to see. It was not a difficult walk or a long one. The trees opened up to another clearing. A similar pattern of stones covered the ground here. But these alternated between a dark and lighter green. Annah's hand went to the gown she had been given by the One Tree. The gown's colors were the same as the stepping stones.

The familiar opening sat in the center of the stones. A tree that Annah did not recognize grew in the gap where the stones were missing.

The bark of the tree was grey. Alauriel pointed at it, saying, "It is a rosewood tree. They are very common in Arcturus where Shorty now lives."

Annah slowly approached the tree. She could see where the shrine was forming in its trunk. The tree's bark there was already missing and parts of the image were clearly visible in the heart of the tree. A human arm reached out from the trunk. Above the arm was the face of a woman that she did not recognize;

Annah wondered why it was important for her to see the image of this woman. She was beautiful. The face was so detailed that Annah almost expected it to speak to her. Maybe the image understood what Annah did not. But the lips did not move and the eyes did not blink. Without taking her eyes from the image she asked, "Who is she?"

When there was no answer, Annah turned to look at the other woman. Alauriel's face was a mask of worry. Annah waited for an answer, but Alauriel only shook her head.

Annah turned back to the tree, puzzled by the look on the woman's face. Her eyes dropped to the only other feature visible on the shrine. She examined the arm reaching towards her. It was long and slender. The palm of that hand was facing up. Annah stammered, "No!" as her eyes traveled up the length of the arm. Stretching from the wrist to the elbow was a birthmark. It was a tree. Her tree. This could not be right.

Her denial came without hesitation, "That cannot be my face. That woman is beautiful. I am just… just me."

Alauriel began to speak but Hunter cut her off, "Dat how boy sees youse. Tree be da boys magics."

Annah could not accept his words. It could not be true. She stepped closer and raised her right hand towards the image growing in the tree. Fear made her hesitate. Annah closed her eyes and let her fingers explore the image. Her left hand came up to trace the lines of her own face. It was easy to deny what her eyes saw, but her fingers did not lie. It was her face growing in the tree.

Annah's eyes opened once more. She stared at the image with curiosity. This was the first time she had seen herself. This image was not the person she imagined herself to be. Annah accepted that this was her image. With that acceptance came more questions. "Why would he make a memorial for me?"

This time, it was Alauriel that answered her, "He believes that what happened to you was his fault. He let you be captured and hurt. He believes that he failed to protect you."

Annah spun around to face Shorty's mother. Annah needed her to understand and believe that Shorty had not failed. "No. That is not what happened. I made him put me down. I ordered him to save Cory and Willie. He left me in that thicket because I gave him no choice."

Alauriel's came and wrapped her arms around Annah. "You do not need to convince me, child. Everyone along the Path made choices. Some chose to save the world. Some chose to save Shorty. Not one of these people regret the choices they made."

Annah melted into the woman's embrace. There were tears in her eyes. "None of it was his fault."

Annah felt Alauriel nod her head. "Now you understand. Every choice in life has consequences. Sometimes those consequences are serious and people die. Those kinds of sacrifices are what makes some people very special. They are heroes. My son has trouble accepting that he is not the only one allowed to make those sacrifices. Sometimes he must allow others to make their own choices. He cannot protect his friends from themselves."

Annah squeezed Shorty's mother before stepping back. "I need to find him before the whole world loses him."

Alauriel smiled and backed away. "Yes, you do. But you need to do more than save him. You must teach him. My son has had many teachers and guides in his young life. I think you are what he needs now. Be his teacher and maybe something more."

Before Annah could understand the woman's was trying to tell her, Hunter barked another command, "Touch! Go ta boy!!"

Worry lines appeared on Alauriel's face. "Are you sure, my Chief?"

Hunter's voice was gentler this time, "Touches, Ann Ah."

Annah did not argue. She turned back and reached again for the image's face. "No!" Alauriel snapped. "You must touch the source of your magic."

Annah examined the arm sticking out from the tree. The birthmark on the image's arm seemed just as detailed as her own. She could see the texture of its bark and leaves. Her fingers reached for that mark. Light and magic flared at her touch…

Chapter 14

A Closed Mind

And then they were gone as quickly as they had come. She almost panicked as darkness claimed her. Had the gift of sight been ripped from her so soon? How would she find Shorty without it? Then a different light, harsh and almost blinding, lit the world around her. It was followed almost instantly by the rumble of thunder. In that brief burst of light, Annah glimpsed a bed and a closed door beyond it. The clearing was gone. She was alone once more.

The harsh light came again, lasting much longer this time. A window rattled behind her as thunder seemed to go on forever. The barrage of sound finally yielded to a steady beat of raindrops hammering the roof mixed with the sharper staccato of it striking glass somewhere behind her. Annah turned slowly, unsure if she wanted to witness the fury of this storm. There, across the room, lit by multiple lightning strikes, was a familiar window. This was the room of her earlier vision and it was the room she had first met Kisa in.

As she watched, crooked fingers of lightning reached down from dark clouds to play across the outer wall of the Keep. At their touch, sharp cracks of power mingled with the rumble of thunder. Annah stumbled back at the force of those strikes, falling onto the bed when it slammed into the back of her knees. Annah's heart raced as it tried to match the tempo of the storm. Her hands clawed for the soft quilt, wrapping it around her like armor against the reverberations of the storm. Was this the end of her quest? Surely, mere glass could not protect her from this kind of devastation.

Individual spears of lightning became sheets as the storm tried to batter down the walls of the keep. Despite their fury, the walls stood proud and tall, too stubborn for even this storm to bring down. Annah could see no sign that the walls even noticed the storms attack. And then, like one of her sisters temper tantrums, the lightning was suddenly gone. Only the echoes of thunder and the pounding of the rain remained.

Annah shivered. Even with Althea's quilt wrapped around her, this version of Stormhold chilled her very soul. This memory was nothing like the real keep. How could a place this dark exist in the same mind as the beautiful forest she had just left? Had the thing that had come for her broken Shorty's mind? She would have to find him to know for certain. She would need to search this version of Stormhold, but that also meant that she might find the thing that Shorty had trapped here. She shivered again, wondering if the quilt would be any better protection against a creature from Hell.

The problem was Annah really did not know her way around Stormhold. She could find her way to the dining room because she had been there. She had counted the steps to the stairs and from the stairs to the table. The rest of Stormhold was a mystery cloaked by her blindness. The only other place she knew how to get to was Shorty's room. His door was only a few steps from her own. It would be best, she decided, to start with what she knew. Besides, what better place to look for Shorty than in his own room.

Annah climbed off the bed. After a moment's hesitation, she folded the quilt and laid it on the foot of the bed. If things went badly, she did not want to stain Althea's needlework with her own blood. Then she walked around the bed and reached for the latch that held the door closed.

The latch was cold, so cold that it burned when she touched it. The latch resisted her efforts to lift it. Slowly, it warmed in her hand and then the door opened. The hallway outside the door was dark, almost as dark as it had been when she was blind, but not quite. All her eyes had to work with was a dim glow that reflected off the well-polished floor. Only silence greeted her, so Annah stepped into that hallway.

After a moment's hesitation, Annah reached back and closed the door behind her.

She turned right, knowing that Shorty's room lay just ahead. A strange reddish light flickered from what should have been the door to Shorty's room. The flickering glow was not bright enough to light the hall, but it was enough to see the shattered wood that was all that remained of the door frame. Annah braced herself and took a step closer. A smell like that of rot and corruption assaulted her nose. Annah swallowed down the bile that had risen into the back of her mouth at the smell. Then she walked to where Shorty's door had once been.

The door to the room was just gone! The frame where the latch and hinges had connected was little more than splinters now. Whatever had done this had been strong, stronger than anything that Annah could imagine. One of the hinges, now little more than a piece of twisted metal, lay just inside where the door should have been. Annah prayed that whatever had done this was not waiting for her inside the room.

She stepped across the threshold and stopped. The smell here was much stronger. The location of the missing door also became clear. It was leaning against the window ledge on the far side of the room. The door was no longer smooth like she remembered it. Several cracks in the wood radiated out from a large hand print. There was something strange about that print. Annah counted twice to be sure, but the hand print had six fingers. Each of them ended in a deep claw mark. Annah knew without a doubt that she did not want to meet the creature that had broken down the door.

Just to the left of the broken door were the remains of a large bed. The mattress and bedding had literally been shredded. Feathers, now matted together, lay in clumps all around the bed. A tapestry hanging above the bed had been reduced to ribbons of cloth. The foul smell that filled the room seemed to emanate from what was left of the bed. Annah told herself that she did not want to know what made the feathers clump together that way.

Annah knew there had been other pieces of furniture in this room. Where had it gone? There was one piece in particular that Annah cared about. She looked for the old rocking chair that her fingers had found so appealing. But it was gone. All that was left of either of the two chairs was a collection of kindling scattered across the floor in front of the windows. But why? Destroying the chairs served no purpose. What had driven this creature to destroy the room's furnishings? Or who, Annah amended.

The flickering light grew brighter as Annah stared at the destruction. The flicker became more rhythmic as the light seemed to dance across the floor. The reddish color became more pronounced, reminding Annah of the color of blood. Annah turned to the right, looking into that strange glow.

The source of the light was clearly visible. Four torches floated in the air at the far end of the room, each crowned by a tear-drop shaped red flame. The torches formed a rough circle that rotated slowly. That sight should have captured her attention, but it did not. It was what hung in the center of that circle that made Annah's own blood turn to ice. A man hung there, suspended from chains that reached up to the ceiling. The torches danced around him, their light seeming to flicker as each passed behind his large body.

Annah's head shook from side to side in denial. The bitter taste of bile returned. She fought to keep her stomach from heaving. In the end, she had to look away. Nothing she had suffered in the slave pens had been this bad. Did the man, or ogre if this was Shorty, still live? The destruction of the room had been bad enough, but to do such things to a person was beyond evil. But, apparently, it was not beyond Hell.

A wet cough told her that the poor soul hanging before her still lived. She forced her eyes back to him. But it was still hard to look at him. Her eyes went to the chains, tracing them to the ceiling where large hooks anchored them to a support beam. Curiosity pulled her eyes back down the chains to where similar metal hooks had been driven through the man's shoulders. The pain of hanging like that was beyond her comprehension.

Those hooks, Annah noted, were only the beginning of what this man had endured. She could see numerous burn marks all across the man's upper body. In places, flesh had been carved from his chest, exposing the white of his ribs. Again, she gagged as bitterness flooded her mouth.

Looking up at the man's face, Annah was surprised to note that it had suffered little damage during his torture. There were dark bruises around his eyes, but little else had been done to mar his broad and simple features. Two large incisors protruded above his lower lip. Tusks like those she had seen on the image of the ogre. She could no longer deny that this was Shorty. He looked just like his father. If only her first look at him could have been different. She did not want to remember him broken like this.

Annah closed her eyes. It was so difficult to see him this way. The aura of the Green Knight shone brightly without the distraction of sight. Familiar greens and blues ran through his aura. She could see scars that had not been there before, but it was clear that his spirit had not been broken. Knowing that gave her hope that they might still win free of this place.

Her eyes open and she began to examine his injuries. She wanted to help, but she knew so little about healing. She looked down to see what had been done to his legs and feet.

Shorty wore little more than the tatters of leather pants. The pant legs had been cut off well above the knees exposing long muscular legs. More burn marks covered his legs and the soles of his feet.

Torture marked him everywhere except for one area on his left thigh. That spot was the site of a massive scar. The flesh there was red and puckered still. The wound did not seem that old. It was a miracle that Shorty had not lost that leg. There were other scars scattered across his body, but this was by far the worst. Her hand reached out to touch him.

She jumped when a dry, pain-filled whisper broke the silence of the room, "Youse… no posed… ta bees dis place." He paused then, sucking in a labored breath, and then he resumed with more strength in his voice, "Try so muches ta protects youse. Now youse dead too. In me head like all da udder ghost. Me fail gin."

His words tore at her heart. Through her tears, she managed to speak, "I did not die, Shorty. You did not fail me. You saved me both times. In the Grove and from the slave market. You protected me despite my own foolish choices."

"Den hows come youse bees in me head? Me ken no keeps youse safe from Avar Ice in dis place. No bees strong nuf."

Annah reached for him again, but stopped. She wanted to touch him, but there was no place that she would not hurt him more. He had suffered enough. "I came for you, Shorty. Someone had to save you this time."

Both of his swollen eyes shot open. "No! Neber! Peoples dat helps me all da times gets dead. No mo friend die fer me. Hurts too muches ifn Ann Ah gets kilt. Better me stay dis place fer ebers."

Annah stared up at the mangled body above her. She could not help herself. She placed her hand on the only spot she thought was safe, the puckered scar on his left thigh. She sensed the powerful spells that had been used to heal the wound. That magic had not been enough. "Shorty, if we do not find a way, this thing will kill you. Your friends still need you."

Shorty began to chuckle, but it quickly turned to a wracking cough that seemed like it would never end. Annah wondered if he would die from simply laughing. Then a thin, wheezing voice continued, "No bees dat lucky. Avar Ice ken no kills me till me lets him out a me head. Ifn me die, him die too. Makes him bery mad me do. One day, me makes him mad nuf dat maybeso him make mistake. Sum day him gonna kills me and den dis game bees done."

Shorty's words were more confusing now than normal. He had turned this into some kind of a game. But the rules of his game had a fatal flaw. "This creature you have trapped in your head, this Avar, he must realize that you will grow weak and die if you stay locked in here. Your body needs food and water. You cannot survive without them."

Shorty slowly shook his head. "It hab muches magics. Bad magic make me lib fer eber an eber an eber. Only way ta stop bees ifn him kilt me in dis place."

She finally understood that he had planned to die all along. He was doing everything he could to drive his prisoner into a rage. He wanted this Avar to hurt him. The destruction in the room and in the hall finally made sense. "You are angering him on purpose. You want him to kill you. You planned to die from the beginning!"

Shorty's lips peeled back in a fierce grin. "Me figger all out. Tink bery hard bouts what me gots ta do. Avar caught in me trap. Now him no ken hurts peoples me lub. Bestus plan eber eben fer ogre. An when me dead, da whole world bees safe." Then he turned accusing eyes on her. "Den youse messes up me plan. Youse come in me head. Now no ken protect youse no mo."

Annah reached up and stabbed a finger into his chest. Anger overcame the guilt as he winced in pain. "Did you ask your friends before you tried this stupid plan? Did you ask me? Did you ever take the time to think that maybe we did not want you to sacrifice yourself. Maybe we wanted to be a part of that fight. Maybe we did not want to lose you."

Shorty closed his eyes and allowed his chin to sink to his chest. "Me knowed all friend bees mad me. One gets kilt betterer den all bees dead. Some bodies gots ta lib so ken fights ebil da next time. All da time bees mo ebil. Dis way jus me gets dead. Den da debil gone fer eber. Bees good trade."

Annah's anger faded at his response. "You are a stubborn man Green Knight." Shorty simply nodded. Annah chose her next words very carefully, "Maybe the world needs you, too, Shorty. Maybe having you beside us is more important than destroying this Avar Ice. You should have asked us first."

Shorty's solemn gaze met hers. "Knowed what friends say. Telled Shorty no. Me no so bery portent. Just bees da ogre. Like youse Mama, muches people jus tinks me da monster. Maybe so gonna eats dem."

Annah clenched her fists. "My mother was wrong about you. You cannot let her words…"

Shorty's raspy voice interrupted her, "No jus bees her. Many say dat bout me."

She wanted to tell him he was wrong. People were not that bad. But were her views any different from his? She did not trust people either. She believed everyone wanted to control her magic. At least she had believed that until she met Shorty's friends. Before she could find the words to make him believe in himself, the sound of laughter echoed down the hall. Something in that laughter made Annah shiver. The thing that made her afraid was growing closer.

A mocking voice came from the hallway outside the room, "Well, well. This is an interesting turn of events is it not my Green Knight? Someone has penetrated your prison. Is your visitor a friend? I wonder if hurting her will open your mind."

Annah turned to see a golden-skinned man entering the room.

Shorty's voice gained some of its old strength. The warrior she had met in the Grove was still here. The protector still lived in him. "No ken hab her!"

Annah felt a force of will and magic latch onto her. The force lifted her from the floor and threw her into blackness. Annah felt like an autumn leaf tumbling in a strong wind. She had no control, no ability to slow her flight. She could do nothing but ride out this new storm.

Chapter 15

Tales from the Passed

The space she tumbled through was an empty void. The void was worse than being blind because there really was nothing out there. Would she spend eternity here? Alone? The very idea of such a future was more than she could bear. Annah's forlorn cry just disappeared into that vast darkness.

Suddenly, unexpectedly, she was no longer alone. A familiar melody called to her through that emptiness. The song of the One Tree swelled until it filled the void. The music wrapped her in its arms and held her close. Her tumbling stopped. Individual notes collided with her, changing the direction of her travel, bit by bit. Far ahead, light blossomed and Annah sped towards it.

The song stayed with her, consoling her, its many harmonies keeping her company. Her headlong dash through the nothingness slowed as light consumed the darkness. The light warmed her skin and chased the fear from her mind. Within the light, far below, Annah saw trees; the green and white ribbon of The Path wound its way through those trees in an endless loop.

She began to descend, drifting along above The Path. The ground came closer and closer as the song faded away. Then her companion was gone. Annah found herself sitting on soft grass. The familiar green and white stones were just out of reach. The Path curved away to her left and right. She could not tell if this was where she had started or if she was somewhere new along the familiar road. The trees growing on each side of the Path all looked the same.

It felt good to have solid ground beneath her once more. Her trip through the void had unsettled her, but not as much as her time in that other version of Stormhold. Everything about the prison Shorty had created bothered her. She could not decide what disturbed her more: the sense of impending doom within the Keep, the vile things that had been done to Shorty, or her friend's desperate desire to die with Hell's emissary locked in his mind. She had no idea how to fix any of this.

Annah stared at the green stone just beyond her booted feet. The answers she needed lay somewhere along that path. She just had to find them. Annah rose and stepped onto the Path. Did it matter which direction she went? She suspected not. The Path seemed intent on showing her things she needed to know. Annah turned left and began to walk. As she walked, she tried to organize her thoughts. There was so much that she needed to know to save Shorty.

It would not be easy to get Shorty to abandon his plan. She was not sure how to convince him not to throw away his life. He was almost fanatical in his need to protect those he cared about. She could only hope that those who had fostered that sense of duty in him had a better idea than she did. If not, her mission might be hopeless.

Annah wondered if all parents indoctrinated their children this way? Her own mother had drilled it into Annah that her gifts made her special. Her magic would be important someday. Were Shorty's lessons on protecting any different? Was his guilt over the death of his friends any different from her guilt at not being able to save Papa? Annah had only failed once. Shorty had lost many friends. How could she expect him to see things differently when she still clung to her own childhood guilt? And why, she asked herself, did the important things in life always have to be so hard?

Annah looked up to see another of the open areas before her. A tree shrine sat in its center. She could just make out the back of a robed figure standing in the center of a cedar tree. Was this another mage? As she got closer, Annah noticed the large hood resting on the man's back. Not robes, but a cowl. She walked around the front of the image. Staring out at her from the heart of the tree was the image of a man. He was clearly human, clean shaven, and with almost no wrinkles on his face. But the wisdom in those eyes told her the man was much older than he looked. The man's right hand clutched a staff that was taller than he was. Something about that staff called to Annah. She stepped forward and ran her fingers down its length. The grain was all wrong for a cedar tree. The staff was made of oak and yet it grew within the heart of a cedar. How strange, she thought.

The staff was unusual in other ways too. Carved along its length were dozens of intricate images. Annah's fingers explored each shape in turn. She recognized each as she touched it, almost as if the staff spoke to her like Shorty's sword did, *Bear, weasel, owl, otter, raven, turtle, wolf, hawk,* and many other names slid into her thoughts. Annah understood then that this man had been a druid. Had he followed Mielikki as she did? As Shorty did? And would she meet him here along the Path? Once again, a voice interrupted her examination of a shrine. Annah froze when a melodious male voice came from behind her. She should have expected someone would show up, but she had been too absorbed in her examination of the staff. Annah turned to see who was behind her.

A tall elf stood there in simple leathers. He gestured towards the image. "His name was Caelum. He was the High Druid of the Valley Region. The council sent him there in punishment. They were fools. Caelum's love for the land around Long Lake transformed the Council's punishment into a blessing."

She liked the elf almost immediately. His blunt assessment of what she assumed was his friend spoke well of the man. The long sword at his belt and the bow that rose over his right shoulder told her that he was a warrior. Around his neck was an intricate medallion depicting a black unicorn with a golden horn. Not just a warrior she amended, a ranger.

The elf smiled at her. "Welcome Ann Ah. I am Sademäärä dit Metsän-Koti. Many humans struggle with elvish names. If you wish, you may call me Rainfall. It is what my friends call me."

She curtsied. "Thank you, Rainfall. My name is pronounced Annah except, of course, by Shorty."

The elf's smile grew even wider. "The common tongue never was his strong point. Perhaps I should have spent more time helping him to master the words, but that would have interfered with his sword practice. Shorty had so much raw talent when Caelum brought him to me. I became a bit obsessed with teaching him the discipline he needed to become a true master of the blade. And now he is a ranger too. I could not be more proud of him. His love of the forest puts most elves to shame."

Questions flooded Annah's mind. Again, she blurted out the first thing that popped into her head. "How did you know Shorty? And why did the elves want to punish your friend Caelum?" Then she blushed at her own rudeness.

"It is alright child. We have time for all of your questions. In my foster son's mind, time has little meaning. I believe our own thoughts run much faster than his do."

Annah perked up at his words. "Foster son?" she asked.

Rainfall nodded and moved to a patch of grass near the edge of the stones. He sat and gestured for Annah to join him. After she sat, he continued, "Shorty escaped from the tunnels of his tribe around the time his real parents died. The Goddess sent Caelum into the mountains where he found something surprising, an ogre boy who lived among a scurry of squirrels."

At Annah's broad grin, Rainfall laughed, "So, he has introduced you to his friends. Well, Caelum brought the boy back to the Valley and his Grove. I lived nearby on the edge of Long Lake. Caelum saw great potential in the young ogre. I think he saw the ranger that Shorty would become. It took me much longer to see what Caelum did." The elven ranger paused, lost in thought. His voice seemed distant as he continued, "Caelum brought Shorty to meet me. Shorty loved the sword and in that we were very well suited to each other. The boy came to live with me and I trained him. In time, he became a son like the one I had lost years before."

The elf sat in silence for a time lost in his own memories. Annah was not sure if she should mention F'lar so she asked again, "Why was Caelum punished? Because of Shorty?"

Rainfall shook his head. "No, that was my son, F'lar's doing. F'lar's mother, my estranged wife, is a powerful magus. She trained F'lar to follow in her footsteps. But my son also showed great potential as a druid. Caelum filled his head with druidic dreams in defiance of my wife's wishes."

Annah looked puzzled. "What is wrong with being a druid too?"

"Elves believe that Arcane magic would corrupt the powers of the Goddess. Being mage and druid is forbidden."

Annah frowned. "That is foolish. Mielikki does not care."

Rainfall chuckled. "Spoken like a human. Caelum said something similar. So, when Caelum initiated F'lar knowing he had already become a mage, he violated Elven law. He had to be censored for it. Then, several days later, F'lar apparently cast a spell that mixed the two magics. Both the Elven and Druidic Councils declared my son a heretic. Caelum and I were sent south to the human lands. Exile was to be our punishment."

Annah grinned at Rainfall. "F'lar does not seem overly concerned about their verdict."

Rainfall seemed amused by her observation, "So, you have met my other son too? My wife also tried to force F'lar to reject his chosen path. She was quite surprised to learn that she was no match for his Goddess. The Druid Council sent several teams after F'lar as well. Apparently, the Goddess stripped them of magic and he made fools of them. Now the elves mostly pretend that F'lar does not exist."

Annah snorted in amusement, "Both of your sons are quite good at getting into trouble. They are also incredibly stubborn and like to stick their noses into everything."

Rainfall laughed heartily. "I have no idea where they might have learned that. I imagine it is all Caelum's fault."

Annah shook her head at the elf's words. She liked Rainfall. She saw many similarities between him and Shorty. Her friend had been blessed with three good parents. Each had pushed Shorty hard, maybe too hard. But each had loved him and cared for him.

She pointed to the image in the tree. "How did he die? And why does Shorty blame himself?"

Rainfall grew suddenly serious. "Caelum and I both died the same way. Minions of the god Set had infiltrated our world. I had gone west into the mountains to verify rumors of a dragon. They were not rumors. I found the ancient black outside its lair. It was not alone. It was working with a powerful necromancer. I tried to get back to the Grove to warn Caelum. I did not make it."

Annah could feel the Elf's pain at that last announcement. "And your friend?"

Rainfall stared up into the eyes of the figure growing in the tree. "They attacked the Grove that night. I do not know who killed Caelum in the end. It might have been the necromancer, or the dragon, or the vampire they had with them. He died with only a few squirrels at his side."

Annah looked around. "Is he here along the Path somewhere? I would like to meet him."

Rainfall shook his head. "No, the necromancer tried to turn him into an undead. Caelum sent his spirit into his land to hide it. The necromancer was very angry about that."

Annah pointed towards the sword on Rainfall's belt. "You both died in battle as did all of the others here."

Rainfall nodded, "Only because we were not together. If we could have joined forces, I think we would have beaten them."

"And what of Shorty's guilt? What could he have done to prevent your deaths?" Annah asked.

Rainfall frowned. "Nothing. Caelum had sent Shorty on a scouting mission over a year before. That boy helped defeat an orc invasion led by another of Set's minions. Shorty killed that damn Troll-Orc abomination in personal combat. Then he helped bring down one of the ancient black's offspring. He could not have saved us even if he had been there. He was not ready yet."

It was that last word that caught Annah's attention, "Yet?"

The elf looked proud. "Shorty and his friends killed the necromancer and avenged mine and Caelum's death. He also helped to kill the ancient black. But that is not my story to tell."

Annah sat quietly for a long time. "Shorty has lost so many people he loves. I do not know how to help him get past that. He truly believes that he needs to make this Avar Ice kill him to save the people he loves."

Annah looked up in surprise as Rainfall's fist slammed into the grass. "Damned stupid plan. I taught that boy to fight, not to die."

Annah's mouth opened in protest, but Rainfall shook his head. "My apologies. Ruler of one of the Nine Hells or not, that boy can beat this thing. He just needs to decide to fight. That is how he will save his friends. He is so much more than he knows."

Annah looked up. "Say that again please? Ruler of one of the Nine Hells?"

Rainfall gave her a patient look and asked, "Is it Ann Ah?" When she shook her head, he continued, "Then who is Avar Ice?"

Annah turned the name over in her mind. She sounded it out, "Avar-ice? Avarice as in greed? That is what he trapped inside himself?"

Rainfall reached over and took her hand. "Yes, Annah. And that is where Set made his big mistake. There is only one thing Shorty has ever been greedy about. Friendship. This Lord of Hell has nothing to tempt Shorty with. He will not give up his honor to this thing. He can defeat this foe. He just needs a good enough reason to fight. Something or someone worth fighting for. Can you be that person, Annah? Will you?"

Annah blanched. "He hardly knows me. Why not one of you? Someone from a shrine. All of you are more important to Shorty than I am."

Rainfall squeezed her fingers gently. "You are the only one who can go to him Annah. We are all bound to our little memorials. You are different because you still live."

Annah sat there thoughtfully. "And your memorial? I assume it is nearby."

A sour look crossed the elf's face. "I would prefer you not see it. I find it a bit pretentious. I was never that impressive as a warrior. I do not know where he got that glorified image of me."

Annah understood his dislike of the shrines, but she had no choice but to visit hers again. "Then can you lead me to my own memorial? " she asked, "I believe it is time to speak with our Green Knight again. I am not sure where my image came from either, but it is my doorway back to him."

Rainfall rose and offered her his arm. "It would be my honor, Annah. And thank you."

She placed her hand in the crook of his arm and he led her into the trees. They walked in silence most of the way there. At the edge of her clearing, he paused. He turned to her and took her hand. "My son cares deeply about you. That may be the only way to reach him. But you must be careful. You have more ability to hurt him than that demon does."

Annah shook her head. "What can I do that compares to what that demon is doing to him?"

Rainfall pointed to her chest. "My son's greatest weakness is his heart. That is the only pain he fears. Avarice can only hurt his body. You can do much more."

Annah stared into the elf's eyes and then nodded her understanding. Then she turned and walked to her image in the tree. "I will do what I can Rainfall. But I am not sure I know enough to protect either of us. I also have much to learn."

The elf stepped back into the trees. "Maybe you can learn together Ann Ah. He has learned to listen to his heart. Have you?"

The elf disappeared as silently as he had come. Annah stared at the image of herself. It was more complete now than it had been. The green gown she now wore was visible on her upper body. Around her neck was a chain with a small sword hanging from it. She had forgotten Tainkintana. She needed to keep her promise to the sword. It needed to go around Shorty's neck.

Annah reached towards the image. She started to touch the birthmark again, but at the last instant, she touched the tiny sword instead.

Chapter 16

Painful Truths

Annah found herself once more staring out the window into heavy rain. Lightning still stuck at the walls, but the fervor of its attack seemed to be ebbing away. The walls of the Keep still stood as if they were impervious to the storm's destructive force. If those walls were any indication, ogres were a very stubborn race.

Annah turned from the window and moved to the bed. The quilt was still folded where she had left it. She sat and wrapped its softness around her. She needed its comfort as she prepared to visit Shorty again.

This quest had become much more than simply finding Shorty and convincing him to take her back to the world outside his mind. They could not just run away and set a Prince of Hell loose upon the land. Especially not one as angry as Avarice was. Rainfall had made it clear that somehow, they had to defeat this demon. Annah could not see any way to win this conflict. Neither she nor Shorty were that powerful. But the only other choice was to spend the rest of her life locked in Shorty's mind.

Shorty's friends had all questioned his decision to fight this thing alone. Annah was beginning to think they were wrong. Maybe Shorty's powerful friends could have defeated Avarice, but what would that battle have done to a land already ravaged by war? That kind of magic and destructive force could not be contained within the walls of Stormhold. Many innocent people would have died along the edges of that battle. Shorty's plan might have seemed crazy, but it had saved many lives.

The question was, what to do next? Rainfall and Hunter both believed Shorty needed to fight Avarice. Could he actually defeat a Prince of Hell? Annah did not know what gifts Mielikki granted her Knight, but she did not think Shorty wielded that kind of power. If she was right, what would it take for Shorty to win? Rainfall believed that Shorty just needed something or someone to fight for. But who or what? He was already fighting for all of the people of Stormhold. Despite Rainfall's conviction, Annah did not believe she was the key to Shorty's victory.

Annah rose from the bed. She carefully folded the quilt and returned it to the foot of the bed. It was time to talk to Shorty again. She needed more information about the demon and he was the only one who had spoken to their enemy.

Annah walked to the door. She paused to listen. There was still nothing to hear except the storm outside. This time, the door latch did not resist her efforts to lift it. The door swung open and Annah stepped into the hallway. It was not as dark this time. She could see up and down the hallway. Deep gouges, claw marks, marred both walls, but none of the doors along the hallway had even been scratched. She suspected Shorty protected his friend's rooms as fiercely as he protected the people in his life.

Closing the door behind her, she turned to examine the entrance to Shorty's room. The damaged doorframe still loomed open. Annah moved cautiously forward. From what she could see from the doorway, this end of the room was unchanged, except that the door no longer leaned against the window ledge. The missing door bothered her. What possible use could the demon have for a broken door?

Annah took a deep breath of the stale air to prepare herself. Then she stepped into the room and turned to see how Shorty had fared during Avarice's last visit.

The four torches still floated in the air, but the chains were gone as if they had never been. The area between the torches now held a large table without any legs. Like the torches, the table seemed to float above the floor. Something lay motionless on top of that table. It had to be Shorty.

She began to walk towards him. She cringed at the thought of what had been done to him since her last visit. The fact that Stormhold was still here meant that he had not managed to get himself killed yet. But what had he endured while she was with Rainfall? Her eyes sought the answer to that question as she walked toward him. Halfway to the table, she stopped. The scene before her was bad, really bad!

Shorty did not just lie on top of the table; he was pinned there. The hooks that had kept the chains in the ceiling had been driven through Shorty's wrists and ankles and into the thick wood of the table. There was no way for him to free himself short of ripping off a hand or foot. And those hooks were just the start of what had been done to him in her absence. Hammers, knives, and other metal tools lay scattered on the edges of the table. Their purpose was made clear by the marks that crisscrossed every exposed inch of Shorty's body.

Her mind refused to acknowledge the things that had been done to him. Her eyes dropped to the edge of the table. A part of her mind fixated on the broken hinge on the long edge of the table. Her gaze followed the table edge to the place where the other hinge had once been. It was easier to think about hinges than it was to contemplate what had happened on that makeshift table. Apparently, Avarice had found a use for the door after all.

Annah managed to not jump when a pain filled voice whispered from the far end of the table, "Youse no shoulda comes back."

Annah could not look up at him, but his voice drew her closer. She took a reluctant step and then another. One bruised elbow lay just above the twisted upper hinge. There was a deep cut right over the spot where she imagined the muscles of his upper arm connected to bone.

Annah watched in fascination as the wound stopped bleeding and scabbed over. How could it heal that quickly? In the span of a few breaths, the scab dried up and flaked away. Pink flesh marked the place where the cut had been. Another breath and the pink faded leaving a thin white scar. The scar quickly darkened until it matched the brown of Shorty's normal skin color. It was as if the wound had never been there.

Her eyes rose to meet Shorty's as she asked in confusion, "Your wounds are healing. How?"

This time it was Shorty who looked away. "Me telled youse afore. Debil hab muches bad magics. It burn in me. Hurt muches ta makes ouches bees gone. Den him gets ta hurts me muches mo time."

Annah snapped at Shorty without really meaning to, "Then why to you just let him hurt you this way? Why not fight him?"

He shook his head as he lay upon the bloody door. "Do dat manys time. Fighted bery hard when me send youse way. No do no good. Avar mo strong den me. Him laugh muches when him beats me. Try ober an ober. Not knowed how ta beats dat one."

Annah felt guilty. He had tried. Maybe Hunter and Rainfall were wrong. Maybe Shorty could not beat their enemy. "I am sorry, Shorty."

She watched as he turned his bruised face back toward her. As his eyes came up to meet hers, he tried to reassure her, "No bees Ann Ah fault. Me knowed it gonna bees bad afore me bring him in me head."

He may have understood what was coming, but Annah certainly had not. She just wanted someone to explain why so many bad things were happening to her. The questions she wanted to ask exploded out of her as demands, "Shorty, Avarice did not come here on a whim. He came here for the two of us! Why does a ruler of one of the Nine Hells care about us? There has to be a reason. What did either of us ever do to deserve this?"

Shorty's eyes lit up then. Whith what? Pride? Yes, the satisfaction in his voice told her just how proud he was of the things he had done. He did not boast exactly, but his words made it clear he would do it all again if asked. "Me do many tings ta makes da bad tings mad. Bees what me do bestus a all. Sum bodies gots ta telled ebil no. Dis time me telled dem no ken hab youse. Takes youse from dem in da Bazaar. Dey no likes dat bery muches."

Annah's heart lurched. He had given her an opening. Even though it had nothing to do with her mission, Annah had to ask, "Why, Shorty? Why did you risk going to that terrible place to save a girl you hardly knew?"

His lips actually twitched with the beginnings of a smile. His words were slow and patient, like those one used with a child who misunderstands something simple, as he explained, "Youse bees me friend. Dat bees bery special. Ann Ah neber sees da ogre when looks me. Only sees Shorty. No got many friend like dat."

Annah found it hard to breathe suddenly. His answer was so… Shorty. His words made her want to scream, and, they made her want to grin like a fool. She would be damned, though, if she would let him see her smile like that. To him, the world revolved around friendship. She was just beginning to understand how valuable his friendship really was. This was why so many people were willing to fight to save him. Annah wanted that friendship for herself, but she knew it was all based on a lie. How could she tell him that before today she had not even known what an ogre looked like? All she had ever seen was his beautiful aura, and she had not even trusted that. She was not the person he thought she was, but she would be a better friend in the future.

 She knew that there were too many things that she needed to say to him, but this was not the time or the place to discuss the past or the future. The words she needed to say were just too complicated. In the end, the words she found were far too simple. They were so much less than he deserved. The only words she could find the air too speak were, "I was blind, silly."

He slowly shook his head. Even now, his words were far too kind, No bees silly. Jus bees no bery smart." His voice held a note of wonder as he murmured, "Youse neber bees fraid a me. Eben Kisa fraid first time her see me. Youse bery good friend."

Annah's thoughts turned inward as she struggled with her own emotions. With an effort of will, Annah set her feelings aside. The only thing that mattered now was keeping them both alive. And to do that, there was more that she needed to know. It was time to ask the only person who seemed to know what was going on, "Help me to understand all of this, Shorty? Please?"

He nodded and Annah asked, "How did you know that Sanctuary was going to be attacked? You came there to protect us. Someone had to warn you. Who?"

Shorty's voice became very animated as he began to tell her about a squirrel riding on a unicorn's head. He rambled on, obviously excited, but his tale made no sense and it definitely was not answering her question. Knowing they did not have much time, she interrupted him to ask, "The squirrel and unicorn wanted you to protect me?"

He shook his head. "No, dem jus comes ta tells me whats ta do. Goddess want me ta protects youse. Lady gib me many job. Dis time her send me ta sabe youse. Green Knight serbe da Lady."

Somehow, Mielikki had known of the attack before it happened. The Goddess had sent Shorty to Sanctuary. But why? She could not imagine any reason for the Goddess to send her champion to defend Annah's family. It could not be her birthmark. Her magic was just too weak to be useful to anyone. Maybe Shorty's mission had to have been to save the Grove not save her. Except the half-orc had come just for her. Annah sighed and tried a different question, "Shorty, who were those men that attacked my home?"

Shorty's lips thinned and those two strange teeth became more prominent. His expression was one that Annah had never seen on his face. It took her a moment to recognize it, hatred. Shorty's words were almost unrecognizable through his snarls, "Dem bees people dat serbe da Bad Cloud. Avar maybeso serve him too."

Annah knew she was missing something important. Shorty was not trying to be vague. "Shorty, who or what is this Bad Cloud?"

"Bad Cloud bees da god name Set. Him no bees bery nice. Me fighted him fer bery long time. Him no like me muches."

Annah's thoughts shot off in a million directions. Set, or Seth as the Treants called him, had come looking for her before. When she was younger, a priest of Set had offered an incredible sum for her capture. Even the half-orc that had been promised a reward from Set. Why was the god Set so interested in her? What was so important about a farm girl named Annah Treemain? Neither Set no Mielikki's actions made any sense.

Then, the rest of Shorty's words sank in. "You have been fighting a god, Shorty?"

Shorty sucked in reply. His breath hissed out as his arms pulled against the hooks that pinned him to the table. Annah could not imagine the pain that simple movement had caused him. It took Shorty a long time before he could answer her, "Only fighted Set one time. Udder times bees dem dat do what him say. Bees muches a dem. Me fighted Orc Chief, dragon, troll king, an da peoples dat hurts Arcturus. Me fighted dem all. Firstus helps Kisa Lady. Den helps Dualis."

Annah shook her head. Was this what Tainkintana had meant when the sword told her Shorty had seen much evil in his life? And why did Set keep sending his followers to do things he could do himself? It made no sense to her, so she asked Shorty.

Shorty's brows came together in what looked like a thoughtful expression. He seemed less sure of himself this time, "Gods no posed to fights wid peoples. Dualis sat dat bees rule. God no eben posed ta fights udder god. Posed ta use sumtin call 'Min Yon.' Dat mean gets udders ta fights fer dem. Set gots many peoples. Forest Lady only gots Green Knight. Bees kay me kills many Set 'Min Yon. Bees funny dat eben gods gots rule. Me glad dem do. Set no fight bery nice."

The whole idea of battling gods and their minions was hard to believe. Who did things like that? But was the idea any crazier than being trapped in someone else's mind with a Prince of Hell? "What does Set want Shorty?" Annah asked.

Shorty did not hesitate, "Him want all. Ebry ting. Bees da boss a dis world an all udder. Him no portent now. Ifn take all den him bees bery muches strong god."

Annah considered all that the Treants had taught her about the Balance. Shorty's explanation seemed to fit with what she knew. Set wanted power. Mielikki opposed Set. Her Goddess was not alone in that effort. Apparently, being a god did not mean you understood the need for Balance. All that aside, there was one piece of this that did not make any sense. "Shorty, if the great ones are not allowed to act against us, how was Avarice able to come here?"

Shorty mumbled something that sounded suspiciously like 'oopses.' Really? Oopses? What had Shorty done? This time, Annah was quite stern when she asked, "What was that, Shorty? I did not understand you."

There was a long pause before he answered her. Whan that answer came, Annah swore he sounded embarrassed, "Bees me fault. When ebil ting at market say dem gonna hurts all me friend, me no likes dat. Me bees no berry smart dat day. Gets muches mad. Maybeso me telled Set ta comes gets me." His voice trailed away then. Annah was about to press him for more when he continued, "Avar Ice bees bery strong, but him no bees a god. Set ken sends him fer me. Maybeso sends him ta teached me ta no open me mouth so muches."

Annah stood there stunned. Not even Shorty was that… What? Stupid? Brave? Self-sacrificing? In the end, he was exactly what those along The Path had made of him. He would challenge Hell itself to protect his friends. And, that also meant he would sacrifice himself to protect her. This situation had been inevitable from the moment she had been captured. Had Mielikki known that when she sent Shorty to Sanctuary? If so, it was a frightening thought.

Annah now understood so much more than she had, but she still had no idea how help Shorty. There was something she could do though. She had made a promise and it was time for her to keep it.

Annah made her way around the table until she stood above Shorty's head. She lifted the chain with the tiny sword from around her neck. She winced when a couple hairs came away with the chain. Gently lifting Shorty's head, she slid the chain around his neck and settled the sword on his injured chest. Once there, the sword and chain faded from sight.

Shorty smiled then. Annah heard him whisper, "Hullo, sword. Youse find way ta sneaks in ta me head too. No bery smart. But me glad youse bees wid me."

Annah heard Tainkintana's response as well, *I missed you too, my friend. I will be ready when you need me, Green Knight. We will stand together in this battle.*

Shorty grew silent. The look of resignation on his face bothered Annah. She surprised herself when she leaned over the broken door and kissed Shorty on his forehead.

Confusion replaced the look of defeat on his face. His hands twitched as if he wanted to touch the place she had kissed. He gave her a puzzled look and asked, "Youse bites me?" He smiled then, the first real smile she seen on his face since she had come into his mind. "Bery nice bite. Tickle. No hurted."

That was not the response she had expected. Annah found herself laughing. "No Shorty. That was not a bite. It is called a kiss." Annah watched his lips form the new word several times.

Then a cultured voice called out from the doorway, "So touching, really." Annah looked up to see a tall, golden-skinned man blocking the way out of the room. Fear shot through Annah at the eager look on the man's face. Her reaction must have shown because the golden man began to laugh. As that ominous sound washed over her, the hair on Annah's arm stood on end. The golden man's presence filled the room and he began to taunt her, "I am so glad that you returned, Chosen One. My Master will reward me when I bring him your soul."

A menacing growl rose from the table before her. That bestial rumble should have been even more terrifying than the sound of Avarice's laughter. Instead, it made her smile. Apparently, that was not the reaction the demon prince wanted because Avarice's face flushed with anger. Annah watched him open his mouth to speak, but his words were lost in the rush of power that filled the room. More gently this time, that power wrapped itself around her. Once again, darkness surrounded her as she was thrown from the room.

Chapter 17

Another Way

Shorty was so predictable. She was back in the void again. This time, Annah remained calm as she tumbled through emptiness. And this, she promised herself, was the last time she would be exiled here. She intended to learn what her friend was doing and how to prevent it. Shorty could not be allowed to make decisions for her. She would make her own choices and control her own destiny. She would never be the helpless blind girl ever again!

The first time she had been here, the One Tree had saved her. Could she save herself? There was only one way to find out. Annah began to hum the song of the One Tree. The melody came out flat. Her voice just did not have the range to get the song right. But, apparently, the void did not mind her limitations. Her efforts were rewarded by an end to the tumbling.

As the sensation of flipping head over heels came to an end, Annah found that she could think more clearly. That was as good a start as any. And, like planting a new garden, the task of countering Shorty's magic had to be tackled one step at a time. The first of those steps was to identify what kind of magic Shorty was using. But how? Could her own magic somehow interact with his? Using her own magic made sense, even if her magic was weaker than his.

Annah stretched her hand out into the nothingness that surrounded her. Neither her arm nor its birthmark were visible in the darkness. Annah called what little magic she had and sent that power into her birthmark. The hickory tree began to glow, lighting the darkness around her. Its leaves began to flutter as if stirred by a breeze she could not feel. The hickory came alive as it never had before. Annah marveled at its beauty. Was this something new or just one more thing blindness had kept her from seeing? She might never know and now was not the time to think about such things. Leaning forward, Annah thrust her arm into the force that drove her through the void.

The magic she sought was not there. Her birthmark continued to glow and the leaves of the Hickory never changed the pattern of their movement. If Shorty had used a spell, she could not detect it. She sensed no magic except her own. There was no trace of Mielikki's power or that of the Arcane. Whatever Shorty had done, it was not born of magic. That unexpected answer left Annah exactly nowhere.

Annah pulled back her arm and studied her birthmark. The magic that was her gift from the goddess Mielikki was unphased by whatever force Shorty had used. Annah was confused. I What secret lay buried in that music? More importantly, how could she use the song to control her own destiny?

She reached for the song again. This time she did not hum the song, she simply let it play in her thoughts. Memory provided a more accurate rendition of the song, but it was still incomplete. As the song filled her mind, Annah felt her thoughts begin to unravel. Sweat beaded on her forehead as she struggled to embrace the music. The song began to falter. In desperation, she sent the song into her birthmark. Again, nothing happened. The glow of her birthmark did not change. If anything, the leaves of the hickory stilled. The song began to fade from her thoughts.

Before the song disappeared completely, Annah felt a presence merge with her thoughts. The One Tree began to sing along with her. She no longer had to bear the burden of singing alone. She realized the song was not meant to be sung that way. The Tree was trying to help her, trying to teach her something important. But what?

Her worries faded and she felt herself grow calm as the song grew within her. The song was not a thing of magic she realized. It was really not a thing of the mind, either. The song surged again as if to encourage her. As a sense of utter peace consumed her, Annah finally understood the truth. She opened her heart and allowed the song inside. The song was about faith and belief. It was a thing of the heart. She felt love and acceptance flow from the tree at her understanding. Then the Tree was gone, but she was not alone, the song now sang within her.

Annah closed her eyes and opened herself to the force that pushed her along. She did not probe it or think about it. She simply felt. Emotions flooded her as the power of that force washed through her. Strong emotions. The intensity of what Shorty felt was frightening. Her heart raced as fear overwhelmed her. Then she realized that the fear she was feeling was not her own. Now she understood the source of her friend's power.

Shorty was afraid. That surprised her until she examined his fear more closely. He was not afraid for himself; he was afraid for her. Fear was not the simple thing that she had always thought it to be. His fear was complicated and it turned on itself at times. Then she realized that he had more than one fear that rode him. His fear that Avarice would harm her or take her was obvious. Hidden beneath the first fear was his greatest fear of all. Shorty was terrified that he might be the one to hurt her, or worse yet, cause her death. Once again, Annah tumbled in the void as the two fears fought for dominance.

Annah smiled as understanding came. The song of the One Tree had not countered Shorty's magic. It had merely calmed his fears enough to release her from their grip. She had found some of the answers she needed, but there was still one question left to find an answer to and it was the hardest question of all. If she was lucky, that answer lay somewhere in Shorty's past.

Annah let the One Tree's song swell in her heart. She shared the melody with Shorty's fears. Her passage through the void slowed as light blossomed around her. Annah sank into the warm glow and the light welcomed her back. The trees of an endless forest stretch from horizon to horizon. Within it, The Path patiently waited for her to return. Hope surged in her heart, carried ever higher by the notes of the song..

Annah's boots sank into tall grass as the last notes of the song drifted into silence. Annah did not mind the quiet moment; she knew the song would return if and when she needed it to. She would not face the future alone, the One Tree wanted this to end as much as she did.

Then, Annah stepped onto the Path, more confident than she had been since entering Shorty's mind. Green and white squares stretched before her and behind. She began to walk, not bothering to look back. The Path would take her where she needed to go no matter which direction she chose. It had not failed her yet. Green, white, and green again passed beneath her feet as the path led her through the trees. Was some part of Shorty's mined guiding her steps? Or was the One Tree helping her in this too? It did not really matter; both served the Balance. Annah just needed to have faith.

As she had known it would, the next open area soon came into view. Annah walked a little faster, curious who from Shorty's past she would meet this time. Annah's eyes sought out the tree that housed the shrine she knew would be there. It was not hard to pick out. The tree was massive, but it was a species that she did not recognize. Its trunk was wider than she was tall and its bark was a dark brown. As she got closer, Annah saw that the bark had a very rough texture, its crevices were deep enough to sink her fingertips into. The branches of the tree did not have leaves or even needles. What hung there looked like braided hair. Annah wondered what the tree was called.

The figure growing in the center of the tree was also huge. Whoever this was, he or she was even bigger that Hunter had been. Was this another ogre? She could not be sure. While Hunter and Shorty stood tall and proud, this person's back and shoulders were hunched over, curving away from her. Despite how the figure stood, it did not appear weak. Perhaps old? Annah moved quickly around the tree, wanting to see the memorial's face.

The opening for the tree was the largest yet. Four stones had been removed in each direction to provide space for the tree and its roots. And, unlike the other memorials she had seen, the ground around the base of this tree was wet and swampy. Annah was not even completely around the tree when a flash of light caused her to stop and stare. A long spear extended out from the front of the tree, the steel at its tip sparkled in the sunlight. Annah knew without seeing the figures face that this person was also a warrior.

Annah looked around, half expecting to see someone watching her. But there was no one there. She advanced slowly until she stood beside the shaft of the spear. Annah craned her neck up to stare into the figures face. It was another ogre, one whose face was marked by wrinkles and age lines. His tusks were clearly visible as he snarled at the enemy he faced. The ogre's nose was bent far to one side as if it had been badly broken at some point in its life. Then she looked into the eyes. They were deep and compelling. Once again, Annah sensed determination in that gaze. This warrior would slay his foe no matter what the cost. He was much like Shorty.

Annah's eyes traveled down the ogre's body, seeking to learn more of this warrior. Age and injuries might have curved its back, but it had not stolen the warriors strength or pride. He was muscular to the point of perfection, or he was until she saw his large bare feet. Annah shivered at what had been done to them. One foot ended abruptly well short of where the toes should have been. It was as if a giant cleaver had removed half of his foot in a single chop. The warriors other foot was even more disturbing. Not only was it missing the two smallest toes, the entire front of the foot was a flat as one of Mama's acorn pancakes. How could this warrior walk, let alone fight?

Annah found herself standing on the edge of the swampy ground, her arm outstretched. She felt compelled to reach out and touch those damaged feet. She knew it was little more than morbid fascination, but she could not help herself. Her left hand grasped the shaft of the spear as she leaned out, reaching with the fingers of her right hand. That, of course, was when the voice spoke from behind her. Her grip on the spear was the only thing that kept her from falling face-first into the murky water around the base of the tree.

"Bees careful, Little Warrior. Dem foots no bery purty ta looks at."

Annah recovered her balance and turned with as much dignity as she could muster. The old ogre stood there leaning heavily on the shaft of a spear that rose several feet above his head. The urge to look was irresistible and Annah's eyes darted down to examine his feet. The image on the tree was not nearly as disturbing as seeing those injuries on a living person. The old ogre chuckled. "No bees lookin betterer on me foot den in dat tree."

Annah blushed again. How did seeing people avoid staring at things they should not? She did not seem to be able to stop herself. "I am sorry. I did not mean to stare. I…" Annah's voice trailed off. She did not know what else she should say.

The old ogre's toothless smile spread across his face. Annah suspected that he liked teasing her. "Ebry bodies looks, Little Warrior. Looks den make sad face. Bees gooder fer me ifn dem lookin me foot an no sees me spear."

She swallowed hard at his bluntness. Annah lifted her chin to meet his gaze and asked, "Why do you keep calling me Little Warrior? I do not even know how to fight."

The old ogre laughed at her, "Fighted ta sabe youse Papa. Fighted fer youse home. Now comes ta fights fer da Boy. Maybeso youse no bery smart. Bery muches bees warrior."

Annah's eyes widened. She had never looked at things that way. Whether he was right or wrong, she liked the way he saw her. "Thank you. My name is Annah. May I ask what you are called?"

"All knowed da name Ann Ah. Bery portent name in dis place," he replied, "Me still gonna calls youse Little Warrior same as me call da Boy's Mama. Me bees," he paused then and lifted the butt end of the spear. He moved the heavy weapon until it hovered over the remaining toes on his left foot.

Annah's brow furrowed as she watched him. Then it came to her, ogre names were very literal. "You are called Three-Toes?" she asked.

He just nodded and grinned at her. Annah noticed that he had few teeth left other than the two large, somewhat yellowed tusks. His tone grew very serious then and he asked, "Youse gonna sabe me brudder's Boy?"

Annah's thoughts stumbled as the words sank in. There were so many pieces of Shorty's life to weave together. "You are Shorty's uncle? Uncle Three-Toe? That makes you Hunter's brother?"

The grin on the ogre's face grew even broader. "Little Warrior get mo smart. Figure out purty gooder. Maybeso figure out how ta beats dat debil too."

Annah had less faith in herself than Shorty's uncle seemed to have. Defeating Avarice seemed way beyond her. She understood gardens and growing things, not fighting evil. Annah doubted she could learn fast enough to keep any of them alive. So far, she felt like a babe learning to walk one step at a time. But if that was the best she could do, so be it. It was time for her next step. What did Shorty's uncle know that she needed to learn? Annah decided to ask her rudest question first, "How did you die, Uncle?"

Three-Toes seemed unphased by her question. He acted like getting killed was an everyday occurrence. The old ogre settled his spear into a comfortable position and leaned his weight against it. He showed no more concern than Mama would have over a little spilled flour. "Gets kilt fer bees no bery smart," he answered with a wink. "Den Boy puts me in dat tree. Dat bees berry muches no bery smart. Now him stuck wid be fer eber."

Did all ogres talk in circles? This was worse than getting a straight answer out of Shorty. Annah tried again, "What killed you?"

"Da big dragon da Boy wants ta kilt," he replied matter of factly. Then his hand traced a big circle around his stomach and hips. "Bited me bery gooder!"

Oh Shorty, she thought, how do you get yourself in so much trouble? Annah knew what was coming, but she asked anyway, "Why would he fight a dragon? That sounds, well, no bery smart."

Three-Toes chuckled and winked at her again, "Boy all a da times tink him gots ta sabe him friend. Tinks it bees kay fer him maybeso gets kilt long as dem all lib."

Shorty had apparently done what he always did, he had battled the monster by himself. But Annah still wanted to know how Three-Toes had died. This time she tried a gentler approach, "Shorty must have fought well. He survived the battle and so did his friends. Did he kill the dragon?"

Some of the light went out of the old ogre's eyes, and his smile faded. "Boy fighted bery gooder. Bery almost win. But old dragon bees tricky. Boy fergetted ta watches tail. Dat tail hits him bery hard. Break him muches. Dragon almost eated him," his voice trailed off and Three-Toes eyes grew distant.

Annah gave him time to continue, but Three-Toes was lost in the memory of that long go battle. He had forgotten about her. Finally, she brought him back to the conversation, "What stopped the dragon from eating Shorty?"

Three-Toes pointed to the figure in the center of the tree. His voice filled with pride as he told her, "Me sabe Boy. No ken lets dragon eated him." Three-Toes lifted his spear in from the ground and spun it around once in the air. The metal tip gleamed in the sunlight. "Fuzzface make dis. Me stick dragon bery gooder wid it. Spear go in it heart."

Annah gave Three-Toes a grateful smile. "Thank you for saving him. Were you hurt?" she asked.

Three-Toes gave an unhappy grunt, "No, Little Warrior, getted dead. Me fergetted ta watches dragon teeth. No bery smart. Dragon bited me. Maked two big piece. Gets me self kilt." Annah watched as his empty hand ran down the length of his torso. Then he began to mutter to himself, "Maybeso should tank Boy fer puts me back tagedder. Two piece no bery funner. Foots walks way an leabe head on ground." Then a cocky grin lit up his face. "Dragon gets dead firstus. Dat mean me win da fight. Dat bees da rule."

Annah looked away as a tear ran down her cheek. "I do not want to lose Shorty that way. What is the point of winning if he still dies. I would lose all of you then."

Three-Toes stepped closer to her and reached out his hand. He gently caught the tear on the end of a calloused finger. He examined the small drop of water before tasting it. Then he patted her gently on the shoulder, saying, "Den finds nudder way, Little Warrior. Finds nudder way bery soonest."

Annah took a deep breath as she studied the wily old ogre. "I am not sure what you mean. What other way is there?"

Three-Toes turned without answering and began to hobble into the trees. He paused and looked back, motioning for Annah to catch up with him. When she did, he began to talk as he limped along, "All a da times dere bees mo den one way. Me jus bees ogre, only knowed fightin. Smart people posed ta knowed mo tings. Maybeso knowed betterer way. Maybeso youse ken bees smart nuf fer ta sabe Boy."

Annah did not feel smart and it seems incredibly unfair to put this all on her shoulders. She was still fuming when he spun to face her. He waited until she met his eyes before speaking, "Long time go, nudder Little Warrior hab biggerest problem. Boy's Mama tinked she gonna gets dead when Boy bees borned. Her bees muches too small fer ta hab him. Her no tinks bees nudder way, but her finds. Youse ken too."

"How did she do it?" Annah asked.

"Magics," he replied with a grimace. "It sabe her an da Boy. Her fighted hard fer ta hab him. Finded nudder way."

"But I do not have powerful magic and Shorty cannot beat that demon. What else can we do?" Annah argued.

He shook a finger at her, "No gibs up!"

"I cannot…" she began.

Three-Toes growled and slammed the butt of his spear into the soft ground. "Ann Ah tinks too muches! Do an lib. No do an bees dead." Then she reached up to place a hand over his heart. "Beliebe, only den ken do. Me kilt dragon cuz dat what me need do. Time fer Ann Ah ta do what her need do."

Annah looked into his eyes. What she saw there surprised her. He believed in her even if she did not believe in herself. Then he stopped and pointed his spear at the gap between two trees. "Me no ken go dere. Muches magic. Bery bad fer ogre."

Annah stepped up beside the old ogre and motioned for him to bend down. When he did, she kissed him on the cheek. "Thank you, Uncle. I will find a way."

He touched his cheek in surprise. Annah grinned up at him. "No, I did not bite you." Then she turned and walked towards where the spear had pointed. She heard his voice as she walked away, "Neber gibs up Little Warrior. Jus beliebe."

Annah stepped between the two trees and found herself standing on a light green stone. Her memorial stood before her. It was complete now. In it, she stood dressed in the green gown and soft boots that the One Tree had given her. The tiny Tainkintana hung on its chain around her neck. Her image's right arm was outstretched, the birthmark clearly visible.

The sight of the completed memorial made her angry. "I am not dead you stubborn ogre. You are not allowed to put me here with the other dead you blame yourself for. Not now, not ever. I am alive and you are not responsible for any of my choices."

Annah rushed to the tree. She wanted to destroy the image. But the face that looked back at her stopped her. No one, not even Mama, had ever seen her this way. The image was beautiful and there was confidence in its face. "I will find a way Shorty. For you and for myself. Then we will talk about the people here. You are not responsible for them either."

Annah stared at herself. The image was her road back to Shorty. But where should she touch it? Then she knew. She needed to be smart this time. She reached towards her forehead. She stopped; fingers just short of the image.

The One Tree had taught her to listen to her heart. Tainkintana had spoken to her of faith. Even Three-Toes had told her to believe. Yes, she needed to be smart. But she had to be more than just smart. Annah raised her other hand and placed it over her image's heart. She touched both places at the same time. This, too, was part of the Balance.

Chapter 18

The Nudder Way

Annah found herself sitting on the edge of the bed. Morning had come to this version of Stormhold, but its light was wan and sickly. Raindrops dotted the window, occasionally sliding down the glass to pool on the outer sill. Lightening still flashed, but it no longer struck at the walls. There was a sense of anticipation, as if the storm was waiting for a signal to renew its assault. Annah was afraid that Avarice was waiting for her return to give that order. She reached for the protection and warmth of Althea's quilt.

She had made a promise to find another way. The words sounded so easy. Just be smarter than an ogre and think of something. Annah suspected that was not as easy as it sounded either. Maybe ogres were not as stupid as people thought they were. Three-Toes has seemed very wise. None of the ogres she had met spoke Common very well, but all three had a very good grasp of the world around them.

Her options seemed very limited at the moment. All of the easy ideas she could think of had already been eliminated. It seemed a bit unfair. So far, they could not just let Avarice go free, they could not just leave, and apparently fighting Avarice would not work. What other options did they have?

Surrender? Could she actually give herself to Avarice and let him take her soul to Set? It would be the hardest choice she had ever made. And if she did, would the demon agree to leave Shorty and his friends alone? Even if he agreed, could she hold him to his word? It was a tangled mess of ifs. Annah chuckled softly when she realized she had missed the most important question of all. Would Shorty allow her to sacrifice herself that way? She doubted it. In the end, she was as much a prisoner in his head as Avarice was. He would force the devil to kill them both before he allowed her to be given to Set. He was rather stubborn that way.

Another choice gone. What was left? Could they negotiate?

Again, that left her the problem of enforcing any agreement they reached. Even if Avarice was willing to make a deal with mere mortals, why would he bother honoring it? A Prince of Hell was as likely to give his word just for the pleasure of breaking it. His kind existed to deceive. To make a deal work, she would need some way to bind Avarice to the agreement. That took more power than she or Shorty possessed.

Annah suspected that she was missing something important. What else did she know? Tainkintana had told her that faith was vital. Both she and Shorty served Mielikki. Could the oath be sworn to the Goddess instead of to mere mortals? Would Avarice risk angering a Goddess by breaking his oath? There was a feeling of rightness to this idea. But how did one forge an agreement between a Goddess and a Prince of Hell? There had to be rules for things like this. Sadly, Annah Treemain did not know them. Or did she?

Rules! F'lar had told her that there were rules that even the greater powers were bound by. Annah tried to remember everything that he had told her. Names had power. Not just names though, what had F'lar called it? A true name. Could she force Avarice to swear by his own true name to the goddess Mielikki to leave them all in peace? It might work. Assuming that she could convince Shorty to try. She wondered how stubborn he was feeling today. Annah did not know if her plan would work or not. But it was another way and it was the only one she could come up with.

Annah ran her fingers across the quilt one last time. This, she realized, might be the last time it ever comforted her. If her plan failed, it was unlikely that she or Shorty would survive. Annah murmured a prayer asking the Goddess to grant Althea the same peace the quilt had brought to her. That small act of gratitude gave her the courage to face her destiny. Annah rose, leaving the quilt piled on the edge of the mattress. No one in this Stormhold would ever notice the messy bed.

She crossed to the door and opened it. This time, the hall was well lit, but the air still smelled foul. More gouges marred the walls. Annah assumed Shorty had been taunting his tormenter again. With a shake of her head, Annah pulled the door closed behind her. Then she turned and headed for Shorty's room. She wanted to talk to him before Avarice discovered her return. Annah used those few steps between the rooms to prepare herself for what she was about to see. There was no telling what Avarice had done to Shorty this time.

Annah stepped across the threshold and turned to find Shorty. The four torches still drifted through the air, circling what Annah assumed was another torture device. Their blood-red flames seemed to wave in greeting as she entered the room. The table where Shorty had been tortured had changed. In the space it had once occupied, two large posts rose from the floor. The heavy door, now split in half, had been mounted between the two posts. Three holes, two smaller ones to the outsides and a larger one in the center, had been cut where the two pieces of the door came together. Shorty's head and hands protruded from those holes. Annah did not think this looked as disturbing as her last two visits had.

She moved closer so she could see Shorty more clearly. The rest of Shorty stood stooped over behind the strange device. His back was bent at what Annah assumed was a painful angle. The three holes were snug around Shorty's neck and wrists. He would not be able to slip out of them, especially not with the chains that held the two halves of the door together. Then Annah noticed the two other chains that bound Shorty's legs to the two posts. He could not even stretch out to relieve the strain on his back and shoulders.

Shorty's eyes were closed; his breathing deep and regular. Annah could not tell if he was asleep or unconscious. She crossed the room looking for a way to release him from the device. The ends of the chains were not visible on the front side of the broken door, so

Annah stepped around the device. Shorty's broad back lay exposed. His shirt and been torn away, leaving little more than bloody strips of cloth. But even those wisps of cloth were not shredded as badly as Shorty's back was. What had been done to Shorty on the table was the work of a child, this…

Annah turned away as her stomach heaved. She found herself on her hands and knees, her stomach releasing Goddess alone knew what. Annah had not eaten since entering Shorty's mind, but her stomach did not seem to know that. It felt like an eternity before the gagging stopped. Annah looked up then, tears in her eyes and the taste of her own sickness in her mouth. That was when she saw the whip that had been discarded on the floor. It was nothing like the buggy whip Papa had kept on his wagon. This whip had three thick leather tails, each braided with hard-looking knots all along its length. Between those knots, Annah saw sharp bits of metal and glass. Bloody chunks of flesh hung from many of those shards. Annah began to gag again.

As soon as she could breathe, Annah jerked away from the whip. She could not bear to look at it or what it had done to Shorty's back. She stumbled backwards until she ran into one of the posts. The wood of the broken door rattled at the impact. A tired voice murmured from the other side of the broken door, "Comed back? Bees jus like ogre. No listen bery gooder. How me posed to keeps youse safe?"

Annah's anger returned in full force. She stepped around the door so she could look into his eyes when she told him off. He had to learn that she would make her own decisions from now on. But, the eyes she wanted to stare into were closed. His face was drawn tight with pain. Her anger flickered out like a candle flame, and it was gone. Her voice, gentle but still firm, held the compassion he deserved, "You cannot keep shoving me away, Shorty. We need to work together or we will both die here."

Ever so slowly, Shorty opened his eyes. Their pale green color seemed dark and troubled. He sounded so tired, but not so tired that he could not argue with her, "No bees nudder way. Only knowed gots ta protects youse. Ifn Avar hurts Ann Ah, da ogre gonna comes out. It no tink, only knowed killin. No helps no body den. Maybeso da ogre hurts Ann Ah. Den what me gonna do?"

Annah heard the fear in his voice. He truly was afraid of hurting her. But she had to make him see that his way was not the only way. "What if Mielikki wants me to help you?" she asked. "Will you tell her no too?"

All of the fight drained out of him. At that moment, he looked so lost. He tried to shake his head, but the opening around his neck was just too tight. She could barely hear his defeated reply, "Me her Knight. Do whats her telled me, all a da times. Jus no wants youse gets hurted. No youse, unnerstan?"

"Why not, Shorty?" she probed gently. "What makes me so special?"

Shorty closed his eyes, no longer willing to meet her gaze. "No gots good word ta tells youse. Likes Ann Ah bery muches. Me needs keeps youse safe. No just fer Forest Lady, fer me too."

Those were not the words she had expected from him. Annah caressed his cheek. "You cannot save me from my own choices, not without making me your slave. The same is true for all of your friends."

The stubborn streak on his face gave way to horror. He sounded defeated when he said, "No wants any bodies bees slabe. Jus wants dem all bees safe."

Annah smiled at him then, "Just like your friends want to keep you safe. Try to remember that."

Shorty closed his eyes again. His features seemed to sag in resignation. "Me jus bees da ogre. Ogre bees one a da monster. No so bery portent ta sabe monsters."

She did not like hearing him talk about himself that way. Would words alone make a difference at this point? She did not know, but she had to try, "Never a monster. I can see you now, Shorty, all of you. I can see the ogre and the Knight, and I am not afraid of either one of them." His eyes flew open in surprise. Before he could recover, she tapped a finger on the end of his nose and added, "And, the big, bad ogre is not going to send me away again! Got it?"

Annah saw that stubborn look creep back into his eyes. She had expected it. What she was asking was not going to be easy for him to accept. Then again, if this lesson was hard, how would he react when he found out he could not throw her into the void anymore?

Annah began to pace back and forth in front of Shorty. They did not have much time before Avarice showed up again. Could she convince him to try her plan? To do so, she needed to put aside her own misgivings about making a deal with Avarice. That meant making sure there were no other options. Annah turned back to face Shorty and asked, "Are you sure that you cannot beat this creature? Even with Tainkintana?"

Shorty raised an eyebrow at her questions, but he answered her anyway, "Ken fight fer long bit, den it getted bad. Avar no get tired. Me do, den gets hurted."

Fighting really was not an option. She had suspected as much. The next option was escape, but that also seemed unlikely. She checked anyway, "I assume we cannot get out of your head without freeing him too?"

Shorty's response was immediate, "No! Me no gonna lets dat debil hurts mo peoples. Me promise ta keeps Arcturus safe."

"Easy, Shorty, I understand that. So, we cannot fight or flee and I am not willing to surrender myself to that thing.?" She just smiled at the growl that came from him at the mention of surrender, then she continued, "Can we make a deal with it? It wants out of your head. Honestly, so do I. The Path is nice, but this version of Stormhold is rather depressing."

The broken door rattled a bit as Shorty tried to shrug his shoulders. "It tell muches lie. No ken trust dat one."

Annah leaned closer. "F'lar thinks there is a way. He says that there are rules that even Avarice cannot ignore, oaths that he cannot break."

"Brudder no always bees smart likes him tink."

Annah giggled as she wondered how F'lar would feel about that calm pronouncement. "I think we have to try, Shorty. Otherwise, this will go on forever."

Shorty shook his head. "Bees betterer ifn me jus makes Avar kills me."

"Do you really want to die?" Her heart ached when he refused to answer her. "Why, Shorty?"

His eyes looked troubled as he stared at the floor. "Bees lone bery long time."

Annah understood loneliness and loss, but she had experienced the real Stormhold and she knew what waited for him there. She just had to make him see it too. "Oh, Shorty. You are so not alone. You have many friends out there." Her hand came up once more to touch his face, her thumb caressed his cheek. "Hush and listen to me. Those people out there are more than just friends. They are your family. They love you like I love Mama and Meerah." Annah paused then, making a decision for both of them, "And, if we live, I will be there too."

A snicker came from behind her. Annah tensed at the sound of Avarice's voice. She had wanted just a few more moments alone with Shorty. But that, apparently, was not to be.

Annah turned to see Avarice sneering at her. Arms crossed over his chest and one foot tapping impatiently against the floor, he made Annah feel insignificant. His voice, when he finally spoke, was demeaning, "Such pathetic, sentimental fools. Friends? Family? What use are they? Power and Strength, those are the things that matter."

Avarice's baleful stare shifted to Shorty then. "And you, ogre, why not be the monster? You should enjoy people's fear. Fear means they respect you. Or, are you too stupid to understand the importance of that fact?" Avarice shook his head at the anger in Shorty's eyes. "Why do I waste my time on you, Knight? It is, as they used to say, like casting pearls before swine. So, let us get back to business. Now that your friend has returned, perhaps we can explore some of your fears, Sir Knight? Will you allow me to entertain the Chosen this time?"

Annah felt the force of Shorty's fear wrap itself around her. She did not wait for it to tighten its grip. The song rose up in her heart, washing her own fear away. The One Tree's many voices joined the one in her heart, their melody soothing even the monster that Shorty thought lived inside him. The storm of Shorty's emotions had no power to move her. Like the walls outside, she was impervious to the storm. It should have felt like victory, but the look in Avarice's eyes made her doubt the wisdom of staying here.

Avarice laughed, "Bravo, Annah. I knew you would eventually stop him. Too bad you cannot stop me as easily."

Annah looked back as Shorty growled softly. She heard the betrayal in his voice as he begged her, "Please, Ann Ah? Dis no bery smart. Go afore him hurted youse."

Annah wanted to tell him it would be okay, but those words felt like a lie. With a sigh, she turned her back on her friend, all Hell was about to break lose and she needed to be ready to face it.

Chapter 19

A Power from Hell

Annah was not sure what she expected a Prince of Hell to look like, terrifying at the very least. What stood in the doorway did not match any of the nightmare images her imagination had created. She would never have expected such evil to be… well, beautiful.

Avarice had golden skin, unblemished and radiant. Ebony horns curled up from his forehead, giving him an air of nobility. And that ingratiating smile, it made her feel like a trusted friend. The only thing that matched her expectations was his size. Avarice was huge, his horns almost touching the fifteen-foot ceiling of Shorty's room. He made the three ogres she had met seem so small. Annah knew she should be afraid, but she was not. If anything, she felt drawn to his beauty. Annah took an unknowing step closer.

The Prince's, no she reminded herself, the demon's lips twitched as if it understood the effect it had on her. His silver eyes locked on her, drawing her in, mesmerizing her. Annah felt lost in his gaze. Thunder rumbled outside as Avarice's laughter filled the room. His voice was a gentle caress as he told her, "I have waited far too long for the pleasure of your company, dear Annah. Your foolish Knight's attempts to keep us apart have tried my patience. Teaching him the folly of that choice was an unfortunate necessity."

Annah forced herself to step back. It was hard, but she made herself remember that this creature was her enemy. Her mind, still captivated by him, finally noticed the long dark spikes jutting out from his knees and elbows, the black hoofs where his feet should be, and the powerful muscles in his arms, legs, and shoulders. It was no wonder Shorty had been unable to defeat this Prince of Hell. Even that first storm had not emanated such power. Avarice was a threat to all that she was, and yet, what she felt most was attraction.

Avarice tilted his head to one side as if listening to her thought. His voice, so reassuring, wrapped itself around her, "You know Annah, that I only wish to be your friend." Annah shook her head, taking another step back. Giving her a sad smile, he said, "But of course, my appearance is a bit overwhelming. Perhaps this will put you more at ease."

The form before her began to blur, its lines melted and reformed as she watched. Annah shook her head to clear her vision. The huge shape that had stood before her was gone. In its place stood a tall man with the same golden skin. He wore tailored pants, a loose shirt, and boots that came to his knees. All were of the same light absorbing black. His features were handsome and nearly perfect. Too perfect. His face had changed, but those same silver eyes stared at her intently. "Is this more to your liking, Annah?"

Annah hesitated, unsure how to answer him. Avarice was so handsome now, and he obviously knew it. She felt like she was being toyed with. Worse, she felt totally unprepared to deal with him on her own. Then, a low, menacing growl began to reverberate from just behind her. Annah relaxed. She was not alone. She had a rather over-protective ogre on her side. His presence gave her the courage to speak, "I do not believe that we have been properly introduced."

Avarice waved his hand dismissively, "I apologize, Annah. I should not have assumed our rather uncivilized host would handle the introductions. As much as he struggles with words, I should not expect him to have good manners or remember names." The demon bowed deeply before continuing, "I am Lord Avarice, Ruler of the Third Hell. Soon, I will also be the Ruler of this pathetic land, once the Knight surrenders his will to me."

Annah shook her head. "He will never surrender his people to you."

Avarice smiled confidently. "Oh, I think he will now, dear Annah. I have you to thank for that. I needed something yon Knight valued more than his own worthless hide, and you have given it to me. I might not have been able to reach you wherever he was sending you, but now you have solved that problem for me."

Shorty's growl grew more bestial. Annah reached back to hold his hand in hopes of calming him, but her eyes did not leave their foe. She wondered if she could use him the way he intended to use her. There were so many things she still did not understand, the most important of which was her own part in all of this. Could she get him to fill in the gaps in her understanding?

"Lord Avarice," she began, "I am truly honored you wished to meet me, but for the life of me, I cannot understand why. What possible interest could a Lord and Ruler of Hell have in a common farm girl like me? It seems so beneath you."

Avarice waved his hand and a throne-like chair appeared behind him. He sat, leaning casually against one of its padded arms. He slowly crossed his legs before answering, "You understate your own worth, Annah. You are a Chosen of the goddess Mielikki. Such a prize has a great deal of value if used properly."

Annah felt a spark of anger at his words. The title of 'Chosen' had never been anything but a curse to her. She had no real power, but everyone wanted to use her. Apparently, that everyone included a god and the power of Hell itself. Annah allowed some of that anger to slip into her voice as she argued, "This particular 'Chosen' has very little power for your Master to exploit,"

He seemed to consider her words and then shook his head. "Perhaps, or perhaps not, dear Annah. It hardly matters though. I believe my Master's real concern is that you might somehow interfere with his plans in the future."

Annah shook her head vigorously. She wanted no part of what he was offering. "I am sorry, Lord Avarice. I am no more interested in accepting this invitation than I was any of the others your Master has made me," she answered as politely as she could.

The smile on Avarice's lips stood out in stark contrast to the note of disapproval in his voice, "You should reconsider, dear Annah. You could be an honored guest. Think of the benefits. Every desire that you ever dreamed of could be yours. Why, you might even be more than a guest. Not queen, but perhaps a consort. I am sure that even your sight could be returned to you. You would never want for anything ever again. Or…" he let the implied threat hang between them.

Annah felt strange. His words droned on, but Annah did not really hear them. Her mind began to drift. Lord Avarice suddenly seemed so reasonable. He only wanted to take care of her. Surely, that was better than being trapped here. Or, she added with a shudder, dying here. Her warm feelings of contentment were interrupted by pain in her right hand. It radiated up her arm all the way to her birthmark where it intensified.

Annah tried to bring her hand in close to her heart, to protect it from that pain. But her hand seemed to be stuck. She tugged harder, but to no avail. Whatever held her hand squeezed even tighter. Annah pulled her eyes from the gaze of the handsome Lord to see what was wrong. As her eyes turned away, a deep rumble filled her ears. Her hand was trapped in the grip of an… Annah's thoughts cleared instantly. Her hand was held by Shorty. He had not, would not allow her to fall into temptation.

Annah nodded to him and whispered, "Thank you."

"Ann Ah go now? Me send," Shorty begged her.

Annah shook her head and turned back to Avarice. This time she made sure she did not look into his eyes. Annah could still feel the pull of Avarice's magic, but now she knew it for the trap it was. She reached for her gift. Her birthmark began to glow. The pull of the hellish magic diminished and then was gone. "That was poorly done, Lord Avarice," she chided. "And, it would have gained you nothing. Neither of us can leave this place without the Green Knight's agreement."

The golden Lord's confident smile returned. "I think he will be easier to convince when I have you in my grasp."

Annah snorted at that, but she managed to push the humor of his words aside as she explained, "I do not think he knows how to be agreeable." Her words were greeted with a dismissive wave of Avarice's hand. That was when Annah realized that the Lord of Hell did not truly believe he could be beaten. To him, this was still just a game, little more than entertainment.

Annah had to convince him he could lose or there could be no bargain between them. She tried to explain, "If you continue to be unreasonable, I will be forced to return to the place the Knight keeps sending me and I will stay there. And yes, I will eventually die." That was when Annah smiled then as she asked him, "And where will that leave you, Lord Avarice? Stuck here for eternity with a stubborn ogre?"

Annah waited for a moment to let her words sink in. Then with a glance at Shorty, she continued, "Eventually, he will make you angry enough to kill him. Then you will both die. We may not be able to defeat you, Lord Prince, but you cannot win either."

Shorty whispered his promise, "Neber lets youse hab Ann Ah. Me keeps her safe. Youse gonna bees dis place fer eber an eber an eber."

Avarice gave Shorty a look filled with mockery. "Then he will be the one to kill you, Annah. Can his soul ever find peace knowing that your death is on his hands? Which Hell will he inhabit knowing he is the reason his precious 'Ann Ah' died?"

Shorty's growl was suddenly gone and Avarice began to laugh hysterically. Annah turned to see the look of confusion on Shorty's face. Before Annah could say anything, Avarice began to taunt them both, "Priceless, is it not? The ogre still has not figured it out. I forget how stupid ogre kin are." Annah saw the pain in Shorty's eyes, but there was nothing she could do to protect him from Avarice's hate filled words. "Let me explain it to you, foolish Knight, you and I can play this little game until the end of time. I will sustain your body as long as I am in your mind. Your 'Ann Ah' has no one to keep her body alive. She will weaken and die. My Master wins whether I bring her to him or kill her. You will lose no matter what you do."

Annah could not meet Shorty's pain filled gaze. Tainkintana had warned Annah, but no one had thought to explained it to Shorty.

To Annah's surprise though, Shorty did not get angry. With understanding came resolve. His sad words caught Annah by surprise, "Bery sorry, Ann Ah. Dies in me head bees betterer den what Bad Cloud do ta youse. Betterer ta dies in me head den ta libs in Hell. Ifn keeps dat one in me head, him ken no hurted me udder friend."

Lord Avarice slammed both palms against the arms of his throne as he surged to his feet. His anger was evident in every line of his face. Annah sucked in a breath as the monstrous form that had first entered the room reappeared. The spikes on his knees and elbows began to grow longer. Annah wondered if Shorty was finally going to get his death wish.

Avarice's voice sounded like rocks grating against each other. His words echoed through the room, "You stupid, idiotic ogre. I will eventually break you. Then I will destroy all that you hold dear. I will make you watch from within my mind as I corrupt everything that you have built in this pathetic world. This land should have died in the first invasion. It will not survive me."

Shorty smiled then, in triumph. Annah had to wonder how sane Shorty was after all he had suffered. The ogre in him was not capable of negotiating with Avarice, it was up to her. Annah faced the golden beast, speaking as firmly as she could, she said, "Think, Lard Avarice. You cannot bully him into letting you go. You know that, right? The more you threaten his friends, the more determined he gets to keep you here. You cannot beat him this way."

Avarice gaze never left Shorty. "Of course, I can beat him. He is only an ogre. I am a Prince of Hell. He will yield. Even a half-witted ogre is not that stubborn."

Annah shook her head. "That is where you are wrong Lord Avarice. He is that stubborn. He has stood against your Master Set again and again. I do not think he knows how to back down. That is one of the reasons why they made him the Green Knight."

Avarice glared at her. "And how do you know that, girl? You only just met him."

Annah looked over at Shorty. "Because I have talked to many of the people who made him into what he has become. Many of them died to forge him. He will never betray their memory." Her next words were not her own, but they were fitting, "Perhaps there is a nudder way to gain at least your freedom, Lord Avarice."

Avarice's voice was filled with sarcasm as he asked, "And what, pray tell, might that be, girl?"

Annah turned from Shorty to face the demon. "A bargain," she replied, "One where each side gains something it desires."

Avarice blurred once more as he lowered himself to his throne. The handsome man sat there with a thoughtful expression on his face. His fingers drummed lightly on the arm of his throne. Annah thought she saw a feral grin on Avarice's face, but it was gone before she could be sure. "If you are correct girl, then the ogre and I are at an impasse and I grow tired of this place and him. What have you to offer that I might wish to bargain for? The normal coin for such bargains is souls. Perhaps yours, dear Annah?"

"My soul is not for you or for any of your kind," Annah snapped. "We offer your freedom and nothing more. What will you offer under binding oath to leave this place?"

The golden figure began to laugh then, long and hard. Silver tears began to roll from his eyes. Annah was not sure what she had said that was so wrong or so funny. Finally, Avarice controlled his mirth enough to ask, "Have you ever bargained with one of my kind before mortal? Your words would be an insult if they were not so ridiculous. What words would you use to bind one such as me?"

Annah prayed to Mielikki that F'lar really knew what he was talking about. "There are rules, Lord Avarice, that even lowly mortals know about. Rules that even one of your station must follow. And, your oath will be made to one much greater than I. My Goddess shall judge your compliance with your oath."

Avarice fingers began to tap again. After a time, he spoke, "What you say has truth in it little Annah. But you must know the proper words to be able to bind me. Do you know them?"

Annah's confidence rose some. The devil had not laughed at her again. "Names have power Lord Avarice. You must swear your oath on your name to the goddess Mielikki."

Avarice released an exaggerated sigh. There was disapproval in his reply, "Your little forest goddess is still sticking her nose in business that is not hers. One day, she will regret her actions." Then Avarice donned a mask of boredom, and yet, there was a gleam of anticipation in his eyes. "What is the price of my freedom, Chosen of Mielikki? What would you bind me to, mortal?"

Annah's mind went blank. She had not expected to ever get this far. She had no idea what terms to ask for or even how to word them. Shorty squeezed her hand then. His voice was still rough, but it was clear, "Me bees da Chief. Me bees da one dat holds youse in dis place. Only Chief make rules. Bees three tings youse must promises."

Avarice's smile grew as he turned his head to study his captor. "Oh, this is good! An ogre wishes to match wits with me. Please, show me your great wisdom Chieftain. What is your first demand?"

Shorty's eyes grew distant as if his attention was somewhere else. He spoke with a cadence unlike how he spoke normally, "Youse an dem youse command neber again comes ta or attacks Arcturus or dem dat lib dere."

Shorty's words surprised her. They were well thought out and she did not see any loopholes that the rulers of Hell could use to get around his demand. What had changed in Shorty? He seemed more confident than he had since she had first found him in this version of Stormhold. Shorty shifted his head and something sparkled on his neck. Annah remembered placing the tiny sword there. Was Tainkintana helping him?

Annah turned her attention back to the throne and its occupant. Avarice no longer seemed as amused as he had moments before. "Interesting choice of words," he remarked sourly. "And your second demand, Chieftain?"

Shorty mumbled to himself and, after a moment, continued, "Youse an dem youse command ken neber agin attack me friends dat lib in udder land or dem family."

Avarice rose to his feet. He began to pace back and forth before his throne, lost in thought. Turning to Shorty, he replied, "Friend is too ambiguous a term. You could twist that to include the whole world. Would you be willing to limit that to those who have helped you in any way during your trips to the Bazaar?"

Shorty tilted his head to one side as if listening again. Then he nodded his agreement.

Avarice settled on the edge of the throne. "Again, your choice of wording has been very interesting," he noted. "It is far beyond what I thought you capable of. Your final demand is?"

Shorty grinned then. "Youse and dem youse command ken neber send udders against Arcturus or dem dat help me in da Bazaar or dem family. Neber."

Avarice raised a golden hand to rub along his chin. Then he lowered it to the arm of the chair. "Well, for three such rules, I would normally bargain for three concessions of my own. But I am not as greedy as my name implies. I will only ask for my freedom and one other concession. You must swear, Knight, to never again enter the Bazaar of Souls"

Annah felt Shorty stiffen. Avarice must have seen it too because he quickly added, "Even you must agree that my demand is fair, Knight."

Annah held her breath. She understood how Shorty felt about slavery. Would he sacrifice his ability to save more victims to end this standoff?

Shorty growled in frustration. Annah watched as Avarice's stare locked with that of Shorty. Neither seemed willing to yield. How long would this battle of wills go on? Surely, her body would die of starvation before either of them conceded the point. Then, the deep rumble of Shorty's displeasure abruptly ceased. He spoke again with the same strange cadence he had used to give his demands, "Me only go back ifn one a me friend gets taked dere. No go ta sabe udders, jus friend."

The two combatants stared deep into each other's eyes for a long time. Finally, Avarice nodded and sat back. "So be it as long as we use the same definition of friend. Now I grow tired of this place and your company, Knight. Let us end this."

Annah was uncertain of what came next, but she did not want to lose what ground they had made. "Your oath then, Lord?"

Avarice glanced in her direction. He seemed amused with the whole proceeding. Annah knew then that something was wrong. But what? He rose slowly to his feet. Placing his hand on his chest, he raised his voice and began to speak as if to an audience, "I, Lord Avarice, Prince and Ruler of the Third House of Hell, do swear to the goddess Mielikki, upon the name of Avarice, to abide by the three rules stated by the Green Knight, in exchange for my freedom and the agreed upon limits to said Knight's access to the Bazaar of Souls. So let it be agreed, so let it be done."

Avarice sat back down on his throne. "Does that meet your needs Knight and Lady?" he inquired.

A near panic overwhelmed Annah. Avarice was too confident. What had she missed? Then it came to her, F'lar's final words, "I cannot tell you when or how to use this…" It all made sense now, Avarice had given in so easily because the oath did not, could not bind him in any way. F'lar had said "True Names" had power. She had to act before Shorty could agree to anything.

Annah pulled her hand from Shorty's and took two steps forward. With a confidence she did not feel, Annah declared, "No, Lord Avarice. It will not do. That oath was little more than a deception. It did not and cannot bind you."

Avarice's handsome face transformed into something far less appealing, his anger at her words distorted his once perfect features. He appeared as one insulted, but his words were not spoken with the same intensity, "My word as a Prince of Hell is not sufficient? You try my patience, mortal. What more would you ask of me?" Annah suspected those words were as much an act as his oath had been.

Annah could only hope that she was reading him correctly. Even if she was, she had no idea what reaction her next words would bring, "More deceit, Lord Prince? Is that all your kind knows? We are not the fools you take us to be, Lord Mammon. To gain your freedom, you must swear by your True Name!"

The air in the room was suddenly gone. Annah lungs heaved, searching for something, anything to fill them. She would have screamed, but even the air that had been in her lungs was missing. Then Avarice transformed again and Annah forgot her urgent need to breathe. This was an aspect of the Demon Prince that she had not seen before. He was still large, but more beast-like. The gold of his skin now appeared tarnished. Long, black nails sprouted from the ends of each of his fingers. The black spikes at his knees and elbows began to drip something dark and oily. And, more frightening than all of that were the black fangs that were revealed by his snarl. He was a nightmare come to life!

Annah did not see him move, but he now stood before her. His hot, fetid breath heated her face despite the lack of air. The cultured voice of the man was gone now. In its place was a guttural voice that promised death, "I do not know where you learned that name, nor do I care. Your mortal lips can only defile what is beyond your understanding. The penalty for even thinking that name is eternal damnation. You would have been better off accepting the false oath I offered and the betrayal that was to come." Annah could only watch, frozen by a terror beyond any she could imagine, as death raised one of its massive arms over her head. Six, long black nails gleamed in the red torchlight as his hand poised to strike.

The hand of her death paused as the sound of wood groaning, stressed beyond its limits, filled the room. Chain links shifted and then whined in protest. Metal shattered in the same instant that wood exploded. Annah was aware of bits of metal and shards of wood flying through the air. Somehow, none of them hit her. Many of the projectiles struck the golden beast, but they all bounced away like leaves in the wind. The beast was impervious to such minor inconveniences.

Annah was still trying to understand it all when an arm wrapped around her. That arm pulled her in tight against a body so warm that it burned away her fear. As her body thawed, Annah's lungs heaved again. This time, air rushed in to fill them. A voice that she knew, but did not, gave her hope again, "Ann Ah bees safe. Me protect youse." It was Shorty, and this time, she trusted him even as that hand with its dagger-sharp nails came at her.

Tainkintana swept in front of her, shielding her from harm. Like green lightning, it came down in a vertical slash, striking the palm of the beast's hand. Pure white light nearly blinded her as a roar of bestial pain assaulted her ears. Through her tears, Annah saw a blur of green come back in a horizontal cut. It must have hit again because a second wave of light stole the last of her vision. Another roar filled the air. Annah blinked away the tears, wanting desperately to see what was happening.

Annah's eyes finally cleared, but she was not sure she could believe what they told her. The deep gashes Tainkintana had left healed even faster than Shorty's wounds had. Except, that the thin white stars did not fade and disappear. The near perfection of the demon's skin was marred by the two white lines that formed a perfect cross on the palm of Mammon's hand. The fact that Tainkintana could actually hurt their foe gave Annah a spark of hope.

The beast stumbled back as if confused by the pain that it felt. Then it blurred again leaving the handsome man in its place. His silver eyes stared down at his palm, searching for meaning in the scars he now bore. His lips moved, but Annah had no idea who or what he was talking to. The few words she could make out made no sense, "Does he move again in this world?"

Mammon backed several more steps as his eyes locked on the greenish blade in Shorty's hand. Again, the Demon Prince seemed confused. "Where did you come by that blade, Knight?" he suddenly demanded. "It is not of this world, is it?" Then with more certainty he added, "It should not be here."

Shorty smiled, his answer filled with certainty, "New Horizons comes from da stars, long time go. Two time, it forge in fire. It bees part a Arcturus now and fer eber."

Mammon looked down at the mark on his palm again, disgust warring with doubt on his chiseled features. When he raised his face again, his arrogant mask was once more in place. His sounded almost eager, almost taunting, as he stared into Shorty's eyes, "You cannot defeat me, even with that sword, but it might actually be an entertaining battle for a change."

Mammon winced them, squeezing his hand closed so the mark was not visible. Annah thought he looked like a child being chastised. The condescension left his voice as he continued, "But, it appears that we will never know, Knight. There are consequences my Master is not willing to risk at this time. I am ordered to give you my oath."

Was it really over this time? Had they won somehow? Annah started to pull away from Shorty, but his arm remained locked around her. Annah smiled and leaned into his warmth. Being protected was not such a bad thing as long as it was on her terms. Annah looked at the Demon Prince, then, In a confident voice, she demanded, "Your oath then, Lord Mammon. This time using your True Name!"

Anger flashed in those silver eyes when she spoke his name again, but she did not care. Shorty stood beside her and Tainkintana hung in the air between them. She and Shorty would be safe now and maybe forever. Then those too perfect lips smirked. The Demon Prince's voice carried the promise of retribution as he reminded her, "Do not celebrate your victory quite yet, mortal. My oath does not bind my Master or the other Princes of Hell. The enemies arrayed against you are Legion."

Shorty pointed the sword at Mammon's closed fist. "Tells dem! Me bees waitin when dem comes."

Mammon nodded. This time when he placed his hand on his chest, it was closed in a fist, hiding the mark Tainkintana had left there. His words, once more very formal, came without hesitation, "I, Lord Mammon, Prince and Ruler of the Third House of Hell, do swear to the goddess Mielikki by mine own True Name, Mammon, to abide by the three rules stated by the Green Knight in exchange for my freedom and the agreed upon limits to said Knights access to the Bazaar." He paused then before adding, "So let it be agreed, so let it be done."

Annah relaxed when her birthmark flowed in response to those words.

Mammon raised an expectant eyebrow. Shorty nodded, his own oath was two simple words, "Me promise."

That, apparently, was enough. The storm outside the Keep died away. Sunlight broke through the clouds. Annah could see that the trees stood, once more whole, outside the windows. Avarice, also known as Mammon, notice their restoration too. With a snort of derision, he turned to Shorty. "Well?" he asked.

Shorty pointed Tainkintana out the now open window. "Go and neber comes back!" he commanded.

Annah expected some kind of dramatic display, some evidence of the demon's power, but Mammon simply faded from view. It was like he had never been there. Then the room began to change around her, healing itself like Shorty's wounds had. Annah smiled as two rocking chairs rose from the piles of kindling, their rebirth a prophesy for the future. Strips of cloth wove themselves into sheets and wall coverings.

In the span of a few breaths, beauty and color surrounded her. She had never seen his room as it really was. What would it tell her about her Knight, the man who lived here? Exotic skins covered one wall. Above the bed was a tapestry that showed a snowcapped mountain. It was all so beautiful. Annah tried to memorize what each piece looked like. She knew that once she left this place, she would be blind again. She would miss being able to see, but she would never again let the blindness define her.

Dirt and filth simply disappeared. The foul stench of evil was replaced by the smell of trees and flowers as Shorty reclaimed his world. Shorty finally released her, but he did not move far from her side. Annah looked up at him. "Are you ready to go back?"

Shorty shook his head. The playful man she had met in Sanctuary had not come back to her, at least not yet. "Needs ta walks in da trees and see me friends," he told her as he sheathed his sword. Then he held his hand out to her.

Annah smiled at that. She wanted to thank each of those who had helped her. And she had a request to make of Shorty's mother. If she could return to this place, she wanted help learning more about her gift. The Priestess would be an excellent teacher.

Annah reached out then, placing her hand in his much larger one. "That would be nice. I like your family. And then what?" she asked.

Shorty waved his hand at the Keep around them. "Den us go home."

Annah considered his choice of words. She wanted a home. And Stormhold would be a wonderful choice.

Epilog

Homecoming

Returning to her body was not at all what Annah had expected. Her first clue that she was back was the pain. Muscles that had not been used for what? Hours? Days? Complained bitterly about their lack of use. She was stiff and sore. Everything at least seemed to be working properly. There was a sour taste in her mouth, she could hear leaves fluttering in the breeze, she could smell the flowers outside the open window, she could even feel the breeze on her face and the warm arm of the rocker beneath her right hand. Her senses were alive, all except for her sight. For possibly the first time in her life, Annah's lack of sight did not bother her.

A new sensation caught her attention. The rough leather under her left hand was an odd contrast to the smooth wood. But the feel of the hilt was just as welcoming to her senses. They had survived. Annah felt the sword shift beneath her fingertips and then a large, warm hand joined hers on the hilt.

Annah slid her fingers from the leather to lie on top of Shorty's hand. It felt right. This world might be dark, but it had its advantages. She had friends here and she had Shorty. That was enough to light her darkness. But she also knew that she could return to a place where she could see. She had friends there as well. More importantly, she had a teacher there who would help her learn about her gifts. Annah would never be alone again.

A golden aura stepped in front of her. Not the cold gold of the Demon Prince. This aura was filled with warmth and love. Kisa's voice whispered in her ear, "Welcome home, Annah. Thank you for bringing him back." Annah smiled as she felt lips kiss her cheek.

Kisa's aura moved past Annah. It merged briefly with the greenish glow that was Shorty. Kisa spoke to Shorty like an exasperated mother, "I am not sure whether to shake you or hug you again. You really scared me this time. Worse than going after that dragon by yourself. Stop doing things like that, please."

Shorty's reply sounded very tired, "Hugs bees muches betterer. Too muches a me gets shaked dis day. Bery sorry, Kisa Lady."

Annah watched the two auras merge again, longer this time. She smiled at the exchange. Kisa had not noticed that Shorty had ignored the request not to do anything like that again. That was something Annah accepted would never change.

Kisa moved back to stand between them. "What do I tell them?" she asked. "If I do not tell them something, they will all be up here yammering at you."

Shorty chuckled and asked, "Kisa Lady gonna protects me? Dat bees funner ta watches." Then his voice grew serious, "Tells dem debil bees gone. Dat one no ken comes back ta me home eber agin. Den telled dem me gonna eats any bodies dat come up me room afore time ta eats dinner."

Kisa pressed him for more, "Did you find a way to destroy it?"

Annah felt Shorty's hand squeeze the hilt of his sword. The anger in his voice made it clear he wished he had killed the demon, "No bees dead, jus gone. It promise no comes back ever. Ann Ah find way ta no lets it break dat promise. Her bery smart. Now it no ken hurts me friend no mo. "

Footsteps crossed the floor as Kisa's golden aura disappeared behind her. Annah heard a door open. It was good to know that the door was back. The footsteps paused and Kisa spoke again, "You both did very well. Now rest." The door closed with a click and then it was quiet. Annah leaned her head back, relaxing for the first time in what felt like weeks.

A deep rumble filled the room. Shorty must have fallen asleep. Annah smiled and leaned her head back as she began to rock. Her eyes drifted shut. Annah dreamed, not of auras this time. Her dreams were filled with trees, clouds, sunshine, and, of course, squirrels.

Annah soon regretted letting the squirrel slip into her dreams. It was so loud and it sounded really angry. It took her a moment to realize that she was not dreaming anymore. She actually was listening to a squirrel. She opened her eyes to see a small aura sitting where she thought the windowsill must be. As near as she could tell, it was the same squirrel that had spoken to her when they had first found Shorty.

Shorty was speaking to his little friend although it sounded more like an argument. Calling her magic to listen to the squirrel was just too much effort, so she listened to just one-side of the conversation. "Youse no bees boss me. No ken do what squirrel say all da times. Sum time gots ta do tings da ogre way."

Annah shook her head when the squirrel began to chatter angrily once more. Why did everyone think they could bully the ogre into doing what they wanted? Did any of them even notice how big and stubborn he was? Please seemed to work rather well on him.

Shorty's voice got angrier, "It no bees broke no more. Youse bee no bery nice. Gets youse own nut. Me done talk wid youse." The squirrel got in the last word before she saw it disappear from in front of her. She assumed it had returned to the tree.

Shorty let go of her hand so he could turn it over. He placed a piece of warm bread in it. "New Horizons make special fer youse. Bees bread an cheese. Sword say youse needs ta eats."

Annah took the bread and began to nibble at it. The bread was good and it made Annah realized that she was very hungry. Shorty got up and brought her a mug filled with cold water. He sat down and took her hand once more.

Annah had just finished her meal when the smell of smoke and something burning reached her nose. She was about to ask Shorty about it when a voice came from behind her on the side of the room.

Annah remembered that there had been a really large window on that side of the room in the other Stormhold.

The voice was childlike and filled with concern, "Mama? Are you all better now? Birdie Max said I was not supposed to come here, but I was really worried."

Shorty rose from his chair again. He began speaking to the voice as he walked away. Love and affection made his aura glow brighter. "Me all betterer, Arlon. Jus bees tired."

"But it is morning, Mama," the voice pointed out. "Why do you want to sleep? Did you eat too much? I get tired too when I eat a whole sheep."

There was the sound of something rubbing against a hard surface, Annah was confused but she continued to rock and listen to the conversation. Why did the voice keep calling Shorty Mama?

"Me protect all da night long. No sleep. Keeps Arcturus safe," Shorty explained to the voice,

"Did you eat the bad thing, Mama?"

"Muches too big fer ogre ta eats. Only big dragon coulda eated all dat. Maybeso no taste bery gooder," Shorty teased whoever he was talking to.

"I am going to help you protect Arcturus when I grow up!" the childlike voice promised. "You will see, Mama. I will be the best protector ever. But I will have to be a red knight, not a green one and I will eat all the bad things. You wait and see."

The rubbing noise came again. "Youse gonna bees da bestus protect eber. Now me needs to rest an youse needs ta go school wid Birdie Max. Kay?"

Annah smiled at the young voice's next questions, "Who is the pretty lady, Mama? Is she going to stay with us too?"

Shorty's voice sounded wistful as he replied, "Dat bees Ann Ah. Me hopes her stay muches long time. Maybeso fer eber. Now go ta school afore Max come an finds youse dis place. No mo bees bad."

There was a noise that sounded like flapping wings and then Shorty returned to sit beside her.

Annah's curiosity ate at her. "Who was that Shorty?" she blurted out as soon as he was seated.

Pride filled his voice as he answered her, "Dat bees me son. Him name bees Arlon. Bery gooder boy."

Annah's heart seemed to skip a beat. Somehow, the thought of him having a wife and family had never occurred to her. As casually as she could manage, Annah asked, "Do you and your wife have any other children?"

Shorty's aura suddenly seemed to draw in on itself as streaks of grey shot through it. "No gots wife," he told her, "Ogre lady bery scary. Me gots picture book. No wants ta gets hurted likes dat."

His words painted a vivid image in her mind of Shorty being dragged off to a cave by a very large female ogre. She could just imagine the ogress with her hand locked in his hair. Relief mingled with the absurdity of it all made Annah laugh. While funny, Shorty's answer left her with even more questions that only Shorty could answer. "So," Annah hesitated as she searched for the right words, "you do not have a wife, but you do have a son that calls you Mama. Men do not have babies, Shorty. Why does your son call you Mama?"

Annah felt Shorty's callused fingers pat the back of her hand. There was humor in his voice as he explained, "Me no hab him dat way. Bery silly. Me hatch him from egg."

Annah knew very little about ogres, but she was fairly certain that they did not lay eggs. Especially not male ogres! Incredulous, she blurted out, "Ogre children hatch from eggs?"

"No, dat bery muches mo silly. Ogre baby bees borned like people baby. Dragon bees hatch from da egg. Arlon no bees ogre. Him bees dragon. Birdie Max help me ta hatched him. Unnerstan?"

Annah most certainly did not understand. "A bird helped you to hatch a dragon from an egg? Really? What is a Birdie Max? And what kind of dragon is Arlon? This is very confusing."

Shorty did not sound confused at all, "Birdie Max bees me friend. Him bees owl made a da metal. Arlon bees bery purty red dragon. Both dem bery mo smart den me."

Annah was more bewildered than ever. Metal owls? Red dragons? What riddle should she solve first? Annah chose to stay on topic, she asked about his son, "Red dragons are supposed to be evil. At least all the ones in Papa's stories were."

The humor left Shorty's voice. Annah got the impression this was an argument he had had many times before. "No baby eber get borned bad. No baby eber get hatched bad. Only bees bad ifn gots bad Mama. Me good Mama so Arlon gonna bees good. Him gets lots lub."

Annah turned in her chair. "I am sorry if what I said sounded mean, but I still do not understand."

His strong hand reached over and took her left hand in his. "Bees bery long story. Maybeso makes youse go ta sleep," he warned her.

Annah sat back in her rocker, enjoying the feel of his hand holding hers. A story would be nice she decided. "Please, tell me about Arlon, Shorty. I really want to know. Besides, we have nothing to do until dinner time. "

"Any udder tings Annah wants ta knowed bout?" he asked,

Annah thought for a moment and then asked, "Who or what helped you to defend Sanctuary? I have never seen an aura like that."

"Me tell dat story too," he assured her.

Annah nodded and began to rock. The gentle movement of the rocker soothed her body and her mind.

Shorty began then. His story did not begin with 'Once upon a time' like the ones Papa used to tell, but his deep voice was animated. Annah could tell Shorty liked talking about his friends. She closed her eyes and tried to imagine all the things he described to her…

Becoming da Mama

Chapter 1

A Day Almost Like Any Other

The ancient city decayed slowly in the gloom of the immense underground cavern where it had fallen many centuries earlier. Despite the passage of time, the city was still mostly intact. Its buildings were now outlined by a pale green luminescence from the lichen that seemed to grow on every surface. The only notable exception was the tall tower at the extreme southern end of the great cavern. The domed roof of that one building glowed with intense magical light. No lichen marred its gleaming white surfaces. The light of that dome was so bright that the gardens around the base of the tower still flourished.

The city appeared to be at rest or even asleep. That apparent peace was pure deception, a lethal trap for those naïve enough to believe the city's lies. Within the city confines, denizens of the deep dark mingled with creatures of the surface world in an endless struggle for survival. Everything that roamed the streets or hid in the shadows was a predator. Only the strong, the ruthless, and the deceitful survived to feed on their victims. Here in the Ancient City, one killed or one was eaten. Those who hunted infested every street and building except for two. The first was the area near the glowing dome. Its light or some other magic repelled the monsters spawned in the darkness. The second area was a small keep in the center of the city. That keep was home to one that even the most dangerous predators had learned to avoid.

A lone figure sat on the edge of a large platform at the top of that keep. The platform was empty except for a pair of heavy oak doors set into the floor on one side of the Keep and the smallish ogre that sat on the far end of the platform, staring intently at the streets below. The platform's only adornment was a faded red circle painted near its center. That circle was big enough for a large flying creature, even a dragon, to land within its boundaries. The ogre ignored the platform at its back. There were no large flying creatures this far beneath the earth. To the ogre, the platform had no purpose other than as a place for him to watch for those foolish enough to enter his hunting ground.

The Keep was not large compared to many of the structures within the city. The platform was only four stories above the ground. If there was a sun overhead, the Keep would be overshadowed by everything around it. Like the Keep, the ogre perched there was small in stature. By the standards of his kind, he was deemed little more than a runt. Still, he sat with confidence in his heavy battle armor. The ogre's body bristled with weapons, the most notable of those being the two swords whose hilts rose above his shoulders. The swords' scabbards ran down the entire length of is back, both easily the length of a tall man. The ogre did not seem to notice their weight or the weight of the field plate covering most of his body. The warrior's heavy, hobnail boots dangled over the edge of the platform. Those massive boots swung in time to the melody the ogre whistled as he watched the streets below. His eyes shifted from building to building as he searched the shadows for what might be lurking within them.

Shorty waited patiently to see if anything would come to challenge him today. Challenges had once been a daily occurrence. But no more. The creatures that had tried to claim his territory had died, quickly and efficiently. It was a lesson that had not been wasted on the more intelligent of the city's denizens. There were still the "no bery smart" things living in the city. They were the easy ones to kill compared to the creatures that crawled up out of the deep dark. As for the others, they waited and watched for any signs of weakness in him. Such a mistake would surely be his last. Then the shadow dwellers would feast on him as they did on his many kills.

Shorty leaned out over the edge as a shadow changed its shape. The long drop to the ground below did not worry him. He still wore the ring of no fall down that his long dead friend had given him so many years ago. He missed that elf. And, he was also mad at him too. Or, maybeso, he was mad at himself. H'aor had died saving Shorty in a battle that had suddenly gone very wrong. Shorty's sword had bounced off the black dragon's scales. The now angry dragon had been about to spit death at Shorty when H'aor had hurt it with his magic. Instead of killing Shorty, the dragon had spit at H'aor. Shorty did not like losing friends. It made him very angry. He did not remember the end of that fight. When the red haze in his head had finally faded, the dragon had been in many, many little pieces. But H'aor was still dead and Shorty was not. Bad H'aor, he thought. But he knew it was his fault and not the elf's.

Shorty hated dragons and maybeso, he was a little afraid of them. Killing them was very hard and people he cared about always seemed to get hurt or dead around dragons. Luckily, there were no dragons down here in the deep cavern where he and Ez'ard now lived with Bone Man. Shorty stared across the vast cavern. He was not really happy here. The cavern was just a place to be. It was not a home. He wanted a home with family and friends around him. He wanted a place where he belonged. He had none of that here. Well, he had one friend, Ez'ard. The little elf was as much an outcast as Shorty was, but he was a very good friend. He just was not a lot of fun most of the time. Ez'ard did not play games and Shorty needed someone to have fun with. He sighed. The real problem with the Ancient City was that there were no squirrels down here. That was bad. He wanted to crack nuts for his little friends and talk to them. He really missed outside very much.

Shorty turned his gaze to the south. He wondered if there were squirrels in the trees around the magic building where Ora Cal lived. There were trees all around Ora Cal's home. Were there nuts and squirrels there in its bright light? Shorty had never gone to the white tower with the glowing dome. He had always wanted to meet Ora Cal, but Bone Man had told him it was too dangerous. Even with that warning though, the trees and bright light were a temptation.

Especially when Shorty was bored. But Bone Man had made him promise and Shorty never broke his promises.

He was really bored and he had no idea what to do about it. There was absolutely nothing to do in the Ancient City except kill bad things. It was good practice, but it was not much fun. How had he gotten himself into this mess? Shorty thought about the road that had brought him here. Magic. It was magic's fault. Once, he had a home with Kisa Lady and Roiland and Thorn. But there had been that magic door. It called to him. He had finally found a way to reach it. When he opened the door, it had taken him far away. He had not wanted to leave, only to see what was on the other side of the door. He had lost the friends that were his only family that day.

On the bright side, he met Ez'ard in the small town where the magic had taken him. Ez'ard had gotten him out of jail. Jail was nice but there was not much to do there either. Squirrels came to visit him in jail, but he quickly ran out of nuts to feed them. So, he went with Ez'ard when the elf had said it was time to leave. They traveled back to the waterfall where the magic door had left him. The waterfall was magic too. The waterfall took them someplace new where darkness and evil hunted. Other people called heroes were fighting that evil. Ez'ard had not been happy when Shorty rushed in to join the fight.

He and Ez'ard had traveled with the new group. They fought many bad things with their new friends. They had even killed a really big lizard that talked and wore a crown. That was when things got ugly. Ez'ard tried on a silly hat with the big purple feather. The others had gotten angry. They punished Ez'ard for wearing the hat. "No treasure for you!" they had told Ez'ard. Shorty picked the hat on his turn and he gave it to his friend. The new people used magic to take them to a place called Delith.

The two groups had parted ways then. Shorty had still been angry about the way they treated Ez'ard. The two friends were left to make their own way in a big city filled with people. Shorty felt lost. There were few trees and no squirrels in that city either. Ez'ard had seen how unhappy Shorty was so he suggested that Shorty get a pet. Maybeso a kitty, Ez'ard had suggested. Ez'ard took him to a place called "Market." There were many things to look at in Market. Shorty got distracted. Well, really, he got lost. A nice woman tried to help, but it did not work. Shorty ended up more lost than he was before she helped.

In desperation, Shorty climbed up on a big crate to see if he could find that silly purple feather. But Ez'ard was nowhere to be found. He sat down on the crate, one very unhappy ogre. That was when a voice asked him what he was looking for. Shorty turned to find an elf with dark skin like Roiland's locked in a cage. Shorty did not understand why the elf was in the cage, but he tried to be friendly. Shorty told the elf he was looking for a pet.

The elf, who said his name was Al Ensidus Dendaire, told Shorty that he knew a place where very special pets could be found. Al, as Shorty called him, offered to show Shorty the way to the pets, but he had accidentally locked himself in his new cage while cleaning it. In his hurry to get Al out, Shorty broke the cage door. Al told him it was okay though and they headed off to find the pet place. The day got even better when Ez'ard showed up just outside market. Ez'ard did not like Al. He liked him even less when Al said it would take several days to get to the special pets. Shorty was so excited. He insisted that they go with Al and Ez'ard, being a good friend,

stayed with Shorty. Al and Shorty were in such a hurry to get to the pet place that they did not even stop for supplies. Because Shorty had to hunt for food, it took three days to get to the mountains and another day to find the tunnel. Ez'ard seemed more and more unhappy about the journey, but all Shorty could think about was getting a pet.

It turned out that Ez'ard was right. Al had lied to Shorty. There was no special pet place. Al had only wanted Shorty to get him out of the cage. He had used Shorty to get away from those who had captured him. The whole trip was just the start of Al being bad. Al led them deep underground with promises that they were almost there. But the place Al led them to was just a small cavern where two of Al's friends waited for him. Shorty had not understood until he was hit by several tiny arrows. The fight had not gone well for Al or his friends. The little arrows had only tickled. Shorty's sword had done much more than that. The fight was over very quickly except for waking Ez'ard up when it was over. Shorty really did not think that a fight was a great time for his friend to take a nap.

When Ez'ard finally woke up, another fight started. This one was fought with words. Shorty wanted to keep looking for the pet. They had come so far already. But Ez'ard wanted to go back to the city. The argument did not last long, and Shorty had won it by being mean. He had refused to lead the way back to the surface. Poor Ez'ard could not smell his way back the way they had come. In the end, Shorty led the way deeper underground. That was how the found the vast cavern with a city inside it.

Shorty and Ez'ard had wandered the city until they found a lone figure in robes fighting two very big lizards with very sharp teeth. Shorty killed one lizard. Ez'ard and the man in robes had used magic to kill the other. It had been quite a surprise when the stranger turned to thank them for their help. What stared out of the stranger's hooded robe was a gleaming white skull. Shorty was even more surprised when the skeleton began to speak. The Bone Man thanked them and invited them to come live with him.

Shorty did not think that was a very good idea. But when the Bone Man offered to teach Ez'ard more magic, his friend said yes without even asking Shorty. Once again, magic was making him do things he did not want to do. That day, they had come to live in the Keep. Shorty soon learned that there were no pets of any kind in the Ancient City. Shorty and Ez'ard had been here ever since. He had no idea how long it had been because there was no day or night in the Ancient City. Ez'ard learned more magic and was happy. As for Shorty, he spent his days defending the Keep. It was a lonely existence, but Shorty was used to that. He had been lonely since he was small.

Shorty leaned back, relaxing. Whatever had moved in the shadow of the building across the street had left. The shadow had returned to its original shape. There would be no fight today, nothing to ease the boredom he felt. Rising, Shorty crossed the platform and opened one of the large doors. It was time to eat. He was very hungry. He stepped inside, remembering to close and lock the door behind him. It was best to keep the bad things outside. Shorty stopped at his friend's room to see if Ez'ard was hungry too. He opened Ez'ard's door and stepped inside before remembering that he was supposed to knock first. Luckily, Ez'ard was not there to fuss at him. The room was quiet and full of interesting toys. Shorty could not resist taking a peek.

He took one large ogre step into the room, stopping at a white line that had been painted on the floor. This was his favorite part of visiting Ez'ard. Just past the line, a mean looking face had been drawn on the floor. It had an upside-down smile. Shorty grinned as he placed his foot on the line. The not happy mouth began to speak, "Do not even think about it, Shorty! You know the rules." Shorty giggled and turned back to the door. This was magic that even he liked. It was fun.

Shorty made his way down the long wide ramp to the bottom level of the Keep. Sometimes Ez'ard practiced magic down here. But his friend was not there. Shorty found himself alone. This level of the Keep, at least the part he was allowed in, was a single large room for magic and sword practice. A well sat in the far corner of the room. Shorty shivered every time he looked at that well. Soon after he and Ez'ard had moved in, something large with many long rope-like arms had pulled Shorty into the well. Shorty had hit the very cold water quite hard. The creature had pulled him beneath the surface and carried him down a long tunnel. There had been no air to breathe as he was dragged through the water.

Shorty was out of air by the time the creature finally surfaced to eat its prey. To eat him! It had not expected him to be alive, let alone awake. But it did not care. Its long rope-like arms were wrapped tightly around him. He had not been able to draw his sword. Thankfully, Papa's dagger was right by his fingertips. The creature had been very surprised when Shorty thrust that small blade into one of its eyes. It had squeezed him quite hard as it bled out. He knew he almost died that day. He had plenty of time to think about just how close he had come because it had taken Ez'ard a long time to come find him. Ez'ard's magic was the only reason he was able to swim back to the well. Shorty had been a good swimmer, but the well was just too far away.

It had not been fun, but he had lived. It had been worth almost dying for though. Shorty's lips twitched in a smile as he remembered the things he found in the dead creature's lair. Shorty's fingers drifted up to caress the large pearl inset on the hilt of the black sword strapped to his back. The sword was very good at killing bad things. It had other magic too, but Shorty did not trust that kind of magic. He had found another toy on the ground beside the sword. The black glove was also magic, but it was a magic that he understood. He slipped the glove on his left hand in that dark chamber. All of the round holes that the creature had made on his arms and legs disappeared while he waited for Ez'ard. The glove healed his ouches any time he got hurt. He just had to be patient.

He really liked the sword and glove. Especially with the beautiful marble on the sword's hilt. Shorty's only regret was that the Fuzz face in town had been afraid of the glove and sword. He said they would make Shorty do bad things. Shorty knew better. He did not want to be the boss of the whole world.

Shorty turned away from the well. He still did not trust it. On the left side of the chamber was a heavy iron door. Normally the door to Bone Man's magic place was closed and locked. Today, it was open and the magic light from within spilled into the outer room. Curiosity about what lay behind that door drew him forward. A quick look through the open door would not get him in trouble, would it?

Shorty moved closer, trying not to be too obvious. Before he got close enough to see inside, a dry, raspy voice called out from within. "Enter and be welcome, mighty warrior."

Shorty hesitated before stepping across the threshold. Bone Man's room was the one place in the Keep that he was not supposed to enter. Bone Man made an impatient sound, so he took another step. He paused again to look around. The room felt wrong and he did not like it. His ears told him the room was very big, but his eyes said that it was small. His eyes also told him that Bone Man was alone in the room. His eyes were wrong. His nose was certain that someone else was hiding in that tiny space. The smell was familiar and yet, it was not. All he could be sure of was that was that it was not Ez'ard playing a trick on him. His fingers itched for the hilt of his sword, but Bone Man would not like that at all.

He drew another breath in through his nose. It did no good. Other smells in the room made his nose burn and his eyes water. He would have backed away, but he did not want to make Bone Man mad. Shorty peered around Bone Man's billowing black robes, hoping to see the unknown enemy. He saw no one. The room was smaller than Ez'ard's room. There was no place to hide. The room was barely big enough to hold the three chairs crowded inside it. None of those chairs matched. One was small and one was large. Large enough for Shorty to sit on comfortably. The last chair was much nicer than the other two. It had cushions and arms. Shorty could see silver squiggles on its arms and back. He knew who would sit on that special chair.

Bone Man motioned at the large chair before stepping back and sitting in the nice chair. As soon as his robed form found a comfortable position, the chair rose into the air. Shorty had to crane his neck to look up into the dark hood that covered Bone Man's head. Nothing showed within its shadow filled opening except for the two glowing red orbs that were all that remained of the skeletal man's eyes.

Shorty walked to the large chair and sat down. Now it was even harder to look up at Bone Man. Shorty settled for staring at the toe bones that were just visible beneath the dark robe. He was already not happy with the way this meeting was going and he did not even know why he was here yet.

Bone Man let the silence drag on as Shorty sat there. Shorty used that silence to listen carefully. He held his breath. Someone else was breathing in the room. Bone Man did not breathe, so Shorty knew it was not the skeleton floating over his head. Before Shorty could locate where the sounds were coming from, Bone Man began to speak, "I have a mission for you. This particular job requires more than just killing things so you will need a partner."

"Ez'ard?" he asked hopefully.

Bone Man released what would have been a heavy sigh if he had the ability to breathe. Shorty did not know what that noise meant coming from a talking skeleton. Shorty reached up and scratched his chin as he tried to think of a convincing argument. "Ez'ard bees good thief," Shorty said encouragingly.

Bone Man just shook his head. "No, your friend really is not right for this mission. Besides, I sent him to town to pick up some magical supplies we are running out of. He will not be back for several days."

The scent he had noticed at the door grew much stronger. Shorty tried desperately to remember where he had smelled it before, but his mind was blank.

Bone Man's arm came up and a single finger of bone slide out of his sleeve to point at the wall beside the empty chair. "I was rather hoping you would be willing to work with a friend of mine. I assume you have no issues about working with an orc?"

Shorty tensed as a dark figure stepped out of the wall where Bone Man pointed. He realized with a start that his hand was gripping the hilt of Papa's dagger. He caught himself before the dagger cleared its sheath. It took all of his willpower to release his grip on the hilt. That oh so familiar scent had the smell of orc sweat. It just was not one of the orcs from his old tribe.

The orc eased himself onto the empty chair, his eyes never leaving the hand Shorty kept near his dagger. While the orc nervously watched Shorty's fingers, Shorty evaluated the teammate that Bone Man expected him to trust on the mission. Shorty did not like what he saw.

The stranger was not all orc. He was clearly a half breed like Shorty was. Half-orcs were dangerous. They tended to lose their temper easily. Bone Man's friend wore black chainmail that did not look well cared for. The armor showed signs of many previous fights. Shorty noticed a mace clipped to the orc's belt. It was also black. Shorty had a feeling his new traveling companion was not a very nice person. This orc would not have been welcome in the tribe Shorty had once ruled. Why would Bone Man want him to trust this orc? Even Shorty was smarter than that. "Better ta do wid Ez'ard," Shorty grumbled.

Bone Man lowered his arm and the finger disappeared back into his sleeve. "Your friend is not here, Warrior, and this must be completed very soon."

The orc's eyes moved from Shorty's dagger to his face. There was a friendly smile on his face, but Shorty did not buy it. The orc's voice was also friendly as he introduced himself, "My name is Erkdratzk. I am both a cleric and a thief."

Shorty frowned at the orc as he tried to pronounce his name. Er…
Erks…" Finally, Shorty blurted out, "Dratz!"

The orc winced at Shorty's version of his name echoed through the
room. The orc's mouth opened to speak but his words were cut off
by the gleeful cackle that erupted from Bone Man. The orc glared at
Shorty as Bone Man announced, "Most excellent, Warrior. Dratz is
exceedingly appropriate. I shall use that nickname for him myself."
The orc gave Bone Man an unhappy look but stayed silent.

Shorty did not understand exactly what Bone Man found so funny,
but he was used to that. Better to find out what he was supposed to
do with a risky partner at his back. "What youse wants me ta dos?"
he asked.

Bone Man's humor died away as he explained, "This mission might
sound a bit dangerous, but it has been carefully planned to ensure
your survival and success. There is a sword that I desire. It is a
powerful magic blade that can be used by wizards such as myself.
It will enhance my magic. The sword is intelligent. You must treat it
with respect."

Something was not right. Shorty just was not sure what. He nodded
his head towards the orc and asked, "Why thief need me help ta steal
sword?"

"Because Dratz is also a cleric. He may not handle the blade," Bone
Man replied too quickly.

Shorty leaned his head back to meet Bone Man's glowing red orbs.
His voice was filled with suspicion as he asked, "Where bees dis
sword?"

Bone Man's eyes burned more brightly as he replied, "In the lair
of an ancient red dragon. Nothing too difficult for one of your
prowess."

Shorty stood suddenly, knocking the chair over behind him. It hit the
wall leaning at an angle as he took a step towards the door. "Me no
fights nudder dragon! Three time afore almosted gets kilt by dragon.
No gonna dos dat gin."

Bone Man raised both of his skeletal hands. "Easy, Warrior. The dragon will not be in its lair. Another team has been sent to draw it away. Your only job is to carry the sword back to me."

Shorty continued to shake his head. "Dem udder peoples bees no bery smart. What ifn dem gets dead? Dragon come back an me get dead too!"

"That group is quite talented. They might even kill the dragon," Dratz argued. The orc's answer did little to calm Shorty.

Shorty tried to remember what he had been taught about dragons. "Dragon knowed when dem toys get tooked. It come back den, eats me."

Bone Man gestured for Dratz to be quiet. "Dratz has magic that will block the call of the treasure. The dragon will not know the sword is missing until it returns. If you follow the plan, there will be nothing the wyrm can do to hurt you."

Shorty seemed unmoved, so Bone Man added, "With this sword, I can teach your friend, Ez'ard, all of the magic he wants to learn. You do want to help Ez'ard, right?"

Shorty righted his chair and sat down again. He was unconvinced, but this was for his friend. The orc spoke again, this time his voice sounded confident. "I have scouted the dragon's lair already. There is a small tunnel that leads into it that the dragon does not even know about. It is too small for her to get into. We can slip in and out without her knowledge. It is perfect for our needs!"

Shorty growled. "Maybeso dragon no do what Bone Man want. Den usn gets bery dead."

The orc started to argue, but Bone Man waved the orc to silence. "The dragon has many beautiful gems, er, marbles. You may keep anything else that you find in her lair. Think of the games you could play with that many new marbles."

Shorty's protests trailed away. More marbles sounded really, really good. And, he would be helping Ez'ard learn more magic. Still, he knew this mission was no bery smart. Shorty tried to figure out if there was anything else he should be asking Bone Man. Then a problem came to him. "How me posed ta finds dis sword?"

Bone man snapped his fingers and a piece of parchment appeared in the air, floating slowly down to land in Shorty's lap. "That is a drawing of the blade and its hilt. It is rather unique, like the marble sword you carry. This sword's hilt is of pure dragon bone and the blade is a dull red color. I am sure that you will recognize it."

Shorty stared at the picture as Bone Man explained the plan, "I will open a portal that will take you to a place Dratz knows that is close to the dragon's lair. Any closer and the wyrm might detect my magic. You will arrive just before sunrise. My associates will draw off the dragon when the sun is completely above the horizon. Once the dragon departs, you must move quickly. Get to the hidden entrance and find that sword."

Shorty felt his eyes drawn back to those glowing red orbs. The desire to help his old friend, Bone Man, burned as brightly as those orbs. A compelling voice whispered to him, "Will you do this small favor for me, Warrior? For all that I have done for you and your elf friend?"

A sense of danger filled Shorty's mind. He knew this was a mistake, but Bone Man was his friend. He was supposed to help his friends, right? A muffled voice deep within him cried out, "No bery smart! No come back dis time!" That last cry triggered a spark of curiosity in him so Shorty asked, "Hows posed ta bring sword back dis place? Who gonna makes magic door?"

Bone Man's hood moved up and down. "Very good, Warrior. I almost forgot that little detail." A skeletal hand reached inside the hood and came back out with a tiny bone fragment. The hand stretched out to Dratz. "Break this and a portal will open around you. Return with what I have commissioned and be rewarded. Fail and I will not be pleased."

Shorty's head pivoted back and forth between the Bone Man and Dratz. "How Shorty gets home?"

The dark hood rippled as a chuckle emanated from its interior. "I suggest that you stay close to Dratz. He is your ride back to me. But, if you get separated…" Bone Man's yellowed finger pointed at something over and behind Shorty's left shoulder. "You have other ways to return here. It is time you learn how to use the other powers of that sword."

Shorty could not think of a reason not to go. That strange need to help Bone Man still filled his thoughts. He just hoped this was not as big a mistake as he thought it was. Would there be enough marbles to make this trip worth the risk? If not, at least Ez'ard would get the new magic he loved so much.

Bone Man waved his hand towards the door. "Get your things, Warrior. Time is of the essence."

Shorty trudged slowly up the ramp muttering. "Ogre bees no bery smart dis day. Gonna gets dead ifn no bees careful."

Chapter 2

The Lair of the Wyrm

Bone Man began his spell by drawing squiggly lines on the floor of the practice room. Shorty and Dratz waited near the old well for Bone Man to finish making the magic door. Shorty made sure that the half-orc was standing closer to the well than he was. Better to play it safe than risk another long trip beneath the ice-cold water. "shAH Ar!" echoed through the room. A pinpoint of light formed in the air where Bone Man had made his funny marks. The light grew, stretching up and widening until it formed an oval in the center of the room. The light rippled, pulses of magic flowing from its center to the outer boundaries of the oval. It was like pond water after a rock had been tossed in. Only pond water was never this bright. Shorty could see his reflection on the portal's shiny surface.

The center of the oval lost its glow. As it faded to darkness, Shorty's reflection disappeared too. Blackness filled the bright outer ring of the oval. A breeze suddenly gusted in the room, bringing the fresh scent of mountain air to Shorty's nose. This was, at least, a good sign. Shorty shifted closer to the oval. Now he could see stars burning brightly in a sky on the other side of the portal. Shorty glanced down at the ground of that other place, wondering if it would be covered with snow. It was not. What he did see not too far away, was a circle of large rocks. If he crouched down, Shorty could hide in that circle. But would it be enough to hide him from a dragon?

Dratz stepped around Shorty and darted through the portal, the half-orc's armor easily merged with the night. Shorty sighed and followed carefully after. He just knew this was going to turn out badly. Once again, magic was taking him somewhere he did not want to go.

Then Shorty found himself outside. It was the best thing that had happened to him in a very long time. The breeze he had felt in the practice room became a strong wind. It was cold and refreshing at the same time. Shorty's long hair swirled around his face. Reaching into his pouch, he pulled out a strip of leather. With a quick twist, Shorty tied his loose hair behind his head to keep it out of his eyes. Then he looked around.

The first thing he looked for was his new partner. Dratz was kneeling inside the circle of stones. Beyond the stones, a dark mass obscured Shorty's view of the stars. Shorty turned back towards the portal and the rising sun. The magic door was already gone. Just beyond where it had been, the ground disappeared. In the pre-dawn light, Shorty could just make out a valley far below. It would be a long drop if he was not careful.

Shorty faced the half-orc once more, making sure it was not doing anything sneaky. Dratz gave him that same friendly smile that Shorty did not trust. With a gesture towards the rocks, Dratz explained, "This is where we will hide until the dragon departs. It is also where we will meet if we get separated. I have my own mission to complete while you find that sword."

The plan, what little of it there seemed to be, was sounding worse all the time. Shorty's way back to the Keep might not be where he could find it. Why was he doing this? Marbles and Ez'ard, Shorty reminded himself. Shorty climbed over one of the stones to get into the circle. He did not trust Dratz enough sit close to him. Shorty slid down the far side of the rock to take a seat on the cold, hard ground. Was a trip outside worth all this? Shorty, keeping one eye on Dratz, studied his surroundings as the sun rose into the sky.

Behind Dratz and the rock he leaned against; Shorty saw a mountain peak rising into the sky. Turning his head, Shorty noticed similar peaks to either side of the dragon's home. Many of them were much taller than the one he stood on. But they were all different. Those other peaks had ice and snow that glittered in the rising sun. This peak was bare of snow. Nothing grew here either. There was nothing but rock and hard packed dirt to see here. He thought it strange that in some places smoke or maybe steam rose up to be carried away by the wind. It was confusing until Shorty remembered that this dragon breathed fire. It could burn him as easily as it did the mountain where it lived.

Shorty eyed his new partner with suspicion. "Where us go ta find sword?" he asked the half-orc.

Dratz pointed, his finger tracing a line along the steep slope of the peak. He sounded like he was lecturing a small child as he replied, "You just follow me. And try to be quiet. I do not need a fumbled-footed ogre announcing our presence to everything still living on this mountain."

Shorty ignored the half-orc's rudeness. He was a hunter. He knew how to move silently outside. Let Dratz think what he would. Shorty pulled a piece of smoked meat from his pouch and chewed on it as the sun rose behind him. It was always a good time to eat after all.

The two unwilling partners sat in silence for a long time. There was nothing to say and neither wanted to turn their back on the other. So, Shorty ate while Dratz played with a worn-down piece of copper. Shorty was not impressed. Ez'ard could do that trick even better than Dratz could.

The uncomfortable wait seemed to last forever. Its end was far more startling that Shorty would have expected. The blue sky to the left of the peak was empty one moment. In the next, it was filled with red scales and beating wings. Each stroke of those wings cracked like a hammer striking an anvil. But louder still was the roar of dragon rage as the ancient beast's flame streaked across the sky. Even this far away, Shorty felt the dragon fear reach for him. Shorty was proud of himself. All he did was tense his muscles at the dragon's unexpected appearance. Dratz fumbled his coin, dropping it to the dirt between his legs.

The excitement was brief. The dragon shot overhead, headed into the rising sun. Luckily it never looked down, never saw the two tiny forms huddling outside its lair. Shorty's eyes tried to track its departure, but the dragon was very fast as it disappeared from view.

Dratz searched for his copper piece, tucking it back into his pocket. The half-orc rose without speaking and slipped back through the gap between the rocks. Shorty was behind him in an instant, moving without a sound on the rocky ground. Dratz blinked in surprise when he turned to see if Shorty was coming. He had not expected Shorty to be that close or that Shorty's massive sword would already be gripped in his oversized hand.

Dratz picked up speed then, moving swiftly along the path he had pointed to earlier that morning. Shorty had no trouble keeping up. If the half-orc expected Shorty to be noisy, he was soon disappointed. They raced around the curve of the mountain, until Dratz just disappeared from view.

Shorty stopped and studied the mountain before him. Then he saw the deep crevice. The dark opening blended perfectly with the surrounding stone. Shorty reached out his left hand to explore the space between the rocks. It would be tight, but Shorty had been in smaller spaces before. He slid his sword back into its scabbard. Shorty turned sideways and slid into the gap.

Dratz waited about a dozen feet ahead. The thief had a wicked grin on his face. Shorty reached down to his thigh and pulled Papa's dagger free. Dratz smile quickly turned upside down as he turned away from Shorty.

Dratz moved deeper into the tunnel, not bothering to make any light. Shorty did not care. The thief's body heat was more than enough to outline him against the cold stone. That advantage was quickly disappearing as the tunnel widened out. Shorty trailed his fingers across the rock wall of the tunnel. The rock was warming up. And Shorty no longer felt the chill of the mountain air.

The tunnel was not short and it was getting uncomfortably warm. Shorty could feel the sweat beading up beneath his armor. He ran his fingers along the wall. It was getting hotter the further into the mountain he and Dratz went. The rock was also strangely smooth.

The one protrusion Shorty found crumbled into dust beneath his fingers. Why were the walls so smooth? He wondered. Then it came to him, fire. The dragon might not fit in this tunnel, but its fiery breath could fill it.

Shorty looked for the half-orc to warn him, but the heat of Dratz body was no longer visible against the walls of the tunnel. Shorty sped up, wanting to find his elusive partner. The end of the tunnel was unexpected and a little painful. The hot wall burned his nose when he smashed it into the stone. Dratz'z smaller body should have been there to cushion Shorty's collision with the wall. Where had the little thief gone?

Then a voice whispered from the side. "Left, you buffoon!"

Shorty reached for the left wall with both hands. He found a much narrower passage through the rock wall on that side. It was smaller than the one that led into this tunnel. Shorty could only hope that the padding under his armor would keep him from getting burned. Emptying his lungs, Shorty sidestepped into the passage. The walls pressed against his chest and back. The heat penetrated his armor making him sweat even more as his armor scraped along the rock of the passage. A dozen steps and he felt cooler air against his cheek. He was about to take another step when a voice hissed at him, "Do not step on me, you oaf." Shorty stopped even though he wanted nothing more than to get out of the crevice he was slowly cooking in.

Dratz began to whisper to in the darkness, "There were no guards the last time I was here. I am leaving as soon as I get what I came for. Find the sword quickly, I am not going to wait for you." Then the half-orc was gone.

Three more steps and the hot stone released its hold on him. The air, though still the temperature of a hot summer day, was a relief after the heat of the narrow crevice. Shorty stared around him, trying to take in the vast chamber that he suddenly found himself in.

Fires burned everywhere, their flames often rising above Shorty's head. Shorty studied the closest of the fires. He blinked in surprise. At the heart of the blaze was a boulder. How had the dragon made rock burn this way? He did not know. Shorty quickly scanned the rest of the room. Waves of glittering light danced along the floor. The light on the dragon's hoard moved with the flickering of the massive flames. The treasure gathered here was more than all of the other dragons he had fought before combined. "Too muches," he muttered softly to himself.

"That is the stupidest thing I have ever heard." Dratz replied from a few feet away. "There is no such thing as too much! Now find that damn sword so I can get paid."

The half-orc slipped into a shadow and disappeared. Shorty took another moment to study the cavern. This was not going to be easy. Small metal circles of silver, gold, and other shiny things covered the floor of the dragon's home. The riches spread around the cavern rose and fell in great mounds and smaller heaps. As his eyes adjusted to the flickering light, Shorty could see many other things mixed in with the round bits of metal. He saw random pieces of armor and weapons. There were larger items, even a wagon that lay on its side, scattered around the chamber. There were bones, many bones, and he could see large tooth marks on all of them. And, of course, there were marbles, more marbles than Shorty had seen in his entire life, mixed in with the other treasures. Each of those marbles cried out for him to play with them. But first he had to find the sword.

There was also a round pit near the center of the chamber. It was filled with piles of the metal called platinum. Other treasures like books and what looked like a horn lay in that circle. This was the dragon's bed, Shorty knew. The outline of its great body was still clear in the treasure pile. He would avoid that nest if at all possible.

He could have stared at the vast treasure for hours, but a frightened voice from somewhere deep inside of him screamed out, "Hurries up afor youse gets eated!" Shorty began to move, staying as far from the dragon's nest as possible.

The search began. Shorty's heavy boots sank into the treasure with every step. Each time he lifted his foot, he was forced to pull his boot free. The bits of metal were harder to walk through than sucking mud. But he trudged on. The effort required to walk made the search seem even more hopeless. And to make matters worse, most of the treasure reflected the flames from the burning rocks. How was he supposed to find Bone Man's red blade in a place where practically everything glowed with the color of warm blood?

Having no real plan, Shorty fought his way to a nearby treasure pile. He began pushing the lose metal and marbles aside, searching desperately for the sword. There were no swords in the pile, only an axe. It had a nice edge on the blade, but the axe was much too small to be useful. The entire length of its wooden handle fit into the palm of Shorty's hand. Frustrated, he threw it at another treasure pile located near one of the burning rocks. Something that sparkled with shades of gold and silver slid down the pile. Curiosity gripped him. Shorty rose and headed that way.

Sweat dripped down his face as he got closer to the burning rock. The heat was unbearable, but he had to see what had fallen to the floor. His eyes searched the floor as he approached the second treasure heap. There, lying on its side on top of a half-buried shield was a familiar shape. Shorty knelt and picked it up. There in his hand lay the body of a tiny metal owl. The feathers of the owl's body and wings appeared to be individual pieces, each woven into the form of the bird. It was beautiful. It would have been perfect except for its missing head.

Shorty looked at the place where the axe he had thrown had buried itself in the pile. Carefully, he began to scoop handfuls of treasure aside. Finding the tiny owl's head suddenly seemed more important than finding the sword. Then his fingers felt something round and smooth. He closed his hand around it and pulled it from the pile. When he uncurled his fingers, two eyes stared back at him over its sharp curved beak. He had found it. It was as perfect as the body except for the bent metal rod that stuck out where its neck should have been. Shorty tucked the two pieces into the pouch where he kept his marbles. He did not have time to play with toys right now.

He rose and stared around. There was just too much for one ogre to search. Where could that sword be? Maybe with Dratz help he could find it. But the cavern was silent except for the crackle of the fires, there was no sign of the half-orc anywhere. What could he do? Then Shorty remembered Bone Man's words. His own sword was the answer. The fuzzface that had warned him about the sword and glove had also told him about the other things the sword could do. It could heal him, it knew how to go pop, and it could help him find things if he knew what they looked like.

Shorty pulled out the parchment that Bone Man had given him. He unfolded it and held it up in the firelight. Shorty then reached over his left shoulder, wrapping his fingers around the hilt of his marble sword. Drawing the blade, he held it loosely in his hand. Staring at the image of the red blade, Shorty whispered to his beloved sword, "Where bees Bone Man's new toy?"

At first, Shorty thought the black blade would not answer. But how could it? The sword had no mouth to speak with. But then the hilt shifted in his hand. The tip of the blade came up, pointing across the cavern. Shorty followed the line of the blade, staring into the flickering light. Halfway across the cavern, a dark alcove was sunk into the wall far from any of the burning rocks. Shorty returned the marble sword to its scabbard and struggled towards that dark opening. The parchment dropped to the ground behind him where it began to smolder.

The alcove turned out to be little more than a small closet shaped opening that was half filled with useless golden circles. There was no sword. Had his sword lied to him? Shorty knelt down, scooping out a mass of gold. There, buried under the metal was the white of fresh bone. That piece of bone was carved though, not chewed like all the others in the cavern. That was when Shorty made an even bigger mistake than coming to this place had been. He reached out and grabbed the bone, the bone hilt of a red-bladed sword, and pulled if from the darkness.

Searing pain shot through Shorty's hand and up his arm in the instant he grasped the hilt. He would have dropped the sword except that it had sunk its power into his flesh. The sword now held him instead of him holding it. Shorty stumbled backwards as an angry voice filled with hatred thundered in his head. *Defiler! You are not a mage. You do not even possess the intelligence to serve a mage. Your touch is an afront to all that I was forged to be. Great suffering is the only way for you to atone for this insult!*

Shorty fought against the pressure in his head. But it was no use, he could no more push the voice from his head than he could release his grip on the sword's hilt. He almost sobbed as he tried to explain to the angry sword, "No fer me! Sword bees fer Bone Man! Him sends me dis place!"

The pain spread into his shoulder and then his chest. His lungs could hardly draw in enough air for him to fight the evil sword. Then the pain eased enough for a single breath as the sword demanded, *Who is this Bone Man? Picture him in your mind, fool.*

Shorty did as he was commanded. He started with the toe bones peeking out from under Bone Man's robes. In his mind, the image rose up the black robes floating in the chair high over his head. Then he focused on those glowing red eyes hidden within the dark hood.

He could feel the sword's excitement as it murmured in his mind, *Lich! One who might be truly worthy of my magnificence.* The sword allowed Shorty to take another breath. *This one that you call Bone Man, you will take me to him. If he is not all that I desire, the next time I hurt you it will be even worse. Do you understand?"

Shorty could only nod in agreement. That seemed to be enough as the pain became bearable. *Find my scabbard in the coins before you. I will not go to this Bone Man in less than my proper attire." Shorty's left hand began to dig in the alcove. He found a white bone scabbard covered in red marbles. As he tried to slide the blade into the scabbard, another pulse of pain shot through his body. *Remember, fool, and do not fail me or this will be little more than a happy memory.*

The sword slid into the scabbard. The pain left him and the voice was gone from his head. Shorty did not like this sword and he suspected that Bone Man was not so nice either. But it was too late. He was trapped. Shorty stood and shoved the small sword and scabbard into his belt. He would not draw it again.

Shorty turned back towards the tunnel that had brough him here. He wanted nothing more than to leave this place. He took a step and then another. Something snagged his foot and he fell to land face first in something that was cool despite the heat of the chamber. The coolness felt good. Shorty pushed his face up from the ground to see what he had landed on. Reds, blues, greens, yellows and even a few white orbs flashed up at him. Shorty had never seen so many beautiful marbles in one place before. One of the yellow marbles even had a small spider trapped inside it.

Shorty wanted them. He deserved something from this trip after what the sword had done to him. But what could he put them in? Shorty reached back to free his foot so he could stand. Maybe he could put some of the marbles in his backpack. His fingers found a leather bag wrapped around his right foot. It was strange because his leg seemed to go too far into the bag. It did not look that big. Shorty took it off his foot to see if it was ripped. But it wasn't, the bottom was intact.

Shorty put the bag beside the pile of marbles and began to shove them inside. He put many, many marbles in the bag. It had to be close to full. Shorty lifted it from the ground. It felt empty. It made no sense. Shorty shoved his hand into the bag. He could feel the cool surface of the new marbles. Shorty put the bag down and began to put a bunch of the useless metal circles into the bag. He lifted it again. It still felt empty. Shorty crawled over to one of the treasure piles. He began to fill his new bag. Only it did not get any fuller. Shorty found a number of potion bottles and pushed them into the bag too. The bag held them easily.

Shorty held the bag in front of him. Could it hold all of the dragon's treasure? He did not know and he doubted he had time to find out. One more pile, he wondered? His thoughts of treasure were interrupted by a high pitched, mewling cry. Then there was another just like it. Shorty looked up. He was much closer to the nest than he had ever intended to get. Staring out of that nest were two pairs of glowing eyes.

"Dragon babies?" he whispered to himself. Shorty stood. From this side of the nest, he could see the remains of two large eggs. Both were now broken and empty. The dragon had been a mama and her eggs had hatched. She would be coming for her babies and she would eat him. Or, maybe the babies would eat him. Shorty did not wait to find out. He moved as fast as the piles of treasure would allow, heading for the safety the crevice and the tunnel beyond. Despite all he could do, that trip across the cavern seemed to take forever.

The strange bag was still gripped in his hand when he pushed his way between the tight walls. If Dratz was still here, the half-orc would be dead soon. One of the three dragons would get him. Shorty was sure of that. In his panic, Shorty barely noticed the heat of those walls. When he made it into the wider tunnel, he began to run. He had to get to the circle of rocks before Mama came back. He would not survive her fire if she saw him outside.

When he reached the exit, Shorty paused to listen behind him, half expecting to hear the cries of the dragon babies coming for him. But the tunnel was silent. Shorty pushed his way back towards the light of day. Cool mountain air bathed his body as he stepped into the morning light. He had not been inside as long as he had thought. Shorty tied his new bag to his belt. Then he began to run back around the mountain towards his meeting place with Dratz.

Chapter 3

Broken Things

As the circle of stones came into view, Shorty crouched down beside the mountain. He scanned the horizon, fully expecting to find red death headed his way. But the sky was nearly empty with just a few harmless clouds floating overhead. Perhaps they could get away before the mama dragon returned to defend her babies. Shorty hoped so at least. It would all depend on whether his unreliable partner was around. The sooner Dratz used the tiny bone to open the magic door, the better. Shorty rose and ran for the opening in the circle of stones.

He need not have worried. Dratz stood in the opening, leaning against one of the boulders. The half-orc had a huge grin on his face. Shorty was not sure what they had to be happy about. Mama was going to be very angry when she got home.

Shorty tried to step past the half-orc, but Dratz did not move out of the way. The thief's eyes moved over Shorty until they settled on the white hilt and scabbard. "Is that it?" Dratz asked eagerly.

Shorty merely nodded. Dratz smiled and pointed at the blade. "That is your prize. Your Bone Man will reward you for it." Dratz took one step backwards and paused again. He raised that finger even higher to shake it in the air. "Keep those oversized hands of yours off my prize. What your boss is going to pay me will make me a king among orcs. Maybe a king among human kind too."

Shorty considered telling his no bery smart partner that orcs did not have kings. They had chiefs. Once, long ago, Shorty had been such a chief. But he had given up that position for the good of his tribe. Shorty brushed past Dratz, but he froze when he saw what was behind the half-orc, sitting on the ground within the circle.

A huge canvas bag, nearly as large as the thief was tall, sat in the center of the circle. The bag had no top, but it did have two arm straps that could be used to carry it. It was not the bag that made Shorty sputter with disbelief, it was the object that hardly fit inside the bag that made Shorty very, very afraid. It was a dragon egg; its pale red shell was dotted with darker red spots. Dratz had stolen one of the mama's babies.

Dratz voice rang with pride as he boasted, "Talk about a sweet heist! I have never had such an easy gig before. Walk in, slip it in the bag, and walk out. I am going to be rich and I do not even need to find a buyer. And better still, I get a bonus because you found that sword."

Shorty stopped listening almost as soon as Dratz began to speak. Most of the thief's words made no sense anyway. Heist? Gig? What also made no sense to Shorty was stealing one of the dragon's babies. What would the little dragon do without a mama? He remembered how it had hurt when he lost his mama and he had not been a baby then. What would happen to this child if it never had a mother? More importantly, what kind of life would it have if Bone Man got his skeletal hand's on the egg. The more Shorty thought about it, the angrier he got. He even forgot to be afraid of Mama Dragon coming home.

Shorty spun on his partner. Shorty's face must not have been very nice because the thief stumbled backwards. Dratz moved to place the circle of rocks between himself and Shorty.

Shorty raised one of his large hands and shook a finger at the half-orc. "Bad Dratz. Bery naughty. Yousc needs a bery hard spank."

Dratz mouth fell open. "What is wrong with you? Are you that stupid? Look, how about we take the egg back and I will give you a share of the take. I can afford to be generous."

Shorty stepped through the opening in the rocks. "No!" Shorty growled at his partner. "Baby need it Mama. Not posed ta steals dat egg."

Dratz shook his head. "It is a dragon, you moron. They are not like us. Who cares if a baby red goes missing or not. Or even if it dies, for that matter, do you know how much the pieces of a dragon sell for?"

Shorty's face darkened at the thought of killing the baby dragon. He took another menacing step towards Dratz. The thief's hand went for the mace hanging at his belt. But before he could free it, Shorty had both his great swords in his hands.

Dratz jerked his hand away from the mace as he backed towards the cliff's edge. The thief raised both his hands up before his body. "Easy big guy. We are friends, teammates, remember? There has to be some way to work this out."

Shorty shook his head as he took another step forward. "Takes egg back!" Shorty answered him.

Shorty could smell the half-orcs fear then. "Hell no! Them other two eggs were hatching when I left. I do not intend to get eaten because you have gone soft in the head."

Shorty took another step forward. Dratz had no place left to go. The thief stood on the edge of the cliff. Shorty was angry enough that he wanted to see if Dratz knew how to fly.

Dratz eyed the two large swords and then he sighed. "This is not going to end well for either of us. I will end up on the run, but what do you think the lich is going to do to your elf friend when you do not return with the egg and the sword. It is not going to be pretty."

Shorty raised his black sword. He would not allow Dratz or Bone Man to hurt Ez'ard. With a snarl of disgust, Dratz reached into his pocket and pulled out the small bone that had been given to him back in the Keep. Then the half-orc threw himself backwards off the cliff.

Shorty rushed forward to see if Dratz did know how to fly. As he looked down, he saw the flash of the magic door and then Dratz and the door were gone. Shorty was alone. Well, sort of alone. He was

on the side of a mountain with a stolen dragon egg that was probably
going to get him killed. Shorty put his swords away as he walked
back to the circle of stones asking himself, "What me gonna dos
now?"

Shorty sat on one of the smaller rocks. He stared at the egg. What
should he do now? Dratz had been right about one thing, if he tried
to return the egg, he was going to get eaten by one of the dragons.
Could he leave the egg out here, hoping the mama dragon would find
it? The cold wind still blew across the mountainside. Even Shorty
knew that cold was not good for the egg. Leaving the egg was not a
good plan.

Shorty's hands moved restlessly as his brain searched for a solution
that did not get him or the baby dragon killed. He stared at his
empty hands as his thoughts followed the same paths over and over.
Sometimes, his head worked better when his hands had something to
do. Shorty reached into his pouch for a marble to play with. What his
fingers found was the metal body of the small owl. The tiny figure
was still warm from the dragon's cave.

Shorty pulled out both pieces of the tiny owl and stared at them. The
place where the head was supposed to go was easy to see, even for
him. But there were problems with putting the owl back together.
Shorty forgot about the egg as he studied a new puzzle that did not
seem so hard to solve.

The big problem would be the bent rod on the head piece. But that
was not the only thing wrong. There were things that had come loose
inside the hole where the head was supposed to go. Two small pieces
of metal flopped around down inside its body. Shorty could see
where they were supposed to go, but his finger was too big to fit into
the hole. How could he hook them into place if he could not reach
them.

Shorty started to pull things out of his pouch and backpack. Most of
his toys either did not fit in the hold or they were useless as tools. He
had a small stick that fit into the hole, but it would not grab either of
the pieces. Shorty became absorbed in his work. He found one of the
small hooks that he used to catch fish. He used the hooks string to
tie it to his stick. Some time later, he managed to stretch both pieces

to the posts where they were supposed to be. When the second one settled into place, Shorty grinned happily.

That only left the bent rod beneath the owls head. Shorty considered it. He had no hammer, and even if he did, he was as likely to crush the head as hit the bent rod. But what Shorty did have was strength. He had bent the metal on Al's cage. Could he bend this piece back without breaking the head? His fingers studied the tiny head, searching for a grip that would allow him to exert his strength against the rod. Finally, he found a grip that felt right and Shorty strained, pushing both thumbs against the bend in the rod. Shorty felt the metal rod give, just a bit.

He tried to put the rod into the body, but it wasn't straight enough yet. He strained again and the rod straightened a bit more. This time the rod slid into the owls body but the head would not go all the way into the hole. Turning the head side to side, he studied the problem but it made no sense. Then he turned the head around backwards and it slipped down into place. Shorty stared at his work. The owl was beautiful, but it looked strange with its head on backwards.

Standing, Shorty set the tiny owl on the stone where he had been sitting. Using one hand to steady its body; he used the other hand to twist the head all the way around. There was a loud click and a strange bussing noise. Shorty's fingers tingled with that buzzing. He released the owl and stepped back.

Several more loud clicks sounded from somewhere inside the owl. The buzzing was replaced by a whirring noise. Shorty watched as the owls body began to vibrate. Light flashed in the tiny owl's eyes and its body began to bounce around on the rock. Had he somehow broken the pretty birdie even more by what he had done? Even at this, Shorty had done the wrong thing. He would soon have a dead metal owl and a dead baby dragon to make him sad.

Magic wrapped itself around him, pulling him for the dark abyss where time had no meaning. His soul had fled to that place of nothingness. But why? His memories were still fragmented. As was his body. He was Maxamillian. But he had given up that name for one less pretentious. Now he was just Max. Sensations from a body that was not the one he was born to returned. That body was as broken as his mind. But the magic flowed through him once more, repairing his body and healing his mind. The magic gave him hope.

As control of his body returned, so did the memories. Memories of being human. Memories of the place of light. Memories of his rebirth as one of The Seven. He remembered his mission, to teach and guide the meek of this world. He remembered the joy that teaching had brought him. And more recently, the memory of his new body being sundered by a servant of the Dark One. Then there was nothing until now. How had this latest miracle come about?

The tiny owl shaped body, an eternal vessel for his soul, was beginning to function once more. Sound returned to his ears, his sight was restored, and more subtle sensations originated in every metallic feather in his small body. Cool, clean air surrounded him. The heat and vile stench of the dragoness was gone. His feathers fluttered in a strong wind and the desire to fly once more was almost overwhelming. Max's mechanical eyes irised open.

Even after over 2000 years in a world ruled by the chaos of magic, the figure looming over him was a surprise. Max had expected to see one of the magical races, perhaps a djinn or even a giant. But it was not. His rescuer was not even a wizard. The individual staring down at him was clearly not human or even one of the longer lived changed known as elves. Why would one of those the ancients had called ogres seek him out? It made no sense. Ogres were more interested in destruction than they were in learning. This looked to be a very interesting discussion.

His new "master" was a bit unusual for one of the lesser changed. Instead of skins, it wore heavy battle armor. Rather than a club, it carried a pair of forged swords, both of which radiated magical energy. Was this creature a would be king or just a wandering adventurer? Based on the aura sword sticking up over the ogre's left shoulder, it was probably evil. It was unlikely to serve the Nameless God or one of his aliases. As long as it did not ask him to violate his oath to that Nameless God, Max would serve it and try to guide it onto the true path. If it demanded more than he was allowed to give, Max would refuse it as he had the ancient red. At least this time, he was unlikely to get his head ripped off for refusing.

The magic that surged through his body and mind dissipated. His body was whole once more. As for his mind, who could tell after all the centuries he had existed. Max liked to think his mind was clearer than that of most in this world, but not all among the Seven agreed with him. Max fluttered his wings in amusement. Only time would tell and apparently, he had just been given many more centuries to find out. The ogre standing over him leaned forward. Max was still contemplating the best way to address what he assumed would be a volatile master when the ogre spoke to him in a voice filled with concern, "Birdie bees kay? Me no breaks sumtin when puts head back on?"

The ogre had repaired him? Preposterous! His mind had cataloged all of the damage the magic had just repaired. How could an ogre…? Max glanced around, noting for the first time where he was. That mountain peak was the lair of the dragoness that he had been forced to serve. He was far closer to the place of his captivity than he really wanted to be. There was, he realized, no one else around. The ogre was the only one who could have put him back together. As was often the case in a magic filled world, reality and logic did not walk hand in hand.

Max decided to try a little flattery on the powerful looking ogre. That seemed the best approach considering the fact that the warrior carried the dark sword and wore the black glove of the World Conqueror. Max could only guess how those two items might affect an overly dominant male ogre. "I am well, Magnificent One. My thanks for what you have done for me."

Max's effort was an utter waste of time. If anything, the flowery title did more to confuse his new master than anything else. The situation became almost comical. The ogre's eyes opened so wide that Max thought his eyeballs might fall out. Max could almost read its mind, "It talks?" Then the ogre spun in place, as if it was trying to figure out who Max was talking to. When the ogre turned back to face him, it knelt on the ground in front of Max. There was pity in its pale green eyes and a sad smile on its lips as it crooned to him. "Poor Birdie. Me musta squeeze head too hard. Maybeso us fid youse friend Mangi after gets way from dragon. Maybeso him knowed how ta fix youse head."

Max started to protest. There was nothing wrong with his head other than the beginnings of an ogre-induced headache. But the ogre just continued to ramble on, unaware that it had insulted one of The Seven who held the knowledge of both the new and ancient worlds in his memory. It seemed almost cheerful as it explained, "Me head no always works so gooder most a da times. Me no gets in too muches trouble. Youse bees kay too." The ogre then leaned in closer and whispered, "Me neber sees a birdie dat ken talks people talk afore. Youse must bees bery smart."

For a moment, Max was at a loss for words. Had the creature kneeling before him cast a spell of confusion on him? It was either that or being beheaded had rattled him more than he thought. No, he told himself. He was not damaged and the ogre had not cast a spell on him. Max knew he should just fly away and leave this creature behind. He needed to get away before the dragoness returned. But how could he abandon someone who was obviously more concerned about Max than he was his own safety. Max had to try once more to do something for the one who had helped to make him whole again. "Good day, Sir Ogre. It appears that I owe you a favor. Is there anything that I can do for you in return for all that you have done for me?"

The ogre's head began to shake from side to side rather vigorously, "No posed ta get nuttin fer helping people. Dat no bees right."

Max's beak opened and closed but nothing came out this time. Who was this creature and why had it sought him out in the dragoness's lair? Max had to be sure he was understanding his companion, so he asked, "There is nothing that I can do for you, Sir Ogre?"

The ogre's head continued to shake from side to side. Then it stopped. Max braced himself for what was to come. The ogre had just been playing him. It needed something that only one of The Seven could provide. When the ogre spoke, his words nearly overloaded Max's circuits, "Maybeso Birdie bees me friend? Plays game wid me sum a da times? Birdie maybeso knowed gooder games?"

Max took a moment to absorb the ogre's request. Even in that long ago time when he had been human, friendship was a rare thing. This could not be real. The next words that Max uttered were unintentional. "Who and what are you? Of all the things you could ask for, you want my friendship?"

The ogre's smile literally lit up his face. "Me bees Shorty. No ken hab too muches friend."

The memories of centuries of masters, both good and evil, flashed through Max's mind. This was the one secret, the one gift, that he had never been asked for in all that time. Had the meek finally inherited the earth while he lay in pieces in the dragon's lair. Max stared at the not so short ogre named Shorty. Having a friend would be nice. "My name is Max, Shorty. And yes, I will be your friend." Max hesitated for a moment before asking, "There really is nothing you want to ask me about? No advice that I can give you?"

The ogre, Shorty, paused for a long moment before he stood and stepped to the side. Shorty pointed to something on the far side of the circle of rocks and asked, "Maybeso, Birdie Max. Knowed what me posed to do wid dat?"

Max's head rotated to the side as his eyes focused on where that finger pointed. A shiver passed through his body. It might have been fear, but that emotion had not been included in the design of his mechanical body. Sitting across that small gap was a dragon egg. Dark red spots decorated the pale red shell, at least the part of it that stuck out of the oversized bag it sat in. She, Saphignis of the First Flame, had laid another clutch of eggs. And his foolish new friend had stolen one of those precious orbs. Max doubted either of them would survive this.

Max did not understand. Even for an ogre, this seemed a bit much. "Shorty, why did you take one of the dragon's eggs?"

Shorty began to shake his head again. "Dratz!" Max's new friend blurted out.

"Drats is quite an understatement, Shorty. That is not just a little oops."

The ogre's head began to move side to side again. Did it know how to do anything else besides shake its head no. "Bees half-orc, no dat under ting."

The headache was growing stronger. And how did a mechanical head ache anyway? Simple questions, Max cautioned himself. "Who is a half-orc, Shorty?"

With another look of pity, Shorty explained. "Dratz bees half-orc. Bery naughty thief. Me bees gonna gib him a spank. But him goes pop."

A thief? Then what was Shorty there for? Surly not to fight the dragon. Max decided to risk another question. "What were you doing while Drats stole that egg?"

Shorty pointed at a ruby encrusted scabbard thrust under his belt. A white sword hilt protruded from the scabbard. It took Max a moment to recognize the blade for what it was. Mage Eater was a vile weapon, evil to its core. It literally ate the magical essence of any creature that it struck. But it was only usable by a mage. Why would Shorty be looking for it? This was making less sense with every fact he dug out of Shorty's brain.

 "I need you to start at the beginning, Shorty," Max suggested. "How about starting before you came here. Tell me how you got here. And remember, we need to get out of here soon."

The tale that spilled out of the ogre would have been unbelievable, except that Max was perched on a rock staring at a dragon egg. The short version of the story had included a lich, the half-orc thief, an intelligent sword that liked to eat magic, and an insane raid into the lair of a dragon. This was what Shorty considered 'not getting into too much trouble?' Max's new friend was at best a magnet for chaos. How could anyone blunder into so many outright disasters and not become a casualty of his own bad luck.

Max was about to suggest they get moving when the next catastrophe in Shorty's tale arrived. It began with a sharp crack that was quickly followed by a childish cry of "Mama?"

Max launched himself into the air as Shorty spun around. Both of them stared at the near perfection of the small red head that stared at them from the cracked shell. Before Max could stop him, Shorty moved to the baby dragon's side. Shorty's hands caressed its small, for a dragon, head removing the inner sac of the egg from around the baby's head. Max sensed it the moment the dragon imprinted on his friend. There would be no going back now.

Shorty looked up at Max. "Me ken no bees da Mama, Birdie Max. Me no bees lady dragon."

Max felt his chest tighten even though he did not breathe in this form. "He does not know that, Shorty."

Shorty continued to caress the small dragon's head. Max watched the ogre's fingers begin to rub the area behind the dragons sensitive ear holes. Shorty gave Max a hopeful look as he asked, "Ken me gib Baby back to its Mama?"

Even Max had to words that could make Shorty understand it meant for a dragon to imprint on its mother. It was a bond that could not be broken. And how could he suggest to Shorty that it would be a mercy to kill the dragon before its evil nature made it do something terrible like eat Shorty. In the end, all Max said was, "The mother dragon will kill it now, Shorty. There is nothing you can do."

The stubborn look that came over his new friend's face was a surprise. Shorty's head began its violent side to side motion again. "No! Me posed ta protect kid, eben dragon. Him bees me son now. Me growed him up."

Max was beginning to see how Shorty got into so much trouble. The ogre's heart was his compass in life and that made him easy to manipulate. Max was not sure if that was a good thing or not. He only knew from his own life that a good heart was a rare thing.

A mewling cry erupted from the baby red, "Mama?"

Shorty looked hopelessly at Max, "What me posed ta dos?"

Max kept his voice calm, "Your baby is hungry. You need to feed him."

Shorty rummaged around in his pouches until he came up with a handful of what looked like jerky. It was not even a mouthful for the dragon. "Needs ta hun," Shorty muttered.

Max circled the pair as he watched Shorty slip his arms into the straps on the large bag. The ogre did not appear to even notice the weight of the tiny dragon as he lifted the bag and waddled out of the circle of rocks. Max had no idea where his friend was going, especially when Shorty turned towards the cliff.

Max flew towards Shorty, catching a thermal that raised him well above Shorty. Was his friend going to drop the baby off the cliff? It might be a merciful end for the dragon, but somehow, Max could not see Shorty doing something like that.

Shorty stared down at the small dragon. "Him bery purtty. Me gonna bees good Mama. Gib him lots lub. Me no knowed haws ta do dat."

Max dipped one wingtip so he could spiral closer to Shorty. He was a bit surprised to see Shorty's fingers caressing the tiny dragon's head once more. What Max was not prepared for was when Shorty stepped off the cliff.

Chapter 4

Finding a Nudder Way

A squawk of surprise reverberated off the side of the mountain as Shorty drifted gently towards the valley below. Looking up, Shorty saw Birdie Max diving towards him. He wondered if telling the little owl that it sounded like an angry chicken was a good idea. Probably not he decided.

Max's wings stretched out wide, slowing his descent. The small owl maneuvered alongside Shorty and his new son. Max seemed a little upset. Shorty was not sure why until Max said, "I thought you were going to die."

Shorty began to shake his head. For a birdie that was so smart, his new friend seemed to need an awful lot of things explained to him. Shorty gave Max an encouraging smile as he explained, "Me knowed no fall down. Bestus magics eber. Bees muches fun to jumps high place."

"I see," was Birdie Max's only response. Max began to fly circles around him and the tiny dragon nestled against Shorty's stomach. The owl's eyes flashed from time to time as it stared at Shorty. Shorty definitely needed to find someone to fix Birdie Max's head.

Shorty watched the horizon as he floated towards the ground below. This was one of those times he wished he could maybe fall a little bit faster. Thankfully, there was no sign of the Mama dragon. Fighting her while in the air would be more than a little bit difficult. The baby dragon seemed to actually be enjoying the drop into the valley. Did dragons come out of their eggs wanting to fly?

Crunching noises filled the air in front of Shorty. That was not the noise his stomach usually made when he was this hungry. He looked down to see Baby clutching a large piece of eggshell between his two tiny front paws. As Shorty watched, the tiny dragon bit off a large piece of shell and began to chew it. Shorty grimaced. He liked to eat eggs, but not the shell. He needed to go hunting before his new son decided to eat the bag too. How much did little dragons eat anyway? Would he be able to keep up with his son's appetite?

Shorty spent the remainder of the no fall down rubbing the back of his son's head and scratching his neck. Whether it was the eggshell he was eating or the petting, a deep rumble of contentment soon came from within the bag. Apparently, baby dragons purred like cats when they were happy. He was glad his son was having a good time. Maybeso he could be a good Mama after all.

By the time they reached the base of the cliff, his dragon was asleep with its head tucked into the warmth of the canvas bag. Based on how much it had eaten, Shorty doubted there was much of the shell left inside the bag.

Shorty's feet came to rest on a rocky ground. The mountain was still steep here at the base of the cliff. Despite how far he had not fallen, he was still high on the slope so there were only a few scraggly trees growing nearby. None of them would hide him from the Mama dragon. The trees he needed were still a good ways down the mountainside. Settling the bag into a comfortable position, Shorty began to run and slide his way down to the forest below. Birdie led the way, his tiny wings beating occasionally to keep him ahead of Shorty.

The sun was well past midday when the trees closed in around them. He struggled on, tired and hungry, until the overhead branches blocked his view of the sky. Then slowly and carefully, Shorty lowered his sleeping son to the ground. Max settled on a tree branch just over Shorty's head.

Shorty slid to the ground beside the canvas bag, pulling off his backpack. He dug inside it for something to eat. But the jerky was all gone, eaten in a single bite by his son. Shorty found a journey cake and began to nibble at the dry bread. After a few bites, he looked up at Birdie Max and asked, "What baby dragons posed ta eats? Baby eated him shell. Bery no so gooder."

The noise that came from the tiny owl might have been a snort or it might have been laughter. Shorty was not sure which. Max sounded confident though when he answered, "It is not unusual for baby dragons to eat their shells. Actually, dragons will eat practically any kind of meat. They are not very particular about their prey. They do not even mind if the meat has been dead for a while."

That last part bothered Shorty. He knew that meat that had gone bad was dangerous. Unwilling to let it go, Shorty asked again, "Old meat no makes dragon sick?" Max should his head and that made Shorty realize just how much he did not know about being a mama dragon. But of all the questions in his head, one worried him more than all of his others. "How muches dragon gonna eats?"

"They eat quite a lot," Max answered him. And then they sleep for a long time and wake up hungry again."

Shorty grunted and rose to his feet. He popped the rest of the journey cake into his mouth and took a long drink from his waterskin. "Times ta hunt den. Watches me Baby please, Birdie. Me bees back soon wid meat."

Shorty walked past his son and disappeared into the trees.

Max stared at the place where the enigmatic ogre has just disappeared. His new master, and maybe friend, was a contradiction in almost every aspect of his being. One moment the ogre was child-like and the next he was deadly competent. Shorty was so eager to please and yet damnably stubborn almost all of the time. Max sensed that it might take a lifetime to fully understand his new friend.

Shorty's equipment was another puzzle that Max would need to sort out. The ring that had allowed Shorty to float instead of fall had been a surprise. It had been hidden among the more powerful magical auras that surrounded Shorty. Max had spent most of their descent studying and cataloging all of the magic on his friend.

What Shorty carried was not insignificant. Two intelligent swords, both evil, had been the most obvious. And yet, Max's own spells had verified that neither blade had tainted the spirit of his friend. Shorty carried a king's ransom in magic, especially the ioun stones. And yet, it was little more than a hodgepodge collection of… Max paused in thought. Toys, Max realized with sudden insight. With everything Shorty carried, he might indeed conquer the world if he tried. But Max doubted that Shorty even wanted that kind of power. Each of those dangerous items was little more than a plaything to his innocent friend. They were dangerous toys in a child's hands.

Max began to laugh as he realized that he, one of The Seven, had been added to that collection of toys. The laughter died away when the dragon shifted in its sleep. That toy chest also now included an evil red dragon. The dragon was a potentially bigger problem that the magic was. The question Max needed to answer was whether there was anything he could do about the dragon. That was just one of many things he needed to figure out while Shorty was hunting.

Shorty had been gone for about an hour when the world was shaken by the bellow of an angry dragoness. Saphignis had returned and her cry of rage caused leaves to fall from the trees. Max said a silent prayer that she would not be able to track any of her missing possessions. High on Max's list of treasure items to be permanently lost was a small owl shaped prize that never wanted to fall into her clutches ever again. He could only hope that the other two babies Shorty had mentioned would keep her busy.

His prey must have known it was being hunted. There was no other reason for it to abandon caution the way it had. It was now heading for the steeper slopes of the mountain where there was less cover. But on the steeper slopes, it would move much faster than he could.

Shorty had been tracking the elusive mountain goat for a while when he heard the angry Mama dragon roar. Was she mad about the missing egg or the things that Shorty had taken. It was hard to know with dragons. That cry frightened the goat more than it did Shorty. The goat reversed its course and charged at him.

One slash of the black sword was all it took to sever the goats spine. Shorty thanked the Lady of the Forest for her gift as he ended the goats suffering. Shorty tossed the goat's body over his shoulder and headed for the place where he had left Max and his son. There would be no great hunting story to tell today. His skill had not provided the food his family was about to eat. He had gotten lucky, nothing more.

Baby was still asleep in the bag when Shorty returned to the small clearing. Shorty quickly hung the carcass from a sturdy branch. Cleaning and draining the goat took only a few minutes. Having no intention to stay here long, Shorty left the less savory parts of the goat's body on the ground. Then Shorty headed back into the trees. He had seen an old dead tree not too far away. It would burn without a lot of smoke. He did not want to tell Mama dragon where they were hiding.

Shorty quickly snapped the smallish tree into pieces useful as firewood. Then he was headed back to camp with an armload of wood. This time, his son was not asleep when he returned. He was not even in the bag anymore. The baby dragon sat beside what was left of the goat's inside parts. His son was eating large mouthfuls of nasty stuff.

Shorty felt his stomach rise up in protest at what his son was doing. Even ogres had more sense than to eat the things his son was gobbling down. How could he explain to his very young son that this was wrong? Would Baby even listen to him? Shorty's mouth opened to lecture his child, but all that came out was, "Baby, no!"

Then an almost unnoticeable weight landed on Shorty's shoulder. Max's voice whispered softly in his ear. "Leave him be, Shorty. There are things in what he is eating that his small body needs to grow strong and healthy."

Shorty turned his face away, unable to watch. "No bodies eat dat stuff. Bees bad!"

"You have to remember, Shorty," Max continued. "Dragons do not eat like you do. They swallow their prey whole. Everything goes into their stomachs, even armor and weapons. What your baby is doing is normal for a dragon."

Shorty shook his head. Then he knelt to pick up the firewood that he had dropped. He did his best to ignore the sounds of the dragon eating as he dug a small fire pit. The dead tree took a spark easily and soon a warm fire burned in the pit. In a short time, long strips of goat meat cooked over the flames, each speared on a green branch Shorty had cut with Papa's dagger.

The meat sizzled as it cooked. The odor might have been appealing at another time, but Shorty had no desire to eat. Perhaps tomorrow he would be hungry again. Baby had pulled his bag closer to the fire and was curled up, sleeping near the heat of the flames. Max still rested on his shoulder.

If there was going to be a time to make Shorty understand the dangerous road he was about to embark on, that time was now. The little dragon's appetite for intestines had really disturbed his friend. It was not much of a wedge between Mama and son, but it was all Max had. Only it still left Max feeling guilty for what he was about to do. Max was not sure if he could get through to the stubborn ogre, but he had to try. Shorty was already staring across the fire at the young dragon so Max asked, "Look at him, Shorty. What do you see?"

Shorty's shrug almost knocked Max of the ogre's shoulder. "Dragon," Shorty answered simply.

"Look at the color of his scales," Max encouraged.

Shorty gave another shrug. "Bees red like him udder mama."

Max choose his next words very carefully. "Red dragons are evil. They hurt people. Your son will grow up to be like other red dragons. He will hurt people too."

Shorty's head began to shake once more, that same stubborn set returned to the ogre's face. "No!"

"He is a red dragon, Shorty. Even their babies are bad." Max tried to explain gently.

Shorty shook his head again. "Neber bees bad baby, Birdie. Only bad mamas. Some mama teaches good. Some teaches bad. Some baby get muches lub. Some not gets no lub." For a second, Max thought he saw a tear run down the ogre's cheek. "Eben ogre ken bees goo ifn him Mama lub him muches."

Max turned to stare at his new friend. What Shorty was suggesting was an age-old argument. Nature verses nurturing. Max would have thought such a concept beyond Shorty. But, considering the type of person Shorty had become, perhaps his friend had more experience in the art of child raising than Max did. And if he understood what Shorty planned, it would appear that Max had another student to teach the ways of the One True Path to.

Max settled his body more comfortably on Shorty's shoulder. "Then you need to name him. Baby might work for the first century, but then what do we call him?"

"Maybeso needs helps wid dat," Shorty replied as he removed some of the goat meat from the fire.

"Why not give him an ogre name?" Max asked.

Shorty began to laugh. It was a good laugh that invited others to join in. "Ogre no so bees good wid name. Me small ogre. Get named Shorty." Shorty gestured towards the sleeping dragon. "Wants me call him Red? Dragon? Or maybeso, Eats Muches?"

Max joined Shorty's laughter. "I see what you mean. Then what kind of name will you choose."

Shorty was silent for a time. "Need name of good dragon. One dat protect many peoples. Needs name ta growed inta. Who bees bestus ta protect ever, Birdie Max?"

Now it was Max's turn to think. There had been many good dragons since the time of the Great Change, but only one fit what Shorty was asking for. The gold dragon, Arlon, had fought against the forces of darkness beside the First Mage and the bronze dragon, Bobo. Arlon had sacrificed himself to save the world. Could this young red survive the burden of that legacy? But choice of names was not Max's to make. "His name was Arlon, Shorty. Arlon the Protector who gave his life so that many might live."

"Good name fer me boy," Shorty replied.

Shorty began to remove the rest of the meat from the fire. He laid it out to cool and began to bury the fire. "Time ta goes, Birdie Max."

"Go where?" Max asked curiously.

"Ta sav Ez'ard!" his friend answered with a grin. "Den ta sees Bone Man. Gonna gibs him dat bad sword, but he no gonna gets me Baby."

Max flapped his wings and flew up to sit on a branch over Shorty's head. "How are we going to get there?" he asked.

Shorty shook his head as he began to stick the cooked goat meat into an oil skin bag. His fingers left the hot meat long enough to caress the pearl set in the hilt of the World Conqueror's blade. "Birdie knowed how ta makes sword goes pop?" Shorty asked him.

Pop? How did a sword pop? Max ran the word through the translation routine he had been building for Shorty's version of the common tongue. Max drew a blank. Then he accessed the information that he had on that particular sword. It could heal, locate objects, and teleport. That was it. Shorty wanted to pop from one place to another using magic. "Yes, Shorty. I think I can explain how to do it."

"Gooder." Shorty slipped his backpack on and moved around the fire. The process of getting his son back in the canvas bag was a touch more difficult than packing the meat had been.

Chapter 5

Dealing with Death

"Close your eyes and picture where you want to go. Then tell the sword to take you there." That was what Max had told him to do. If only Birdie understood how hard that was going to be. Miles of tunnel stretched from outside to the ancient city. It was all very dark. Shorty had no idea what most of it looked like. He also had no idea where Ez'ard might be on his return journey.

Then again, maybeso it was not that hard after all. Ez'ard only knew one path down from the surface world. So, Shorty just needed to get to the place where the tunnel entered the great cavern. Unlike the tunnels, the cavern was filled with the strange plants that made green light. Shorty remembered the broken door on the building closest to the tunnel he wanted. Shorty focused all of his thoughts on building a picture of that door in his head. "Go dere!" he whispered to the sword.

The fresh air of outside was replaced by the stale, dusty smell of the long dead city. They found themselves in a world filled with pale green light and many, many shadows. Shorty spun in a slow circle, checking each pool of darkness for danger. When he was certain that they were safe, he loosened his grip on the sword just a bit. "Where bees Ez'ard?"

As it had in the dragon's lair, the sword shifted in his grip. The tip of the blade pointed into the darkness of the tunnel. He had gotten here in time. Now all he needed to do was gather up the last member of his new family. Then he would make a deal with Bone Man.

The black blade slid into its scabbard with a whisper of steel against steel. Shorty settled the canvas bag against his stomach as best he could. There would be no petting his son for now. He would need his hands and sword if they met anything besides Ez'ard in the tunnels.

Max's feathers rustled on Shorty's left shoulder, but he did not want the owl flying ahead. It was no bery safe in the darkness. This was Shorty's world and he was the most dangerous predator in it. "Stay wid me, Birdie," Shorty ordered. Then Shorty slipped into the darkness. He knew where he wanted to wait for his missing friend.

The passages that led down were silent and dark. Silent was better than filled with the roar of some beast that was hell-bent on eating him, but the silence did not mean safe. Too many things down here knew how to wait in ambush. Ez'ard moved with the silence of a well-trained thief. He was also invisible thanks to his spell. But he had no magic that would hide his scent and that was what the monsters in the darkness would use to find him.

Once again, he lamented the fact that the lich had not taught him the teleport spell yet. The "you are not yet ready" routine was getting old. Did Shorty's Bone Man understand that Ez'ard would take Shorty and leave as soon as he had that spell in his spell book? Probably. The lich was not stupid. But neither was Ez'ard. If he did not get the spell soon, he and Shorty would disappear into the dark tunnels. Long dead wizards gave him the creeps even if they were teaching him useful spells.

"Focus!" Ez'ard whispered to himself, immediately regretting making even that much noise in the silent tunnel. This trip was stressful without Shorty along. He felt so much safer with a five-hundred-pound ogre protecting him while he cast his spells. He just needed a few minutes to sit and relax. Luckily there was a small side cave not far ahead. That was the place where he and Shorty had been ambushed long ago. Now it was just a place to sit, rest, and get a bite to eat from his supplies.

Ez'ard picked up the pace. The Drow cave was well over halfway back. He reached the dark chimney that led down to the cave. It was an easy climb down. Ez'ard hardly slowed as his fingers and toes located the familiar holds. Turning, he stepped out into pale light.

Ez'ard stumbled back. Magical light leaked from the small cave into the wider space where he and Shorty had fought the Drow. The small Drow cave was occupied, probably by something very hungry for elf meat. Then someone chuckled from right outside the crevice. Ez'ard was rather proud of himself. He did not scream, he did not faint, and he definitely did not lose control of his bladder.

The laughter died and a voice he knew all too well said, "Hullo, Ez'ard."

"Damn it, Shorty! That was not funny!" the words exploded from his lungs, definitely louder than they should have been. "Why are you here?"

"Bees waitin fer youse," his large friend replied.

"I do not need you to babysit me!" Ez'ard snapped despite the fact that he actually was relieved that Shorty would be with him for the rest of the journey back to the Keep. "Why the light? That is not like you."

Ez'ard stepped out of the crevice again, looking composed and confident. It was a wasted show of bravado. He was still invisible after all. All Shorty had to go on was Ez'ard's familiar scent. Ez'ard ended the spell as he watched Shorty shuffle his feet nervously. "Me gots sumtin ta shows youse."

Shorty turned and led him into the light coming from the side cave. He knew Shorty had done something wrong. He just could not figure out what kind of trouble the big guy had gotten into in his absence.

Shorty stepped aside and waved Ez'ard into the chamber. This time he might have screamed. But only a little. No, he assured himself. It had only been a small squeak of surprise. And why not? The toothy grin of the little red dragon had not been anywhere on the menu that Ez'ard had used to plan his day. He did not even notice the mechanical owl while he was trying not to get eaten by the dragon.

It was hours later before he finally thought he understood it all. As normal, Shorty's version of the story had been fairly confusing and utterly useless. But the little owl was quite intelligent and it explained most of what had happened to him. It was a hard tale to swallow even with Shorty involved.

"So, let me get this straight. The dragon is your son?" Shorty nodded and Ez'ard groaned and went on. "You went into a dragon's lair to steal treasure and magic?" Ez'ard pointed at the mechanical bird for emphasis. "And, you not only did not invite me, you took up with another thief not half as good looking as I am?"

"No bees me fault!" Shorty grumbled, "Me comes ta gets youse but youse no bees in youse room."

Ez'ard frowned. "Did you go into my room?"

The "Oops!" from Shorty told Ez'ard all he needed to know. The guilt was clear on Shorty's face as the big guy looked down at his feet.

"Yeah, right! Oops," Ez'ard said with a hopeless sigh. Then he shook his head. "So now what? The lich has got to be looking for you. We cannot just go on the run. Half my stuff is back at the Keep."

Shorty's eyes hardened. He pointed at a ruby encrusted scabbard leaning against the wall. "Me trade dat fer yer toys."

Ez'ard recognized that look. It meant the steel trap in Shorty's brain had closed. There would be no changing the ogre's mind on this. They were in trouble. Ez'ard tilted his head towards the sleeping dragon. "The lich is going to want him too."

Ez'ard actually felt cold at the look Shorty gave him. "No," was all his friend said.

Ez'ard sighed. There was no argument left to be made. The ogre was back. Ez'ard started to rise. "Best to get this over with then."

"No!" echoed through the chamber again. Ez'ard looked at Shorty. "You cannot be serious. You are going to negotiate with a lich by yourself? If we are lucky, he will only cast a charm spell on you. And besides, what am I going to do while you are off being stupid?"

"He is not going alone," the owl quickly corrected. "I am going with Shorty."

"Youse gonna takes care a me baby," Shorty added.

Ez'ard stared at the small dragon. This was a really bad idea. He was not babysitter material. And he did not like the idea of being a dragon chew toy. Then again, the alternative was letting the lich fry his brain. How did he get into these messes all the time? Never mind, he knew the answer to that. Shorty was involved and that was usually all it took.

The Keep seemed more menacing than it ever had before. The shadows were darker, more like dead eyes watching for his return. The building itself had not changed, but Shorty no longer felt welcome there. This place had never been home, but it had at least been a place to live. Now it was a threat to all those that Shorty cared about.

The two metal doors on the ground level had been swung open. That was not normal. They should have been closed and barred on the inside. The faint shimmer of magic lined the top and bottom of that dark opening, almost like teeth prepared to snap closed on a tasty ogre morsel. That would not be his path. Not unless he had no other option. He moved to the side of the Keep, Max soaring just over his head.

Shorty found the familiar hand and foot holds. That much had not changed at least, or had it? The stone felt cold in his hands. He scampered up the side of the building, not wanting to touch it any more than necessary. The top of the Keep was much as it had been a little more than a day ago. The red circle still marked the center of the platform. Was the red darker than it had been the last time he was here? Was it more like the color of blood than he remembered?

Wing tips brushed against his right ear as Max settled on his shoulder. It was strange, but that small form seemed to calm his nerves. Shorty crossed the platform to the double doors leading down into the Keep. He bent down, grabbing one door handle, and lifted. The door opened easily. It should have been locked. He was not liking this at all. It felt like he was walking into a trap and he suspected that he was the intended prey.

The ramp and the halls that opened off it were all well-lit. There was nothing he could see waiting for him. As with any good trap, everything appeared safe. Shorty stepped from the ramp into the hallway that led to his and Ez'ard's rooms. His own door was closed as it should be. But when he turned the handle, the door refused to open. That made no sense. His room did not have one of Ez'ard's lock thingies. Shorty gave the door a good rattle, but it still would not open.

Max's voice was a soft chirrup in his ear. "It is magically sealed. It will not be easy to force it open."

Shorty nodded and turned to the left. Ez'ard's door was a short walk away. "An dat one?" Shorty asked.

Max was quiet for a moment before answering, "It is also magically sealed. I don't think you were meant to get into either room."

Shorty slowly pulled the white scabbard from where it was tucked into his belt. He gripped it tightly in his left hand. "Den bees no udder way. Must makes deal wid Bone Man."

The walk down the ramp seemed to take much longer this time. When he reached the bottom, the well sat where it always did. Shorty would rather face another trip through the icy water than the monster that he knew waited for him around the corner.

"I will be close," Max promised and then the small owl launched himself into the room. Shorty steeled himself for what was to come and then took that final step. Then he turned to face Bone Man's door.

As he expected, that door was wide open. Was it an invitation or a challenge? After what he had done, would he dare to face Bone Man? Shorty really had no choice. His family needed him to bargain for their freedom. Shorty tightened his grip on the scabbard. The red marbles along its surface dug painfully into his palm. Would the sword be enough to satisfy Bone Man? He was about to find out.

Shorty walked to the door and peered inside. The room was much bigger this time. The chairs were gone now, even Bone Man's fancy one. The room was empty except for a high marble slab and the robed figure that stood on top of it. The slab was the white of bone except for the three dark steps that led up to the top. Those steps were as black as the robe draped around Bone Man.

Shorty was still staring when Bone Man's cold, raspy voice filled the room, "I think you have kept me waiting long enough, Warrior."

Shorty met the red orbs that shone within Bone Man's black hood. His voice was calm as he replied, "Had ta makes sure Ez'ard bees safe afore come here."

Bone Man stared at what Shorty held in his left hand. A skeletal foot appeared from under the robe as Bone Man lowered himself to the first stair leading from the marble slab. His voice seemed curious as he enquired, "Is that my sword? From what Dratz told me before I punished him, I did not think you would ever return."

Shorty did not like the tone in Bone Man's voice. He would not allow Bone Man to hurt those he cared about. Dratz was not one of those under Shorty's protection, but that did not mean Shorty was not interested in what happened to his one-time partner. "Punish how?" he asked tentatively.

Bone Man chuckled and waved a hand. A small pedestal appeared in the center of the room. A cage was perched on its marble top. A large, black rat sat in the cage, its tiny front paws gripping the bars as its hate filled eyes glared at Shorty. Shorty sighed. Even Dratz did not deserve to spend his life in a cage. The rat part of the punishment was only fair as far as Shorty was concerned. Did rats have kings? Maybeso that would make Dratz happy.

Shorty held out the scabbard for Bone Man to see. "Me keeps promise. Brings sword. Me takes Ez'ard's tings an me tings too. Den me go. Ebry bodies gets what dem wants."

Bone Man floated down the last two steps. He stood beside the slab, staring at Shorty. Shorty watched one of his robed arms come up. A boney finger came out to tap at the place where Bone Man's chin should be. "Let me think about this. The sword for your own possessions. Hmm."

Bone man took several steps towards Shorty, his burning eyes focused on the sword Shorty held out to him. "It is an interesting offer, but we do have another trade to negotiate before I agree to your proposal."

Shorty shook his head, not understanding. "What udder trade?"

Bone Man's laughter filled the room. "What do I get in exchange for letting you and your friend live?"

This conversation was not going the way he had planned. There had to be some way to protect those he cared about. Shorty just had no idea how. Hoping for some other way he asked, "What youse wants?"

"My egg!" was Bone Man's angry retort.

Shorty swallowed hard. "Bees no mo egg," he tried to explain.

Bone Man threw an angry glare at the rat sitting in the cage. Then he snarled at Shorty, "What happened to my egg, Warrior?"

"No me!" Shorty protested. "Baby dragon breaks it. It get borned."

Anger was replaced by excitement as Bone Man asked, "You have the hatchling? You saved my dragon?"

The ogre began to rise from the depths of Shorty's being. It had freed itself from the cage he kept it locked in. Shorty did not like the ogre that lived in him. It was mean. It was always angry. It hated. Thankfully, it did not escape its bonds often. Shorty felt his lips shape words as the ogre screamed at Bone Man, "No fer youse!"

Bone Man's laughter filled the room for a moment. When the laughter stopped, the skeleton's voice proclaimed, "Then you and the elf will die. Then I will take what is mine. That dragon shall serve me or I will use its organs to power my magic."

A red haze began to cloud Shorty's vision. Through it, he saw Bone Man's skeletal hand come up. Strange words came from within that dark hood, "naw-than maw VETH!" Bone Man stepped forward to touch Shorty.

Shorty heard the ogre scream out its rage, "No me son!" The ogre reached for the closest weapon. Shorty tried to warn it that the white bone hilt was a bery bad idea. But the ogre did not listen. The red blade erupted from its scabbard, swinging across in a horizontal slash. A blast of red light merged with the haze in Shorty's eyes as that blade hit the place where the hood met Bone Man's robes.

The hood fluttered to the floor, empty. The skull that it had covered flew across the room. It struck the pedestal hard, bouncing back to land at the ogre's feet. The pedestal leaned for in the other direction. The cage fell to the floor and, the rat bouncing around inside. Then the pedestal tipped the rest of the way over. Its stone top hit the cage breaking it open.

That was when the familiar pain from the red blade washed over Shorty. Even the ogre could not withstand that onslaught. Shorty and the ogre dropped to their knees. Shorty found himself staring into the flickering eyes of Bone Man's skull. "Your son?" the unattached skull asked. Then magical energy began to stream from the skull into the red blade. "The last thing Shorty heard before his world when white with pain was Bone Man's "Oh Shit!" as the light of his eyes went out.

The sword began to scream in Shorty's head. "He was mine you fool! With him I could have ruled the world. I WILL make you suffer for this!"

The pain flared brighter and hotter. Shorty knew the sword was killing him. The ogre retreated down into the depths of Shorty's being, leaving him to suffer alone. The red blade's hatred was consuming him a piece at a time. A pure white light began to pulse. At first, that light was small. But with each beat of Shorty's heart, it grew brighter and larger. It pushed away the glow of the red blade. It drove back the pain. Then another voice joined the link between Shorty and the red blade. This voice spoke with calm assurance. "Release the hilt, Shorty. You are safe now. Just let the blade go."

Instinctively, his right hand rose up and thrust the blade back into its scabbard. After long years of practice with a blade, his muscles knew that motion without needing his brain's assistance. The blade screamed out its protest and then it went silent as the scabbard surrounded it. Shorty unclenched both his hands and the hated blade fell to the floor. As peace reclaimed him, Shorty made sure that the ogre's cell was locked once more.

"Tank youse, Birdie?" he muttered. Shorty looked around. Bone Man's body was gone. A pile of white dust was just visible within the dark robe. There was nothing left where the skull had been. His small family was safe. And they had a home now. Without Bone Man, this place could be their refuge for as long as they chose to live here. Then Shorty noticed the broken cage. There was a large hole where the table had snapped several of the thin metal bars. Dratz was gone.

"Where da rat goes, Birdie?" he asked.

Max seemed confused. "What rat?"

Ez'ard climbed up out of the well, cold and very, very wet. The trip through the icy river to that hidden cave where Shorty had found his black sword was not pleasant. It was even worse when a megalomaniac sword was alternately begging, pleading and then threatening him. It would serve that cursed blade right if it spent the next millennium alone in the almost watery grave.

Ez'ard leaned back against the half-wall that surrounded the well. He was tired. It had been an even longer swim coming back from the underground prison against the current. And now his favorite clothes were as wet as he was. But there had been no arguing with Shorty when his friend had handed him that oilskin wrapped bundle. The sword had to go, and it had to go right away. Ez'ard shivered as he looked around the practice room.

The first thing that caught his attention was the mountain of gold, platinum, and gems piled in the corner across from the well. It was a thief's dream come true except that none of it was for him. Instead, Shorty's pet dragon was sleeping happily in the center of the pile, its head resting on the small leather bag that had been attached to Shorty's belt when he returned from his "mission." Ez'ard shook his head as he watched the tiny red dragon swish its tail through the coins. No matter what Shorty said, he was not going to be cleaning up dragon poop. No Sir. Not happening.

That was when Ez'ard noticed Shorty staring at him expectantly. The ogre had one hand behind his back. Did Shorty really think Ez'ard would notice how big the treasure hoard behind him was? Not bloody likely! Ez'ard sighed and answered Shorty's obvious question, "It's done. The sword is hidden in the back corner of the chamber where you were trapped. Happy?"

"Gooder," Shorty replied with a smile.

Feeling more than a bit unappreciated, Ez'ard snapped, "Did you give him all of the treasure?"

"No all," Shorty replied with a grin. "Me keep some nice marble fer ta play wid."

Ez'ard felt his temper beginning to flare. "Why did you have to give the rest to a dragon that does not even know what coins and gems are good for?"

His friend obviously did not understand sarcasm. Shorty's answer was dead-pan serious. "Bees good fer making a bed. Dragon likes ta sleeps on useless metal circle. Sides, Ez'ard no likes ta play wid marbles."

"Wonderful choice, nothing for your cold, tired, and very wet best friend who just swam an underground river for you." Ez'ard groused as he looked down at his wet clothing. That was when the warm, soft towel that had been hidden behind Shorty's back hit him in the face.

That gift was hard to complain about. Shorty turned and walked towards the lich's room. "Wen gets dry, comes wid me."

The towel helped a lot, not that he was going to let Shorty know that. He dropped the wet towel on the floor. He was as dry as he was likely to get without changing clothes. Now it was time to see what else his friend had been up to while he was down in that well.

Ez'ard walked to the entrance to the lich's room. Even he had not been allowed to explore Bone Man's domain. Each time he had been allowed inside, the room had been a different size and shape. The old, dead wizard had liked to play mind games. What Ez'ard saw now from the doorway was vastly larger than he had ever imagined. The illusions had all been stripped away to reveal a magical laboratory beyond any guild hall that Ez'ard had ever visited. Lab tables and equipment were spread out in a pattern that Ez'ard did not understand. At least not yet. He was going to claim this room for his own. And he would figure out each of the lich's secret experiments in time.

Shorty was sitting on the corner of an ancient stone desk. His friend had a smile on his face. Ez'ard was not sure if that was a good sign or not. When Shorty crooked a finger and motion for Ez'ard to join him, that smile grew bigger. What the heck, he might as well find out what the big guy had in store for him.

Ez'ard sauntered over to the desk, pretending not to be interested in whatever Shorty had planned. "What now, all wise and knowing ogre?" Ez'ard muttered with all of the sarcasm he could muster. It had no effect on his friend. It never did.

Shorty just pointed an oversized finger at the wall near the corner of the desk. "Birdie say push dere," was all Shorty would explain.

Shorty stood up and moved out of Ez'ard's way. The wall seemed to be slightly discolored in the spot that Shorty pointed to. Had some experiment splattered the stone? The color difference was too minor to be important. That spot really did not look any different than the rest of the walls. Ez'ard decided to humor Shorty. The sooner he got this over with, the sooner he could explore the lab.

The stain sank in when Ez'ard applied pressure to it. Lines appeared on the stone wall above the desk, two horizontal and one that was vertical in the center of the desk. The lines grew into cracks as two doors swung open. A thick stone shelf slide out of the opening to cover the desk. On that slab was a large, open tome. It was the lich's spell book. It was a treasure beyond anything Shorty had given his dragon. The heavy tome rested on an ornate oaken lectern.

Ez'ard stepped closer to examine this wonder. Shorty sounded rather proud as he announced, "Fer youse me friend. Birdie say him ken helps youse reads da squiggly line ifn youse needs helps."

Ez'ard started to lean over the book to see what spells the lich had been studying last. Shorty's hand closed on his shoulder, holding him back. His friend's long arm reached past him to press on the corner of the lectern. A drawer slid open on the base of the lectern revealing three wands. Shorty's breath was warm against his ear as his friend warned, "Birdie say no touches da magic sticks till him telled youse what dem do."

The hand on his shoulder released him. Ez'ard could not take his eyes off of the spell book. Shorty's voice came from somewhere over near the door. "Hab fun Ez'ard. No fergets, bees youse turn ta cooks da dinner." And then his friend was gone.

Ez'ard leaned over the tome, reading the spell that was so carefully inscribed on the right page.

רוּשׁ

TRANSLOCATION

This was the spell he had practically enslaved himself to the lich to learn. With it, he could teleport anywhere in the known world. Or at least anywhere he had been to. With this spell he would never need to walk through those dark tunnels to get back to Delith. With this spell, he was truly free. No one could ever control him again. He could never be imprisoned if a job went bad. He could go anywhere he wished with one simple Arcane word.

One question nagged at him as he stared down at the page. The lich would not have needed to study this spell. He never left his keep. So why was the book open to this page? Had Shorty turned the book to this page? But his friend could not read common, let alone the Arcane. No, it had to be Max. The owl seemed to know a great deal about magic. "But how did the owl know I wanted this spell?" Ez'ard muttered out loud.

A slightly mechanical sounding voice answered that rhetorical question from somewhere behind him. "I did not know. Shorty told me what to look for. He said you wanted to be able to 'pop.'"

Ez'ard turned slowly. Max sat on a lab table in the middle of the room, his tiny taloned feet clutched an empty beaker stand. "And how would Shorty know that?" Ez'ard demanded. "I have never said anything to him about what I wanted."

The voice that came from Max this time was a perfect imitation of Shorty's. It was an exact match of Shorty's tone and cadence. "Me bees him friend, Birdie. Me will all da times be him friend." There

336

was a slight pause and Max continued on his own voice, "And now, apparently, he is my friend too."

Neither elf nor bird spoke again for a long, long time.

Chapter 6

Home and Hearth

Max had watched with amazement as the ancient keep became a happy home. The transformation began with the purging of its former resident. Max had known that destroying the lich's body was not good enough. They had to find Bone Man's phylactery. It had taken a combination of ancient spells that Max knew and several unusual spells that Ez'ard had found in the lich's spell book. The soul gem had been hidden among hundreds of similar gems on a chandelier in the main entry hall.

Thankfully, Bone Man's soul was not within the gem. But would Bone Man return there in an attempt to reclaim his lair? Max did not know. He could only hope that the evil of the sword had destroyed the lich forever. To keep them all safe, Max knew the gem needed to be destroyed. But how? Phylacteries were highly resistant to magic. Max did not think his spells would harm the dark gem. To Max's delight though, soul gems were susceptible to other forces like overly large hammers wielded by strong and highly motivated ogres. Shorty's maul had left only dust when he brought it down on the soul gem.

Once the threat of Bone Man's return had been eliminated, an almost magical series of changes began. Shorty single-handedly turned dark and somber into a place of light and happiness. The small dragon had more love and attention than any child Max had ever known. Shorty did not spoil Arlon, but the tiny dragon never had a reason to doubt he was loved.

To no one's surprise, Ez'ard became obsessed by the new spells at his fingertips. The elf was not to be spoiled either. Shorty made him cook and join the family for meals. Ez'ard went to town regularly for supplies and things to make the Keep more like a home. Ez'ard always complained about the cost of the things Shorty wanted. Mama Shorty always had a bag of gold and gems handy to pay the bills. The lich's treasury was more than enough to cover their needs as long as Ez'ard did not figure out where Shorty had found it.

As for Shorty, his days were filled with activities too. The ogre had a son to love and play games with. He had much to learn about being the Mama. Shorty spent time each day wandering the streets of the ancient city, hunting to feed his son. The skills of the warrior had no opportunity to become rusty. Shorty was surrounded by people he loved and that was more than enough for him.

And that just left Max. He had three pupils now. Max had a dragon that was almost frighteningly intelligent. As Shorty had predicted, the dragon was not evil. And he loved to learn. Max's only worry was that the world might not accept a good red dragon. Max also had a wizard to instruct in the ways of magic. The elf's idea of right and wrong was a bit more flexible than Max liked, but he could be guided to the True Path. Especially with the help of Ez'ard's friend. And lastly, there was Shorty. Shorty would be a lifetime project. But what he lacked in intelligence, the ogre made up for with an innate understanding of what was truly important in the world.

Max realized that for the first time he could ever remember, he was content, happy even. His pupils were not royalty or wannabe kings. They were what used to be called the salt of the earth. His friends just wanted to make the world a better place. And that was what The Seven existed for. He would help his new family whether The Seven agreed or not.

On da Way ta Market

Dedication

This story is dedicated to the incredible Baby Penelope. Her little heart was so amazing that the doctors had to actually see it with their own eyes. Within days of her birth, she went through more than many people do in a lifetime. With the love and prayers of her mob of a family, she continues to overcome peril after peril. Th-thump, th-thump! Such a wonderful sounding heartbeat. It was your struggles that helped me when I was stuck at the end of this story. Thank you for being part of our lives, little one.

Preface

The door of the fancy room was not his friend.

He threw his ball at the floor just in front of the door he did not like.

The ball skipped off the floor, hitting the door before returning to his waiting hand. Th-Thump!

He caught the ball easily.

He did not like the door because it was locked and there were guards outside to make sure he stayed inside.

He threw the ball again. Th-Thump! His large hand already knew where the ball would go.

He had not done anything wrong. They did not need to lock him up. Fancy or not, he did not like this room.

Th-Thump! He had been throwing the ball for a long, long time now. The guards had given up telling him to stop.

How had he gotten into this mess anyway? He had tried so hard to be good.

Th-Thump! Th-Thump! There was nothing else to do except play ball.

Th-Thump! Th-Thump! Play ball and think about what he might have done differently.

Chapter 1

Accidents and Errands

Six… Seven… Eight… Th-thump! Ez'ard winced as the next sound to reverberate through the room was that of glass shattering on stone. Then came the inevitable "Oops!" followed by the sound of heavy boots crushing glass fragments into dust. Ez'ard added the last two particles of bat guano to the beaker as it bubbled on his lab table. He stirred the mixture until it turned a uniform black color. He steeled himself for what was to come before turning to glare at his oversized friend.

The half-ogre was still staring down at the remains of one of Ez'ard's expensive new flasks. Surprise and regret were evident on Shorty's face as he looked up to meet Ez'ard's frustrated stare. "Sorry, Ez'ard. Was accident."

"You are not supposed to touch anything in my lab, Shorty. Many of the things I work on go BOOM." Ez'ard motioned towards the shattered glass. "Or they break into a million pieces and I have to buy new ones. Again!"

Shorty shrugged. "Udder time it go boom no hurted bery muches. Only burn me little bit. Me marble make ouch all gone when me wakes up."

The smaller elf sighed and shook his head. "I am not worried about whether you think getting blown up hurts much or not. You always seem to survive your accidents. I am not a muscle-bound ogre. So, I AM worried about whether or not I survive your oopses."

Shorty nodded solemnly. "Maybeso youse no stands close me den."

Ez'ard wanted to scream, but it was unlikely to do any good. He could picture Shorty jumping back at his scream and knocking over several lab tables. Ez'ard took a deep breath. He needed to get Shorty out of here before someone, most likely him, got hurt.

Ez'ard turned and removed the beaker from the small flame before he ruined his potion. As he stirred the mixture one last time, he asked, "Why are you down here Shorty? There has to be something more exciting for you to do."

The ogre gave a disgusted grunt. "Nuttin ta do. No places ta go. No monster ta fights. Me bees a board, Ez'ard."

Ez'ard groaned and turned to face Shorty. You are not a board, you are bored." Ez'ard stopped when he saw the confused expression on the ogre's face. "Never mind, Shorty. Why not go play with Baby or Birdie? They might play a game with you while I work."

Shorty shook his head sadly. "Birdie teachin school fer Baby. Telled me ta go way so Arlon ken learn ta bees good dragon. So, comes ta helps youse."

Ez'ard's hand slid up the back of his head. His fingers curled in his long hair. He wanted to pull it hard. At least then there would be a good reason for his head to hurt. His brain spun as he searched for a way to keep Shorty entertained. Then an idea came to him. Ez'ard marched across the room to his desk. Where was that list of spell components he was running short on? There! He grabbed up a large scrap of parchment. He should have thought of this sooner.

Ez'ard rummaged through the top drawer and came up with a small pouch. He began to count coins into it as he spoke, "Shorty, do you remember the magic shop in the capital?"

Shorty nodded slowly. "Dat fuzzface wants muches me marble fer him toy. No bery nice."

Ez'ard growled softly as he tied off the pouch. "No, not that one. The other shop where the sell the things for my magic. You know, the one with all the funny colored sand?"

Shorty smiled and nodded vigorously. "Me member dat place. Bery mean gnome. No let me touches him tings."

Ez'ard motioned to the broken glass and Shorty blushed. "Oh, dat hows come?"

Ez'ard grinned as a lesson seemed to sink into the ogre's brain. Then he stepped forward and handed the parchment to Shorty. "Take this to the shop. Do not go inside the shop! Give the list to the gnome at the door and wait for the bag he will give you. Then give him this pouch to pay for it."

Shorty lifted his left hand and began to wiggle fingers. "One… Two… Four…" Shorty geld up three fingers. "Bees sure, Ez'ard? Take me four day ta gets dere." Shorty lifted his right hand and compared it to his left. He raised two fingers and then a third. "Den takes nudder four day ta comes back. Dat make…" More wiggling fingers. "Lots a day dat me bees gone."

Ez'ard chuckled at the thought of lots of days without a very bored ogre under foot. "I am sure. It would make up for breaking things in my lab."

Shorty glanced back down at the broken glass. "Kay. But maybeso bees betterer fer Ez'ard ta go pop? Get dere fast den."

Ez'ard shook his head. "No. I am very busy right now Shorty. And, I now have to clean up this mess too. Besides, I do not have teleport memorized today so I cannot just go pop." Ez'ard thought for a moment and then added. "Besides, this will get you outside. Maybe you will get to talk to a squirrel while you are on your way to the market."

A look of excitement spread across Shorty's face. His smile could have lit up the room. "Youse tink maybeso? Dat bery good plan. Me ken go now."

Ez'ard watched Shorty's broad back rush out of the room. Th-thump! The door slammed hard as Shorty ran for the ramp. He felt a twinge of guilt for manipulating Shorty that way. The guilt only lasted a heartbeat before he glanced down at the glass that covered the lab floor. Six days without interruption seemed like a very good idea.

Ez'ard muttered, "Paw-sas Ehbed." When his servant had materialized, he set it to cleaning up the broken glass. Then he turned back to his beaker. He had several hours to go before the oil of slipperiness would be ready. After dinner, he would try it on several of his practice locks to see if they opened more easily with a magical lubricant.

Chapter 2

Ta Market Me Go

The trip to the surface was very familiar to Shorty. He traveled this way a lot, sometimes just to spend a day outside. Going pop was much faster, but then he missed all the fun things like fighting monsters and maybeso meeting squirrels. Sadly, there had been no monsters to fight this time. There had been nothing to do but walk. He was getting tired after the long walk. Without Ez'ard to keep watch, it was no bery smart to sleep.

A small pinpoint of light appeared as Shorty came around a curve in the tunnel. Sunshine. The spot of light was no bigger than his finger, but it signaled that he was almost outside. He would be able to sleep soon.

Shorty began to move faster. There were no side tunnels from here to worry about so he started to run, enjoying the th-thumps of his feet against the floor of the passage. He felt more awake as his heart beat faster. He was almost to outside where the squirrels lived. Th-thump, th-thump! Just this one last long tunnel and he would bc there.

The pinpoint of light grew to the size of his hand and then larger still. Shorty was happy. He liked outside. He was about to start whistling when his nose caught the faint scent of smoke. Shorty forgot about being tired. Someone had found the entrance to the tunnels and that was not a good thing.

Shorty slowed. He needed to be very careful. An ogre bursting out of the dark tunnel was bound to cause problems no matter who had started the fire. Before he caused a panic, it would be a good idea to figure out who had camped in the cave near the exit. Were strangers still in the cave or had they moved on?

The darkness of the tunnel made it easy to stay hidden. Sand and hard-packed soil covered the tunnel floor so even his big feet did not make much noise. Shorty kept his eyes on the growing light, hoping to see who had found the tunnel entrance. He came to a stop still well back in the darkness. Something was different about the lines of the cave ahead. He sniffed the air blowing from the exit into the tunnel. In addition to the scent of smoke, there was an acrid scent that burned his nose. He knew that stink. Troll!

He studied the cave as he crept towards the exit. There were new lumps and bulges along the walls of the cave. Whatever lay there was not big enough to be sleeping trolls. It took him a moment to realize that the new shapes were bedrolls and blankets piled against the walls near the exit. A firepit had been dug in the center of the cave. Shorty continued his careful advance. The trolls had to be close. They would not leave their bedrolls behind.

The bedrolls lined both sides of the cave. He did not bother counting. There were enough of them to be a problem for just one Shorty. This could be bad. Shorty chuckled softly to himself, at least he had found something exciting to do. No more being a board. Seeing nothing moving within the cave, Shorty slipped inside. He knelt by one of the blankets and lifted it to his nose. The reek of troll was fresh. Shorty dropped the blanket as his mind raced. He would need to kill the trolls somehow. He could not let them control the path to his home.

Shorty considered which sword to draw. It was hard to be sneaky with both swords out. The troll sword worked really well against this particular enemy, but the black sword would not be happy if it did not get to do some of the killing. Shorty did not want an angry sword, so he reached over his shoulder. His fingers caressed the large marble on the pommel before closing about the hilt and pulling the sword from its scabbard.

Someone began talking out in the ravine. Shorty recognized the rumbling tone of a troll. He crept to the exit, keeping his body pressed against the rock wall. Shorty peered out into the tiny ravine that concealed the cave entrance and the tunnel that was no longer his secret.

A group of mountain trolls stood in the center of the ravine. Each was nearly ten feet tall. One of the trolls wore dirty robes. It must be a magic troll. That was not good, fighting trolls was hard enough without being hurt by magic. Standing before the magic troll was a line of larger trolls. There were as many of them as he had fingers on one hand. Shorty did not know what that number was. Maybeso it was called trouble.

The larger trolls wore heavy chainmail and carried swords at least as big as the ones Shorty used. Shorty realized that these trolls were not just wandering around looking for a new home. This squad had come here for a reason. Shorty sighed as he realized things had just gotten harder.

The magic troll began to speak. The robed figure was facing away from Shorty so he could not make out everything the troll said. The magic troll pointed at the two trolls to his right. "…door guards… quickly… dead." Then the troll gestured towards the other armored figures. "King's guard… yours... eliminate… magic… kill king…"

Th-thump, th-thump! His heart beat faster at all the talk of killing.

Shorty had no clue what a king was, but he was pretty sure it did not deserve to be killed by the trolls. More importantly, it sounded like a lot of people were about to die. He could not let that happen. He had promised Mama that he would protect. Trolls were bad and he could not let them get away with whatever they had planned. The problem was there were too many trolls for him to attack. Shorty thought. Thinking was never easy. Could he draw them into the tunnels where he could fight them one at a time? Even that would be dangerous since the trolls had magic.

As he considered his options, the armored trolls separated into two groups, one to each side of the magic troll. The robed troll raised its hands and did something strange with its fingers. The troll's next word echoed through the ravine, "shAH-Ar!" Shorty tensed as a blood-red light began to shine behind the armored trolls. The light was shaped like an egg, but it was bigger than the largest of the trolls.

The first two trolls stepped into the egg-shaped light. They did not come out the other side. They were just gone. Shorty guessed this was a door of some kind. He gripped his sword's hilt more tightly. His leg muscles tensed as he prepared to spring. His chance to stop the trolls would come soon.

Shorty watched as the remaining armored trolls turned and walked into the light one by one. As the last one stepped towards the light, Shorty charged. Even if the last armored troll turned back, the magic troll would be caught in the middle. Too bad for it. Shorty did not want it hiding behind the warrior and using its magic. Shorty grinned as the last armored troll disappeared too.

He was a dozen paces from the robed troll's back when his foot came down on a stick. There was a sharp crack as it snapped beneath his boot. The troll spun to face Shorty. Raising one hand, it shouted, "shEH-laKH!" Shorty barely had time to register the crimson bolts before they began to slam into him. Th-thump, th-thump! He did his best to ignore the burning pain as each hit him in a different place. He just concentrated on his foe.

Shorty's left hand clamped down on the magic trolls shoulder. He jerked the troll towards him as his right hand drove the black blade deep into the troll's stomach. The force of his charge drove the blade in to the hilt. Both ogre and troll stumbled back into the red light. Shorty used his left hand to push the troll back so he could pull his blade free. Then he drove it in again, its tip angled towards the trolls heart.

Shorty felt the troll go limp in his grasp. He released it and watched as it slumped to the floor. Its head hit with a hollow th-thump. Its eyes were open, but Shorty did not think it saw anything anymore. Shorty gazed around him. He was not in the ravine any more. There was no red light behind him to retreat into.

He now stood in a well-lit hallway. It was a big hallway, but not big enough to use both of his swords. A door slammed shut and Shorty looked up. It was a nice door, with much shiny gold on it. He might have enjoyed looking at it except for the bloody human lying on the ground before it. He could not tell if the human was dead or not, but the man looked to be in bad shape.

Just past the door, another battle was taking place. One of the armored trolls was hammering at a human soldier with its huge sword. The human was bleeding from several places. One arm hung uselessly at the soldier's side. Before he could move, the human dropped to his knees. The troll's laughter echoed down the hall as it raised its sword and chopped down.

The soldier managed to get his blade up in a near perfect parry. The troll's strike was powerful though and Shorty knew that human bones were not meant to withstand that much force. There were several small cracking noises like tiny twigs. The soldiers sword clattered to the floor. He grimaced at the sight of the soldier's broken hand.

The troll laughed and raised its sword. Shorty's voice was a harsh whisper that carried down the hall. "Maybeso youse should no picks on little peoples. Ifn hits him agin, me gonna bees bery muches mad. Den me really gonna hurts youse."

The troll spun around; Shorty could see the surprise on its face. The human looked up at him in confusion. Shorty understood the man considered Shorty to be as much an enemy as the troll. He did not have time to explain things to the injured man.

The troll did not hesitate. He could see the dead magic troll behind Shorty and the blood dripping from the black blade. The troll charged; its sword extended in a lunge. The tip of that long blade came straight towards Shorty's face. It was a no bery smart move, one easily countered. Shorty did not bother to parry the blow. He simply dropped to one knee as he extended his own sword towards the troll, waiting for its lunge to carry it onto his own point.

The troll's blade passed over his head just before the troll's body slammed into his sword. Shorty was ready for the heavy impact of the troll's body. He flexed his elbow to lessen the strain on his own grip. The troll stopped and stared down at the blade now embedded in its chest. It staggered back two steps. The troll coughed and Shorty saw black blood on its lips. But the troll was a warrior and it raised its sword as Shorty stood once more.

Shorty did not give it time to think. He stepped forward and began to hammer at its blade. The swords met once and then again. The troll knew it had lost. Shorty could see it in the creature's eyes. At Shorty's third strike, its sword went flying. The troll tried to snarl at him, but more blood bubbled from its mouth. Shorty struck again, driving his sword into the troll's neck.

The troll fell to the ground. It would never hurt anyone again. The relief he felt at his quick victory did not last long. The clash of sword on sword and the th-thump of weapons striking living bodies told him that a battle still raged on the other side of the door. He wanted nothing more than to burst through that door so he could fall on the trolls from behind. But he could not leave the two humans to die from their injuries.

Shorty moved up beside the kneeling soldier. He ignored the hatred in the man's eyes as he knelt beside him. The soldier's head stayed proudly erect as he growled out. "Just kill me and get it over with. I deserve to die. I have failed my King."

The humans eyes widened as Shorty set his black blade down so he could reach into his belt pouch. Pain mingled with confusion on the man's face. As Shorty's hand rummaged in the pouch the soldier asked, "Why did you kill the trolls? Are you angry because they got here before you did?"

Shorty finally found the small vial that he was searching for. He pulled it out. This would be the hard part, Shorty knew. With difficulty, he peeled the small wax seal from the vial. Dropping the wax beside his sword, Shorty raised the vial towards the soldier's mouth. The man shook his head defiantly, pressing his lips together. Shorty had not expected the soldier to refuse healing.

Shorty sighed and whispered, "Drink so youse ken sabe youse friend." The soldier turned his face back to Shorty. Hope battled disbelief in the man's eyes. In the end, the soldier opened his mouth and drank the potion. Shorty watched as the flow of blood slowed and then stopped.

Reaching back into his pouch, Shorty searched until he found his last vial. He placed it on the ground before the soldier. Then Shorty took his sword hilt in hand and stood. He pointed at the second vial with his sword. "Sabe youse friend. Me gots troll ta kills." Shorty gestured back to the two troll bodies that were already beginning to twitch. "Den burns dem."

Chapter 3

Me sabe a King

A scream penetrated the heavy door. Shorty forgot his plan to slip quietly into the room at that pain-filled cry. He needed the trolls focused on him, not the humans who were being slaughtered. He drew the troll sword with his left hand, raised one hob-nail boot, and kicked out at the door. Th-thump! His foot impacted the point just below the handle that opened the door. The door rattled hard, but did not open.

It was a good door. The metal-covered surface did not even dent. However, the doorframe had splintered. Bits and pieces of the wooden frame fell to the floor. Shorty kicked a second time. Th-thump! This time, the door exploded inward showering the room beyond with large pieces of the frame.

Sounds of battle filled the hallway; warriors grunting as they struck or were hit. The sharp clang of steel striking steel drowned out the sound of mere mortal pain. Shorty stepped into the chaos of the room unnoticed despite the noise he had made. The warriors inside were too involved in their own struggle to survive.

The battle within the room had been fierce. A human in fancy clothes lay dead just inside the door. An armored troll lay in a pool of blood near the center of the room. Beyond the dead troll, several soldiers lay on the floor. At least one of the soldiers was dead. His head lay several feet away from the pile of bodies. The killing was far from over.

His eyes tracked the battle sounds to the far corner of the room. Things did not appear to be going well for those the trolls had come to kill. Three of the huge monsters still battled the very few soldiers still on their feet.

A pair of trolls stood toe-to-toe with the last two human soldiers. The last troll, bleeding heavily from a large cut in its thigh, hung back behind the other two. Blood actually spurted from the wound with each beat of the troll's heart. For a human, or even an ogre, the wound would have been fatal. But not for a troll. Shorty knew the troll would heal quickly. It would be back in the battle soon. Trolls were a problem that way. Few weapons did lasting damage to trolls. Without magic like his troll sword, trolls had to be burned to keep them from coming back.

For a brief moment, Shorty's eyes locked on the two remaining soldiers. The one on his right, a large human male, swung a battle axe. The man was good. His axe knocked the trolls sword aside over and over again. It was the smaller figure at his side that drew most of Shorty's attention. The other soldier was not human as he had assumed. She was an elf. Her sword was small, but it struck so quickly that the troll she faced spent most of its efforts defending itself. Shorty liked the female warrior. She was very, very good.

Shorty almost missed the thin, much older human standing behind the two soldiers. He had no armor to speak of, only a funny shaped metal hat on his head. The old man held a metal rod in one hand. The rod was made of gold and had lots of pretty marbles on it. Shorty did not think it would hurt the trolls even if the old man could hit one of them.

The two uninjured trolls continued to hammer at the two soldiers. Shorty did not think the fight would last much longer unless he did something quickly. The Lady Elf was good, but she was obviously defending the old man. She could not move around and take advantage of her speed without getting the man killed. She would not last if she kept trying to protect him.

The trolls kept the pressure on the two soldiers. They were just too big and powerful. It bothered Shorty that none of the combatants had even noticed him yet. He decided it was time to get everyone's attention. A grim smile appeared on Shorty's lips. Getting everyone's attention should not be too hard. He was an ogre after all. He just needed more than a broken door to announce his arrival. Shorty drew in a deep breath. "Aaaaarroooooooo!" The war cry of a bull ogre rang through the room.

"Aaaaarroooooooo!" The second battle cry brought the fight to a stop. Everyone in the room turned to face Shorty. Even trolls were not foolish enough to ignore an angry mountain ogre at their backs. Shorty raised both of his swords and smiled. "Me no bees tiny warrior dat troll ken pushes round. Me ken fights betterer den no bery smart troll. Ogre no smell bad like troll do." Shorty met the gaze of the Lady Elf and winked. It was the only signal he could think of to give her. Then he stepped closer to the trolls. "Me no likey troll. Whiches one a youse wants gets kilt firstus?"

Shorty got the attention he was hoping for. One of the uninjured trolls turned and stomped in his direction. Shorty noticed the injured troll limping around to Shorty's left side. He had pulled two of them away from the soldiers. It was the best he could do.

Unfortunately, the remaining troll used the distraction of Shorty's battle cry to strike at the human soldier. The man went down in a spray of blood. Shorty hoped the Lady Elf could hold her own. He did not have time to watch her battle. He had his own battle to fight to win against two experienced troll warriors.

Shorty did not wait for the trolls to attack. He cut a vicious slash at the uninjured troll and then spun to his left. The move placed the injured troll between him and its squad mate. Its limp was bad enough that he should be able to keep it between him and the more nimble troll.

The injured troll thrust at Shorty as soon as he came within its reach. The strike lacked power as the troll could not step into its attack. Th-thump! Shorty easily knocked it aside.

The troll's next swing was a diagonal slash that Shorty blocked with his troll sword. The two blades slid across each other with a screech of steel. As the two cross guards slammed together, Shorty stepped in close and shoved the off-balance troll into the path of the uninjured troll.

The charging troll's sword came across and cut down its injured teammate. Shorty was caught by surprise as the badly injured troll fell in a spray of blood. Shorty dove to the side in a desperate attempt to avoid the remaining troll charge. Shorty avoided being run down, but a line of pain ran down the back of his leg. He rolled and came back to his feet. Blood trickled down his left leg into his boot. The troll spun back to face him with a snarl on its lips.

The two combatants came together in a flurry of blades. The three swords moved in a blur of bright metal as each tried to overpower the other. Shorty struggled to find an opening in the troll's defenses. He finally managed a shallow slice on his opponent's arm with his troll sword. The troll howled in agony as the sword's magic bit deeply. The troll stared at him in shock. "It burns. Why does it burn so? I will mount your head on that blade soon enough."

Shorty just grinned at his foe. The troll raised its sword high over its head. Its left hand came up to join its right on the hilt of the gigantic sword. Then it stepped forward, bringing its blade down with all its strength and weight behind the sword. Shorty crossed his swords overhead catching the trolls' blade between his own. This time he did not try to match strength with the troll. Shorty allowed the power of the blow to drive him to the ground. The troll roared in triumph as it raised its sword for another strike.

Still on his back, Shorty kicked out with all of the power he had used on the door. It was a no very nice way to fight, but it was necessary if he was to help the Lady Elf. The heel of his boot smashed into the side of the troll's knee. There was a wet popping noise as the knee suddenly deformed. The upper and lower parts of the leg were no longer lined up properly. His foe stumbled, dropping its sword as it grabbed for its injured leg. The troll leaned forward and Shorty drove his troll sword deep into the troll's neck. There was no scream this time, only a gurgling sound as bloody bubbles erupted from its throat.

Shorty kicked out once more, driving his boot into the troll's chest. The body flew away, freeing his sword. Shorty rose to his feet. He stepped over to the second troll he had fought and ran the troll sword through its heart. This troll would not get back up either.

Now that both his opponents were dead, Shorty checked to see how the Lady Elf had fared with the final troll. She was injured, but at least she was not dead. The old man stood at her side, supporting her. The last troll lay at her feet. Her sword jutted from one of its eye sockets. She had done what she needed to do to protect the old one. Shorty respected that. Now, though, both of them were staring at Shorty with strange looks on their faces.

Shorty was about to say hello to the nice people when someone cleared their throat behind him. The sound was more like rocks grinding together than something that should have come from a living person. The awful noise made the hair on the back of Shorty's neck stand up. He turned to face the door. He needed to see what kind of trouble had come for him now.

Three figures stood just inside the broken door. These were not just guards or common soldiers; they were warriors like him. He could tell by the way they stood that they fought the bad things that soldiers could not. They had come here to kill trolls and foolish ogres who went places they did not belong.

The warrior standing closest to him was a fuzzface with hard brown eyes. Long brown hair hung from his face all the way to his belt. The hair not only hid most of his face, it also covered his heavy plate armor. The hairy little man carried a huge axe in one hand. Shorty suspected that axe was sharp. He had a bad feeling that he was about to find out exactly how sharp it really was.

Behind the fuzzface stood two more problems for Shorty. On the right was a human in robes. Robes like that meant one thing: the man fought with magic. Shorty hated magic. It usually hurt. Beside the human stood an elf with skin as dark as his friend, Roiland. The elf was also dressed like a mage, but carried a short sword. Shorty was not sure what that sword meant, but he doubted it would be much fun.

The fuzzface began calling out orders as he studied the bodies scattered around the room. Shorty guessed that he must be the boss of the team. "Trysk, protect the King. Better yet, get him out of here.

Ye can teleport him to the Audience Chamber. That is where the rest of the guard is forming up."

The dark elf darted around Shorty staying out of the reach of Shorty's swords. Shorty did not try to get in his way. He really did not want to fight this group. The old man began to speak, "Wait a mo…" then there was the soft sound of rushing air. Shorty looked back to see the old man and both elves were gone. Magic. But at least he now only had two people left to get past if he was going to escape.

The fuzzface gave another order, "Morteft, see if ye ken save any of the injured soldiers."

The human did not move right away. "I think that is your job, Warwick. You are the cleric, not me."

The fuzzface shook his head. The hair hanging from his face swayed back and forth. "Do yer best, please. I have something more important to take care of."

The human began to move around Shorty towards the bodies of the soldiers. He did not seem to like being told what to do. "What is more important than healing these men?"

Shorty felt a moment of panic as white teeth smiled through the hair on the little man's face. It was not a nice smile. "I am going to play a game called twenty questions with yon ogre. If I do not like his answers, I am going to introduce him to me axe. It has been far too long since I last played with one of his kind."

Shorty's head darted around looking for a way out. No doors had magically appeared to let him escape. He was trapped with an angry ball of hair between him and the door. If he wanted out, he would have to fight the fuzzface. Even if he won that battle, he knew he would just get in even more trouble. This was all Ez'ard's fault. He should not have sent Shorty to market.

The fuzzface began to move forward. But the strange little man did not walk. He seemed to float across the floor. Was this what happened when you had too much hair? Shorty could only stare as the small warrior floated closer. It was a neat trick. Shorty backed towards the wall but the small warrior continued to crowd him. He wondered if he could talk his way out of this. "No wants to hurts youse. Me just go home now. Kay?"

The hairy nightmare let out an evil-sounding chuckle. "Ye do not need to worry about going anywhere. We are going to talk whether ye like it or not. I doubt yer are good enough to hurt me. Shall we start with me first question? Who are ye and who sent ye and yer troll friends to kill the King of Delith?"

Shorty shook his head. That was two questions. Which was he supposed to answer? Since the fuzzface had already moved on, Shorty tried to answer the second one. "No me. Dem not bees me friend."

The fuzzface darted closer to Shorty. The axe came up so quickly that it seemed to blur. Shorty tried to block the strike, but it came in much lower than he expected. Another line of pain ran down his lower leg to his ankle. More blood ran into his boot. He did not like the wet feeling gathering in there.

The fuzzface continued, "Meet Giant Cleaver. Yer a bit smaller than a giant. Actually, yer a bit small fer an ogre too. But me axe will be happy to take small bites out of ye. Listen carefully now. Ye did not answer me question. Who sent this group to assassinate the King?"

Shorty did not know which question to answer anymore. He had forgotten the first question and the next two sounded the same to him. He tried to stick to the truth. Mama said telling the truth would keep him from being punished. "Me no come wid dem. Me no like troll."

The fuzzface darted in again with his wicked axe ready to strike. This time Shorty brought his black sword across in a solid parry. The sword hungered for the small warrior's blood. Shorty ignored it and struck out with his boot instead. Th-thump! His kick connected, but the small warrior was heavier than Shorty had expected. The kick only created a small space between him and that axe. It also left a smear of blood in the middle of all that hair. The hairy nightmare seemed to get angrier at that.

The warrior's only response to the blow was a softly muttered, "Good. Maybe ye can make this fight interesting after all."

Nothing was going the way Shorty had wanted it to. Killing trolls was always a good thing. Fighting these others was not going to turn out well. He was going to lose no matter how this ended. Why not just let him leave? He would gladly hide in the underground city for a long time. But the fuzzface would not listen. That axe came in again. Shorty managed to block two more strikes. Both of his own swings went over his opponent's head. Fighting something that small and fast was hard.

The short warrior raised his axe again. "Tell me who sent ye after the King or ye will feel me axe again."

Shorty had no idea how to answer that question. No one had sent him here. He had decided to kill the trolls. They were dead and he just wanted to go home. He would never let Ez'ard send him to market ever again. But first, he had to get away. He realized his only way to live was to kill the small warrior. Shorty dropped to one knee and slashed at the small warrior's legs. The fuzzface rose in the air. Shorty's blade passed under his boots. It was just not fair. The fuzzface had cheated.

Shorty looked up to see that horrible axe poised to come down on his head. Both of his swords were low and out of position. He would not be able to parry this strike. Shorty stared up at the axe as it came down. He watched death come for him.

Something hammered against the stone floor. Th-thump, th-thump! Then a commanding voice called from the doorway. "Warwick, NO!" The axe halted in mid swing. Shorty froze as well. He knew that voice. It was one he had hoped he would never hear again. Maybeso getting killed by that axe was not such a bad thing after all.

Chapter 4

No Me Fault

The axe hung there, just above his head. It seemed close enough that if he sweated, he would get the blade wet. The sharp edge centered between his eyes. When he stared at it, his eyes saw two blades instead of one. Shorty decided to just close his eyes; one axe was bad enough.

The gruff voice of the small warrior sounded frustrated as it muttered, "I assume you have a really good reason for stopping me, Arch Mage. Good people died today. The only thing that I can do for the dead now is to kill the last of their butchers."

Shorty wanted to argue that he had only killed trolls, but he did not want to anger that voice from his past. He seemed to have a talent for making the one called Arch Mage mad at him. He had never needed to try very hard to get fussed at. Was there anything he could say now that would not get him in trouble again? Probably not. And if he did open his mouth, would the fuzzface just hit him with that axe to shut him up?

The voice from his past spoke again, "It would appear that the ogre you are so intent on killing saved the King, the Guard Captain, and several soldiers."

The axe drew back. Shorty held his breath as he waited for the axe to descend again. It was obvious that the fuzzface did not believe that

Shorty had been good. The voice of the Arch Mage was sharper this time, "Let him be, Warwick! He is known to me."

The sound of grinding rocks filled Shorty's ears again. But the fuzzface, and more importantly the axe, floated away from him. Shorty was finally able to see the door he had broken open. A tall human filled that opening that Shorty wanted to run through. There would be no escape that way.

Shorty stared at the one he considered to be a tormentor. Braided red hair fell to the waist of the human's black robes. A short sword and a long sword were belted at his waist. Shorty met the piercing green eyes of the man who had led him and many others into the lair of the salamanders. The one they had called Arch Mage of Delith had not changed. Dualis still liked to boss people around.

Shorty's memories of that time were not very clear. So much had happened since then. They had won the battle, but then there had been an argument about a silly hat that Ez'ard had liked. The team called Ez'ard a thief. They sent him away. Shorty called Dualis no bery smart. Both he and Dualis had gotten angry. In the end, Shorty had taken the funny hat as part of his share of the treasure. He had walked away from the team, Dualis, and the missions Dualis wanted his help with. Shorty had chosen to stick with his friend. Ez'ard needed him more than Dualis did.

It had not done him any good. Dualis had found him again. Shorty had a bad feeling about this. Would he be able to escape Dualis's plans a second time?

The green-eyed tyrant motioned towards the bodies of the soldiers and the fuzzface floated that way. Shorty hoped the small warrior could save some of them. Shorty tried to ignore the Arch Mage. He would rather watch the healing of the soldiers, or better yet, sneak out of the room.

But ignoring Dualis never seemed to work. Neither did arguing with him. The man was more stubborn than a female ogre. Dualis spoke softly from just behind Shorty using that tone of voice that Shorty always hated, the one that sounded like Mama scolding him. "How do you manage it, Shorty? Every time things seem to be going to hell, you turn up. The Temple Elders get kidnapped and you burst out of a dark tunnel to save them. The King gets attacked and here you are cutting down trolls to save him." Dualis stepped up beside Shorty and waved a hand. A single finger motioned around the room as he asked, "How much of this destruction is your handiwork?"

Shorty stared around him. There was a dead human near the door. Two dead soldiers in the center of the room. Three badly wounded soldiers that the fuzzface was working to save. And, of course, four dead trolls. There were also the two soldiers out in the hall and two more dead trolls. Shorty could only think of one response to that question. He looked at Dualis and said, "No me fault dis time!"

Dualis shook his head and sighed. "Of course not." One hand rose to massage his temple. "That is the same thing you said when we found you standing over the Temple Elders. And now I have a headache just like I did that day. Why does my head always hurt this way when you are around, Shorty?"

Shorty considered for a moment before answering. "Youse tinks too muches. Dat bees bery bad fer youse head."

Dualis simply glared at him.

A squad of human soldiers entered the room with their swords out. Dualis held his hand out towards them with a single finger raised. "Shorty, a lot of people are afraid right now. You are one of the things they are afraid of. Will you lay down your weapons and go with these men. I promise that you will be safe and your things will be returned to you."

Shorty stared at the soldiers. He did not want to fight them either. He nodded and slid both swords into their scabbards. He removed the two scabbards, his axe, and the large hammer from his back. He piled them on the floor. Then he pulled Papa's dagger from his boot and laid it beside the other weapons. Shorty touched the hilt of the black sword with its large marble in the pommel. "Dis one no bery nice sum a da times. Dem no should touches."

Dualis nodded, "I will make sure no one touches your sword. Please, go with these soldiers."

Dualis lowered his hand and one of the soldiers turned and left the room. Shorty followed him. The rest of the squad fell in behind

Shorty. They led him down many levels to a room with a heavy door. Shorty entered the room to find it was very nice. A large, comfortable looking bed filled most of the room. He turned to face the door. Th-thump. It slammed closed as he watched. A loud click came next and Shorty knew the door would not reopen for him. He was trapped once more.

Shorty sat on the floor and got as comfortable as he could. There was not much to do in the room. He thought about playing marbles, but there really was not enough space. Besides, the soldiers probably would not like it if he drew a circle on the floor with his chalk. With nothing better to do, Shorty pulled up his pant leg and watched the deep cut on his leg begin to close. The black glove's magic was working. He always enjoyed watching his ouches go away. It was like fixing a hole in his sock without all the hard work.

Eventually, the soldiers brought him food and a jug of water. The th-thump as they slammed the door in his face had not been very friendly. He guessed that they were still not happy about him being here. Shorty finished off the food very quickly. Peoples never seemed to understand just how hungry ogres got. And it had been a long time since his breakfast at home. Shorty tried to make the water last a little longer, but that idea did not work so well either. He was still thinking about home when he fell asleep leaning against the soft bed.

Th-thump! The door hit Shorty's outstretched feet. It woke him up. Shorty stood as the door was pushed open a second time. Shorty sighed. He had hoped the soldiers were bringing him more food. But it was only the Arch Mage. The man stood there with that knows everything look on his face. "Come with me, Shorty."

He followed the Arch Mage down the hall to another room. This one held a table with chairs all around it including one large enough for Shorty. Three of the chairs were already occupied.

Dualis sat at the head of the table and gestured to the large chair. "Sit, please. Shall we start with introductions?"

Dualis began to talk in that tone that told Shorty this was going to take a while. He did his best to pay attention. "Shorty, I would like you to meet my new team. The dwarf is Warwick. He is a fighter and a Priest. To his right is Morteft. Morteft is a mage and an alchemist. He is quite skilled in battle and at research. The dark elf is Trysk. Trysk is also a mage. He has other skills that I will let him reveal to you if he chooses. These three are the specialists that help me keep the land of Delith safe.”

Shorty looked at the trio and smiled. “Muches nice ta meets youse.” Then he turned to Dualis. “Udder team bees kay?”

Dualis hesitated. “Most of them are well, Shorty. The team did not stay together long after the battle with the salamanders. Several went their own way and the rest decided they did not want to start again with new teammates.”

Shorty whispered softly, “No me fault.”

Dualis shook his head and then gestured towards Shorty. “This is Shorty. He is a fighter who joined one of my teams on an important mission a year or so back.”

The fuzzface warrior named Warwick grinned. The look was not as scary without the axe in his hand. “Sorry about our last meeting. The King explained that ye were not responsible for what happened. I should have listened to ye.”

Shorty grinned. “Bees kay.” Shorty pointed to the black gauntlet on his right hand. “Dis make ouches bees gone. Me all betterer now.”

Dualis turned a hard gaze on Shorty. “We have heard from the guards who survived, Lady Gwynda, and the King himself. There are things I still do not understand. Can you tell me what you know of this attack?”

Shorty shrugged, “No knowed bery muches. Me jus bees on da way ta market…”

Dualis finished his summary, “That is all we have been able to determine so far, Your Majesty. The spell the troll used to penetrate the castle wards was unusual. I suspect whoever sent the trolls provided them with the spell.”

The King sat back in his chair considering what he had just been told. "What of the ogre?"

Dualis sighed heavily, "Shorty just happened to be in the wrong place at the right time. He is harmless."

The King began to laugh. "He followed an assassination team into my palace. He took on five well-trained troll warriors and a powerful troll mage. By my count, he killed four of them including the mage. I hardly call that harmless."

Dualis smiled but did not join in the King's laughter. "He is a liability, Your Majesty. Do not put too much faith in him."

The King gave Dualis a knowing look. "You do not like him, Arch Mage. May I inquire why?"

Dualis sat up straighter in his chair. "It is not that I do not like him. I find him frustrating. He depends too much on his feelings and intuition. I know he is only an ogre, but he refuses to think things through."

The King nodded. "I see," he replied, his tone was quite serious but his eyes were filled with humor. "Have you ever considered how a little intuition and gut-instincts might benefit your team? This Shorty seems to have a nose for problems that need fixing."

The King noted the sour expression on the Arch Mage's face and moved on. "Who you use on the team is your affair, old friend. Forgive the meddling of an old man. I want to reward this ogre. We owe him a great deal. I need your help with what Gwynda has in mind. The Captain of my Guard's idea has merit, but it requires some negotiation that you are best suited to handle."

Dualis rose. "As you wish, Majesty."

Chapter 5

The Gift

She extended her front legs, stretching across the floor of her lair. Her belly was sated, but not her mind. The boar had not been the challenge she had hoped for. It had died too quickly and her need for a good game had gone unfulfilled. Why had she expected so much from her prey? She was Cat and the boar had only been a male. Its flesh had been succulent and sweet, warm and tender, but it had failed to satisfy her greater need to play the game.

So, what now, she wondered. What great challenge was there for her? She was Cat. She was the Prime, the ultimate predator in the Pride. Was there anything left this day except the drudgery of Pride politics? Was there anything in her world that would make her feel alive? Anything at all to challenge her mind as well as her body? Did all of the past Primes suffer from boredom as she did? Perhaps a nap would take her mind off her boredom. Perhaps her dreams would provide more challenges than the real world did.

Cat slept, but not so deeply that she did not sense the ripple of magic outside her lair. Her claws extended in anticipation. A purr of excitement vibrated in her chest. Had a challenge worthy of her come at last? She drew in a deep breath through nose and mouth. The smell of a human mingled with the taste of powerful magic. Her ears perked up as she listened to the prey. Its breath was slow and steady. She could just make out the beat of its heart. Th-thump, th-thump. This human was neither excited nor afraid. Cat's claws retracted as she grew more interested in her guest.

Cat sat up, assuming a regal pose. To her surprise, the polite cough of a supplicant came from her ledge. This human knew the ways of the Pride. Most interesting. Cat growled softly to indicate that it should enter.

The human that entered her cave was unusual. First, it had no armor to protect its soft flesh. Not that two-legs tasted good anyway. It wore lose robes as if to invite her attack, but Cat sensed the magic that wrapped itself around this prey. It would not be an easy kill. As with most humans, this one was furless except for the top of its head. What fur it had was a brilliant red that hung halfway to the ground. Its fur was carefully knotted. Long like a snake with a tuft at the end, it reminded her of the tail of a hairy tuskers.

Cat met her visitor's gaze. Its eyes were old, containing much knowledge. This one considered himself her equal. That, of course, was preposterous. He was a male. But perhaps he would be the challenge she sought. Maybe he was more than she should dare. She felt her own heart begin to beat faster as boredom departed her lair. Somehow, she knew her world would never be the same after this meeting.

"Greetings, Prime." The stranger's voice was cultured and smooth. This one was well versed in negotiations. But, what did it want?

"I come to negotiate the payment of a debt of honor," the stranger continued. Cat owed no debts. She had never been foolish enough to accept obligations of any kind. Debts were for those who had not mastered the Great Game. She was Cat and there was no game that was beyond her.

Cat growled in warning. She did not like the way this conversation was going. But the stranger reached into a hide bag hanging at his middle. Slowly, as if daring her to watch, it drew forth a white shape. It was a stone, beautifully carved to represent one of the Pride. The figure was that of a female. The human placed the stone form on the ground before her. Cat studied it carefully. The She who it represented was strong, powerful, and quite beautiful. In many ways, the near perfect feline form reminded Cat of herself.

Cat took an involuntary step towards the thing that the human had placed on the ground. It was magic and that magic called to her. Anger sparked within her and she came to a stop. No thing would control her. She was Cat. She would not stand for it. She hissed at the small version of herself and then glared at the human.

The stranger was staring at her as if she were a field mouse to be played with. His murmur seemed more for his own benefit than hers. "So, it calls even to you, leader of the Pride." She backed away from the small carved feline, unwilling to risk touching it. But that did not mean that she could not reach the one who had attempted to control her. He was well within the range of her spring.

The human met her angry gaze and raised his hands as if to placate her. "Long ago, even by the standards of the Pride, a disease attacked your kind. It would have wiped out the Pride. A human king named Alexander offered his aid. He brought clerics who found a cure for the curse that had been laid on the Pride. He asked nothing for what he did, but your predecessor was a proud feline. She would not be obligated to this King or his descendants."

The human waved his hand at the small figure of one of the Pride. "So, they bargained. That Prime decreed that one and only one member of the Pride would serve as the King desired. And so, this figurine of power was created. It was lost in a treasure vault for many generations. Now, a new King requests the aid of the Pride."

Cat, as did all adult members of the Pride, knew of the time of the Great Shedding. Handfuls of fur fell out of those afflicted with the curse. Great open sores formed where the fur was lost. Pain, suffering, and death would follow. Any who came in contact with one of the afflicted became sick as well. What none in her day had known was of the bargain that had been made to preserve the Pride and its pride. And now that debt of honor was being called in.

A querulous sound erupted from Cat. It shamed her, but she had not been able to keep it inside. The stranger shook his head, clearly understanding her question. "No, you will not serve me or even the human King. He, like your Prime of ancient times, owes a debt of honor. He wishes the Pride to serve the one to whom he owes that debt."

Cat sniffed the stranger. She smelled only truth in his words. Her ears perked up in curiosity. "The one to whom that," the human pointed at the stone carving, "will be given is a hunter and a warrior of no little skill." At her chuff of disbelief, the stranger smiled. "No, he is not your equal, but for my world, he is quite skilled."

Her ears twitched in question. His reply was immediate. "No one expects the Prime to abandon her duties for this service. You may select any that you deem appropriate as a companion for this warrior." The stranger's lips curled oddly for a moment and then he continued, "This one is involved in many great games in my world. His foes are great and powerful. The challenges he faces might be beyond him even with one of the Pride at his side. Choose wisely, great Prime."

The human squatted, keeping a watchful eye on her, as it retrieved its magical toy. It backed respectfully from her lair. Standing on the ledge outside her lair, he paused, "This gift will be given at midday here in your world. You must choose before that time." Another word formed on the stranger's lips, one that she did not comprehend. Then the stranger was gone.

Cat lay down once more. Thankfully, none among the Pride came to annoy her by whining about things they could do for themselves. She was left with nothing to do but consider the stranger's words. Who should she select for this onerous duty? Would it be a punishment befitting those who sought to manipulate her for their own benefit? Or would this duty be a blessing to chase away the monotony of games too easily won in her world? Just how great were the challenges faced by this warrior to whom the figurine was about to be given? Cat's mind raced as she weighed her options. But she did not make this decision alone. Her greatest enemy, boredom, was there with her. They were soon joined by the greatest weakness of her kind, curiosity.

Th-thump! The ball shot back to his hand. Shorty glared at the empty bowl sitting by the door. He aimed the ball at the thin line between the floor and the door. Th-thump! Ogres did not eat soft, mushy stuff. Unless of course they were very, very hungry. Th-thump! Ogres needed meat and lots of it. Th-thump! The tiny pieces of pig meat mixed into the porridge did not count. He could not even taste them in the nasty mush they had given him to eat.

Th-thump! Shorty caught his ball as the lock on the door clicked. Were they going to give him real food this time? Shorty was on his feet before the door came fully open. He slid his ball back into his belt pouch before the guards could see it. They did not like the sound of the ball hitting the door. They might try to take his ball like they did his swords.

A different group of soldiers stood outside the door this time. He did not smell any food. That was disappointing. The soldier who had opened the door looked familiar. It took Shorty a moment to recognize the soldier from the hallway, the one that that had fought the troll. The man stepped forward and took a knee.

"I owe you a debt of honor, Lord Ogre. You saved my life and that of my companion." The man bowed his head.

Shorty looked down at the man in surprise. No one knelt before an ogre, especially not him. Embarrassed, Shorty spoke softly. "Stand uped. Me no bees lard. Just bees Shorty. Youse welcome. Bery brabe soldier. Fight troll no bees bery easy."

The man stood meeting Shorty's gaze. Somehow, he seemed taller after Shorty's words. Pride shown on his face. "Thank you for that, Sir." The soldier stepped back and another, older man, took his place. The older man bowed his head to Shorty, saying, "Your presence is required in the King's audience chamber. Please follow me."

Shorty had no idea what an audience chamber was or why he needed to bring a present. Hopefully a nice marble would do because he did not have anything else to give as a gift. Shorty scooped up his backpack and followed the older man into the hall.

Shorty followed the older man with the three soldiers right behind them. They walked through many hallways and down several flights of stairs. They finally made their way into a large room with many pictures on the side walls. Most of the people in the pictures had those funny metal circles on their heads. The wall on the far end of the room was not really a wall at all. Two large doors filled all the space between the two corners.

That was when his day got much, much worse. Waiting for him beside those two large doors was the one person he had hoped not to see today. The older man led him towards the Arch Mage. With the soldiers right behind him, Shorty had nowhere to hide.

Dualis studied him as Shorty walked towards him. There was mild disapproval on his face. Dualis sighed as Shorty came up beside him. "You could have at least cleaned up a little before your audience with the King. You smell like… well, an ogre."

Shorty was not sure how to answer the Arch Mage. He was an ogre. What else was he supposed to smell like? And how was he supposed to clean up? There was no bath in his room, only that extra pitcher of water which he drank almost as quickly as the one that had come with his dinner. The second pitcher of water had tasted funny and it smelled like flowers. But it had been wet and he was very thirsty after all the fighting he had done.

Dualis gave a hopeless shrug. "You will just have to do. It would take more time than we have to clean you up, let alone teach you the things you need to know for a formal audience. If I am lucky, we can give you a few manners before you embarrass the realm."

Shorty had no idea what Dualis was talking about. "No wants man tings. Bees too small fer ogre." Shorty pointed at the old man now standing against one of the side walls. "Him say me posed ta gib presents. Hows come? Me no gots nuttin cept fer marble ta gib."

Dualis began to rub his temples, a pained look on his face. "This is going to be a disaster," the Arch Mage muttered.

Shorty leaned in close and whispered, "Maybeso lets me sneaks way? Me go home and no comes back? Ebry bodies bees happy den." Shorty grew hopeful when Dualis actually appeared to consider the idea.

Dualis shook his head and stood straight and tall. "I can do this. I am an Arch Mage. The powers of the universe are at my command. I can overcome the limitations of a single ogre, even you, Shorty."

Shorty actually felt sorry for the man. "Youse gonna bees kay sum day," Shorty whispered to him.

Dualis glared at Shorty. "I do not understand why, but the King is rather set on rewarding you for saving his life." Dualis gestured toward the large doors. "The King and his court are inside that room. He intends to thank you for what you did. What do we say when someone thanks us, Shorty?"

Shorty thought long and hard, wanting to get this one right. "Bees welcome."

Dualis groaned but knew that there was no way he would ever get a 'Your Majesty' out of Shorty. Best to focus on the things he could achieve. "The King is also going to give you a gift. What do we say when we get a gift, Shorty?"

Shorty grinned. He knew this one. "Tank youse bery muches!"

Dualis nodded, but the wrinkles on his forehead grew more numerous as he considered the next piece of the lesson. "And what do you say when you get introduced to the King?"

Shorty hesitated. The only other King that he had ever met was the Salamander King. He had not really spoken to that King unless hitting him with a sword counted. He did not even have his sword to hit this King with. Besides, he had a funny feeling that was not the right thing to do. That only left one answer so he gave it a try, "Hullo, King?"

Dualis frowned. "No, Shorty. He is not some guy you just met in a bar."

Shorty did not understand. "Jus wabe ta him? Maybeso shake him hand? But no squeeze hard."

Dualis just groaned and threw his hands up in the air. The Arch Mage walked over to stand by the large doors at a loss for words. Shorty wondered if that was really as good a thing as he thought it was.

Then the doors began to open slowly. An old man with grey hair stood in the gap between the doors. The man held a large staff in his hand with an iron tip on its bottom. The man whispered something to Dualis. The Arch Mage of Delith gave a shrug and then gestured towards Shorty.

The old man nodded before raising the staff into the air. He brought it down three times against the floor. Th-thump! Th-thump! Th-thump! Then in a booming voice, the old man announced, "His Majesty, the King of Delith, welcomes the Warrior, Shorty, to his court."

The doors continued to swing open even further, each one being pulled by a pair of human soldiers. The room beyond the door was far larger than anything Shorty had seen in the castle so far. Shorty wanted to stare around the room, but Dualis cleared his throat and motioned Shorty forward. Shorty began to walk towards the open doors, still uncertain what any of this was all about.

The old man continued to stand in the doorway, only now he faced into the room. Shorty stepped around the old man and into the room. But that was as far as he got. The room was far wider than the two doors. The area to each side of the doors was packed with people. There had to be hundreds of them now staring at Shorty. Colors that Shorty had never seen before seemed to compete with each other to catch his attention. Each seemed to scream, "Look at me! Look at me!" Men wore fancy robes or marble covered armor that would never withstand a single sword strike. Women with skinny arms wore poofy dresses that made them look fat. The sight overwhelmed his senses and made him want to run and hide. He did not belong here.

The crowd had been silent when Shorty stepped into the room. But now, people began to whisper to each other. Others laughed and still others pointed in his direction. Someone must have said something funny, but he did not know what. The joke must have been very gooder though as more and more people began to laugh. He wished someone would tell him the joke so he could laugh too.

The old man slammed his staff into the floor several more times. Th-thump! Th-thump! The crowd became silent once more. Shorty felt a hand on his back. It was Dualis. The Arch Mage gave him a gentle shove towards the far end of the room. Shorty began to walk along the wide pathway through the middle of the crowd. He had never felt this many eyes watching him before, not even in battle. He did not like the feeling.

The far end of the room was blocked off by a line of soldiers. Each held a loaded crossbow in their hands. A few of the soldiers watched the crowd, but most stared at him, their eyes cold and hard. He would need to be very, very gooder in this room. Beyond the soldiers, a wide set of stairs led up. One, two, four, lots. The lots of stairs led up to a stone chair inlaid with gold and silver. The old man with the funny metal hat sat in that chair. The old man had a smile on his lips and kindness in his gaze. His were the only friendly eyes in the whole room it seemed.

To the old man's right and down one step stood the Lady Elf. Her ouches seemed to be all better now. Shorty was glad. The Lady Elf stood straight and proud. Her sword hung from her belt once more. She nodded at Shorty as he came to a stop well short of the line of soldiers. Then her gaze returned to the crowd. Shorty saw anger in the look she gave those people. Better them than him, he thought.

Shorty stood nervously, waiting for something, anything, to happen. Then the old man spoke. His voice seemed to carry through the room. It was surprisingly loud for such a tired old man. "Be Welcome, Good Ogre."

That was not one of the things he had practiced with Dualis. Shorty considered the three answers that he had practiced. None of them really fit the old man's words. He would just have to guess at the right thing to say. "Hullo, King. Muches good ta sees youse bee safe."

The old man's smile grew even bigger at that. Shorty relaxed hoping he had done well. The old man leaned forward on his big chair and said, "I am safe, in large part, because of you, my large friend. Thank you."

Shorty sighed in relief. That, at least, was something he knew the right answer to. "Muches welcome, King!" Even Dualis had to be happy with that answer. But Shorty did not turn to see if the Arch Mage was smiling or not.

The King turned his head towards the Lady Elf. "Proceed, Commander!"

The Lady Elf turned sharply to her left, took one step forward, turned again and knelt before the old man. Shorty saw the old man lift something large and white from the chair beside him and place it in her hands. The Lady Elf wrapped whatever it was in her arms. At a wave from the old man, she rose and walked down the stairs.

The line of soldiers parted before her as she reached the bottom of the stairs. Her body was very rigid, unlike the agile elf he remembered from the fight. Then she was standing before him, a sad smile on her face. Her voice was barely a whisper as she apologized, "I am sorry. Sir Ogre. I only wished to honor you. I forget sometimes how petty the court can be."

Shorty was unsure what she was apologizing for, but she seemed to need him to say something. "Bees kay," he told her. "No youse fault."

She smiled at him then with both her lips and her eyes. Apparently, he had said the right thing again. This time when she spoke, her words were loud enough to be heard by everyone in the immense room. "For bravery in battle, a battle that was not yours to fight, His Majesty, the King of Delith, extends to the Ogre, Shorty, the gift of friendship. Not just his own friendship, which you have from this day forward, but the friendship of a companion for the rest of your life."

Shorty felt a small nudge from behind. He was not sure what he had been given, but there was only one of his practiced answers left to give. "Tank youse bery muches, King."

There was a scattering of applause and then the Lady Elf extended her hands. Shorty stretched out his own hands and she placed the white object in them. The object was made of stone, cold still to the touch. It was not like a marble; it was something much more than that. Shorty stared down at the gift he had been given.

His eyes and fingers traced the line of the shape he now held. The white stone had been carved in the image of a cat. It was not like any cat he had ever seen though. This cat had two very large front teeth. Despite its strangeness though, she was beautiful. Shorty was not sure why he said she, but he knew that he was correct. He was not sure how even a pretty rock like this could be his friend, but there were many things he did not understand. The cat in his hands seemed real enough except that it was made of stone. Perhaps he could talk to her when he was lonely.

The Lady Elf retreated to the line of soldiers; her eyes still locked on him. Then Dualis whispered to him in that same bossy tone he always used, "That is powerful magic, Shorty. Place the figurine on the ground and ask her to come to your aid."

Again, still, Shorty did not understand. But he knew that tone that Dualis had used. The man would not stop hounding him until Shorty did as he had been told.

Shorty lowered his right knee to the floor. He placed the beautiful carving before him. Running his hand down the cat's long back, Shorty murmured, "Please ta comes, purty cat."

Shorty snatched his hand away from the cat figurine as white mist began to billow from the stone. It quickly hid the figurine and then spread out to cover an area almost as big as Shorty was. Shorty was left wondering what he had done wrong now.

Chapter 6

Servant or Something More?

Cat stood on the highest ledge on the bluff. It was hers, the one right outside her lair. From this vantage point she could see almost the entire valley. These were the Pride lands. They were hers for as long as she could protect them. It stretched from the bluff where she now stood to the ice wall that slowly retreated to the North. Her domain ran from the great salt sea where the sun came up each day to the rolling hills where the sun set each night. She ruled here as the Prime and would remain so as long as she continued to be the most dangerous predator in the Great Game.

She was Cat. All was as it should be in her world. She should be content. And yet, she was not. The valley-her valley-seemed a small place of late. The games that had made life interesting had become repetitive. There were few if any opponents that challenged her. Without that challenge, the Great Game seemed pointless. She could not become more than she was because she seldom had to strive for victory. Even the creatures of the high plain behind her had become easy prey.

The Pride did not need her either. Not really. Those who came to her were simply too lazy or stupid to play the game as it was meant to be played. She had warned off three such supplicants already this day, unwilling to listen to them mewl like kits. Her dissatisfaction had grown by leaps and bounds since the human had disturbed her peace just after the sun had risen.

Was she a fool for listening to him? She could have picked any among the Pride, even a lowly male, to serve the call of that figurine. But she had not. The human mage had tempted her with the possibility of new games and greater challenges. Had it all been a lie? She had smelled only truth in his words. She had chosen to take the burden of that ancient debt of honor upon herself. And soon she would learn if her choice had been wisdom or folly.

Cat glanced up at the sun. It had reached its zenith. The mage had told her midday. Cat turned her back on the valley she both loved and hated. She entered her lair so that none in the Pride would see her disappear. Best not to give certain over ambitious females more reasons to scheme than they already had.

Without warning, Cat felt the pull of that stone carved into the shape of one of the Pride's females. The pull of that object had been strong when it sat within her lair. It was stronger now, more compelling. Instinct drove her to resist it. Th-thump, th-thump. Her heart beat faster as she strained against that call.

A gentle breeze began to blow from the back of her lair. There was no opening there for a breeze to come through. Mist floated on that breeze obscuring her sight. A voice whispered to her in that breeze, "Please ta comes, purty cat."

The summons was no longer a demand. It was a request couched within a compliment. Cat realized that with that change, she could resist if she choose to. But did she want to resist? Was this call the Game she had desired for so long? There was only one way to find out. Cat stepped into the mist that was gathering at the back of her lair. The wall that should have been there was gone. Cat found herself in a place between worlds. She could smell her way back into her lair. Or, she could follow the pull of the voice that had called her purty cat.

Faced with a past that did not excite her or the possibility of something more, Cat began to move through the mist, seeking this other world.

Cat stepped from the place of mist into a world filled with light. This new place stank of fire and too many of the two-legs. The figurine that she expected to see sitting on the ground was not there. Instead, it had become a part of her and she a part of it. She was bound by the choice she had made. Now she must find out if that choice was a good one or not.

She looked around at the large cave where she stood. Many, many two-legs were in the cave, most of them well back. She could smell their fear. Two of the cursed creatures were right in front of her. One was the human that had come to her lair wrapped in its magic. She still did not know if it had lied to her or not.

The second two-leg was different, larger, than the others. It did not smell of fear. It smelled of blood and death. Cat filled her lungs with the scent of him. The one who crouched before her had killed more than once in the past day. She could smell the blood of his prey on him. Cat tasted that scent; it was a scent she knew. This one had fought trolls and won. That it had killed more than one was impressive. Trolls took much killing before they stayed dead. And this one had killed more than one of the brutes.

Cat glanced hopefully at the red furred user of magic. Had he told her the truth?

She studied the one who now controlled the ancient debt of her kind. It stared at her with such hope and joy. Oh, no, she realized. It was but a kit. She was not being asked to join with a true hunter. She was being asked to raise another's young. That was a burden she would not take on. Still, it had killed powerful prey.

Cat debated for less than a heartbeat before turning away. She would not do this, not even for the honor of the Pride. She would assign another to watch over this kit.

The youngling spoke again, "Us bees friends, purty cat? Maybeso?"

Not her, she told herself. It would be another's problem. Then the kit spoke again, "Me knowed many game, purty Cat. Youse like game? Games bees bery muches fun."

Cat froze mid step. No kit knew of or understood the Great Game. And yet, this kit asked her to play at its side. Moreover, she had never heard of a two-leg that knew of the Game or comprehended its importance. Yet this one, smelling of the blood of powerful prey, spoke of the game as if it was part of his daily existence.

Cat turned to study this anomaly. He was big, but that meant little in most games. She sensed that it was strong. That was good. But it was the blood of the trolls that intrigued her. The kit had no injuries on its large body. Even she was unlikely to kill multiple trolls without being injured. Cat strove to push aside the interest that was growing within her. The question was, how intelligent was this kit? Could it learn?

The two-leg whispered softly, "Ken me gives youse good scratch?" Its hands came out as if to touch her. Cat raised a paw, prepared to slap its hands away. But the kits fingers paused, waiting for her permission. It was at least smart enough to understand that there were rules and consequences.

Cat stepped forward, brushing against its hands. Those fingers moved quickly to the spots that she could not scratch on her own. The pleasure that caress brought was intense. The kit whispered to her, "Usn bees bestus friend. Friends helps eaches udder. No bees bossy."

Cat did not hesitate this time. She surged forward, rubbing her neck fur on the kits face, scent marking him as hers. She would take this kit as her own. She would teach it and train it in the Great Game. She would protect the kit and keep it safe until he was able to hunt on his own.

Cat leaned in close, listening to the beat of the kit's young heart. Th-thump! Th-thump! Th-thump!

Its steady rhythm told her that all was well.

Epilog

The smell in the room was overpowering by the time he finally dumped the mass of lavender petals into the strainer. The liquid that it had been soaking in for the last four days flowed into the wide-mouthed beaker. Ez'ard used a pestle to press the rest of the fluid out of the sodden mass. The petals got dumped into the trash and the beaker was moved to the next station. He settled it onto a stand and lit a flame beneath it. It took a few moments for the steam to begin rising into the air. It would take at least an hour on the low flame to concentrate and purify the sleeping agent for his daggers. The time did not matter. It was quiet and peaceful in his lab.

Then he heard the th-thump, th-thump of heavy feet running down the ramp. That could only mean one thing, Shorty was back from the market. Ez'ard dipped a glass rod into the beaker and began to stir. Shorty was two days late. Hopefully none of the spell components he had asked the ogre to pick up had spoiled along the way.

"Ez'ard! Guesses what?" Shorty's excited voice demanded.

Continuing to stir, Ez'ard guessed, "You actually managed to get everything on my shopping list?"

"Oopses," was Shorty's mumbled reply. "Fergetted ta goes dere."

Ez'ard released a frustrated sigh. He should have known. "Then what did you do at the market, Shorty?"

"Me do whats youse tells me ta do long time go," Shorty blurted out.

It had been a long time since Ez'ard had heard his friend this excited. He turned to face Shorty then. The ogre's eyes were lit up like a small child's. His big smile showed both of his tusks clearly. Having no idea what good advice Shorty had finally taken, Ez'ard was forced to ask, "And what was it I told you to do?"

Shorty did a little dance. "Youse telled me ta get a cat. Me do dat."

Ez'ard groaned. He had hoped the pet nonsense would have been satisfied when Shorty sort of adopted a baby red dragon and a mechanical owl. Apparently not. Now there would be dirty little feet walking across his lab table, contaminating all of his work. Just great. Ez'ard's eyes narrowed as he glared at Shorty. "I am not cleaning up after your cat either. And it is to stay out of my lab. Now where is this furball you brought home instead of my spell components?"

Shorty moved out of the doorway. A tawny yellow form bounded into the room. The 'cat' was slightly taller than Ez'ard was. That was bad enough, but the two obviously razor-sharp teeth that extended at least a foot down from its upper jaw were truly frightening. Ez'ard stumbled back against the lab table. His right hand reached for one of the daggers on his belt.

Unfortunately, his elbow hit the now hot beaker. The beaker fell from its stand and shattered on the table. Ez'ard's arm shot forward as he felt his elbow blister from its contact with the hot glass. Ez'ard's pain-filled gaze locked with that of the sabretooth Cat standing right in front of him. Its eyes were both intelligent and… amused.

There was only one thing that could have made the situation worse and those words were not long in coming.

"No me fault!"

Author Bio

Major Ursa's love of fantasy and science fiction began as a child lost in the worlds created by Andre Norton. Her characters were true heroes. They walked the paths of honor even when it came at a price. That lesson became a part of Ursa's own life.

Major Ursa made his first forays into fantasy gaming in 1980. Soon, he was creating worlds and adventures to entertain friends and family. The games became stories to entertain his children and grandchildren. Somewhere along the way, entertainment turned into teaching about honor and sacrifice and ways to persevere when things were hard. Now, the old bear is putting his favorite tales in print. The world needs heroes, even fictional ones, that are willing to put the needs of others before their own desires.

Major Ursa was medically retired from the US Air Force after 20 years when his eyesight had deteriorated enough to affect his performance. Upon retiring he moved to Vermont and took up teaching before retiring full time to focus on family and writing.

To find out more about Major Ursa and his stories please visit his website at www.ursabooks.com and his Facebook page at Ursa Books.

You will also find a free downloadable companion short story, For Love of Games, posted in the website's books section.

Major Ursa's previous published works:
> Tapestry of the World, a collection of short stories
> Short Path to Becoming Heroes
> Beautiful
> Virus-C